Marry Your Husband

Jacqueline Rohen was born in Essex. She worked in television and musical theatre in London, before moving to Uganda with her fiancé where they set up the Bulindi Chimpanzee & Community Project to conserve wild chimpanzees by supporting local households living alongside them. *How To Marry Your Husband* was her first novel. Tragically, Jacqueline passed away just before the book's publication.

Jacqueline Rohen

How to Marry Your Husband

arrow books

1 3 5 7 9 10 8 6 4 2

Arrow Books
20 Vauxhall Bridge Road
London SW1V 2SA

Arrow Books is part of the Penguin Random House group
of companies whose addresses can be found at
global.penguinrandomhouse.com

Penguin
Random House
UK

First published in Great Britain by Arrow Books in 2020

www.penguin.co.uk

A CIP catalogue record for this book is available from
the British Library.

ISBN 9781787464582

Typeset in 11/15.85 pt Charter ITC Std
by Integra Software Services Pvt. Ltd, Pondicherry

Printed and bound in Great Britain by Clays Ltd, Elcograf S.p.A.

Penguin Random House is committed to a
sustainable future for our business, our readers
and our planet. This book is made from Forest
Stewardship Council® certified paper.

For Maggie and Andrea – both of whom said to aim for the stars, and provided the stepladders to reach them.

For Joyce.

And of course for my very own nearly-husband, Matt.

Prologue

It started with a kiss.

Rachel spotted her husband on the high street. Such a lovely surprise. With a flutter of excitement, she wondered if she'd caught David picking up an anniversary present for her. She looked for a parking space where she could pull over. They could start their celebrations early; she had bought an expensive silk chemise especially for the occasion. There was one night left free for the two of them to celebrate together, followed by a weekend of festivities. The opportunity to see friends and family en masse was sacrosanct; everything was prepared.

When David kissed the woman standing in front of him, Rachel almost crashed her car. She stomped on the brakes and the Chelsea tractor behind responded with an angry blast of the horn. Uncharacteristically, she considered replying with an obscene hand gesture to convey: *Hello? Give me a pissing break. I've just this moment discovered that my husband is a cheating bastard.* Instead, she threw up her hand to apologise and pulled over in a bay marked DELIVERIES ONLY. She tasted bile in the back of her throat. When he'd said not one hour before that he had errands to run, Rachel had stupidly assumed that meant buying a last-minute gift for her. He'd omitted any mention of this flame-haired beauty on his to-do list.

David was oblivious to everything but the girl; the kiss had ended and he was now deep in conversation with her. Even the cacophony of traffic noises didn't distract him. Why did he have to kiss her in front of Sylvie's bakery? On their anniversary … their fifteenth wedding anniversary, for fuck's sake! Rachel was drowning under waves of emotion, lapping faster and faster, one on top of another, attacking from all angles. She was upset. And sad. And angry. And baffled. And downright furious. *How could he? What was he doing? Was he trying to get caught? Who was she? How long had it been going on?* The questions piled up, her bewilderment mounting.

Rachel pulled at the necktie of her blouse, a stylish bow. The knot wouldn't budge and was now suffocating her. If she couldn't soon untie it – it'd be listed as *cause of death*.

Just breathe, just breathe.

Rachel grabbed her phone and called her husband's number. She hoped he would let her in on the joke and hastily explain that he had bumped into a beautiful woman and they accidentally kissed on the street – one big misunderstanding. *Ha ha ha!* No such luck as the worst possible scenario played out before her. David retrieved his phone, glanced at the screen, cancelled the call and returned the phone to his jacket pocket. His voicemail announced: *You've reached David …* Rachel watched as her husband's hands returned to caress the woman's shoulders.

What. The. Actual. Fuck?

Rachel waited impatiently for the traffic to subside; the stream of cars and cyclists was relentless. She wiped her eyes. The dislodged eye makeup left sweeping Rothko trails on the back of her hand as she tried to stem the flow of salty tears. They wouldn't stop but ran down her face and onto her neck, stinging the tender skin.

She tried the number again. This time it went straight to voicemail. *You've reached David …*

Rachel couldn't wait any longer. She scrambled over the gearstick and toppled out of the passenger door, confident that she could walk and breathe at the same time. David had disappeared; she couldn't see in which direction he and the girl had gone. She tried his mobile phone again. It seemed to take years for the call to connect and once more it was sent straight to voicemail.

Just breathe, just breathe.

They couldn't have gone far. She searched the swarm of pedestrians for her husband and a woman who looked startlingly like a young Nicole Kidman: wild red curls, tall and slim. And young. Bloody young. Much younger than Rachel's thirty-four years. The meditative breathing hadn't worked and panic started to take hold. It was such a cliché. Her older husband was cavorting with a woman half his age.

Rachel was worried she might faint. Her knees wobbled as she searched the four corners of the town square for clues. No sign of either of them.

Defeated, she returned to her car.

She tried David's number. Again it clicked to voicemail. *You've reached David …*

Rachel mimicked the recorded message. *You've reached David but I'm too busy cheating on my hapless wife to take your call …* She threw her phone into her bag.

From somewhere deep within Rachel a primitive wail escaped. She sobbed as she thumped the steering wheel. *Lying. Cheating. Bastard. Shit!* Through tear-blurred vision, she flinched at her reflection in the rear-view mirror. She was a mess. Mascara tears had already stained her shirt collar with inky blotches and soaked the hair framing her face, making the ends of her neat bob curl. She searched her handbag for a packet of tissues or a stray grubby paper napkin that sometimes loitered at the bottom; she couldn't find anything suitable.

She rummaged for her phone to send a text message to her cheating, lying bastard of a husband.

Rachel: Please don't forget to pick up the cake. Patisserie Sylvie's – all paid for. X

David would have to cover his tracks and re-emerge from wherever he and his lady friend had disappeared in order to collect the cake before the bakery closed. Rachel wiped the remaining tears from her face and took a deep breath. *Why had she added that kiss at the end of the text?* In the rear-view mirror she spotted a traffic warden at the end of the high street marching in her direction. The warden's hand was already primed with the ticket machine to write her up for illegal parking. Rachel turned over the ignition and accelerated towards home.

She tried David's number again. It clicked to voicemail. She gave no thought to using the hands-free and if the police caught her using her phone whilst driving it really would be the icing on the cake.

'Pick up your BLOODY phone!' she screamed into oblivion.

You've reached David …

Rachel tried to recollect what she had actually seen. She didn't want to believe it. But David had clearly kissed another woman and gone off with her. And on their anniversary too. Their marriage was wholly monogamous. They had a strict set of rules, and kissing other people was not permitted. And it's never just a kiss, is it? You don't go around kissing people without it meaning something. Not beautiful women who are not your wife.

It was a miracle she and the car made it back in one piece. She could expect a telling off from the Neighbourhood Watch committee at the next meeting. They lived in a strict twenty-m.p.h. zone and Rachel had clocked at least forty coming into Sycamore Rise. She imagined Mr Renwick, the Neighbourhood Watch chairman, would refer to her as Jenson Button for the foreseeable future.

Rachel

1

Rachel pulled into the driveway and picked up her phone. She needed to call someone, but who? Rachel and David lived in the quaint riverside town of Richmond, thirty minutes by train from London Waterloo. It would be a lie to say the social scene there was buzzing.

There was no one on her contacts list who could a) offer a shoulder to cry on, or b) actually give good advice. Most of her best friends were scattered around the world, in Australia (emigrated), Mexico (travelling *Eat, Pray, Love*-style) and East Africa (saving the world). She never felt thousands of miles away from them thanks to Facebook, Twitter, Instagram, WhatsApp, Pinterest. But today she might have well been on Jupiter. David's infidelity would hardly be a welcome topic on their monthly split-screen Skype call. She tried an impromptu call with Becca in Brisbane but couldn't bring herself to say the words aloud. Instead she said she'd called for a quick chat. Becca asked if Rachel was okay; she blamed the long distance for the catch in her voice. Becca couldn't talk for long. She was taking one of the boys for a swimming exam. They promised to catch up properly soon.

Rachel checked her Facebook account: 763 friends and still no one to call upon. Did she even know seven hundred people? She scrolled through her online acquaintances. Obviously, there were close chums and family, and then friends she went to school, college and university with. Colleagues, David's colleagues and friends, her mother's Bible group, clients, employees. A nice Irish girl she met on a yoga retreat in 2010. Her brother's neighbour from five years ago. Her dentist! As she went through the list she started to delete people she didn't actually remember or indeed like. It was a welcome distraction until the realisation dawned on her that she had few if any friends completely independent from her husband. Her best friend Jojo was her husband's sister, for God's sake. Everyone in her immediate circle was inexorably linked to David, and ultimately would they, could they, be loyal to Rachel? There was Cathy who was (unhappily) married to Aaron, one of David's closest friends. And Jessica – David was godfather to her and husband Tom's two girls. Then there was his best friend Barry's soon-to-be-ex-wife, Gina. But they split up and got back with each other more often than Rachel got a pedicure.

How had she never noticed this before?

*

Rachel opened the front door and let out a shrill sarcastic, *'Honey, I'm home!'* The house was cold, as usual. It was too big, too old and impossible to heat. She had been so thrilled when they had first moved into their terraced Georgian house. Now, the vast emptiness of their home was a metaphor for their marriage; a grand-looking, worthless chasm.

Rachel took in the interior of their home. It was not so much designed, more an accumulation of things from the life they had built together. The lounge was filled with memories. Framed prints of Edward Hopper paintings complemented their mix and match furniture. Inexpensive IKEA items stood next to designer pieces they had collected and cherished over the years. The classic 1950s sideboard was their first joint furniture purchase. The huge, oversized dining table was accidentally acquired when David ordered a four-metre table instead of a table that seated four! They kept it anyway, and now Rachel loved its overbearing, ostentatious presence. She squeezed the armchair that needed reupholstering, and straightened the colourful rug inspired by Mondrian's compositions.

Rachel toyed with a chilled bottle of white wine from the fridge. She never normally drank alone. But, by God, she wanted a drink and a bath, ideally both at the same time.

An anniversary present from Eva sat on the kitchen counter in its brightly coloured gift bag: organic oils. Thoughtful but unsurprising. On any given day at work, Eva would pull out at least two bottles of essential oils from her handbag, inhaling and exhaling deeply, before waving the pungent vials in Rachel's face and insisting that she do the same. Eva swore by the benefits of aromatherapy and had promised the oils would relax Rachel, who sometimes found it difficult to take serious advice from her peri-menopausal nymphomaniac office manager, but Eva's no-nonsense attitude was hard to ignore. Hoping that she was right about their miraculous properties, Rachel picked up the gift bag and brought the bottle of Chardonnay along too, just in case. She drew a bath and allowed the chamomile and sandalwood to lull her into a temporary state of calm.

Three hours before, Rachel had ended an upbeat staff meeting with applause, thanking her team for a job well done. She'd capped her new Montblanc fountain pen – an early anniversary gift – and concluded work for the day. Now, in the depths of their bath designed for two, she despaired. Rachel couldn't help but obsess over the mysterious woman she had seen locking lips with her husband. *Who was she*? It was no one she'd recognised. But then again, she had experienced quite the shock. Her memory of the event was already fading. Rachel closed her eyes and tried to concentrate, mentally listing the fragmented details she could remember:

- The redhead was stunning. More than pretty, she was categorically beautiful.
- Her skin was translucent. The way her milky complexion offset her long thick hair was mesmerising. With her wide eyes and small, pouting mouth, she looked like a doll.

- She was the sort of woman you noticed on the street; cool, hip. She was wearing a denim jacket, teamed with navy linen dungarees. *DUNGAREES!* Rachel would be mistaken for Super Mario in that outfit.
- The woman was young.

The last point was the worst of all. Rachel knew she shouldn't make excuses for her stupid cheating husband, but she got it. She understood why he – why any red-blooded heterosexual man – was interested. *So what if she's drop-dead gorgeous and my husband drinks from the fountain of her ...*

Stop it, Rachel, she admonished herself. She was fresh out of lucid deliberation. She topped up the hot water a further three times.

An hour later, when her extremities had shrivelled to official prune status and half the wine was consumed, Rachel finally pulled herself from the bath. She caught sight of her panda eyes. *Waterproof, my arse,* she thought. Why couldn't mascara stay on her lashes when it had no problem with sticking to the bags under her eyes?

She stood in front of the large steam-free mirror and prepared herself for the pep talk of her life. She knew that it would have been terrible to see David kissing anyone, but did he really have to pick someone so young? To date, Rachel hadn't minded getting older. When her friends fretted and obsessed over every little facial line and new grey hair discovered, Rachel was usually the first to remind them that 'age is just a number'. She hadn't rejoiced when the speed of her metabolism nosedived at the end of her twenties, or to learn she needed double the hours of sleep to function, but she hadn't lost her head over it. Rachel looked like a thirty-four-year-old woman, and that was fine – she *was* a thirty-four-year-old woman.

Rachel took a deep breath and pulled at her neck. She hadn't given her décolletage much attention until a Facebook advert inconsiderately pointed it out to her. It was the start of a neck-shaming phenomenon, she was sure of it. 'Stop it!' she told herself as she massaged her skin with moisturising cream.

It was the only thing that had slightly rattled her about passing the big 3-0. Aside from that, Rachel had confidently leaned into her thirties, and found that there was actually a lot to be said for shrugging off the trappings of her twenties. She no longer wanted to follow fast fashion. She didn't want to wear jeans with purposely ripped holes in them or pay more for the slashed versions. She didn't want to dye her hair grey AS A FASHION STATEMENT! She didn't want to straighten her hair to within an inch of its life or fill her lips in with pencil and over-gloss them into a frozen, fishlike pout. She didn't want to wear anything mustard in colour. And she didn't want Botox injected into her forehead, her laughter lines, or anywhere else for that matter. She was happy with her lot – or had been until precisely eighty-nine minutes earlier. Now she felt and looked like death. She'd make a note in her diary, she decided, for this was the day she started to hate her thirty-four-year-old face.

Maybe her friends were right all along. Why hadn't she been checking the progress of the lines on her neck? No such evasive action now. Neck-centric self-loathing came rushing back full force. Hands shaking, she dotted serum along the lines, counting them like growth rings on a tree. She pushed down the sob building inside her and let out a deep, aching sigh. *What was the point?* The serums, the waxing, the twelve-weekly cut and highlights. Why was she bothering with any of it? Why was she starving herself twice a week on the 5:2 diet if her husband was going to run off with someone half his age anyway? She had wasted the majority of her adult life dreaming of and rejecting the desire to eat cake when what was the point?

Rachel had thought she kept sex with her husband exciting, and regular enough. *Wasn't it?* She blushed at what she had planned for her evening in with David, the new lingerie and their own special anniversary celebration – how embarrassing; a wife thinking she was going to blow her husband's mind with lace and stockings while he was at it with . . .

God, the thought twisted her stomach.

David – her stupid, philandering husband – was tall, dark and still handsome despite the fact that he was more than ten years older than her. Even as they aged, men retained the advantage. David modestly acknowledged his good genes, but kept himself in shape and always smelled amazing. And he listened, he was a laugh. He was a good husband, or so she'd thought. He was certainly adept at acting like a good husband.

She loved being Mrs David Chatsworth. She loved David, warts and all; her love for him had never wavered, though he had tested her patience over the years. Friends had had their doubts about whether the relationship would last, but she and David had not only survived, they had flourished. Not that he was perfect by any means. She accepted David's flaws and loved him more for them. Like the time he'd *accidentally* tried cocaine on a stag night. In a state of paranoia, he'd called her at four in the morning to collect him from an outdated holiday camp in Bognor Regis. Then there was the way he could never replace a depleted toilet roll. He was oblivious to dishwasher etiquette. He left his toenail clippings on the side of the bath. When incensed by the neighbour's dog using their garden as a toilet, he'd embarrassed the entire street by hollering from the front door, 'HONEY, THERE IS A STRANGE DOG TAKING A SHIT ON OUR LAWN,' ignoring the fact that the offending Dalmatian was literally attached to their neighbour by a lead. And the time he forgot Rachel was allergic to apples, which resulted in a visit to Accident & Emergency. And even then, they still managed to laugh. They'd had years of happiness together – or so she had been led to believe.

Not once, in all their years of marriage, had she suspected David of having an affair. Where were the warning signs? He had been spending less time at home recently, it was true. He was working late at the office, preparing for the buy-out of his IT company. Rachel wondered if the sale would happen at this rate, or was he drawing out the process to gain extra time with his mistress before he announced that the deal had fallen through? In the last few months he had swapped running for attending the gym. *The gym!* she thought. It was surely a ruse to climb upon his gym bunny thrice-weekly. The redhead had the body of a personal trainer. Rachel Googled David's gym and searched the website for the staff section. She swiped through all the beautiful profiles. No redhead.

Back to the drawing board.

When friends complained about cheating spouses, they were almost gleeful about spotting the blatant philandering, as if their marriages were cosy crime dramas where the 'butler/husband did it'. There had been nothing visibly amiss in Rachel and David's life together though. True, they'd both been busy at work, David preoccupied with the buy-out and Rachel accepting more clients than she should have, afraid to turn away new business. They were tired in the evenings and intimacy was largely replaced with TV box sets while sex was sometimes substituted with chocolate Gü pots. They still had sex though, still kissed each other goodbye in the morning, still spooned in bed. David hadn't become secretive or changed his passwords. He was such a terrible liar. However, when it really counted, Rachel had not suspected a thing. On reflection, it was clear he'd used text messages and notes left on the kitchen top to keep her updated with fictitious movements, resulting in few to no lie-detecting opportunities.

Rachel regretted not confronting her husband and his new squeeze right then and there on the street when she had the chance. What if she'd run them over? Would the police have believed it was an accident? Probably not. She could see the headline: **Husband and MUCH younger lover mowed down, wife says it was an ACCIDENT.** There wasn't a jury in the world that would find her not guilty.

Still, how could she have just sat there and done nothing? She should have jumped out and unleashed an almighty verbal assault on them both. But she hadn't. Ultimately, it was the right call. If she had caught her husband in the act and confronted him there and then ... now it would be game over! Some marriages survive infidelity, but she'd always assumed she was the sort of person who wouldn't tolerate a partner's affair. She'd never seriously thought she would have to contemplate such a thing, though. Of course, that was if David wanted to save their marriage. A damning thought occurred to her: what if he was madly in love with the mystery girl? What if he'd already planned to leave Rachel, and shack up with the twenty-something redhead and live happily ever after with her?

It was clear to her now that she was destined for jaded divorcee-spinsterhood. She'd wallow in self-pity, drown in wine, and warn young people never to fall in love. She would stop being invited to weddings for fear she would make a scene. She'd adopt an unreasonable number of cats and become a modern-day Miss Havisham. She had always wanted an excuse to wear her wedding dress again. It was last seen in the attic. She picked up her phone to Google *how to upcycle a wedding dress*.

The phone buzzed in her hand. She saw Eva's name pop up. She had sent a picture of a deep purple manicure and a text message:

Eva: What can I bring tomorrow night? X

A new husband? Or perhaps a gun? Eva was resourceful, she would know how to get her hands on weaponry. Instead Rachel replied:

Rachel: Just yourself. Rx

She was reminded that in less than twenty-four hours approximately forty of their nearest and dearest would descend on the house for a bonanza celebration. She contemplated her options; she did not want to cancel the anniversary party. She had a kilo of defrosted Marks & Spencer's sustainably farmed smoked salmon in the fridge that she wouldn't eat on her own and didn't want to waste, and she was not ready to explain to all their guests that the selfish and rampant behaviour of one David Chatsworth had ruined their marriage. No, she wouldn't cancel the party. What was one more day of pretence? She let out a sigh and added more serum to her neck.

All she wanted was to return to the state of blissful ignorance that was formally known as her happy marriage. Rachel would have to keep David's infidelity to herself for the time being. She was determined everyone was going to bloody well enjoy the weekend and then her life could unravel in private.

She heard the front door close.

Her prodigal husband had returned.

2

For their anniversary date night, Rachel chose a slim-fitting teal dress and applied her luxurious red Hourglass lipstick. While getting ready, she had primed herself for a swift announcement from her husband that he was leaving her so he could set up home with the red-haired temptress instead. It was the only way to cope. Rachel wasn't going to cry, she wasn't going to make a scene. She would keep her head held high and not let David see the cracks. She would dictate an amicable split, stage-manage a 'conscious uncoupling'. And above all she would not become hysterical, because if she became hysterical, and he then called her hysterical, she might actually kill him.

Rachel wondered if false eyelashes would be too much. She decided not. She applied glue to them and, while she waited for the adhesive to become tacky, started to make a list of her settlement demands.

Rachel wanted:

1) the food processor and the coffee machine;

2) the new charcoal-coloured corner sofa – with the chaise end – that they had on order from John Lewis;

3) the cats.

How had she chosen the cats third after kitchen appliances and furniture? She really had lost the plot.

Rachel fixed the eyelashes and finished her outfit with the pair of pearl earrings David had bought her for their first wedding anniversary. At the bottom of the stairs she took one last glance in the mirror. She was ready.

'You look nice,' David said.

Rachel smiled. Nice? NICE? NICE!? Peonies look nice. Boats harboured in a marina at sunset look nice. Paintings by nine-year-olds look nice. When did Rachel become nice and – more to the point – when had David ever settled for nice?

He placed his hand on her neck. Rachel held her breath and stared into his eyes as she tried to move away from his embrace.

'Your dress is . . .'

Rachel's dress was open an inch at the top. David closed the zip to the nape of her neck and delicately kissed the naked skin above.

'There, that's better.'

A small shiver passed through her body, igniting goose pimples and awakening her erogenous zones like a steel ball ricocheting through a pinball machine. She tried to clamp down the confusion caused by his touch.

David fought melodramatically with a magnum of Prosecco as if the bottle was a crocodile she needed saving from; one of their in-jokes that he liked to break out on every possible occasion. It seemed stupid that she'd ever found the charade remotely funny. He topped up two flutes already packed with brandy and bitters and a brown sugar cube each.

CHAMPAGNE COCKTAIL RECIPE
100 ml Champagne (Prosecco/sparkling wine may be substituted)
15 ml Cognac
1 splash of Angostura bitters
1 brown sugar cube
1 maraschino cherry to garnish
Note: If one has the time to make homemade Angostura sugar cubes, one has too much time on one's hands.

'To us – and our happy union.' He kissed her on the cheek.

The words 'happy' and 'union' tightened the knot in Rachel's stomach.

'Fifteen glorious years. Cheers!' Their glasses touched and the high-pitched clinking sound echoed against the high ceiling, filling the silence. Rachel wondered what he would do if she hurled the crystal flute towards his head. David took a sip of his drink and smiled his self-satisfied, lupine grin.

Dickhead.

On a normal evening, Rachel would ask after his afternoon. She would waffle on about her own day, but tonight small talk felt perfunctory; small talk for her small life. It was all too much. She was busy concentrating all her efforts on not crying.

Within seconds, Rachel was competing for attention with David's phone.

'So you found it? I tried calling you earlier.' It felt like pushing a bruise. It hurt but there was a sick sense of gratification in watching him squirm.

'Did you?' His voice was uncomfortably high. 'It must have been on charge'.

Lies, lies and more lies. David's phone display was alive with activity and the case vibrated against the marble-topped surface of the coffee table. He scrolled through the notifications. Rachel nodded for him to take the call but her eyes asked if it was more important than their special evening. He turned over the device.

'It can wait – it's our anniversary!'

She raised an eyebrow as if to enquire what or who could wait but he didn't furnish her with any further information. Rachel's anger threatened to boil over.

Come on, just do it already! End the marriage. Walk out. Leave!

It was *The David Show* and she was demoted to a bit part in his life. Soon she'd be written out entirely with another woman cast as his love interest. She took a deep breath, fighting down both anger and pain. Their marriage was a sham. *How could he even look her in the eye?*

David had mentioned going to their favourite restaurant – El Salvador – but apparently by the time he called to reserve a table it was fully booked. They reverted to their weekly Friday night takeaway. Rachel ordered the hottest curry on the menu to distract her heartache by punishing her taste buds.

She wondered if her husband still fancied her. She watched him intently as he discussed the dull particulars of the company buy-out. His eyes didn't drop from her face. No looks, hidden or otherwise, at her cleavage. She purposefully dropped her napkin and bent over. David didn't give her bottom a single glance. She held her posterior in the air and let the pose linger. No, nothing.

'New earrings?'

No! They are not new. You bought them. For me. When you still loved me. Eejit!

'Maybe.' Rachel fingered the jewellery to give the impression she couldn't remember which pair she was wearing. Had she thought that they could magically rekindle his affection for her? That he would notice the pearls and remember their first year of marriage and realise the error of his ways and beg for forgiveness? There was only one idiot in this relationship, and that was herself, Rachel thought.

There's a reason Indian food is never cited as an aphrodisiac. The delicious dishes – butter chicken (extra hot), vegetable biryani, saag bhaji, aloo muttar, poppadoms and naan bread with lashings of garlic oil – left Rachel feeling full to bursting.

Since David hadn't announced his departure from the marriage, and gave little sign of doing so, she had to wonder if he was the sort of man who could live with conducting an affair. What if this wasn't his first? What if he was exactly the sort of man who had AFFAIRS?

She wondered if her husband's libido had been sucked dry by the flame-haired seductress. God, the thought of that harlot fellating David was too much. Grief washed over her again and there was a lump in her throat that wouldn't dissolve. She wanted to prove to her husband she was still a worthy contender for the role of wife. *What if it wasn't too late to win him back?* What if she found a cushion and used it to protect her knees as she dropped to the plush carpet? She could unbutton his fly and … She tried to think when she had last given him a blowjob. Was it as long ago as Christmas? Or before that even? There was of course his birthday blowjob, but had she last year …? Or was it the birthday before that?

Her reverie was interrupted when David kissed her on the nose and told her he'd had a long day and suggested they cuddle in front of the television. Rachel wanted to query what part of his day off work was so exhausting but instead she nodded and pushed down on the corners of her eyes to hold back the tears threatening to make an appearance. She escaped to the kitchen for a liquid breather. David raised an eyebrow when she returned with more wine. He could be a judgemental bastard at times. Didn't he realise that this was his fault? It was *his* behaviour that had driven her to drink.

Neville appeared in the doorway, trailed by Oscar his black-and-white friend. Oscar jumped up onto her lap while Neville draped himself across her feet. Did she imagine it or were they trying to lift her mood with their mewing and purring? *Did the cats know about the other woman? Had David brought her here? Had she met Neville and Oscar?*

Rachel wasn't sure what constituted an affair but even snogging other people was a definite no-no so far as she was concerned. She mentally reviewed the incriminating facts so far while David soon fell asleep in front of the finale of *Masterchef*. This too was added to the growing list of evidence against him:

– the kiss on the high street (Concrete proof);
– cuddle in front of the television in place of anniversary marathon bonk (Anecdotal);
– exhaustion from all the extramarital sex (Hypothesis).

David started to snore. She moved away from him until not even their elbows were touching. It was petty but at that moment it felt like a small victory. Rachel stayed in front of the television without watching the programme. She couldn't give a flying fig which pompous amateur whisked up the best meringue. *I've not tried this recipe before; I hope it turns out well.* As if anyone would go on national television – a cooking show no less – having never tried that dish before. It was such bullshit.

Rachel had read enough magazine articles informing her that her good years were behind her. Scorned women shouted in films: '*HE TOOK MY BEST YEARS!*' The thought of dating again terrified her; she physically shuddered at the prospect. She wondered how difficult it would be to find another husband. If David was bonking someone twenty years his junior, Rachel calculated she would have to start man-shopping in the over-fifties aisle. It wasn't going to be easy; she'd have to trudge through heaps of divorcees. And there could be the trials and tribulations that came with being a stepmother, as well as perhaps being the second or third or fourth wife.

Plus there had been a worldwide sexual awakening in the last decade; she blamed Internet pornography.

She heard nightmare stories from friends, and friends of friends, about online dating. They were adult fairy tales told to warn others. Stories involving a catalogue of unbridled men expecting fellatio or, worse, desiring anal sex on a first date. And then not phoning afterwards! And then there was ghosting, orbiting, breadcrumbing ... she wasn't sure which was which; they all sounded awful.

Rachel convulsed at the horrific thought of having to get to know a new penis. She knew David's appendage; they were old friends – or 'besties', millennials might say. Rachel couldn't actually picture another penis. She refused to check the Internet for penile images; she didn't want that request seared on her search history for all eternity. Even when you delete something it's never quite erased allegedly. Anyway, as she recalled, they were an ugly bunch with protruding veins. It was more the personality of David's cock she had warmed to over the years. She had got used to his angry-looking cycloptic phallus.

David opened his eyes to find Rachel staring at his crotch.

She downed her glass of bubbles with gusto.

'Rachel …' David said. His voice was quiet and gentle. 'Please don't freak out. Sit still.'

This was it. Confession time.

'And don't move.'

Rachel took a deep breath.

Don't cry. Don't cry.

'I don't want you to worry but …'

Rachel didn't want to cry. She wasn't going to cry, she ordered herself. As David lunged at her, she moved her head back.

'What the fuck, David …?'

'Stay still – you've got a spider on your cheek.'

Rachel screamed and slapped both sides of her face. 'Get it off, get it off!'

David gently picked the squashed black mess from her cheek and Rachel realised that in his hand was a crushed line of false eyelashes.

David didn't notice. He didn't notice it wasn't a spider. And he didn't notice Rachel's lopsided eye make-up. *When had he stopped looking at her?*

'Don't hate me but I forgot to pick up the cake.'

'Not to worry, I can collect it in the morning,' Rachel said in a sarcastic sing-song tone. She jumped up, scaring away both cats in the process, and released a silent scream into the depths of the fridge. *Come on, Rachel, you can do this. You just need to keep it together for another forty-eight hours.*

3

Rachel's mother Norma was late to the party, as usual. When she arrived she smelled like a hair salon and Rachel noticed that they had somehow managed to get matching haircuts; both of them had light brown hair bobbed to shoulder-level with similar subtle highlights. It was another reminder that Rachel was on track to turn into her mother, a thought that was simultaneously reassuring and petrifying.

Norma was always impeccable. After sixty-one years she had perfected the art of looking like she woke up divine. Rachel knew better; she could see her mother was wearing a new outfit and would have spent hours to achieve that flawless hair and makeup. Her mother kissed her on both cheeks and waved a half-hearted hello to David in the background.

Norma had never approved of her son-in-law. She didn't like him when they first met, and after fifteen years of her daughter being married to him, Norma's mind was unchanged. She was a staunch believer that eyes were the windows to the soul. Before they were married, she had warned Rachel multiple times that David's were categorically shifty. Norma had never got over the ten-year age difference between Rachel and her husband. She hadn't trusted him when he first set his sights on her then nineteen-year-old daughter and nearly had a stroke when they eloped on a fancy island holiday, less than six months later. She never missed an opportunity to reiterate her devastation at missing her only daughter's wedding, but Rachel suspected that Norma's real gripe was not having had the chance to talk Rachel out of it.

'Are the boys here?' Norma asked.

'They're in Geneva with their mother,' Rachel said. She was certain she saw a flicker of relief cross her mother's face when told that the boys wouldn't be joining them. *That's not very grandmotherly*, Rachel thought. Norma was not shy about stating she had already had her quota of grandchildren with Kevin's teenage sons who were loud, annoying and always hungry. Norma didn't know why her friends from the Bridge Club banged on about their own little blighters as much as they did.

'I suspect you're going to announce your own addition to the family any day now,' she said suspiciously to her daughter. 'This is *just* an anniversary party, isn't it?' she added in a conspiratorial whisper.

Rachel didn't think her heart could drop any further but her mother's words were like a punch to the gut. She and David had always said that they would start a family, once the time was right. And that time was supposed to be now.

After their anniversary weekend the plan had been for Rachel to cut out alcohol and increase her vitamin intake and folic acid, then they'd have endless bonks. It was planned – they had bought the thermometer and ovulation tests. She had downloaded a fertility app and had started tracking her daily temperature. David hadn't stopped teasing about them getting lots of practice in. Now it seemed the joke was on her. *Hilarious.*

Rachel pinned her smile back in place and directed her mother through to the conservatory that was already filled with guests, circumnavigating David in the kitchen. He was hopping around, searching for the secret ingredient for his punch. It wasn't much of a secret, hardly in the same league as Colonel Sanders's signature fried chicken recipe. The drink was another in-joke, stemming from one of their many Paris trips. It was a story that was too filthy to repeat. It made Rachel's neck turn red whenever she heard David offer a guest a taste of Parisian Sunrise.

PARISIAN SUNRISE PUNCH RECIPE
100 ml Vodka
100 ml White Rum
300 ml pink grapefruit juice
500 ml pineapple juice
500 ml bitter lemon
10 ml Triple Sec
One dash Grenadine
One pipette vanilla essence

David ferreted through drawers and cupboards. He couldn't find the all-important vanilla essence. Rachel wondered if this was another excuse for him to go to the shops. He was always popping out for things she didn't know they needed or had run out of. Yesterday it had been toothbrush heads. Rachel was no longer sure if they had been her suggestion; his treachery had fogged her brain.

Remembering her electric toothbrush pissed her off even further. It had been a Christmas present from David. It was no wonder he was having an affair. He had bought his wife a toothbrush for Christmas! A toothbrush! As her main gift! Had her teeth ever been cleaner? No, but it was an alarm bell ringing if ever there was one, and she had missed it. And that Montblanc pen – yesterday she had viewed it as the most exquisite fountain pen she had ever seen, while today it seemed heavily symbolic. Rachel was the kind of wife you buy a pen for. After fifteen years, all she was worth was a fucking pen!

She struggled to suppress the anger. It surged into her throat and she took three swigs of Prosecco to push it down. Once upon a time, David rooting around in cupboards on their anniversary would mean he was arranging a surprise for her. Well, she supposed, he had surprised her this year – his affair was something she definitely hadn't seen coming. God, this afternoon was going to be difficult. One last hurrah projecting an image of marital bliss, and then she would have to let the cat out of the bag and inform everyone that their marriage was over. What was the etiquette for admitting to your friends that the last fifteen years had been a lie and your husband was leaving you for a younger woman? No matter how it was spun, it was humiliating.

'Rachel?'

She ignored David's call and the scuffling noises coming from the kitchen.

'Don't worry! Found it!' he shouted.

Found what? Rachel sneaked her head around the doorframe and saw David standing in the kitchen laughing with a woman. *Was he fucking her too?* And then backpedalled as she saw that the woman was his sister and Rachel's best friend, Jojo. Rachel realised that she hadn't actually seen Jojo in person for ages and her friend looked amazing – she'd restyled her hair, with blonde curls now bouncing on her shoulders. She was practically unrecognisable without her trademark scrunchie top-knot. When Jojo saw Rachel, she gave her a huge smile and rushed over to give her a hug. How long had it been since they'd actually met? They talked most days, or sent silly memes and messages. They both apologised for not making more time for each other and in unison said they needed to catch up.

'Big news,' Jojo said with a wink.

Rachel gave an over-enthusiastic clap of her hands and tried to keep smiling.

For a brief moment, she wondered if she should simply throw her husband to the wolves, announce the news of his affair to his sister there and then, loudly and mercilessly, with their family and best friends watching. A dramatic exit from the marriage made even more piquant by the fact that it happened at their anniversary party. She knew that wouldn't be fair. But then, his behaviour was hardly reasonable. For a moment she wished she was on a Saturday night game-show, where David's punishment for infidelity was about to be decided by a public vote ... The punch, wine and subsequent Prosecco had gone to her head, she thought. *Keep it together.*

Rachel planned to concentrate on her guests and avoid David as much as she possibly could. Easier than one might think considering it was their anniversary. Except for a quick speech, she wouldn't need to interact with him at all. Leaving him to his cocktail-making and shaking, Rachel and Jojo joined the other guests. Rachel could see that cliques had already divided the guests. Her friends sat perched on the wicker furniture in the conservatory. His family stood nearest the buffet. Hers were inspecting the pictures. She wondered if any of the guests knew? *Did they feel sorry for her? Was she a laughing stock?*

From the window, she watched David join his friends who were milling about in the garden. Rachel spied him taking a crafty drag from his best friend Barry's cigarette. She rolled her eyes at Jojo. Barry was a terrible influence on David. They had met at university and were still thick as thieves. So David still smoked on occasion? Yet another thing he had been keeping from her. Yesterday Rachel would have been appalled, but today she simply didn't have the energy to confront him about it. What did it matter if he had started smoking again? So what if he contracted a vicious strain of lung cancer? His new girlfriend could nurse him; it was no longer Rachel's responsibility.

She caught David's eye and he gave her a small wave. She could overhear Barry's Sid James boom emanating from the garden and the tail end of a well-worn cliché about how Dave would have done less time for murder. Rachel liked Barry, in a warts and all way. He was very agreeable, charming even in his own fashion, and sincere. A decent bloke who remembered which one of your parents was ill and asked after their diagnosis. He always thought to wash up and Hoover, and she'd even caught him tending to a blocked toilet at her mother-in-law's one Boxing Day. But she knew he had the potential to be a bad influence. Barry's own marriage had imploded like a stack of cards only months earlier. Was that it? Had he been filling David's head with the joys of bachelorhood refound?

Rachel was surprised to hear the doorbell. Surely everyone was here. She opened the door and was relieved to see Eva and her date, Terry. Eva was undoubtedly #Team-Rachel. Rachel hugged them both and gushed a welcome as she showed them in. Rachel often invited her staff to drinks and barbecues at her home and, in spite of polite nods of thanks, usually received last-minute excuses. She got it – who wanted to socialise with the boss at the weekend?

Eva had blossomed since her divorce. Terry the Fireman was twelve years her junior. He was also Eva's consolation prize after the split from husband number three. Terry wasn't marriage material apparently, but Eva boasted about her new boyfriend's sexual prowess at every opportunity. Would Rachel find herself a younger lover after she and David separated? Someone with a carefree attitude and a love for long walks in the countryside?

Rachel thanked Eva for the aromatherapy oils. Eva then went into too much detail about how other oils could be used – not that Rachel had to worry at her age – when things started to dry up. She mouthed the words 'down there'. Rachel nodded and prayed to a God she no longer believed in for Eva to stop talking quite so loudly in the vicinity of David's mother. Lillian pretended to be deaf when it suited her but Rachel had established, at certain times, that her mother-in-law in fact had the auditory capacity of an owl. Rachel excused herself to top up glasses, namely her own. Norma was fidgeting and vying for her daughter's attention. Rachel saw that her mother couldn't help herself from straightening picture frames and brushing invisible crumbs from the table. It was Norma's tell; Rachel's mother was quite likely to drop a bombshell or throw a grenade into polite conversation, but Rachel already had enough to worry about. For the sake of her own sanity, she tried to dodge Norma until cornered by her next to the buffet.

'I need to talk to you.' She bustled Rachel away from prying ears. Rachel meanwhile tried to keep one eye on David's movements.

'Can you give me a minute?' Norma insisted.

'In a moment,' Rachel replied.

She found her brother and tugged on his sleeve.

'Please, Kev, look after Mum.'

Kevin filled a sherry glass to the top and headed towards an irate Norma. Rachel gave her mother an apologetic wave and ignored the eye roll from Kevin.

Suddenly, David appeared behind Rachel and patted her left buttock. It was the ultimate test of strength for her not to slap his hand away. She didn't trust polite words to leave her mouth; instead, she pecked him on the cheek. He positioned his mouth to meet her lips but she swerved away. The idea that any part of her could touch the mouth that had recently kissed someone else's made her stomach turn.

'I love you, Mrs C,' he whispered softly in her ear. 'Come on, it's time for the toast!'

She could taste the tobacco on his breath and was startled to see he was wearing his wedding ring. She hadn't taken hers off since the day they were married, but David complained the gold band aggravated his skin. The sound of it chiming against the Champagne-filled flute to attract attention and summon their guests was almost too much for Rachel.

David reminded everyone of the story of how they first met and said how happy he still was all these years later. Rachel winced as the lies streamed from his mouth like a string of magician's handkerchiefs. She wanted to tear apart his untruths one by one and ask everyone to leave; instead, she smiled a tired smile then covered her face with one hand to allow the muscles controlling her false expression a moment to relax. She hoped friends and family would assume that any tears that escaped were tears of joy. In a room full of loved ones, Rachel had never felt so alone in her life. She looked around at all the familiar faces and the picture seemed to tilt before her eyes. *Jeez, how many glasses had she drunk?* She stood next to David. There he was – eulogising their years together in front of all of their closest friends. Little did they know they were witnessing the final chapter of their marriage.

David's speech seared her to the heart. Sadness turned to anger; his words were cheap and their sentimentality worthless. She raised her glass to his and they clinked. 'Cheers!' The guests followed suit and cheered their own salutations. Rachel spied one of Sylvie's famous chocolate fondant cakes on the table and was tempted to smash it into David's face. The room started to spin. She swapped her glass of bubbles for iced-cold water; that was enough alcohol for one day.

By the end of the night, everyone was tipsy and Eva was visibly drunk. Rachel spent ten minutes at the front door with her trying to say goodbye. Their extended farewell was due to Eva's deciding that their parting was the perfect moment for her to divulge to Rachel how much she liked her as a person and not because she was Eva's boss. Eventually Terry the Fireman saved them both from the situation by throwing Eva over his shoulder and carrying her out into the night.

Rachel filled the dishwasher and left the remaining mess piled up in the sink. She said goodnight to David and his friends, who had started to play poker in the conservatory, and retired upstairs. Rachel wasn't ready to sleep. The party had been the ultimate distraction. Now that it was over, there was nothing left for her to think about but the other woman.

When David delicately opened the door to their bedroom, Rachel pretended to be asleep. She heard him gargle mouthwash and brush his teeth before getting into bed. He started to snore seconds after his head hit the pillow. Rachel thought back to Eva gushing about her boss's *perfect life* and her cheeks burned with embarrassment. Rachel's life was a charade.

She woke a couple of hours later. The bedside clock glared a demonic red – 04:13. Champagne-induced dehydration pounded behind her forehead. It was no use, she wasn't going back to sleep. She thought about the times when David had been romantic – he would send her letters and cards even after they lived in the same house. On the occasions she went away without him, she would find that he had secreted a love note in her suitcase or her passport holder. Or when he went away, she would find notes in her underwear drawer or under her pillow. She was certain David had loved her once. Not being able to believe he did now left a painful black hole in her heart.

She pushed down the anxiety she felt about him not using condoms with the flame-haired bombshell ... what if that meant Rachel herself had to be tested for sexually transmitted diseases? She would be mortified to go to the doctor's with a mysterious itch. Was she just imagining she could feel an irritation there already? She pushed gently against the cotton gusset of her knickers. *Were bacteria already multiplying down there?*

She picked up her phone again and searched the Internet for reasons why a man cheats. Google returned more than 179,000,000 results. The scale of these findings confirmed her worst suspicions. It was never good news for the wife. *Quelle surprise.* Rachel wanted to confront David and demand to be told what the hell was going on. Her recall of the details of the kiss in the street had already started to fade. She couldn't remember what either of them had been wearing or how long the kiss had lasted. She couldn't remember how they'd acted with one another and she didn't know where they went afterwards. Rachel had spent the last couple of days in a haze, which she put down to post-traumatic shock. She was exhausted from it all.

Rachel's brain took over from her broken heart and she resolved they needed a quick divorce, like ripping off a plaster. That's all there was left to do now the trust was gone. When she heard David stir, she slid her phone under her pillow and pulled the silk sleeping mask back over her eyes.

4

By the time Rachel woke up again and wearily descended the stairs she had two missed calls from her mother. She knew that she would have to tell Norma about David soon, but wasn't ready to face the predictable 'I told you so'. It had been years in the making. She could almost hear Norma's voice saying something scathing about 'wandering lips and travelling hips'.

Rachel and David had plans to meet friends for Sunday lunch but the middle-aged hangovers caused one couple to cancel and another to beg forgiveness and postpone. David and Rachel were both secretly grateful that they didn't have to pretend to be sociable and were allowed to soothe their own sore heads.

Rachel distracted herself by reading the Sunday glossy mags. She turned the pages and stared at photos without getting past the headlines. Confronted with an article about anti-ageing serums, she pulled distractedly at her face. She couldn't concentrate; she'd read the same paragraph a hundred times. Something about the importance of circular motions ...

Rachel's phone buzzed. *Mother Dearest* flashed across the screen and she was tempted to send the call to voicemail.

'Hi, Mum, did you—'

'I think it's time,' she cut in. No 'hello', no 'How are you?' Norma always got straight to the point.

'Time?'

'Time for me to, you know, get out there again.'

'Out there?'

'Annie has met a man on the Internet. Can you believe it?'

'Annie ... From choir or Bridge Club?'

'Anne is choir, Annie is Bridge Club. You know, purple hair, only one good leg,' Norma clarified, as if Rachel should have a photographic memory. As if one could forget Annie with one leg; the woman was a wonky Rottweiler. And that really was being unfair to Rottweilers.

'Really?'

'Really. She only has one leg, she's rude and hates everyone and everything. And in spite of all that, she's gone and found herself a man. And to make matters worse, she's incredibly happy and, dare I say it, he's rather nice, Annie's new boyfriend. He's living in that fancy retirement home ... you know, the one that serves wine with dinner.'

Rachel did know. It cost a fortune.

'. . . so you think it's a good idea?'

'What? Yes, it sounds fine to me.' Rachel was only half-listening and didn't know what she had agreed to. 'Wait, do you mean for Annie?'

'No. For me!' Norma huffed, and Rachel could picture her mother rolling her eyes.

'You think you're ready?'

'Your father's been de— gone ten years,' Norma added matter-of-factly. David was right; her mother had all the warmth and empathy of an iceberg.

'You were married for thirty years.'

'That's by the by.'

'If that's what you want, you know I worry about you being on your own. Whatever makes you happy'

Norma released a massive sigh of relief. 'Look, I've got to go.'

The call had already ended. Rachel found herself saying goodbye to an empty line.

David called out as he closed the front door. Rachel caught the tail end of '. . . be back soon'.

'Where are you going?' she shouted after him. It was too late, he was gone. This was ridiculous, she thought, and opened a browser to Google 'Divorce'.

About 722,000,000 results.

She followed this up with:

'How to divorce'

'How to divorce UK'

'Divorce lawyer Richmond'

'How long to divorce'

'Divorce tips for cheated on wives'

'Divorce for cheated wives UK'

'Divorce cheated on wife no children split assets'

'Divorce tips for cheated on wives no children split assets no pre-nup UK'

'Does wife get half in divorce'

'How to get everything in divorce'

'How to get everything in divorce UK'

The search results threw up innumerable legal professionals offering three feasible routes. She divvied the local companies into the main categories: Lions (Take him for everything he's got), Sheep (Be nice and go along with everything) and Sloths (Get left behind). The following day was Monday. She was going to have to get herself a lawyer.

5

The following morning, Rachel's whole body ached. She gulped down a sob, feeling a visceral ripping sensation inside her. Her throat was raw. *Was it possible to die from a broken heart, literally?* She contemplated phoning in sick. It was her company, no one would complain, but the thought of staying in the marital home all day made her feel worse.

Rachel had been trapped for seventy-two hours, floating in and out of four of the five stages of grief – all but acceptance. Today, she was stuck in anger. She was a little ball of fury; she scared herself by how enraged she was. She didn't know how she made it into work. She slathered on too much make-up, in an attempt to cover the hollow eye sockets and the bags under them, and wore an oversized t-shirt and yoga trousers. Yes, some could consider her outfit leisure-work attire, but Rachel's get up was less *fitness fashion* and more an urgent cry for help. When she finally sat down at her desk she noticed she was wearing odd shoes. They were very similar, both black strappy sandals; though sisters and not twins. She had seen that wearing mismatched earrings had become absurdly fashionable. Would it be too optimistic to think that the same rule applied to footwear?

Rachel's company provided marketing and events management. They had two big upcoming events in the diary: a vodka brand launch and the opening of a refurbished boxing hall. They had recently recovered from organising the wedding of a politician, the Hon. Joseph Longneck MP, a relatively high-profile event for Rachel and her team. The small office were naturally sworn to secrecy so far as the world outside was concerned, but also forbidden from using the politician's name in any written communication. This resulted in the in-house code words for the respective families of Mr & Mrs Mouse (Bride's) and Mr & Mrs Giraffe (Groom's). Afterwards they had sworn off weddings for the foreseeable future.

Rachel slumped in her office chair, her head in her hands, the weight of anxiety seemingly too much for her neck and shoulders to bear. She'd never noticed the clock's noisy mechanism before but now it was screaming into the silence of her office. Tick! Tock! Tick! Tock! Tick! Tock! She felt the minutes of her marriage run out. With each tick, her ovaries dried a little, and with each tock more lines developed on her neck. She stifled a yawn and accepted her fate as a childless spinster. Rachel couldn't concentrate on work but she couldn't go home, frozen in her own personal Purgatory. Instead she opened her mailbox. *Mistake!* Two hundred and twenty unread emails. She couldn't deal with them today. She turned to her calendar. *Mistake!*

09:00 Team catch-up.

Rachel checked her watch – 09:43. *Ooops – missed that!*

11:00 Conference call with florist. *Must cancel.*

12:00 Meeting with Bruce Johnston. *Must cancel.*

16:45 Meeting with Champagne company. *Ask Lydia to check if they are bringing tasting bottles. If not, cancel.*

Rachel couldn't face any sort of work. She closed down the browser and attempted to count slowly to ten. By the time she'd reached six, Eva was knocking on the glass wall and opening the office door. She complimented Rachel on a wonderful spread at the weekend then sheepishly apologised for getting tipsy. Eva didn't *exactly* remember leaving the party but Terry the Fireman had said she might want to consider saying a few words to excuse their ungainly exit. Rachel was halfway through reassuring Eva that she had nothing to apologise for when her phone buzzed. She looked at the phone but didn't take in the message. She could sense Eva staring at her and it made her self-conscious. Rachel would have to go home, she was a mess.

'You okay?' Eva asked.

Rachel nodded. She could feel her bottom lip start to quiver.

'What is it?'

'Nothing.'

'No. Not nothing. Something … you're wearing odd shoes for starters.' Eva had a natural talent for calling out bullshit.

Rachel tucked her right foot behind her left to conceal the diversity of her footwear.

'It's fine. Anyway, it's nothing work-related.'

Eva waited for her to continue. When she didn't, Eva opened her notebook and began reciting the attendees for the vodka launch. By the time she reached F on the alphabetised list, Rachel was trembling. Her face was hot and tears pricked at her eyes.

'He kissed someone else,' she whispered.

Eva looked up suddenly.

'Who – David? Kissed someone? I don't believe it. What kind of kiss?'

'It was a my-husband's-mouth-on-another-woman's-mouth kind of kiss, then a hug. I think.'

'Seriously?' Eva said, and frowned. Her head dropped to one side in puzzlement. 'Are you sure it wasn't one of those moments where you both go to the same side and your lips accidentally meet in the middle?'

This was not the reaction Rachel had been expecting and she was stunned into silence. Eva was a realist, ergo she was the most pessimistic, cynical individual Rachel knew. She hadn't expected to have to explain that lips plus lips equals kiss. And then kiss plus kiss equals affair. It was simple arithmetic, wasn't it? Her husband had kissed another (much younger) woman on the eve of his wedding anniversary – it didn't get much worse than that. Eva stared at her calmly and Rachel rejected the implied message. This wasn't an overreaction. 'He kissed someone else!'

'I'm sorry, Rachel,' Eva said, finally. 'It sounds awful.'

'It *was* awful!' she said, her voice warbling sanctimoniously. 'They were at it on the high street. Smooching and hugging. In broad daylight. In full view of EVERYONE!'

Eva raised an eyebrow.

'And she's young, Eva. I mean, she's *really* young. She had red hair straight out of an advert and puckered, kissable lips. And an *I'm so pretty, look at me* smile. I tried to follow but I lost them.'

'You lost them? When?'

'Friday.'

'This happened on Friday, before your party? And you kept it together all weekend. Well done you! I would have razed the place to the ground.'

'What did I do wrong? I starve myself two days a week to fit into my jeans. TWO BLOODY DAYS A WEEK! And for what? I do yoga AND Pilates. ... well, I tried Pilates a couple of times, it's really difficult, you know. But we have sex every week,' Rachel added feebly, before saying, 'I thought we would be okay, I thought it was enough ...' She tried to keep hold of the fury. At least anger was a good, cathartic, appropriate emotion. She couldn't cope with the commiseration in Eva's expression.

Stay angry, she resolved.

Stay angry and you won't cry.

Eva could see that Rachel was on the edge. She made them both coffee.

*

41

'So …' Eva started as she put the I ♥ MARKETING mugs down and closed the office door behind her.

'I think it's over,' Rachel whispered on a shuddering breath.

'Are you sure?' asked Eva.

Rachel nodded.

'Because—'

'Eva,' Rachel said, holding up a hand to silence her. She tried to give the impression of being in charge. 'I know that some people can forgive an affair, but I'm not one of them. I never have been, and I never will be.'

'But you don't *know* that it's an affair …'

'Eva!' Rachel cut in, more sharply than she had intended, and then taking a deep breath said, slowly and clearly, 'It's never *just* a kiss.'

Eva nodded slowly and walked over to Rachel, wrapping her arms tightly around her shoulders. A hot tear escaped from the corner of Rachel's eye and fell onto Eva's blouse.

'I know what you need.' Eva quickly straightened up and left Rachel's office. Through the glass wall Rachel could see her extract something from her desk in the outer room. Eva's Marie Kondo-ed, minimalistic desk space was the opposite of Rachel's paper-laden jumble. Moments later, Eva was back and handing her a business card: *Stefan Stratos Esq. Family Law,* it read, above a local address and phone number all embossed in a thick black serif typeface. Rachel envisaged a faceless man with the printer choosing the weight and colour of these business cards. The cream parchment felt expensive.

She assumed his fees would be likewise. The word 'family' hit her like a punch in the ovaries. She and David would not now be having the family that they had planned. The one upside: divorce was much easier when you didn't have children.

'Call Stefan, he's brilliant,' Eva said. She nodded towards the business card. 'He really is the best. I got to keep the house, the car, the dog. And these.' Rachel wasn't sure if these meant Eva's necklace, her teeth or her rather splendid bosoms. Rachel smiled all the same and gave a half-nod before returning the card.

'I don't know—'

'Phone him – or pop into the office, he's local. In town, opposite Boots,' Eva said.

'You don't have to commit to anything, but you should know where you stand. Tell him I sent you. And don't be put off by the hair ...'

What did that mean – don't be put off by the hair?

Rachel nodded.

'Before you have a complete breakdown, shall we do a little work today? I know you're not up to much but ... I need to prepare you,' Eva said softly. 'Bruce called to say you hadn't sent something, and it was urgent, and ...' Eva made a rude gesture with her hand and tongue. 'He said he's been calling and calling.'

Just then Lydia entered Rachel's office with a notepad and pen poised. Lydia was an amazing assistant. She was enthusiastic and intelligent, and nice and friendly to boot. She wore her long blonde hair in a ponytail that swished from side-to-side when she got excited. She resembled a

Disney horse – a very pretty one, with huge eyes, long eyelashes and impressive teeth.

'Not now, Lyds,' Eva said without turning around.

'But—'

'I know I said that you could start management training, but it's a bit full on to be shadowing me at the moment – can we start next week?' Rachel pleaded with her eyes.

Lydia looked crestfallen, but nodded as she removed herself from the glass-walled office and closed the door.

'It gets worse. Bruce called and he's on his way in. Rachel? Rachel, are you listening to me? He wanted to make doubly sure you hadn't forgotten your meeting.'

'Yes, missed calls, Bruce ... what did you say?'

'Bruce. Bruce Johnston? The formidable Bruce Johnston! He's coming in for a meeting at noon, he'll be here in an hour.'

'Shit!' Rachel looked down at the comfortable assortment of cotton jersey she had shrouded herself in. 'He can't see me like this, can you take the meeting?'

Eva shook her head. 'Mr Johnston was quite adamant that it was you he had to see – he insinuated that you've been dodging his calls.'

Rachel couldn't even remember seeing any messages. They must have got lost between the flurry of *Happy Anniversary* wishes and an excess of medicinal Martinis.

She checked her phone: Bruce Johnston – seven missed calls.

Double shit.

'I'd better go home to change. Please can you do me a favour and cancel my other appointments for today?'

6

The house was quiet. When David had said he was working from home today Rachel had suspected it was another lie, so why did the truth hurt? She presumed he was out with his young mistress, having post-sex brunch and making plans for their happy-ever-after future. Laughing together about the fact that Rachel had no idea.

She called his mobile and to her surprise heard the *Match of the Day* theme ringtone echo throughout the house. She cancelled the call and shouted up the stairs, 'Hi, it's me!' And after a pause, 'I didn't realise you'd be in.'

David was in their study. Rachel climbed the stairs and poked her head around the door. Their home office was split into two very distinct halves. Once they decided to make the room a shared space, they proceeded to choose their own furniture and decoration like teenage siblings who had been forced to share a bedroom. Rachel's side was full of pastels and bright colours and framed pictures. David's half was simply leather and dark wood. Rachel knew how it must seem to outsiders – hideously mismatched – but she had always liked the contrast.

David was deep in concentration. She watched him pound his fingers against an oversized calculator and let out a deep sigh of frustration. He had been struggling with work lately. Despite how furious she was with him, Rachel couldn't help but feel for him. The sale date was drawing nearer, and every day there seemed to be a new complication that needed to be resolved or a fresh concession to be made.

'You look tired,' she said, stopping herself from walking over to lay a hand on his shoulder.

David moved her out of the way, saying that he needed a coffee. She hated the sound of his feet plodding away down the stairs. In the old days, they were a team. He would have asked her advice on whatever situation he was struggling with and they would have found a way through together. Now, he didn't have the will or the energy to explain it to her. Rachel realised that another kind of trust had been mislaid. She fingered the business card loitering in her pocket. The only sane thing to do was to make an appointment with the divorce lawyer. Eva was right; she needed to know her options. Rachel called the number and allowed a soft female voice to calm her thoughts. She found a pen and made a list of documents that she needed to find. Rachel located the paperwork and made a table of the pros and cons of leaving her husband:

Pros	Cons
Do what I want, when I want	The betrayal
	The betrayal
	The betrayal
	The betrayal
	The betrayal

Rachel changed out of her comfortable clothes and into a suit worn with matching shoes this time. The three-quarter-length trousers flattered her figure and the heels elongated her legs. She added a small squirt of perfume to her neck and wrists and left the house without saying goodbye.

Rachel stood outside the offices to Stefan Stratos Esq., Family Law. While she deliberated, she called Bruce who was very unhappy she was running late and ordered her to get back to the office pronto. After Rachel had offered her sincere apologies, he sacked her and her team, announcing: 'Your services are no longer required.' She tried to explain it was a difficult day but he had already ended the call. Rachel sent a text to Eva to say they had lost the Bruce Johnston account, followed by a row of happy face emojis.

Rachel stared at the lettering on the frosted glass panel; the gilded font matched the embossed text on the thick cream business card.

Stefan Stratos Esq.
Family Law

She pushed open the door and stepped into an open-plan office with three smaller conference rooms leading off it. The ticking of an invisible clock was audible throughout the room. A short, stout man smiled at her. Eva wasn't kidding: Stefan Stratos was the hairiest man Rachel had ever seen. If she had to hazard a guess, he was at least eighty per cent fur. He had hair sprouting all over his neck and out from between his shirt buttons as well as from his cuffs. She was reminded of a hedgehog, with hair in place of spines.

'I'm Stefan Stratos.' The hirsute man extended his hand for her to shake. In spite of his heavy-set physique, he held her hand in his with the delicacy of someone handling a rare orchid. He showed her to a conference room.

'Rachel? Eva mentioned you would be calling by.'

'Eva's great, isn't she? She said you were one of the good guys.'

Rachel regretted gushing like that. *One of the good guys?* She hoped he didn't take it as patronising. She handed him a folder containing the paperwork she had been asked to bring.

'Eva *is* great,' Stefan Stratos replied. Then he went through the documents one by one, saying, 'You're here for marital advice?'

Rachel nodded.

'Husband? Wife?'

'Husband.'

'When did you marry?'

'Fifteen years ago.'

'You still live together?'

'Yes.'

'I have to ask, do you still share a bed?'

'Yes.'

'Children?'

'No.'

Did she detect a pause there, longer than in between the other questions?

'My husband has been unfaithful,' she blurted out. Stefan Stratos looked up from ticking boxes on a form.

'I'm sorry to hear that,' he said softly. 'A recent discovery?'

Rachel nodded.

'I know that this must be difficult for you, Rachel, but can you explain the circumstances to me?'

Rachel described the kiss she'd seen. Even as she said the words aloud she knew they sounded silly. As a divorce lawyer, Stefan Stratos must have seen degrees of infidelity far worse than a public kiss! But if he thought her complaint trivial, he gave no sign. Stefan Stratos nodded along and made notes. He called for his assistant to join them. Sophia was young and enthusiastic, petite and pretty with olive skin. Her hair was an impressive bouquet of shiny, black curls held in place with a red ribbon to match her blouse. She took Rachel's documents and returned with two sets; photocopies and the originals. Stefan Stratos said the important thing was to start the ball rolling.

'May I offer some advice?'

Rachel nodded. She thought that was what she was paying him by the hour for.

'The heart is a fickle thing. And I can see you're in pain, a lot of pain. It's easy to lash out in reaction. Think about what you want in the future. The number one regret of too many of my clients is not taking the time to resolve both the head and the heart.'

'But he cheated on me,' Rachel managed to whisper.

'I know. And right now it feels as if it's impossible for you to forgive his misdoings, but in the long term how do you want to handle the relationship? If you're sure you want to separate, we would need verification of his infidelity. He would likely deny all wrongdoing,' Stefan Stratos explained. He placed his hand over hers and left it there until she had calmed. He reassured her he would be available to help in whatever way he could. Rachel was comfortable with being represented by him. He was, as Eva had said, a bloody nice bloke. She wondered how many clients he had talked out of a divorce. Surely reconciliation must be bad for a family law business?

Rachel checked the notes she had made:

1) not to make any rash decisions;
2) start quietly collecting tangible evidence of the affair.

Whatever she decided to do, knowledge was power, and if she did decide to file for divorce then she would need all the evidence she could get.

Rachel had assumed that the moment she had arranged an appointment, that would be it – the decision made. But she left Stefan Stratos's office with more questions than answers. *Could she really see herself forgiving David? Could they move on past the affair? Did she want to be a divorcee and start again at her age? She could almost hear her biological clock screaming from inside. TICK, TOCK, TICK, TOCK.*

7

Rachel announced to Eva she had retained the services of a divorce lawyer. D.I.V.O.R.C.E. The big D. Divorce. The word still felt foreign in her mouth.

'I told you Stefan was great, didn't I?' Eva placed a cup of tea on Rachel's desk. 'Sorry, we've run out of biscuits.' This was a polite way of reminding Rachel it was her turn to buy chocolate digestives. Another thing that she had forgotten in the madness of *Kissgate*.

Eva sat down next to Rachel, with her own *What would Madonna do?* mug in hand. She continued carefully, 'look, David isn't my cup of tea.'

'I thought you liked him?'

Eva didn't answer. Instead she took a sip of her tea and exhaled deeply before she continued. 'As the survivor of multiple divorces, do you want my advice?' She raised her hand in a formal gesture, to emphasise her point. 'It could have been a harmless kiss; maybe he's not having an affair.'

Rachel rolled her eyes. 'You don't believe that.'

'I don't. But I've been known to be wrong. You need to hire a private detective.'

'Where do I find—'

Before Rachel could finish her sentence, Eva had started to scribble on a post-it note. 'The first and second ones I have used personally; both of them are very good. The third, my neighbour used when her husband went missing.'

'The one who was living on a fishing trawler in Iceland?'

'That's the one. And it was those guys who found him there.'

Rachel thanked Eva with as much sincerity as she could muster. Speaking to her had helped, though this was not the reaction Rachel had anticipated. She had wanted the ball-busting Eva; had expected the number for a hitman, not a private detective agency.

'You know where I am if you need to talk,' Eva said, and left Rachel alone with her confused thoughts. She scrunched up the list of names and threw the paper into the wastepaper basket only to scout it out again ten minutes later. She went for the third company first. She liked the story about the Icelandic fishing trawler and it couldn't have been an easy find. She dialled the number and a gum-chewing voice answered and asked how she could help.

'I need to hire your services. I think my husband is having an affair.'

Having an affair. The words devastated her again and Rachel stopped talking as they caught in her throat. The girl on the other end of the call took some details. The routine nature of the conversation chilled Rachel to the core. It was akin to ordering a pizza: *evidence of one philandering husband, please, with a side of photographs of the young mistress, thank you.*

'Miss?' the voice said. 'Are you still there?'

'Erm, yes,' Rachel managed eventually. 'Yes, sorry, it's all a bit ... I've not done this before.'

'I understand,' the voice said coolly. 'I'll go through some of the packages we offer, shall I? Obviously each case is different but our detectives need to know what level of engagement you expect and what services you're willing to pay for, and we can build an invoice for you. What do you need evidence of? We start at £45 per hour plus VAT and expenses.'

Rachel hurriedly told the woman she had changed her mind. A private detective was a step too far. She was conflicted about having her husband followed. Of course, Rachel preferred to think it was just a solitary kiss and that her husband wasn't banging the beautiful redhead, but what were the chances? Had hell frozen over? She checked the sky for flying pigs. If Eva was right, that David was innocent until proved guilty (one kiss does not a philanderer make), then he should be given the benefit of the doubt and the chance to clear his name. And she was also uncomfortably aware that hiring a professional was something you couldn't come back from. It wasn't at the same level of deceit as cheating, but it certainly wasn't showing good faith.

Rachel saw Eva had overheard the conversation and wondered if she could style it out without having to address it. She couldn't. Instead, she said that she wouldn't hire someone to follow her husband at great expense when she could do the legwork herself with a minimal amount of sleuthing. The Internet listed a few basic steps that could be undertaken from home: by checking joint finances for unusual credit-card activity or large cash withdrawals, Rachel could see for herself if anything was amiss, and maybe put in some harmless tailing of David too. Check he was at the office when he said he was at the office, for instance.

'Did you say Tuesday was his "gym night"? How about we check he's actually going there tomorrow?' Eva asked, her eyes filled with glee.

8

Rachel sat on the toilet and waited until she could will enough urine to splash onto the plastic stick. Would the test show a stupid smiley face? Of course it did; she was ovulating. *Ding ding ding – we have a winner!* She updated the app with the news and stared at her fertility graph. There wasn't much point in it, she knew, but she would be damned if David would take her perfectly plotted ovarian chart away from her, as well as everything else. Still with her knickers around her knees, she checked her temperature. That too was added to the data. The phone buzzed in her hand. She had a new text message.

Eva: I'm at the end of your road, parked outside number 6.

Rachel called her as she pulled up her knickers and wriggled back into her black skinny jeans.

'What are you doing? Come to the house,' she whispered.

'I can't park outside because he might notice my car and we can't take yours because it's a pillar-box on wheels. He'll spot you a mile off. Come on, Rach, this isn't amateur hour!'

'Okay, I'll let you know when he's going.'

Eva was wearing sunglasses and looked stunning, dressed head-to-toe in what appeared to be a black catsuit. Rachel shook her head in disbelief.

'What are you staring at? I never get the opportunity to wear this,' said Eva as she checked her blind spot and pulled the car out and onto the main road. She told Rachel the plan was to stay two cars behind David.

'Have you done this before?' Rachel asked.

'Here, put these on.' Eva handed her a pair of oversized sunglasses.

Rachel put them on; they really suited her. She had packed her SLR camera complete with a zoom lens. She rarely used it, but it was the closest thing she had to binoculars, and if she needed to collect evidence, it would take a clearer shot of David than the camera on her phone. Eva nodded to the back seat; she had stocked up on 'stake-out essentials', buying water, iced coffee, honey-roasted peanuts, chocolate brazil nuts, crisps and grapes.

'How long are we planning on being in here?'

'As long as it takes,' Eva said gravely.

'I'm not sure this is a good idea.'

'You didn't want to pay a private detective, I get that—'

'It's not the money.'

'But, Rachel, you need to know.'

They followed David through the winding streets for fifteen minutes. Rachel loved the twinkly lights of Richmond at dusk. The shops were closing. Warmth glowed from windows of cosy pubs and moonlight glimmered on the River Thames. This was home. She couldn't imagine living anywhere else.

Rachel was relieved when she saw David park his silver Prius outside the gym. Her shoulders released and dropped a couple of inches. She had figured he was using the place as an excuse. There was no way he had time for both squats and sneaking off with his mistress. Perhaps he wasn't having an affair? Eva was evidently thinking the same, as she caught Rachel's eye.

'It's not proof that he's not ... you know,' Rachel said thinly. 'But at least he's telling the truth about something.'

Eva nodded and then said, 'Hey, do you want to get something real to eat? I'm not sure if I fancy the camping fare.'

'Tapas?' Rachel suggested.

Eva had already reversed the car out of the parking space when Rachel spied David in the rear-view mirror. He had walked right past the gym entrance. She gasped and reached out to grab Eva's shoulder but accidentally grabbed the steering wheel instead.

'Rachel!' Eva slammed on the brakes.

'Shit! Sorry!' she said as she held up her hands.

'There is no gym bag.' Eva managed to manoeuvre an impressive U-turn in spite of Rachel's flapping, pointing and bellowing. 'THERE IS NO GYM BAG!' Rachel repeated in a screech.

They watched David approach a three-storey apartment building and push a button on the intercom. After what seemed like hours, but was probably only seconds, he was buzzed in. The door opened onto a dimly lit foyer and David disappeared from sight.

Rachel had been so shocked that she had forgotten to take pictures of him entering the building. Retroactively, she tried to get a close-up shot of the building number or the door but Rachel's zoom lens was hopeless; the picture was dark and blurred and she couldn't identify any useful detail. Eva darted out of the car and nonchalantly approached the intercom display. She shook her head as she walked back.

'No names, only a list of apartment numbers,' she said as she got back into the car.

Rachel nodded. Eva was stoically calm but Rachel's imagination ran wild as she imagined the different ways David and his mistress would be enjoying each other's bodies. *Would there be foreplay or would they get straight down to it?* It was all too much. She looked at the dashboard clock. Four minutes of mental torture was exhausting. She was already drained. Eva opened a bag of crisps and Rachel shot her a murderous look.

'What?' she said innocently. 'We might be here a while.' Eva pointed out that David and the woman were probably only having a drink and hadn't even undressed. Rachel was too wounded to respond. The sound of Eva's chomping was unnecessarily loud in the silent car. Rachel opened one of the iced coffees. It was cold and tasted good but sweet in a sickly way.

After half an hour spent in silence, Rachel admitted, 'I think it's more than just a kiss.' She said the words so quietly she didn't think Eva had heard her until she felt her hand being squeezed.

The coffee-in-a-can wasn't enough. Rachel wanted a real drink. She wasn't sure how long it would be before David would eventually return home, but she imagined Eva and herself could easily polish off a bottle of Sauvignon before his marathon love-making session was over. Rachel stared out of the car window. She was glad she'd had the foresight not to wear mascara.

Her phone buzzed in her hand and made her jump. A banner flashed at the top of the screen alerting her that she had a new email from Stefan Stratos.

'That was quick,' Rachel said. *Was it too quick?* 'I've got an email from Stefan Stratos.'

It felt impossible for her not to use his full name. It couldn't be Mr Stratos. Or Stefan. It had to be Stefan Stratos.

'I told you he was brilliant,' said Eva proudly.

'Oh, God.'

Eva's expression said, 'Wuss!' She gently took the phone to read the email. 'He has some news but says it's best to meet in person.'

'That's bad news, right?'

'Not necessarily. He says you're welcome to pop by tomorrow, before nine. I can come with you?' Eva offered.

'Thank you, but it's alright. I'm done with the hand-holding for one day.' Rachel found she was glad to have discovered a good friend in her kind if eccentric office manager. Rachel tried David's number, she didn't know what she was going to say but she couldn't sit there and do nothing. The phone rang, and rang, and rang, and rang. Eventually, his voicemail clicked in. *You've reached David . . .*

'I think it's time to call it a night. Please can you take me home?' Rachel asked.

'Sure?'

She nodded.

'Are you going to be okay? I can stay and keep you company until he gets back,' Eva offered when Rachel unbuckled her seatbelt and opened the car door.

'I'll be fine, really,' she said. 'I want to be on my own.'

Rachel thanked Eva again and walked up the path to the front door, hoping she hadn't come across as rude.

Once inside, Rachel went straight to the bathroom and collected every gadget, supplement and accessory that was even remotely connected to their pregnancy plan. The ovulation kits, vitamins, the thermometer, the books – everything was thrown into the big, unsightly council bin outside and dragged to the kerbside for collection the following morning. She reached for her phone, located the fertility app and deleted her profile.

Finally, she collapsed on the sofa, wine glass in hand. She regretted leaving behind the crisps and chocolate brazil nuts in Eva's car.

When David eventually returned her call two hours later, she didn't have the energy to question his whereabouts.

Rachel felt destroyed, her mind frazzled, her body deflated and her heart broken (again). She was beaten to the point of inertia. She lay near-comatose on the sofa watching a shopping channel, unable to muster the strength needed to find the remote.

'You rang – everything good?' David asked with a chipper inflection.

'Yeah, I wanted something but can't remember what.' *Self-esteem maybe? Or a loving husband or anything other than her current life.* 'How was the gym?'

'Might have a quick post-workout pint, I feel like I deserve it.'

'You knock yourself out,' Rachel said sardonically.

'Love you,' David added.

She fought back the bile at the back of her throat as she made an affirmative noise and ended the call.

9

The door to Stefan Stratos's office was closed. Rachel tried a push and a pull, but it was firmly locked. She looked at her watch; the brisk walk to his chambers had taken her seventeen minutes. It was 08:49. She knocked gently on the door and with her finger traced the words *Stefan Stratos* that were etched with a gold finish on the frosted glass. She was about to leave when the door was opened by Stefan himself, who continued to hold a conversation on his mobile phone. She was cheered by the waft of freshly brewed coffee. He nodded towards the reception area. She stepped inside and he locked the door behind her.

Stefan Stratos finished his call.

She hoped her face hadn't given away the apprehension she felt. 'All credit is due to Sophia. She was logging your documentation.' He pointed towards his assistant's empty desk. 'And she noticed that you were married on an Indonesian island. Bali, I believe?'

Rachel thought back to Bali. The memories had lodged in her mind. 'It was gorgeous. Idyllic.'

'I'm sure.' Stefan Stratos allowed Rachel to spend a moment in quiet reflection.

'The thing is, we can't see anywhere that the marriage was, how should I put it, *validated* by either the Indonesian or the British government.'

Rachel frowned.

'Let me be clear: you were under the impression that you were entering a legal marriage contract?'

'It was an official ceremony,' Rachel insisted defensively as she watched Stefan Stratos scribble notes. 'David paid the fee and there were witnesses. The local priest even sacrificed a chicken in honour of our union.'

The moment that the words left her lips, Rachel realised how absurd this sounded. Absolute lunacy. There was a pained silence in which Stefan Stratos nodded and adopted a carefully non-judgemental expression.

There was no correlation between a chicken, dead or alive, and the completion of a legal procedure.

'Are you sure there's no other paperwork?' he asked gently. 'Could you maybe double-check your records?'

'I can certainly check,' Rachel said, although she was certain there was none.

'We've seen this problem before, not only with Indonesian islands. And it's not always for nefarious reasons.'

'What do you mean?'

'I'm sorry to be the bearer of bad news, but in the eyes of the law you are not actually married.'

'Not what?' Rachel was stumped. 'Say that again?'

Stefan Stratos pushed a box of tissues towards her. He didn't repeat himself but let the words sink in. Rachel stood up and paced the office, her heels imprinting on the thick carpet.

'I'm not …' she thought she might explode '… married?' she whispered.

Rachel looked at the delicate ornaments displayed around the stylish room. She imagined throwing the paperweight through the window and pushing the computer from the desk.

'I'm not married,' she repeated. 'I'm not *married*.' She laughed when Stefan Stratos moved a crystal vase out of her reach.

'This is a lot to take in. Please come back to see me when you're ready to talk about next steps. Until which time – I'd advise you not to leave the marital home …'

Rachel scoffed.

'… and as well as collating firm evidence of adultery. And to help with dividing the assets, it would be good to start pulling together proof that you are Mrs Chatsworth, according to common law.'

This was like a bad dream. Too much for her to take in. Too many questions and home truths were flying at her. But the bottom line, however she framed it, was that she and David were not married.

Rachel had never officially changed her name – had that been her idea? She was young, David said. It was good to keep a sense of her own identity, he had said. They thought it would be better for business reasons. David Chatsworth and Rachel Keatley. He said it sounded more professional. This was at the beginning when the two of them were working together from their kitchen table.

How had she been so stupid?

Rachel was Mrs Chatsworth to all intents and purposes – except the bloody legal ones! She was determined not to cry. Until she did. And then, finally, she accepted the proffered tissue from the box on Stefan Stratos's desk.

David

10

One Week Earlier

David had the day off to take full advantage of their wedding anniversary. It was terrible timing, what with the sale of his company rapidly approaching, but he wanted to give Rachel his full attention for at least one weekend. He always looked forward to their anniversary – the little rituals they honoured, Champagne cocktails and a romantic dinner, the retelling of their stories. This year was a special one too, their fifteenth celebration. It's true: time flies when you're having fun.

He set a brief and vague out-of-office and allowed himself to sleep in. When he had exhausted the news his iPad had to offer he got out of bed, stepped into a cold shower, then made a start to the beautiful day ahead. He began by grinding coffee beans. He poured himself a glass of grapefruit juice and breakfasted on granola with low-fat yoghurt. It was going to be a good day, David could feel it. He had spotted a hidden anniversary surprise in Rachel's side of the chest of drawers. It was wrapped in cream tissue paper and felt light and soft; underwear, he imagined excitedly. That was one of the things he loved about Rachel. Even when she was organising everyone else and playing host to dozens of people, she would always plan something private for the two of them. David would enjoy the day a little more, if that were possible, in the knowledge that he had this extra present waiting for him.

David pottered in the garden; he mowed the lawn and installed the pop-up gazebo for the weekend's celebrations. Then he locked the back door and left a note for Rachel:

Gone to collect the cake x

He walked along the river towards the town centre, trying to keep up with the rowers practising their lengths. It really was a glorious day. His step fell into the rhythm of the cox's short sharp shouts – 'left, right, left, right'.

The main street was busy with yummy mummies and their extravagant child carriers. His own father, David Senior, had never wanted children and said they ruined his life. The words had haunted David. But he knew he would be ready when his time came. And that time was now.

David found himself assessing the design of buggies and prams in the same way he used to shop for cars. He spied men dressed in their athleisure dad uniforms with babies strapped to their chests and wondered how long it would be until he was one of them. A man with a baby in tow. A family man.

He didn't see the woman approaching him.

'This is a nice surprise!' she said, and before he had a chance to react, there was a hand cupped around the back of his head and she was kissing him on the lips. Her own pouting mouth was as soft as rose petals and tasted of vanilla. She left behind a creamy pink residue on his mouth when she pulled away and finished with a hug.

Fuck.

The girl.

Fuck!

David was stunned. His mouth opened and closed but no words formed. She giggled. He held her shoulders; needing to keep her at arm's length while he tried to execute an escape plan.

'Sorry, David, didn't mean to startle you.'

The use of his name unsettled him. 'What are you doing here?' He was having trouble comprehending what had just happened. The woman, the street, the kiss … 'How did you find me?'

'Find you?' Amelia-Rose's smile faltered. She looked confused.

David's phone rang in his pocket. He juggled it like a hot potato and checked the screen – Rachel. *Shit!* He couldn't think quickly enough. He sent the call to voicemail and switched the phone off. At school, he had had a good javelin arm; maybe at this distance he could get it into the bin forty metres away. David took hold of Amelia-Rose and ushered her into a narrow lane between two high-street shops.

Her wild red curls bounced when she laughed.

David looked at Amelia-Rose's pretty, cherubic face. She was grinning.

He had never meant to spend the night with her. From the moment he'd met Rachel, he'd never wanted to sleep with anyone else. He married her within months, that's how sure he was.

However, last December, on a cold, winter's day at a mind-numbing bore of a conference, he'd been briefly distracted. He spent the afternoon gazing into the sparkling hazel eyes of a young woman who laughed at his stupid jokes and touched his hand when she asked for advice. When she suggested having a drink afterwards, he was flattered. He should have taken the praise, gone home and boasted to his wife: *You'll never guess who asked me out today? I know! And she's only twenty-two years old! Ha ha ha!* They would have bought a bottle of Champagne and made a toast to the life (still) in the old dog yet! But he hadn't. Instead, he'd told his first white lie to Rachel and shared a bottle of red wine with the alluring Amelia-Rose. It was only meant to be one ego-boosting drink; he had never thought she would actually be interested in him. Her youth and enthusiasm were captivating and all-consuming. Amelia-Rose was booked to stay overnight at the conference; she had a room upstairs. And she led him there. Thinking back, it was so surreal it was like an out-of-body experience. As if it wasn't him. Except, of course, it was.

He felt pathetic when he recalled how alive she'd made him feel. He was weak. He was the physical embodiment of that Robin Williams joke: *God gave Man a brain and a penis, but not enough blood to run them both simultaneously*. The fact that his mind had even summoned the reference made him feel old. Amelia-Rose probably didn't even know who Robin Williams was.

The sex was okay, but not great. It surprised him how difficult it was to discover a new body. He couldn't get her to orgasm easily. And he suspected that she wasn't entirely honest when she said she was there. He found women had changed since he was last single. There was no time for exploration; Amelia-Rose knew exactly what she wanted. She was so outspoken. She directed him to her clitoris. It was hard going, like navigating Milton Keynes – full of roundabouts and one-way systems. *Left a bit, yes, oooh, right, harder, gently, gentle, back a tad, nearly, nearly, gently, just there, no, you had it a second ago.*

Ever since that night, David had been consumed by self-loathing. He didn't deserve a lovely wife, a house, a job, or even his life. He had since taken to watching Rachel sleep in the morning and couldn't believe he had been *this close* to ruining their marriage over a silly fling, a one-off. He wanted to confess all and be absolved. He wanted Rachel to rap him on the knuckles and tell him what a fucking idiot he had been. David returned home riddled with guilt, but he was adamant he wasn't going to let one terrible mistake ruin his life.

'Do you want to go for a coffee?' Amelia-Rose asked

David was stuck. No, he didn't want to have a coffee. He wanted to invent a time machine, travel back in it and erase any interaction with this woman. But he found his voice saying yes. The truth was, he wanted to know why she was here, and what she wanted from him. Amelia-Rose then actually apologised, with absurd British politeness, for not calling him after their night together, before she told him about going through a tough time at work recently. David didn't point out that they hadn't in fact swapped numbers, and then panicked that she would ask for his now. The idea of stamping on his phone in front of her to prove his commitment issues towards technology was probably the only way to get out of coffee unscathed; either that or he could hand over his number and then immediately change it or else fake his own suicide.

It turned out Amelia-Rose didn't want anything. She'd seen him and had time to kill before her train. The relief was stupendous. He didn't know what there was left to say between them. He was petrified that anything nice he said would be misconstrued as flirting.

With the realisation that Amelia-Rose had not been hunting him down, was not pregnant, nor threatening to ruin his life, David panicked he was having bloody coffee with a woman where anyone could see them together. What if Rachel walked in? And why had she just called him? David hurried Amelia-Rose along. Drink up, he motioned. He threw a tenner down, and told the waitress to keep the change and instantly regretted his rudeness. The bill came to £9.97, she probably thought he was taking the piss, or else he was a smug arsehole, or both. In fairness, she'd be right.

David held Amelia-Rose's elbow as he walked her to the train station. She had less than ten minutes left to catch her train. He dithered. Should he wait with her? No, that would seem over the top. But if he didn't, he wouldn't know she had actually left. Maybe Amelia-Rose was like the Glenn Close character in *Fatal Attraction* and only playing cute and casual to get him to relax before she boiled his bunny!

David waited with her, asking more questions in those seven minutes than during the entire evening they had spent together. He wanted to know where she lived (Kingston – six stops on the train), where she worked (Teddington – four stops on the train), how often she came to Richmond (every couple of months) and, finally, all the places she liked to frequent. Coffee houses (Costa), supermarket (Tesco), department stores (House of Fraser). David made a mental list of all the establishments he would never set foot in again.

The train arrived, she reached over to kiss him on the cheek, and he stepped sharply out of range of her mouth and shook her hand instead. He waved her off like a child being evacuated in the Blitz.

Amelia-Rose gave a feeble wave goodbye, and as David retreated, called through the window, 'I'll send you a LinkedIn request.'

Fuck, NO!

David forced his face into a sort-of-smile and half-nodded, resigned to his fate. This was karma. He searched the platform for anyone he knew, and more importantly, anyone who knew Rachel. He saw a blonde with a horsey ponytail and wondered if she could be Rachel's assistant, but without his glasses he couldn't identify the young woman's features. Still, he turned away quickly and walked off, in case it was Lydia and she recognised him. He sloped out of the station, having to produce his credit card to exit.

Once on the street, he realised he had just paid to escort Amelia-Rose to the station platform. What if Rachel saw the amount on their bank statement? What if she questioned where he was on their anniversary? He made a mental note to intercept the post. What if someone saw them, put two and two together, told Rachel, and she left him? He was spiralling again. Nothing in his life worked without Rachel. She was his true north, his guiding star. She was his soulmate. Whenever anything bad happened, there was Rachel to help him through; whenever anything good happened, there was Rachel to celebrate with. The one person he could rely on, day in, day out, was Rachel. And that was without mentioning the way she did everything necessary to keep him in clean clothes, wholesome food, and regularly caffeinated.

David's chest tightened painfully at the thought of losing his wife. What was he to do? His heart noticeably raced. *Was this a heart attack?* His father had died at the age of forty-five from problems with his heart. Perhaps this was the karmic consequence of infidelity for David.

He tried to catch his breath but it was impossible. There was nowhere for the oxygen to go. He walked back to the riverside and headed home, switching on his phone as he walked. Five missed calls from Rachel. *Shit!* He didn't have any excuse. What could he say? He was tempted to throw his phone into the Thames and tell her he had lost it.

Rachel looked incredible in a turquoise dress he hadn't seen before … or had he? Her face was alluring, the red lipstick she wore shone. David wanted to drop to his knees and beg for forgiveness. He took his time closing the zip at the top of her neck and left behind a small kiss.

The comfort of the Indian food warmed his body. He allowed the cucumber and mint raita to cool his tongue. Rachel suggested another bottle of wine, but he declined with a small shake of the head. Another drink would have him confessing all. David knew he should make an attempt to woo Rachel into bed, but his libido was well and truly extinguished after this afternoon's unwanted encounter. Had his wife mentioned something this morning or the day before about coming into her ovulation window? He was stifled by a renewed surge of guilt thanks to the unexpected encounter with Amelia-Rose. David closed his eyes in an attempt to think clearly. *What was he going to do? What could he do?* He sensed Rachel move away from him and an immediate sense of loneliness engulfed him.

David opened his eyes and found Rachel staring at him. It was unnerving. *Did she know? Could she see into his soul?* He quickly closed his eyes again.

'Don't hate me but I forgot to pick up the cake,' he said to distract her.

He felt Rachel bounce off the sofa in a huff, although her words said otherwise. In those few seconds on his own he knew he wouldn't be able to cope if he ever had to live without her. *Don't leave me, Rachel. Please don't leave me. What am I going to do?*

David loved hosting parties at home. Rachel oversaw the food and he was in charge of drinks. Barry arrived early and wanted to get stuck into a six-pack, but David wasn't in the mood for drinking. Yes, one or two would probably help, but he was scared he would divulge his infidelities and end up losing his wife on their anniversary; a confession still hovered precariously on the tip of his tongue. *Loose lips sink ships.*

David didn't hear Norma arrive, but he saw her pashmina swish past like a dragon's tail. After the many years of barely disguised hostility he had learned not to expect any warmth from his mother-in-law. He had enough on his mind tonight without attempting to interpret Norma's not so thinly veiled digs. He would try his hardest to stay out of her way.

Once he had finished making the cocktails David went outside to pinch one of Barry's cigarettes. The crackle of the lighter ignited a memory, and the first inhalation reintroduced nicotine to his lungs. *Hello, my old friend.* David promised himself it was only one cigarette (these were extreme circumstances after all). *God, that felt good.* It had taken countless attempts for him to quit completely. He had been a smoker for twelve years when he dramatically threw away his last pack on the night of their wedding. He acknowledged he had spent more time as an adult without tobacco than with. Though every so often he was ashamed to admit that he occasionally lusted for a cigarette. There was nothing quite like a warm evening with a cold beer and a smoke. That was before the health warnings on the packets: SMOKING INCREASES THE RISK OF IMPOTENCE and photographs of mouths riddled with cancer.

He looked back to the house to check he hadn't been spotted. He saw Rachel and gave his boldest *no-I-haven't-been-smoking* wave. Now he was guilty twice over; Rachel hated smoking.

David needed to talk to Barry, but one look at his old friend's face told him that Barry had enough on his mind. His wife wasn't sick – the reason he'd given for Gina's absence from the party – they'd broken up again. And, apparently, for good this time.

The two friends agreed to have a couple of beers later in the week and chat about how Barry was coping since Gina had chucked him out and changed the locks. Answer: he wasn't. David already craved another nicotine hit. Instead, he kept his fingers busy by picking apart precious flower heads.

When the time for the speeches came, David ran upstairs to find his wedding ring. The metal irritated his skin, but maybe the gold would protect him in some way, like in *Lord of the Rings*, or maybe he was misremembering that? He had prepared a short speech, peppered with affectionate light-hearted jokes, but when it was time to deliver it, he decided to speak from the heart instead, and unlike other occasions this speech wasn't garbled or rambling or repetitive. Telling the truth about his love for Rachel was relaxing, felt like a meditation. Everything he felt, he was able to say truthfully. The soppy and silly stories that he told their friends and family, which would once have made him feel self-conscious and clichéd, now made him invincible. He loved Rachel and wanted everyone to know it. She never needed to find out about Amelia-Rose and he was certain he would never stray again. His head was not for turning. He saw the pain of utter regret cross Barry's face, which threatened to break into tears. David quickly raised his glass and called out: '*Salut!*'

The next morning, David's head was banging. Mixing the grape and the grain had given him a horrendous migraine. He inhaled the scent of Rachel's anniversary blueberry pancakes, regretting he couldn't opt for the well-proven hangover cure of eggs, bacon and sausage. He tried to work out his worries. He was no closer to shrugging off his burden of guilt. Even the business section of the *Sunday Times* couldn't distract him from his nagging thoughts and regrets.

Barry messaged to say he'd headed to the White Hart pub for a *swift half*. In under quarter of an hour David had joined him there and the hair of the dog immediately soothed their aching heads. After the first beer, both men visibly relaxed. David sat for two hours listening to Barry explain, through sniffs and sobs, how much he missed Gina and how he wished she would take him back. And how not seeing the kids was killing him. It was embarrassing, Barry told him. He'd had to sneak in on sports day to watch his youngest fall over in the relay.

David listened to him explain about asset separation and divorce papers while all the time thinking about Rachel. His own infidelity had hit him like a bullet to the brain. Every night since, he had been haunted by thoughts of Rachel burning his clothes and calling in a locksmith.

Barry was now living in a bedsit opposite David's gym on the outskirts of town, which gave him an indication of the sort of place any new bachelor could expect to find himself living in. It was grotty, with next to no furniture but for a microwave with a friendly resident cockroach Barry had named Cocky.

After three pints David called time and walked home slowly. He sought comfort from Rachel and held her tight in his arms on the sofa, praying he would never lose her. The violence and betrayal they watched in *Game of Thrones* only increased his inner turmoil and anxiety.

David was the founding director of a bespoke IT firm. This was the company he and Rachel had started from scratch together years earlier before she had diverted to marketing and event management. He was now on the brink of selling the company to a multi-national. It should bring in enough to pay off the mortgage and buy the place by the sea that he and Rachel both coveted. It was a deal that had been in the works for over two years and part of the plan was for David to continue to work in a non-executive advisory role. The incoming Chief Executive would have the benefit of the company founder's opinions and strategy without needing to accept any input in the managerial side of things. It would be hard for David to keep to an arms-length approach though. DC Computing was his company; it would always be *his* company even when, as it transpired, it belonged to someone else.

David was checking the final heads of agreement when he heard the front door open and shut. Rachel was home unexpectedly in the middle of the day. *Was she ovulating? Had she come home to demand sex?* He was wearing his working from home attire: grey baggy joggers and an old t-shirt. He slipped his hand into his boxer shorts. *Come on, ol' boy. This is it. You've been in training your whole life.* He started to think about Rachel and looked at a photo of the two of them on their wedding night. They were young and full of hopes and dreams. *You can do this, easy does it.* Amelia-Rose popped into his mind unexpectedly. *Go away!* Back to Rachel . . . he imagined – taking off her bra His favourite black lace one. *Yes, feeling good!* A notification popped up on his screen. One new email: You have a LinkedIn request from Amelia-Rose Springer. *Fuck off!* It was no use. He'd have to feign a headache. When he heard Rachel run up the stairs he pretended to punch numbers into the barely used desk calculator.

David was relieved when she said she had to change quickly and return to work. He raced down the stairs and set the coffee machine to work. When he heard the front door slam shut, he felt his chest tighten alarmingly.

The doctor, a locum David had never seen before, invited him to take a seat. David described his chest pains and the doctor asked him twenty questions about his general health and lifestyle. Alcohol (four times a week, probably too many units), food (healthy), red meat (less than average), exercise (runs three times a week, recently joined the gym), anxiety (high), stress (lots). His blood pressure was healthy, very healthy.

'However, as a precautionary measure considering your family medical history, I think we'll refer you for an assessment with the local heart clinic.'

He was made to feel like he'd wasted his and the doctor's time.

David said thanks and goodbye, lingering for a moment as he thought about airing a secondary problem.

'Ah, the old door handle.'

David was confused.

'Sometimes, Mr ...' the doctor checked the computer monitor '... Chatsworth, people aren't forthcoming about their primary cause for concern until they are halfway out of the door.'

David sat back down. He explained the situation with their plan to start a family, and the anxiety of having to be ready to go, at any moment. He admitted that he'd thought it would be a fun time – trying for a baby – but now his thoughts were interfering with the inner-workings of his ball sack.

'See how you go with these.' The doctor prescribed him a low dosage of Viagra, *just in case*. David had never felt less sexy in his entire life. He left the surgery with a nagging sense of unease.

At home, David found Rachel in the hallway peering past the curtain into the road. She was whispering into her phone. When she saw him she rushed upstairs and continued her call from the bathroom. He stood outside their en-suite bathroom and could hear her talking. *Who was she talking to that she had to take the call in private?* He pressed his ear against the door but couldn't make out any of the words. Was the sink blocked again? Rachel had an annoying habit of calling in her brother Kevin to fix things when she had a perfectly incapable husband at home. Technology was David's thing. Pipes and plumbing definitely were not.

He checked his watch – it was getting late – Tuesday and Thursday nights were his gym nights, for legs and arms respectively. He had intended to tell Rachel that he was going to Barry's instead of the gym but she was still in the bathroom.

David parked outside the gym. He crossed the road, not watching where he was going, and nearly walked straight into a white van. He could have sworn he heard the driver shout 'wanker' in his direction. David pushed the buzzer to Apartment 3C. The lift had an Out of Order sign. 'I know how you feel,' he said to it, and headed for the stairs.

Barry opened the door and David stepped into his best friend's grim bedsit. There were a number of brown cardboard boxes with Scandinavian names on them piled up against the wall. Flatpack furniture waiting to be assembled, with one box doubling as a coffee table and covered with empty lager cans. The bin was overflowing with takeaway containers.

Up until recently David and Barry watched the football at Barry and Gina's, but Barry no longer had a TV, let alone a fancy sports package, and the Arsenal game was on Sky Sports.

They started to open IKEA boxes. David was still distracted by Rachel's bathroom phone call.

'Why does it always take longer to read the instructions and identify the right screws than it does to build the bloody things?' Barry complained.

Between the two men, they managed to put together a table, a couple of chairs, a bookcase and a bed frame.

'Let's go for a beer and catch the end of the match.' David was desperate to get out of the tiny man-flat.

On the way to the pub, he saw a missed call from Rachel and quickly returned it. She was barely audible, her voice low. He told her he was going for a post-gym pint. The fib caught in the back of his throat and he saw Barry roll his eyes. David told Rachel he loved her, but it didn't make up for the white lie.

He forgot to ask her who she was speaking to in the bathroom. What if it wasn't her brother? What if Rachel was being unfaithful? What if she was planning to leave him? Where was she? Was she even at home? What if she …? *Stop, David, you're spiralling again.* He felt his chest tighten at the thought of her packing her bags and told himself to concentrate on his breathing.

Breathe in, breathe out.

The pub was full. Football on a weeknight was a treat. An extra game for the sporting calendar. In the time Arsenal had scored a goal, relined their defence and nearly scored a second straight away, David had formed a plan, a strategy fuelled by a four-pack of Stella Artois and a pint of Amstel. He was going to swallow the guilt, suck it up, and no matter how terrible he felt, he was not going to ruin his marriage by telling Rachel. And he was definitely going to stop wallowing in self-pity. David bought another round of drinks.

'Mate!' He passed Barry his pint. He tried to talk through his idea with his friend amongst the noisy crowd; Barry had to bend his head closer to hear.

'I'm sorry about you and Gina.'

Barry clinked David's glass with his own.

'Hold on to Rachel, mate.'

David clinked his glass against Barry's and gulped down his anxiety.

'I'm going to be a better husband. I love Rachel, I'm not going to ruin it. I'm not going to end up in a bedsit – no offence.'

'None taken, mate. If any good comes from me fucking up my life ... take it! Have it!'

'I'm going to go home and get her pregnant,' David said loudly.

Barry gave him the thumbs up. And the tall man standing next to Barry congratulated David on his plan.

When Arsenal were awarded a last-minute penalty the pub erupted. David repeated to Barry and their new friend that right now he needed to go home and impregnate his wife. The penalty was scored and the final whistle sounded. The pub descended into chaos. Glasses clashed and beer spilled.

Their new best friend started a chant, 'GO, GET YER WIFE PREGNANT ...' The rest of the pub starting singing along. 'GONNA GO AND GET YER WIFE PREGNANT.'

David took a mini-bow to thank them for the encouragement. More cheers were unleashed.

Barry slapped his best mate on the back and wished him luck. 'Before you go – could you lend us twenty quid? I wouldn't ask but ... you know ...'

David raised his left eyebrow.

'Gina, mate. She's stopped all my cards.'

David checked his wallet and handed Barry the contents: ten crisp £10 notes.

'Thanks, Dave, I'll pay you back.'

As David slipped out of the door, he heard the final hurrah as a man bellowed, 'THREE CHEERS FOR THE BLOKE WHO'S GONNA GET HIS WIFE PREGNANT!'

Rachel

11

Rachel didn't want to go home but Stefan Stratos had instructed her not to leave the house so as not to lose her rights to the property. But how could she stay? She would once have trusted David to be fair in the divorce settlement, separation, splitting of assets, or whatever on earth they called it. But then again, he was hardly trustworthy of late.

Rachel would try to act normally if only to discover what the hell happened fifteen years earlier to cause him to pull the wool over her eyes about their marriage. She joined her never-husband for a cocktail.

ESPRESSO MARTINI RECIPE
50 ml Grey Goose Vodka
35 ml coffee liqueur

1 shot (25 ml) of freshly ground coffee, strong blend
Ice

'Cheers!' they said at the same time as they clinked glasses. Before Rachel had the chance to take a sip of her drink, David opened his laptop. *Hello?! I'm right here*, she thought.

'Do you remember our wedding?' she asked.

'Is this about our anniversary? I already feel bad enough about not booking the restaurant in time.'

'Why did we go to Bali in the first place?'

'I don't—'

'Was it your idea or mine?' Rachel moved closer to see the laptop screen.

'I can't remember.' He slammed it shut before she could see what or who was capturing his attention. 'By the way, about the weekend ... there's a small chance I may have to work.'

Rachel opened her hand and let the glass drop to the slate floor. The 1920s-style Champagne saucer smashed. Splashes of chocolate brown liquid plastered the duck egg blue wallpaper. The wall resembled a shit-stained Jackson Pollock.

'Oh my God, are you alright?' David asked. He ran to the kitchen and returned with paper towels. He blotted the wall but it was too late; the dark liquid had already taken hold. It had permeated the wallpaper and seeped sideways. There was nothing more David could do to salvage the damage. Rachel was satisfied with the destruction. She would worry later on about whether the colour and design were still stocked by Laura Ashley and who she could get to rehang the paper.

'I'll make you another one,' David said.

'It's okay, I've lost the taste for it,' Rachel said.

Anger bubbled inside her; her hands were shaking after dropping the glass. She wanted to tell him she knew about the other woman. She wanted to hurl all the bottled up anger at his face. She wanted to declare that she knew everything. She wanted answers.

But she didn't say anything. Mainly because she knew she couldn't trust a word that came out of his mouth.

'Actually I'm not feeling that well. I think I need an early night, sorry.'

David kissed her on the forehead and followed her upstairs with a glass of water and a selection of painkillers. Rachel thanked him and cocooned herself in the duvet. She was mentally and emotionally exhausted from the thoughts churning endlessly in her head.

The next day Rachel thought she could hold it together until she burst into tears in her yoga class. When the Swedish instructor hugged her, she only sobbed harder. The physical contact was too much; she took her mat and wet sleeves out of the hot sweaty exercise studio.

She saw a missed call from Jojo and replied with a text message:

Rachel: Busy day, you okay?
Jojo: All good here – we have to catch up soon.
           Miss your face xxx
Rachel: Miss yours more. Xxx

*

At home, Rachel heard the cat flap squeak and her two cats appeared, mewing for attention. She was still wearing her coat and hadn't turned on the lights. Dusk shrouded her and as she sat down in the dark, gloomy room, her foul mood started to resurface. *Where was he?* David's every movement demanded investigation and should be treated as suspicious. *Where was he?*

She collected herself and resolved to go through his online accounts, line-by-line. She didn't know what that would confirm since he was a methodical and calculating bastard. Rachel didn't find anything obvious. Stefan Stratos had offered the name of a forensic accountancy firm she could use to locate any money David might be hiding. She doubted he was, though. For one thing, she did their accounts and tax returns. The profits from selling the company were going straight to pay off the mortgage.

Rachel looked at the framed photos in their home office. Now forever to be known as their *common-law* home office. The picture on her desk was of her and David sat on the bank of the River Thames. They both looked happy, wearing silly Union Jack hats, and drinking fizzy wine from plastic flutes in honour of the Queen's Diamond Jubilee.

She decided that now was as good a time as any to search the rest of the house. They shared every space, in every room. Their books were mixed together on the bookcases, they used the same medicine cabinet and all their paperwork was in their communal office.

There were limited places to hide things from each other. She opened the bank statements; a dozen or so envelopes had piled up. She really should stop them and go paperless. She didn't know why she was surprised to discover that he'd been taking out cash, £100 at a time, here and there, nothing she would have noticed normally. David didn't usually like to use cash and always preferred to pay by card. She double-checked the withdrawals against the desktop calendar. They were made on different days, but they were all on the wrong side of town; nowhere near their home or his office.

'Call me Miss Marple,' Rachel said, winking at Neville and Oscar.

David was a specialist in IT and still he was woefully lazy with regard to his digital security. Most of his passwords were random digits written on post-it notes stuck around the edge of his monitor. This was almost too easy. Rachel used her phone to take photos of the fluorescent slips of paper. She checked his blazers and found nothing. In the back pocket of a pair of indigo jeans, she found a prescription for Sildenafil. She Googled this and found its more common name: Viagra. She appropriated the flimsy piece of paper. She didn't know David had ever used Viagra; she liked to think she would have known if he'd used it with her.

At the back of his side of the wardrobe she spied a plastic bag that she didn't recognise and opened it. It contained a French Maid's outfit David had bought her last year. She couldn't remember how that came about but she remembered not taking it seriously. He'd said it was a joke gift and she'd laughed. She hadn't given a second thought to the shoddy nylon outfit.

Was that it?

The sign? The beginning of the end. If she had dressed up for him in the cheap, transparent lace costume, would he have been satisfied? Would he not have strayed? The tears welled once again. Was this really her fault? She allowed guilt to wash over her. Her anger was put on hold as she tried to comprehend and grasp her actions and inactions, and their consequences.

Rachel took a quick look through the medicine cabinet; there was no trace of any blue diamond-shaped tablets. It was her instinct to twist the bottles so that the labels were facing out. However, she was careful to return them back to the angle at which she'd found them and did one last check to ensure that everything was in its rightful place. She was getting better at snooping. She turned and jumped as she saw Neville and Oscar in the doorway judging her. She bought their silence with tuna treats.

Rachel remembered the words of Stefan Stratos. She opened their life-admin cabinet and took photos of pertinent documents on her mobile phone. The mortgage was in both their names, as were the deeds to the house. She found a bill for a credit card she knew nothing about – why was she not surprised? However, after inspecting the list of purchases (domain names and computer supplies) and extensive Googling indicating the purchases were work supplies, deemed it unworthy of further investigation. She nearly binned the Mickey Mouse 'marriage certificate' Stefan Stratos had declared null and void. Instead Rachel found some passport photos of David and scribbled devil horns and silly handlebar moustaches on them. She felt calmer then until she realised with a pang of irritation that, thanks to the council's ridiculous recycling policy about printed paper, she couldn't recycle these and deposited the defaced prints in her pocket.

The stages of grief were wavering in Rachel. At times she was in denial about David's betrayal, at others she felt she needed to make the obvious decision and quickly rip off the Cellotape keeping their marriage together.

Leave the bastard. Leave the bastard. Leave the bastard.

What Rachel wanted more than anything was a time machine. She wouldn't use it to unsee the kiss, but to go back further to investigate why her husband had got bored of her in the first place. Or even better, to go back fifteen years to when she neglected to check if their wedding was legal.

Rachel was desperate for some sleep, but she also wanted to know precisely what time her wayward husband returned. When she heard the front door shut, she lay in wait, her spine rigid. David always smelled of his signature aftershave. But was it different tonight? It was a blend of scents that pleasantly evoked the sea. He collapsed into bed and was asleep in minutes. Sneaking home after visiting his mistress? The man was shameless.

When she finally drifted off to sleep, she had a dream that David had died and she was at his funeral. Rachel was fighting the redhead for the right to be chief mourner. When her mother-in-law chose the side of the mistress, Rachel awoke in a cold sweat.

There was no way she could get back to sleep. She needed a plan. There was no marriage; ergo, there was no need for a divorce. They could divide their belongings in a civil manner. They were both grown-ups, there needn't be too much animosity. She made a list of people to see.

Stefan Stratos was first and foremost. She would have to tell him that she was resolved in her decision to separate from her husband and he should get the ball rolling on whatever legal steps she needed to take.

Next it would be the estate agents: she would like to find a small cottage. She would also need a financial adviser; they had amassed various assets and the rest of the cash was accumulating in a generous pension fund. Their plan had been to retire early when David turned fifty-five.

Rachel closed her eyes and practised meditative breathing. She silently chanted positive affirmations.

Stupid fucking affirmations.

12

When the home landline phone rang, Rachel knew it would be one of two options: Norma or an automated sales call. She picked up anyway.

'Please can I phone you back, Mum? I'm taking Neville and Oscar to the vet's.'

'Yes, yes, but do phone me back this time.'

Rachel rolled her eyes. 'I always call back!'

Norma scoffed at this.

'Bye, Mum.'

Rachel hung up the phone and called out for David who had promised that he would go with her to the vet's; wrangling their cats demanded back-up. David was nowhere to be seen, however. He really was proving to be the worst non-husband ever.

Oscar adopted an instant air of mistrust as he saw Neville being jailed. Rachel tried to bribe him with salmon biscuits, but he was wily as a fox and just as vicious when cornered. He didn't trust random, middle-of-the-day treats. By the time he was captured in his travel basket Rachel looked as if the Beast of Exmoor had savaged her left arm. She stood at the kitchen sink with her arm under the running tap. One-handed, she dressed her injured limb with an overabundance of bandages.

At the vet's, the receptionist, a young man wearing a name badge that read 'Paul', welcomed Rachel and her pets. Paul had a jet black Mohawk. He also had those stretching rings in his earlobes, ones she would have been able to poke a finger through. The thought made her queasy. Rachel glanced at the magazines in the waiting room. She picked one up and put it back down. The dog-centric issue proclaimed **How to Get the Best Dog Selfie** and **What Your Dog Wants You to Know** articles.

Dr Luke Parry-Wilson entered the reception area to identify his next patient. He called out for Neville and Oscar Chatsworth. Rachel put up her hand on behalf of her pets. Luke walked them to treatment room three.

'Where's Trevor?' she asked after her usual vet.

'He's retired to a farm in the Cotswolds.'

Rachel thought it was in poor taste to say that Trevor Benterman had retired to a farm in the countryside. It was exactly what she had been told as a child when the family dog disappeared. Years later she'd learned the truth – that he had been run over by a brewery van.

Dr Luke Parry-Wilson introduced himself and supplied some background information on his training and how much he was enjoying working at a new surgery. He had recently completed a PhD concentrating on the importance of play for dogs.

'And who are these handsome felines?' he asked, leaning towards the cages.

'That's Oscar,' Rachel pointed with her non-mauled arm, 'and this one is Neville.'

'Adorable,' he said, and flashed her a friendly smile.

'Do you have cats, Dr Parry-Wilson?' Rachel asked, and smiled back at him.

'God, no!' He chuckled. 'And please call me Luke, or Dr Luke if you must. Alright, Neville, Oscar, let's take a look at you.'

Rachel held the cages still while Dr Luke extracted the cats, telling Rachel at length about his pair of adopted veteran military Alsatians. Apparently they had worked with the British Army and completed two tours in Afghanistan. Veteran dog-owner or not, Rachel took an immediate dislike to the new vet. She thought it plain rude to tell a woman that he was a dog man while he was handling her cats

Dr Luke gave both animals a thorough examination, taking almost twice the time Trevor normally did. Rachel wondered if it would be double the cost. He mentioned that they were both at the top end of the weight scale and if they got any heavier they would be classified as obese. Rachel couldn't believe Dr Luke was actually fat-shaming Neville and Oscar! They were big-boned, that was all. At the end of the appointment, however, he complimented them on their beautiful coats adding that they were clearly well looked after. The subtlety was not lost on Rachel and she was able to read between the lines that he was telling her (again) her cats were too well-fed.

Rachel felt betrayed by Neville and Oscar as she watched them allow Dr Luke to house them in their respective travel boxes with ease and without disagreement from either cat. Her arm still throbbed from the attempt to confine Oscar.

Rachel thanked him and there was a moment when she looked closely at her new vet. If she didn't already dislike him, she might think him attractive. He was tall and dark-haired; she guessed a few years older than her, maybe forty at a push. She wondered, if she looked at him long enough, would she be able to lose herself in the magical emerald hue of his eyes? She smiled and flushed at the eye contact, bumbling her way from the treatment room and out of the surgery. Rachel deposited the cats, still caged, on the back seat of the car and mouthed 'sorry' before shutting the door and marching towards the dry cleaners-cum-key cutters-cum-alterations booth at the train station.

As David was in no rush to inform her of his intention to leave, and was going to torture her by keeping his mistress, Rachel decided to have a little fun too.

The machinist, a small Greek man, welcomed her. He put down his newspaper, happy to have a late-morning visitor. She handed him a bag of trousers and shirts, explaining that for the trousers she wanted an inch taken in from the waist and an inch from each leg. And for the shirts, she wanted the chest taken in an inch. She stopped at a small pharmacy on the corner, not her usual one near the GP's where Rachel knew the pharmacist by name.

She produced the snaffled Viagra prescription and waited for the pills to be dispensed. The gaudy women's magazines distracted her while she waited to pay. This was what she needed – vapid celebrity gossip. She wanted nothing more than to read a slew of articles about beautiful famous people whose marriages were also falling apart. It didn't have to be true, it only needed to be entertaining tittle-tattle. **Beacon of Hope for Jen** with a picture of Brad Pitt holding Jennifer Aniston's arm at a recent award ceremony. And the Z-list celebrities' Circle of Life: one normal-sized woman puts on weight and loses weight, supplemented with obligatory pushed-out-stomach before pictures and glamorous Photoshopped-to-an-inch-of-their-lives after pictures. **My Husband Married Both My Sisters & Then My Mother.** *Seriously, where did they find these people?* The bottom cover story caught her attention: **10 Reasons Your Man Cheats.** She folded the glossy magazine and added it to her shopping. On her way back home, her attention was drawn to a chocolate cheesecake – David's favourite – in the window of a bakery. She was going to buy a slice but opted for the whole dessert.

Before David returned home, Rachel went to the bedroom and removed one sock from each pair and threw them directly into the large wheelie bin outside. Then from the kitchen she collected a side plate and located the spice she needed: ground chilli. In the bathroom, she opened David's expensive musky face wash. She emptied the cleansing paste onto the plate and added a dusting of chilli powder, mixing it until the powder dissolved. She unscrewed the lid and spooned the mixture back into the tube. She pumped a little paste onto her finger, to check it didn't look or smell tampered with. And for the finale, she added one scoop of hair lightening bleach – reserved for her lady moustache – to his shampoo and one scoop to his conditioner. She stopped short of contaminating his shower gel with hair-removal cream, however tempting it was.

Finally, she put the cheesecake in the fridge and started to prepare dinner.

David was very regimented about what they ate. He was a creature of habit and had a weekly preferred menu he liked to live by:

Monday	*Pro-greens salad (no wine)*
Tuesday	*Fish (with wine)*
Wednesday	*Chicken (no wine)*
Thursday	*Vegetarian (no wine)*
Friday	*Takeaway (with up to three, preferably European, beers)*
Saturday	*Italian (with wine)*
Sunday	*Sunday Roast – a rotation of lamb, chicken, beef, chicken (with wine)*

He liked to have at least three days a week without alcohol, mainly to prove he could. Cocktails didn't count apparently! It was a Wednesday evening and Rachel had prepared an organic chicken breast. She thought of their fixed routine. When did they slip into their roles? Rachel did cooking and washing, David did bathrooms and gardening. She wasn't at all surprised their marriage had stagnated. She allowed sadness to wash over her and then anger once more replaced her melancholy. She wished he had said something. She would have joined him in a quest to be more spontaneous and exciting. *What if she wasn't the boring one?* Good luck to the second Mrs C., having to conform to David's strict routine.

His behaviour had muted Rachel. She no longer felt like the sexy young wife; she was the downtrodden, forgotten old wife, and realised she had started to dress accordingly. Her blouse showed no cleavage and her skirt hovered below the knee. She looked like Old Mother Hubbard; all she needed was a shawl and a cotton mobcap. Rachel would normally have changed out of work clothes for dinner, but not tonight. *What was the point?*

She had to up the ante. She vowed to keep the fridge stocked with at least one of David's favourite desserts at all times, knowing he couldn't help but indulge. It seemed he had no willpower for anything that was right in front of him. She swapped sugar for his sweetener. She switched his low-fat yoghurt for a full-fat version and started adding cream to his coffee. She told him it was organic skimmed milk prepared with an electric milk-frother and he hadn't questioned it. David was oblivious to the fact she was on to him. The idiot deserved everything he got.

David

13

David's first love was Lieutenant Stephanie Holden, *Baywatch*'s very own goody two shoes. He liked her short hair and small pert breasts and was distraught when his mother wouldn't let him have a poster of her in a high-cut swimming costume for his bedroom wall. Instead, he kept a small photo of her in his wallet, cut from the *Radio Times*.

In real life, he had four, what one could call proper, girlfriends before he met Rachel. Lisa was his first. They lost their virginity together and were inseparable during A-levels, and only broke up when they were accepted into different universities at opposite ends of the country.

At university David met Fiona during Freshers' Week and spent the rest of his undergraduate years with her, much to his best friend's chagrin. Barry said it was sad to see a man go down so early, but at least it left the rest of the ladies free for him, Aaron and Jim. Dating in his twenties had been easy for David. When he moved to London there was no shortage of girls in bars, pubs and clubs. This was at a time before the Internet managed romantic engagements. David was shy and geeky, but that only seemed to endear him more to women. He didn't set out to have one-night-stands, but it was easy pickings. Barry was wingman extraordinaire when they were out to ensnare the ladies, his rough and tumble presentation highlighting David's tall physique, sharp sense of humour and blue eyes. His friends called him the *accidental monogamist*. He liked love, he liked being in love, but most of all he disliked the unknown. He was hopeless at the rules. *Could he call? Should he call? How long to wait to call? Why couldn't he say how he felt? Why did everything feel like a trick or a test?*

David was single for three weeks after his graduation before he met his next girlfriend. He met Emily at a party. She was spectacular. He was sure he didn't stand a chance with the likes of her, so was able to talk to her like a normal human being rather than a tongue-tied lothario. Emily had trained as an actress. After years of stereotypical thespian struggle she was disheartened by the theatre world. The relationship ended amicably when she moved to New York for the chance to work on Broadway.

And, finally, there was Karen. They were at secondary school together and she was his first kiss with tongues. Twelve years later they ran into each other on their respective annual Christmas visits to their hometown. Over drinks, they reminisced over old times, teachers they'd shared and the school bullies they hoped had received their just deserts. The relationship went sour after a few years when one Saturday morning Karen proclaimed she wanted children and according to her calculations they should start trying at her next ovulation, which was in six days' time.

David had ambitions to set up his own business. He'd saved enough money and had registered a company name. He wasn't sure he wanted children. At twenty-nine years old he wasn't ready for them, emotionally, mentally or financially. He was still discovering the man he wanted to be; still enjoying living the way he pleased. He'd booked tickets to Glastonbury, for God's sake. David simply hadn't given a thought to settling down. He asked Karen for a little time to consider, but it was no use. And for months after that he tried gently to extricate himself from her, while all the while his penis felt under siege and he feared that at any moment there'd be the announcement of a happy accident resulting in a bundle of joy. In the end Karen left, and though David had been pretty devastated at the time, he understood that she was doing the right thing.

David was a serial monogamist. Less than one month after finding the balls to tell Karen how he felt, he picked Jojo up from her halls of residence and spied her roommate, Rachel. She was no longer his sister's quiet little shadow; she'd turned into a beautiful swan. The ghost of Karen still haunted him. Why didn't he want to settle down with her? Why had he run away from commitment? Anyway, Rachel was too good for him. She was young, she was happy, and she was gorgeous. He'd never wanted a woman like he wanted Rachel.

Rachel

14

Rachel's daydreams preoccupied her. Eva talked and Rachel nodded along but wasn't really listening. She was preparing an alibi for when the police questioned her about crimes against marital harmony. These fantasies usually resulted in David being incarcerated for relationship fraud. She'd take on the role of prison wife, visiting him fortnightly at Her Majesty's Pleasure.

Eva interrupted her reverie. She was complaining that Terry the Fireman didn't like black-and-white films or those with subtitles. Rather than agree that he was a complete philistine, as Eva wanted her to do, Rachel suggested she introduce him to *Raging Bull* and expand his horizons. What with Martin Scorsese's fight scenes and Robert De

Niro at his finest, Terry probably wouldn't notice the movie's lack of Technicolor.

'Which is best? To marry a man who has married three times or a man who has never married?'

'I didn't think it was serious with Terry?'

'It's not but—'

'*Maybe* you should find someone closer to your—'

'My what?' Eva sounded offended. 'My own age?' she finished the sentence for Rachel. 'I'd love to – don't you think I've tried? I'm forty-six-years old and I look great for it. So I should, I work hard to look this way. But do you know what?' Eva left no space for Rachel to answer. 'I'm on tablets that regulate the hormone levels in my body. All they do is stimulate a constant state of horniness. I don't know whether I'm coming or going, no pun intended. So when a thirty-three-year-old fireman finds me attractive, who am I to disagree?' Eva's eyes were fierce. 'Because do you know what men my age want? To shag twenty-five-year-olds. No offence, but it's what your husband is doing!' She looked at her watch. 'He's probably having a post-fuck shower as we speak.' Eva stood up. 'I'm sorry, I shouldn't have said that.' She collected her notebook and left Rachel's office.

Rachel was shell-shocked. Now that Eva had gone she could think of any number of retorts that would have been better than standing there with her mouth agape. And what she'd meant to say was that it didn't sound like the toyboy fireman was fulfilling all of Eva's wants and needs.

Rachel was smarting from Eva's verbal attack on David's fidelity, or lack of it. She wanted to remind Eva who was the boss. She also wanted to hug her and tell her she was sorry. Rachel's phone rang then. Saved by the bell. Until she saw the caller ID: David. She didn't have the energy to listen to more lies, so let the call go to voicemail. She looked back towards Eva's desk; it was empty. Eva had left the building.

'Lyds, do you know where Eva went?'

Lydia pulled out her earphones and glanced up from her colour-coordinated spreadsheet and looked around – she hadn't heard Eva leave.

Rachel drafted a dozen text messages to Eva before she deleted them; none of them could convey how she really felt. Her life was such a mess. Normally Rachel hated confrontation but this was different: Eva had become her rock. She couldn't bear to lose her now. Rachel's phone buzzed. It was David, letting her know that he was playing squash, and then a second message arrived to say it made sense for him to get dinner at the Country Club. *Since when did David play squash? He was useless with a racquet.* She tried his number to catch him out in what she expected was a lie, but the call went straight to voicemail. She left a message for her never-husband to call her back. She was surprised she still cared. She reread the message and wondered if she should pop into the Country Club to surprise him. But then Rachel remembered Stefan Stratos's instructions which were to allow enough time for evidence-gathering and, importantly, not to give David any pre-warning advantage of their pending split.

Later that night in bed, Rachel thought about Eva; how she had managed to bounce back and move on after all of her dating disappointments. Rachel doubted that she was as robust. She didn't know how to go about being Rachel Keatley. She had been Mrs David Chatsworth for so long she couldn't remember who she was before him. And she couldn't even imagine being with another man. She'd had opportunities to cheat on many an occasion, but hadn't. There was the time that a very handsome client asked to hold her hand and then suggested they celebrate their new working partnership in his hotel suite. He had a lovely smile but she'd admonished him for being naughty and he had taken the brush-off in his stride. It had been easy to say no. And then there had been David's friend Aaron, who had kissed her on the mouth when he was drunk. He'd told her she was beautiful and that he had always wanted to kiss her. That had been bad, but it hadn't been her fault, and although she liked and cared about Aaron, she didn't think of him like that – first and foremost he was David's friend. She tallied up the extramarital sex she could have had over the years. There were more instances than she had fingers, but she hadn't because she valued the sacred vows she had made. Was it short-sighted not to have bonked all and sundry? They *were* right – the films and the magazines – David had taken her best years.

Rachel heard the front door open and imagined David trying to creep in quietly. She heard a pause as he tried to avoid the noisy step at the bottom of the stairs and failed. She was, for once, glad the annoying squeak hadn't been fixed.

It was late. He joined her in bed.

'I tried calling earlier,' she mumbled.

'Sorry, I got caught up in something.'

Rachel could only assume he was delayed in the bedroom of a nubile young woman. She added it to her internal tally of David's lies. Somehow these hurt more than the infidelity itself – or so she told herself. She struggled not to express her anger.

'Night,' she slurred. Her eyelids were pharmaceutically heavy. She pulled down her silk eye mask and turned away from him. The waves of slumber washed over her. She heard her husband gulp down his glass of water in one go. Rachel smiled as she remembered the two caffeine tablets she had crushed into it and then gave in to sleep.

15

Rachel awoke feeling hazy and groggy, a residual fog from the sleeping tablet. She was in no state to go to work, and messaged Eva to say she'd be working from home. David was already up and about. She ignored the temptation to press her face into his pillow and inhale his musk. She splashed cold water on her cheeks and moved a cotton wool pad of rejuvenating toner around her features. She didn't look revived.

She was at the age where she was told by every magazine, every television advert, every reality star's Instagram, that she should be 'keeping it tight'. She should be moisturising her face at forty-five-minute intervals, to compensate for the inevitable ageing of her skin. There was probably an app she could download to remind her. She should post to Facebook a public apology for the effects of gravity upon her and then wait for an acquaintance to mansplain the science behind it. The media constantly reproached her for being the wrong side of twenty.

Downstairs David sat at the dining table with his iPad. looking wild-eyed and manic. God, he was a gorgeous mess. He was rabbiting on about something; she squeezed his shoulder in support and made herself a coffee. David was still waffling. He announced he didn't sleep well and repeatedly prodded his touchscreen. Something was wrong with a financial report. The numbers didn't convey the expected results. Rachel tried to add sympathetic sounds and nods in the gaps between his bursts of prattling. His eyes were red and his hair askew. Rachel suspected this was the knock-on effect from messing with his sleep patterns. Evidently, it had had the desired effect; he was wrecked. David eventually left for work, having to return three times to pick up his phone, his wallet and then finally his car keys.

She picked up the magazine that was loitering on the side. She flicked through the pages until she found the article **10 Reasons Your Man Cheats**. As she could have predicted, it was all her fault.

She didn't fuck him enough.

She certainly didn't blow him enough.

She had become too independent

She had allowed herself to age.

Rachel had paid £2.50 to be informed she was a selfish, past-her-prime, bad wife. The print consolidated all the doubts and suspicions in her head. It was quite simply her fault. She flicked through the other articles and noted the few tips on which foods make semen taste disgusting (suggesting that it is delicious the rest of the time?) and how natural foods (grapefruit, kale, milk, black liquorice) can affect medicines (Sildenafil, Warfarin, antibiotics, Digoxin). Overall, not a complete waste of money then.

Truthfully, though, she had no clue when it came to what men did or didn't want. She had married at nineteen and had no real point of reference when it came to sex before her relationship with David. She'd had a few flings and one proper boyfriend before she met him, but they could all be classified as *teenage fumblings*. Rachel and David were at it twice a day at first, four times a week when they moved in together, and then more recently regular as clockwork on Sunday nights. *Was that normal?* She thought they were doing okay. She recalled friends saying they didn't have sex for months or in some cases years after having their first child. Was that an exaggeration? The seven-year itch, was that a real thing? She had read an article that said research had found that no couple (straight, gay, old, young) could uphold sexual attraction past ten years, could that also be true? For Rachel, *honestly*, none of these thoughts had crossed her mind during her non-marriage. She still fancied David. She still loved him. She still wanted him.

She took the magazine upstairs and drew a hot bath. Lying in it, she descended into a state of oblivion. David's philandering mouth crowded her thoughts. David's good shape and increased 'gym activity' (read: extramarital shenanigans) had caused him not to notice the inch taken in from his clothes. She imagined the Olympic bonks keeping him trim.

Rachel couldn't stay relaxed in the bath. She skimmed magazine articles that concentrated on how to coast through life. Pills for feeling better, exercises for feeling better, food for feeling better. The whole world was against women. Too fat, too old. If not too fat, then needing to lose even more weight for a thigh gap. If not old, then too inexperienced, too stupid. Together with the having-it-all yummy mummy advice: put on your Cath Kidston apron and bake cookies for neighbours you secretly resent while your baby sleeps during the day and all through the night. Their Stepford smiles haunted her. Maybe that was the problem; while everyone was trying to be better there was a big looming omnipresent voice with a million reasons why YOU should feel like shit. She threw the magazine against the bathroom wall and enjoyed watching it fall into a heap in the corner.

She'd finished rinsing the bath when an evil thought blurred her judgement. She picked up David's electric toothbrush and used the double pulse feature to scrub the toilet bowl. It was satisfying. When the euphoria subsided she was disgusted with herself. She looked for replacement heads but was unable to find them.

Rachel: *Where are the new toothbrush heads?*
Rachel: *X.*
David: *Must have forgotten them. X*

The reply infuriated her. She wanted to scream. David needed to get his lies in order. He'd said he was going to buy some, and it was obvious to her now that it was a cover to bonk his young girlfriend.

'DAVID, YOU FUCKING WANKER!' The words and the volume exorcised her stored anger.

Rachel fed Neville and Oscar rabbit-flavoured treats before she popped to the shops to buy replacement toothbrush heads. How she hated David at that moment. The depths she had descended to unnerved her. She walked to the shops in an attempt to calm her nerves. Rachel had started to relax after the two-mile round trip. She almost returned with a spring in her step. When she attempted to open the front door, she discovered that the Chubb was unlocked though she was sure she'd double turned the key on her way out. She spied David's jacket draped over the banister and could hear water running. She ran up the stairs.

'What are you doing home?' she asked through the closed bathroom door. It sounded accusatory but she couldn't help herself. She banged on the door when an answer wasn't forthcoming. She tried the door; it was locked.

'I came home to have a quick shower,' he shouted.

Rachel almost laughed that David was asking her to believe he would have a shower *before* playing squash. His lies were piling up. David opened the bathroom door, allowing a mass of steam to escape. He had a towel wrapped around his waist and showed more of the weight he had put on. *Ha!*

David started to dry himself. Rachel tried not to look at his body. She felt herself blush as she followed the abdominal strip of hair from his navel to his pubic mane. *Had he trimmed his cockbush?* He was practically bald down there. She looked away as she realised she couldn't remember when she'd last seen his penis. Even shrivelled from the shower, she missed the contact. She missed the intimacy. She felt a blush burning her cheeks as she tried to avert her gaze.

'Wait, have you brushed your teeth?' she asked.

'Of course.'

'When?'

'Earlier.'

'Earlier this morning or earlier since you got back?'

'Earlier.' David was distracted. She wondered if he was trying to conjure more lies.

Please no, please no, no. Please don't have used the toothbrush.

She didn't question that David wasn't dressed in his gym gear. She didn't know why she was avoiding confrontation. Was she still in denial? She wished for it to be a big joke so that she could forget all about the beautiful redhead. Then she and David could live happily ever after, as they had vowed to once on an exotic Indonesian island fifteen years ago. She was naïve to think then that she would only marry once and it would be for life.

'I bought some new heads for the toothbrushes.'

'Great. Thanks, love, I'll see you later.' David went to kiss her goodbye. Rachel violently jerked her head away from his mouth. He caught her right earlobe. After he left, she rushed to check David's toothbrush, it felt damp-ish but not dripping wet. She hoped the moisture was condensation from the hot shower. She hoped to God that's all it was.

Rachel didn't get a wink of sleep. Her head was filled with dental nightmares. Huge crumbling teeth the size of the cliffs at Dover threatened to bury her. She arrived in the office early and was immediately overwhelmed by her ever-increasing to-do list, and her acute lack of impetus and inability to complete a single task.

Rachel was looking at the coffee machine, internally debating whether to make a third coffee, and panicked when she saw Eva sashay through the door. All Rachel wanted was to talk to her but they hadn't spoken properly since their argument. Eva sat poised to start work as she waited for her computer to fire up. Eva was a real-life goddess; she had great posture, her hair was perfectly coiffed and Rachel could see a small flick of flawless eyeliner. Rachel pulled at her own blouse and pinched her cheeks for natural blush.

She stopped by Eva's chair and took a deep breath. 'I want to say how sorry—'

'Please. Don't be.' Eva quietly added that she was embarrassed by her own recent outburst.

'*I'm* the one who should be sorry.'

'But I want you to know that I *am* sorry. And that I've missed you. And thank you for putting up with all my crazy . . .'

'Please let's not mention it again.' Eva swatted the conversation away with her hand. She tried to keep a poker face before abandoning it and giving Rachel a bear hug. She drank in Eva's smell. She always wore classic Chanel No. 5, but Eva, as with everything else, made it her own. 'I need to explain—'

'Eva, you have nothing—'

'I have a confession to make. You've only known me ... what? Eighteen months – two years, at most? This isn't me. The hormones are driving me potty. I used to like nothing more than gardening and Zumba. Then early menopause hit. I'm waiting for it to end so I can get my real life back.'

Eva let out a huge sigh. Rachel waited for more. It was hardly the revelation of the century. *What was wrong with gardening and Zumba?* She presented Eva with a packet of milk chocolate digestives.

'Anyway, I need to tell you something,' Eva said, in between mouthfuls. 'I was having drinks last night and Lydia ...' She left the conversation hanging as she filled two mugs with hot water.

Stop! Rachel thought. Eva and Lydia aren't friends; they have nothing in common. Nevertheless she felt a pang of jealousy at the thought of them out together. Were they having drinks without her? And then she suspected that if they had got together, it was almost certainly to discuss Rachel's insane behaviour. Were they going to leave and set up their own brand new marketing consultancy and take all her clients with them? Further rejection to contend with. God, she was a paranoid wreck.

'When I say drinks,' Eva continued, 'we were in that new cocktail bar Happy Hour separately waiting for our friends and—'

Rachel felt better about the short-lived drinks. She wouldn't have to fire either of them now. Ten minutes earlier she was admittedly inundated but had at least passed for sane.

'Look, I can see how much you're still hurting. Now you have no purpose in life and you're turning into a miserable spinster. By the way – seeing as you'll no longer be needing it, have you booked your fanny in for cremation or burial?'

Rachel hid her smile and tried to interrupt with protestations of innocence. Eva held up her hand. Rachel pulled a faux-sulky face.

'It's no use, I know too much. I have seen your mad twin; it's too late to try and sweep her under the crazy carpet. Anyway, guess who walked in?'

'I give up.'

'Your husband.'

'David? Did you have drinks with him too?'

'Put that forked tongue away. Don't be horrid.'

Eva was right. Rachel *used* to be a lovely person. She used to do fun runs and sponsored walks. She used to volunteer at the local charity shop, collecting bags of donated clothes from the posh roads in town. That reminded her – in the boot of her car she had the coats and blankets for the homeless shelter. Since the discovery of David's infidelity, Rachel's exuberance was altered beyond recognition. She used to laugh and smile – ALL THE TIME! And in its place resided a petty spitefulness that could give the Wicked Witch of the West a run for her money.

'I'm horrid?' Rachel whispered.

'No, sorry, I shouldn't have said that. Don't do that. Stop your bottom lip going ...'

Rachel placed a finger on her mouth to steady the wobble.

'Think nice thoughts and *try* to be less ... horrible?'

'You think I'm a horrible person?' Rachel hid her face in her hands.

Eva was trying to placate her, telling her people have bad thoughts but that doesn't automatically mean they are bad people.

'You're not horrible,' she soothed Rachel.

'Dare I ask,' she whispered, 'who he was with?'

Eva clapped her hands and announced that David was there with another bloke; they both looked sweaty, they both were wearing sports attire. 'I don't know his name but I recognised his friend – you know – short, squinty, hair thinning, teeth that would look right in a small child.'

It was a caricature version of Barry's less flattering features, but he wasn't *that* bad. In the right light he was cute in a garden gnome kind of way.

Rachel fiddled with her expensive pen. She doodled a line of question marks. 'It gets worse,' she admitted. She realised that somewhere in the hurt and the pain, she'd forgotten to tell Eva this. Was it because saying it aloud made it real?

'How can it get worse than Mr Computer cheating on you? Wait, is she pregnant?'

'Oh, God I hope not. No, get this – we were never married.'

'What the actual fuck?' Eva blurted out. 'I did *not* see that coming.'

Rachel explained in the quietest of voices all that Stefan Stratos had relayed to her. Rachel watched as Eva went through the five stages of grief, but on fast-forward compared to Rachel's own shock, surprise and dismay. Eva said she was impressed that Rachel hadn't imploded completely, but she too supposed it would be difficult to change the locks to the marital home once she had found out there were no marital vows. Rachel knew it was over, and told Eva so.

'We were never married, we were never married,' Rachel repeated again and again. 'We were never FUCK-ING married!' She was becoming near-hysterical. She calmed her breathing before it threatened to speed up into a full-blown panic attack. Eva pushed a biscuit on her, and then a second. Eva looked at the ingredients list and quickly turned the packet over. She told Rachel that *grief biscuits* were void of inconveniences such as fat, sugar and calories.

The marriage was over and it never was. It was the *Schrödinger's cat* of relationships.

Eva suggested that Rachel should get her revenge by shagging David's best friend. Rachel was adamant that was not an option. Eva nodded as she ran through poor Barry's flaws again. 'At your anniversary party, he was wearing an awful purple shirt that made him look like a bruise.'

Eva was unperturbed. She had other revenge strategies:

- add laxatives to his meals
- mix diesel in his petrol engine
- cut the crotch out of his underwear and trousers
- use a burner phone to intercept the messages intended for his lover (Eva had been re-watching *The Wire*).

Some of the ideas had already crossed Rachel's mind. She wanted him to suffer; but she didn't want to kill him. *Did she?* Rachel didn't admit all the tomfoolery and havoc she had wrought so far but confessed to Eva about the tailoring and adding cream to his coffee, which – of course – Eva found hilarious. Rachel omitted to mention that she'd drugged her husband with caffeine tablets or that she'd intercepted his Viagra prescription. She hadn't told Eva she could quite easily have killed the man she had loved for her entire adult life. She hadn't conveyed to Eva quite how much she had lost the plot. She was a deranged soon-to-be cat lady. Rachel was embarrassed at the depths of depravity she had already reached. At this point, Rachel didn't need an accomplice; she needed an intervention.

Eva suggested they celebrate and commiserate over cocktails, asserting that:

- Their favourite wine bar had a buy-two-glasses, get-the-rest-of-the-bottle-free offer.
- Rachel was unshackled from the chains of marriage! It was time to celebrate!
- She was unmarried. (Hence untainted, unlike poor mistreated American divorcee Meghan Markle.)

- She was still young(-ish), i.e. she was the right end of thirty.
- She had her whole life in front of her.

Rachel nodded as she chewed on the inside of her cheek. She sent a text message to David to say she would be having drinks on the way home from work. Instantly, she regretted informing him of her movements; she would have liked him to wonder what she was up to for a change.

After drinks, Rachel tried to recreate a divine artichoke dip, but what she'd thought would be a simple recipe was full of lots of different ingredients. Namely, artichoke hearts, three different fats (cream, Parmesan, Comté), two fresh herbs (rosemary and thyme), none of which she had. And French mayonnaise? *Ha!* Everyone knew Hellman's was the best. Instead she prepared an aubergine risotto. Guilt infiltrated the taste of one of David's least favourite dishes; he had what she deemed was an irrational dislike of aubergines. Then there was the guilt she felt about drugging his nightly glass of water. Guilt about taking in his trousers. Guilt about tampering with his shampoo, his face wash, his waistline. *Why couldn't she stop?* She added more salt to every meal. She served grapefruit for breakfast after she'd read it reacted adversely with Viagra. And she frequently added asparagus to their dinners – under the guise of varying their five vegetables a day – after she'd read it made semen taste disgusting. *How do you like that, Little Miss Redhead?*

When she received a text message to say David was, for once, going to be back in time for dinner, she looked at her aubergine dish with shame. Not only did she not like who she'd become, she was thankful she hadn't killed the poor man. She finished her glass of white wine. She'd only opened the bottle for the risotto (honestly!) and then filled a glass for heart-numbing purposes, so it was essentially medicinal.

At bedtime Rachel dwelled on her monstrous actions, before remembering again they were NEVER MARRIED! A tsunami wave of anger crushed her heart. When David came to bed, she pointedly faced away. She dreamed about him being mangled by a cartoon anvil.

16

While David was in the shower, Rachel scrolled through his phone – no new messages or emails from unknown women, not much of note at all. Was that in itself suspicious? She gave herself permission to access his GPS location from her own mobile phone.

Rachel called through the bathroom door and suggested making David a cup of decaffeinated coffee. Not that it would make a difference; he was still affected by the chemical manipulation of his sleep patterns. He was both tired and wired.

She took his water-lashed grunts for an affirmative. Amidst running through to-do lists in her head, she made him a coffee and honestly couldn't recall if she'd used the caffeinated or decaffeinated beans. She looked at both coffee canisters standing innocently side-by-side. She tasted the dark bitter drink. It tasted like coffee.

Rachel poured organic orange juice into a tall highball glass. She took a small packet from her cardigan pocket and ground one Viagra tablet into a fine powder. She added the sex dust to David's juice and stirred vigorously.

Rachel played with her phone, scrolling to Jojo's number. Her thumb hovered over the call button. Jojo answered on the first ring. Rachel cleared her throat before she let out the first chorus of 'Happy Birthday'.

'Awwwww, thanks, Rach.'

'Another year wiser ...'

'The flowers are gorgeous!'

'I demanded they put in sunflowers, were there sunflowers?'

'Loads of the buggers! I have so much to tell you. But not now, I need to see your face when I do,' Jojo said.

Rachel silently concurred but Jojo's birthday wasn't the day for bad news.

'See you in a couple of hours!' With an effort she summoned some joy into her voice.

Rachel stood under the shower. *What was she doing? How long did she think she could punish him? She was acting like a madwoman. What if she was a madwoman? Had she always been mad?* She leaped out of the shower and grabbed a towel. She rushed downstairs dripping water and soapsuds on the floorboards.

David had the orange juice in his hand.

Stop!

'Wait!' Rachel wrangled away the half-empty glass and poured the contents into the sink.

'What did you do that for? I hadn't finished it.'

It was too late. Rachel had stooped to depths she had never envisaged. But the mirror didn't lie. It was she who had done it. She was a monster.

David followed her upstairs asking for an explanation. What could she say? *Don't mind me – I'm a lunatic!* Rachel dried the remaining soapsuds from her shoulders and they both got in each other's way preparing for a new day. She wondered when David had stopped watching her get dressed; the lack of interest or excitement as she stood in front of him in matching lingerie destroyed her confidence further.

David's family tradition was to celebrate Easter on Easter Monday and this year it coincided with Jojo's birthday. Lillian had called a few times during the week to confirm and then re-confirm the details. She would prepare lamb; she had seen a full leg (frozen) on offer at Morrisons.

David was in no fit state to drive; he was still tired from his dysfunctional naps. Rachel packed chilled Prosecco and presents for her sister-in-law. *What did people do before Prosecco?*

Rachel never usually had to think of things to say to her husband. But now the metaphorical cat had her tongue. She had forgotten how to *be* normal around him. It was a state so far removed from how she was feeling. Had it been so long since they had been alone without the distraction of gadgets and box sets that they had forgotten how to converse or interact? *What did they used to talk about?* She wanted to make him laugh or to impress him, to woo him, to turn him on. Rachel settled for bog standard small talk, even the weather was mentioned. David closed his eyes in hope of a power nap.

She gently squeezed his inner leg and, to her surprise, a small moan escaped under his half-awake, half-asleep breath. David opened his eyes, relieved that he had managed at least ten winks.

'Hello, sleepy. We're about to pass that B&B, do you remember?'

'The you-know?'

'The you-know!'

'Where you and I...?'

'And then some!'

'Best New Year's Day ever!' The corners of David's mouth lifted and he closed his eyes again.

Rachel and he had first consummated their relationship in a small Cotswolds cottage. Rachel sighed as she recollected their romantic getaway all those years ago. David had planned the weekend perfectly. He brought a picnic basket packed with Rachel's favourite nibbles. He chilled Champagne and lit what must have been a hundred tealights. David had made it clear he expected nothing physical from her. He wanted her to feel ready. The mind plays tricks with memories and there was no recollection now of their initial awkwardness, or the futile attempts to get into the right position, or how David's hands trembled with excitement when he couldn't pull the condom over his erection and they both got the giggles. She recalled the moment they found a working rhythm and tempo as their bodies melded. The relief and strength of her orgasm had surprised the inexperienced Rachel. Being with David was different from being with other boyfriends. At nineteen years old she knew it was the turning point for her. She had matured from girl to woman.

From the corner of her eye, Rachel saw that the material over David's crotch was tightening. His genitals were squashed against the stiff indigo denim, trying to escape but to no avail. David fidgeted to get comfortable. Had she not still been angry with him, she would have been rather turned on. It seemed a waste to leave his erection high and dry.

David and Jojo's mother Lillian had lived in the same house her whole life. Rachel retrieved the gifts from the boot of the car as she left David to navigate himself out of the passenger seat. The protruding outline of his crotch fascinated her. David attempted to cover his groin area with his hands, in the position adopted by footballers defending a free kick. Lillian was delighted to see them and stood waiting impatiently at the door. David's mother was small and round. She wore a constant, uneasy smile as if she was sitting on something uncomfortable. She walked slowly with her elbows held high. Her pink and purple striped housecoat reminded Rachel of a knitted tea cosy.

David and Rachel were the first to arrive as Jojo and Beth were delayed in traffic. Rachel kissed Lillian on both cheeks and David followed them into the house awkwardly.

Jojo was beaming when she and her girlfriend Beth arrived. They were both gorgeous blondes, with huge smiles, exaggerated with red lipstick. Rachel wondered if they wore the same shade. Jojo whispered in Rachel's ear, 'I've got a surprise!'

She called for her mother and brother to sit as she presented the still flat stomach of her fiancée Beth. They were pregnant AND they were getting married!

Beth explained in her Texan drawl they were nearly fifteen weeks pregnant, hence she was still wearing her normal jeans although they were getting tighter, while Jojo tried to interrupt with key points. They'd had to choose which one of them would undergo IVF. Beth had a real job with maternity benefits, while Jojo was freelance. They chose the sperm donor from a catalogue. He was a professor of something, practically a rocket scientist. And who knew it would work first time!

What the fuck? A baby?

Rachel thought about her own empty womb as she realised that Jojo had not confided in her about this and tried not to be offended. How long had Jojo and Beth been planning this? A baby, an IVF baby, no less, takes time. She worked out the dates going backwards. Fifteen weeks pregnant plus two weeks for implant, a month or more for IVF drugs and testing, a couple of months of consultations to begin with. Before that choosing a clinic. Discussing it like adults. THAT MADE THIRTY-THREE

WEEKS! They had been planning it since last year. *Stop being selfish, Rachel*, she chided herself.

Rachel couldn't remember saying more than hello to Beth at the anniversary party, she had been so wrapped up in her own life. And here Jojo and Beth were going through life-changing events.

'I'm so happy for you!' Rachel hugged them once, twice, and then attempted a third time before Jojo said that was enough.

'Was it planned?' Lillian asked and then realised her mistake. 'Of course it was planned, otherwise ... I mean, I'm so happy for you both!' She was going to be a grandmother for the first time. She said the words 'first time' while frowning at David. It was a nod to the fact that she was the last of her friends to have a grandchild and that was something her son could have remedied years earlier. It was becoming a bone of contention. Jojo and Beth hadn't wanted to announce the pregnancy until after the crucial three months, and then they had wanted to do it in person.

'When are you thinking of getting married?' Lillian asked. 'Will you wait until after the baby—?'

'We were thinking in the next couple of months. As soon as possible,' Beth said, while she looked to Jojo for a reassuring nod.

'Well done, sis. Rachel can organise your wedding.'

Rachel glared at David. Weddings were hard work and fraught with problems. She did not want to lose her best friend over a stupid tiered cake, the wrong dress, or the fallout from the chief bridesmaid bonking the best man.

'Yes, of course, please let me,' Rachel said through gritted teeth.

Lillian asked after Beth's health, her blood pressure, if she was getting proper rest and eating enough green vegetables?

Jojo basked in the interest her mother was showing in her fiancée.

'Fiancée!' Jojo repeated. 'Doesn't it sound great: *have you met my fiancée*?'

She grabbed the cushion that David was using to hide his erection and used it to help prop Beth up. David yelped at the sudden unmasking of his crotch then smiled with relief.

'Yes! It's gone!' he exclaimed to a puzzled audience.

Lillian entertained everyone with how she'd told her fellow team members at the bowls club about her lesbian daughter, and how she had met her lesbian daughter's lover and now she could tell them all about the lesbian baby on its way. She asked if there was a babygro colour-preference for lesbian babies. When Jojo asked if the gravy would be lesbian-friendly, Lillian blushed and asked if she had said something 'politically incorrect' (yes, she raised her fingers for the quotation marks). She explained how she'd read in the *Daily Mail* that 'the gays' had been getting upset about certain labels. David rolled his eyes, for Jojo's sake. He didn't have the patience to explain LGBT etiquette to their mother again! It was difficult to stay annoyed with Lillian when she repeatedly ambled into politically incorrect cul-de-sacs while trying so hard not to offend.

Rachel quickly defused the atmosphere by opening the bottle of chilled Prosecco and prepared Sham-Chams and non-alcoholic Sham-Shams for designated drivers (Rachel and Beth) and mothers-to-be (also Beth).

SHAM-CHAMS RECIPE
(an inexpensive alternative to Champagne CHAM-CHAMS)
150 ml fizzy white wine
*10 ml Chambord raspberry
    liqueur*

SHAM-SHAMS RECIPE
10 ml raspberry cordial
150 ml soda water

Rachel let her panic at the prospect of a TWO-MONTH WEDDING PLANNING EXTRAVAGANZA subside as she noted how much pregnancy suited Beth. She had its telltale glow. They toasted Jojo's birthday and the newest baby-bump addition to the family.

Rachel helped Lillian serve lunch. Her mother-in-law cooked the best roast dinners and they were a benchmark of traditional English cooking. Rachel was pretty sure the secret was good old-fashioned lard. Lillian had cooked roast lamb that melted in the mouth. Bone marrow gravy. Fresh mint from the garden. Roast potatoes cooked with rosemary sprigs. Huge, crisp, freshly made Yorkshire puddings. Lillian wouldn't allow any frozen muck in her Sunday lunch.

She stayed close to Beth's stomach and tried force-feeding her leftover Yorkshire puddings. Jojo pointed out that Beth was only eating for two, not two army platoons.

Despite everything, this was the life that Rachel wanted: time with family and loved ones, and good food. David's hand had been on her left knee since dessert and his touch warmed her. She returned the gesture and gave his knee a small squeeze. They shared a knowing smile and for a second Rachel forgot she hated him. She looked at the expanding Chatsworth family and her heart sank at the thought of leaving them.

David

17

David went downstairs to read the morning papers armed with his iPad and waited for the coffee machine to warm up. He tried to remember where he had put the Viagra prescription, although after yesterday's stonking middle-of-the-day erection he knew he wouldn't need the tablets any time soon. The virility of his teenage years had returned, and to celebrate he tried to high-five an unwilling Oscar who swished his tail in disapproval.

Despite nearing his forty-sixth birthday, he would always be his mother's special little soldier. He had left Lillian's with an armful of Easter goodies plus a bottle of finest single malt. He'd already demolished the After Eight egg and looked forward to cracking open the six-pack of Cadbury's creme eggs. *Were they getting smaller? They looked tiny in his hands.*

David had been blessed with the metabolic rate of a teenage athlete and had taken it for granted all his life. But now, after he had adopted a healthier lifestyle, it seemed Mother Nature was having the last laugh. He'd have to work harder at the gym and maybe book a couple of personal training sessions to identify more effective exercises. He looked at himself in the mirror. Karma was out to get him. Ever since he'd slept with Amelia-Rose he had been the unluckiest man in the world. As if the Greek god of marital affairs wouldn't let him have his cake and eat it. It was a stupid one-off. He'd not fallen in love with Amelia-Rose, it wasn't even about her; it was about how she made *him* feel. Alive and young. That only made the guilt worse, his action all the more selfish. He knew he was a walking cliché. She'd been so youthful and full of energy but David regretted being steered by the contents of his pants; he knew she had merely stroked his ego, and then some.

He questioned where the intimacy he used to share with Rachel had gone. When had the romance disappeared? His wife used to do sweet little things for him and then it stopped. She was distant. She had pulled away. None of this was enough to excuse what he did, though.

He didn't know where to look when Rachel dropped her towel to get dressed for work. He snuck a quick peek when she turned away and then quickly left the room.

When David asked if Rachel wanted to accompany him to an IT conference, she'd said she couldn't have time away from work, but it sounded like an excuse. They loved going to conferences together, or they used to, mainly because it meant staying in a fancy hotel. They would choose somewhere with a spa and a Michelin-quality menu. He tried to remember the last time he'd had his wife's full attention. He put it down to *him* being busy; he was distracted by the buy-out and hadn't been paying her enough attention. He didn't even know now if he wanted to sell the company. Of course, there was the money to look forward to. And it was agreed he's be on hand a few hours a week. But what would he do then? Would he look for another job? Would he start something new?

It took David most of the day to get his head into his work. And then before he knew it Rachel was home. She kissed him on the forehead and mentioned something about an early dinner. He had squandered the day being busy but accomplishing nothing. David was about to shut down his computer when Rachel's phone screen danced. He unplugged her phone from the charger and was going to call out to her but stopped when he saw the display. He presumed it would be Norma, or Jojo, or Eva calling, but he didn't recognise the caller's name. David could hear Rachel hoovering on the stairs. The vacuum crept closer, one step at a time.

He sat at his desk and quickly Googled 'Stefan Stratos'. There were a number of people with that name in the results. But on a map showing an area less than two miles away was the entry 'Stefan Stratos – Family Law'. David clicked through to the website:

> *Stefan Stratos's Family Law. Experts in dealing with divorce, the breakdown of family relationships, cohabitation or civil partnership. Areas of expertise: how to separate. Resolution negotiation. Code of practice promoting a sensitive approach ... likely to result in an agreement.*

The words 'divorce', 'breakdown', 'separate', jolted him. Panic washed through his body. Maybe it was the wrong number? But how could it be a mistake when she had his name saved in her phone?

He called the number back.

A smooth voice answered the call immediately.

'Rachel, hi, thanks for calling back. Listen, about your separation agreement, I have one quick question about—'

David hung up the phone.

Separation agreement? Rachel was going to leave him. *Why? What did she know?* The noise from the vacuum affected his ability to think. *How did she find out about Amelia-Rose? Had he been talking in his sleep?* What on earth had a forty-five-year-old been doing with someone twenty years his junior? Amelia-Rose didn't know his music; she had no point of reference to a life before the Internet. She wasn't born when he left home for university. He was the archetypal dirty old man. Self-loathing suffocated him. And now he could only presume that Rachel now knew what he'd done.

She was metres from the office. The door was ajar. His heart was thumping. He quickly deleted the calls (missed and dialled) from the log. Maybe it would buy him some time. Time to do what, he had no idea. He locked the screen and put the phone back on charge where he'd found it, deliberately askew, and waited for her to push the Hoover through the door. He sat in his leather chair with his legs crossed at the ankle and perched on the matching footstool. He tried to appear nonchalant. He waited, his pallid face blotched red with guilt. He could hear the edge of the Hoover bump against the door before it moved noisily away along the hallway and towards the bedroom. He let out a sigh.

The bottom had fallen out of David's life. It was destroyed. And the worst part of it was, it was entirely his own fault. He felt nauseous. His lunch and three chocolate creme eggs were threatening to make a reappearance. He ran to the downstairs toilet and retched.

One possible scenario was that Rachel knew everything. But that didn't make sense. She would have blown her top. Or she'd have organised a conscious uncoupling meeting had she wanted to separate. Or, heaven forbid, demanded a divorce. She would often compile lists and objectives for their relationship. She'd start with communication strategies from marriage counselling through to holidays "to reconnect". There would be months and months of talking through their problems. No, Rachel couldn't know what he'd done. BUT OF COURSE SHE

KNEW SOMETHING – WHY ELSE WAS A FUCKING FAMILY LAWYER CALLING HER?

When he went back upstairs, Rachel had finished in the office. He gave her a sheepish smile and patted her bottom affectionately, which left him with a lingering feeling of awkwardness. *Was he still allowed to touch her?* He loitered, waiting for her to finish. She took the Hoover downstairs but returned straight away, making him jump. She reminded him that she had a video-conference scheduled and needed to use their office. It was a call with Australia – it was already tomorrow there. David made a point of double-checking that the Ethernet cable was attached for the best connection with the other side of the world.

He needed to keep his hands and his head busy; he went to the kitchen to make cocktails. Rachel came downstairs to get a glass of water while she was waiting for her call to start. He presented her with a tropical cocktail, complete with umbrella and cherry.

'What's this?'

'A Bali Bombshell!'

'A what?'

'You must remember, from our wedding.'

'In Bali?'

BALI BOMBSHELL RECIPE
25 ml Vodka
25 ml White Rum
15 ml Watermelon liqueur
35 ml pink grapefruit juice
75 ml pineapple juice

'Yes, in Bali.'

David took a sip and was instantly transported back to their wedding night. It was a bitter-sweet reminder. Rachel's face didn't reveal any sign of uncertainty or duplicity. *Who was this woman?* Once he could read his wife like a book and her voice had been a measure of her mood. He kissed the back of her neck, aligned his body with hers and snuggled in. She didn't outright push him away but she nudged out of his immediate personal space and said something about needing to join the video-conference; she'd only come down for water. She left the untouched drink on the side. He knew this was a bad sign.

David needed to know how long Rachel had been feeling like this. He was loath to think that during their anniversary weekend she'd had doubts about their future. Had she already set an official separation in motion? He felt betrayed and rejected. The irony of this was not lost on him, though it was submerged by fear. Fear of being found out. Because if Rachel was seeking a divorce, it was only a matter of time before she found out David's biggest secret.

He paced the kitchen. *Think, man.* David was determined to fight for his wife. Marriages had survived worse, hadn't they? A terrible realisation dawned on him then. Rachel might forgive a one-night stand if he promised a lifetime of apology and no repetition, but if she found out they weren't actually married – there would be nothing to stop her from walking away.

Rachel

18

On the whole, Rachel was a cheerful person. She wasn't one of those ridiculously chirpy people who floated through life on a cloud of unicorn dust, but she woke up most mornings on the right side of the bed and walked with a spring in her stride. Or she used to. This was yet another morning when she'd had to drag herself out from under a dark cloud.

She looked at her never-husband, his head gently balanced on two thick pillows. She visualised how easy it would be to take her own pillow and push it down against his face ... The fantasy both thrilled and disgusted her and she was snapped out of it by the unmistakable sound of one of the cats knocking the fruit bowl to the floor. She had recently bought a metal one from Habitat. Neville and Oscar had smashed enough pottery to teach her a lesson.

Rachel left David sleeping and tiptoed down to the kitchen. By the time she reached the bottom of the stairs the cats had scarpered. Rachel couldn't remember ever before experiencing such inner turmoil or feeling actual hatred. Because wasn't that what this was? Hatred? It blackened not only her heart but also her every waking minute. She wanted David to suffer, she wanted him to feel incredible pain and indignity, and she wanted him to beg and beg for her forgiveness. Then, and only then, could Rachel leave him. She needed to find her happy place. Sadly, David and the home they shared was no longer that.

The kitchen was the epitome of extravagant living. There was a bronze food processor on the birch worktop: a lavish appliance chosen to complement their self-indulgent lifestyle. It had come at an exorbitant price, costing more than Rachel's first car. The worktop was also expensive and so delicate that any liquid would stain the finish. The wood needed oiling every two months. It was an impractical worktop for anyone who liked to use the kitchen for cooking or, heck, even reheating food.

She wanted to make herself a coffee but didn't want the noisy built-in bean grinder to wake the selfish bastard sleeping upstairs. She wasn't ready to stretch her facial muscles into a smile, nor to act normal in front of David. She wondered how they would split their life in two. Rachel would rather die than let him have both an affair and the coffee machine. She thought of her mother and of the traditional, nuclear family in which she had raised her children. Soon both of them would have experienced divorce. Rachel had two teenage nephews, but she rarely saw them. Isaac and Hendry were always on the continent somewhere with their glamorous and very French mother, Elena. Kevin's ex-wife had been granted full custody as part of the divorce settlement. He was the parent-in-absentia who followed them from country to country for weekends, much to the annoyance of Elena's newly acquired fifth husband. Rachel couldn't imagine getting married again, let alone another four times.

She heard David's footsteps overhead. His heavy-footedness irritated her. His every movement annoyed her. He trudged down the stairs and complained again about his disturbed sleep. Rachel insinuated that his 'habit' was to blame for his sleeplessness. She even suggested research into the half-life of coffee, but David was having none of it. She left the house after using the fewest words possible to ascertain that they would both be at home for dinner.

Eva had interrupted Rachel's daydream about her formerly happy marriage. The time when David was still in love with her. She was relieved her thoughts were moving away from hate and vengeance. The truth was, she didn't want a new husband. She wanted her own husband back; the original Mr David Ross Chatsworth. The formerly loving, funny, attentive David.

Eva pulled down the blinds to Rachel's glass-walled office. The blinds that hadn't been used once since they'd moved in. The creaking and comic slowness of them failing to cover the glass panes adequately was painful. Rachel could see Lydia trying to spy on them over her monitor.

'I've got some bad news,' Rachel said.

Eva was stopped in her tracks. 'What else could possibly go wrong? How many mirrors did you break in a past life?'

'Jojo's getting married.'

'Isn't that good news?'

'Yes and no. David's volunteered my, ergo *our*, services to organise it.'

'Shit!'

'Yep.'

'I didn't think we were doing any more weddings. Do you think your friendship with Jojo will survive?' Eva, as always, was blunt and to the point.

'I really don't know.'

Eva reverted back to the task in hand and nodded towards the open-plan office beyond the blinds.

'Lydia is drowning in work – she needs some direction. Timothy is afraid to come into the office and is making every excuse under the sun to work from home. He's only here today because he wants to close month-end.'

Timothy was an enigma to Rachel. He came in, did his work and went home again. He was a stealth accountant. He had three book-keeping jobs. He worked two days a week with Rachel at Keatley Marketing, two days a week at a private art school and one day a week for an urban farmers association. In the early days, he had told Rachel he liked working with her the best and that if she could offer him more hours, he'd take them. Rachel knew she frequently forgot about invoices and yesterday only authorised the staff salaries at the very last possible moment. And that was after four very polite email reminders from Timothy.

'And Wendy hasn't been given any freelance work in months.' Eva clicked her fingers under Rachel's nose; she had already zoned out. Eva laid down the law to her boss. 'Time for some tough love.'

Rachel nodded in agreement. She was in another world though.

'Cards on the table? I can run the office with my eyes closed but it's dead boring doing it on my own.'

Rachel nodded again, having nothing of value to contribute. She promised to do better, to be better. Lydia wasn't the only one who was out of her depth. Rachel was five foot and three inches underwater. She would have to talk to her PA and book-keeper and ask for their understanding a little longer. Lydia was far too good to lose, and Timothy was great. He never complained about anything and worked autonomously without questions or errors. And she would think of a small project she could throw to Wendy who liked being freelance, charged good rates, and didn't complain when things were too busy or too quiet.

Eva added that she'd seen Lydia lingering over the job pages in the free paper on the morning commute, and that it wouldn't take much more rudderless behaviour from their boss for the whole team to start looking elsewhere. Rachel wondered if that was Eva's way of saying she too was eyeing up other jobs.

Rachel's phone buzzed. It was David. He was going for drinks after his squash game and would be back late.

Rachel hung up, frowning, and explained this was another lie from her never-husband. 'You know, he doesn't even play squash!'

Eva immediately toned down her bad cop tactics and, with a twinkle in her eye, suggested drinks after work.

The restaurant had a garden bar that overlooked the river. Instead, Eva persuaded the waiter that they needed a booth at the back, out of sight but, importantly, by a window so they could see the people coming and going at the country club opposite. The two women waited there for David to finish his "squash game".

Rachel opened the GPS app and found the blinking blue beacon that signified David's location. He was less than two hundred metres from where they sat. Eva asked the waiter to turn down the music. Rachel was silently relieved. Her taste in music hadn't changed much with the passing years. It wasn't that she didn't like contemporary music, she didn't understand it – felt no connection to it. There were a handful of songs she genuinely liked and even fewer albums. She could think of only one CD she'd purchased in the last few years: Michael Kiwanuku's *Home Again*. Was that what happened when you got older? You bought albums based on the BBC's coverage of Glastonbury? Whatever happened to going to festivals? As he got older, David liked the idea of festivals more than the reality and had listed complaints about the camping, the mud, the noise.

Rachel had always liked her older brother's favourite bands: The Cure and The Smiths. She loved George Michael and Prince. She still liked to dance to Whitney Houston's 'I

Wanna Dance with Somebody' and Cyndi Lauper's 'Girls Just Want to Have Fun', and not in an ironic way.

'It's only been a few minutes, and already I'm sick of staring at an empty car park.' Eva waved to the waiter.

She ordered a bottle of Pinot Noir. Rachel was in awe of Eva's self-assurance. She was a force of nature, attractive and strong. And her taste in wine was impeccable – the bold red tasted sublime. Rachel picked at the label of the wine bottle.

'*Salut*!' said Eva,

'To not being married,' Rachel added, and they clinked glasses.

Rachel checked her phone. The flashing blue beacon hadn't moved.

She lamented overlooking the parking spaces when there was a fabulous view of the river from over by the bar. The wine bottle was soon emptied and Eva ordered two cocktails. When four glasses arrived the waiter announced it was happy hour and buy one, get one free. The cocktails were meant as cover for their espionage but the lychee martinis tasted divine.

LYCHEE MARTINI RECIPE
50 ml Vodka
25 ml Lychee liqueur
25 ml Lychee syrup
Fresh lychee and its juice

Rachel watched a tall, handsome man walk into the bar. He smiled in their direction. Eva glanced at Rachel who was smiling back. 'It's my … the cats' vet and I think he may be a vet … eran too. Army maybe. Dr … Perrier-Water, something like that. Anyway, he doesn't like cats.'

'Look at you – catnip to the dishy bachelors in town! And how can a middle-class urban vet not like cats? Go and speak to him.'

'I wouldn't know what to—'

'Practise on me,' Eva demanded. 'Come on, quick.' Rachel tried her 'sexy' pout while fluttering her eye-lashes.

'Why are you doing a Mick Jagger impression? Put your lips away. Don't try to flirt with him, talk to him like a normal Earthling. Are you drunk?' Before Rachel could answer the attractive man was at their table.

'Hi, Doctor P. This is Eva,' Rachel introduced them.

'I'm Luke.'

'Eva.' She didn't shake hands and ignored Luke's attempt to do so.

'Luke doesn't like cats.'

Eva admonished Rachel with her eyes.

'What? I love cats.'

'You don't like my cats.'

'Your cats are great. Beautiful coats as I recall.'

'But you said they were fat.'

'They are on the portly side. But I only said to put them on a diet because I want them to live a long time. And I want them to live a long time because they make you happy. And I want happy patients.'

'I thought you said Neville and Oscar were the patients. I liked that.'

'You're absolutely right. Think about it. If you were the patient, I wouldn't be able to socialise with you like this.'

'Is that what this is?'

Rachel tried her seductive pout again while Eva waved a dismissal at Luke, who looked a little confused and said he hoped the women enjoy their evening before excusing himself. Rachel could have died from acute embarrassment. She mimed hitting her head against the table. Glancing over, she could see the vet was out with his staff; an odd-bod collection of pierced and tattooed animal lovers. She allowed herself to wonder if Luke had any bodily adornments himself.

'I bet he's a vegetarian. Why am I such a loser?' she asked.

'You did really well!'

'It was awful. He's too perfect ... handsome and a vet. Why are the beautiful men even single? What's wrong with them?'

'They've got their own shit to deal with – often they're divorced with crazy ex-wives, or else they're serial killers, or both.'

'Will I be a crazy ex-wife?' Rachel asked.

'Probably.'

'But the thing is, Eva, it's over and I know I'm better off without David. Mentally, I know that. So, physically, emotionally, why does it still hurt so much?'

Eva raised her glass in a toast: 'As the saying goes: *how you get them is how you lose them*. Good luck to whoever she is!'

Rachel felt melancholy seeping through her. She didn't want to watch David with another woman. She didn't want evidence of shared laugher and stories being exchanged, but she couldn't help but wait to witness it. Like a bystander at a car crash, her eyes were trained on the scene, awaiting further developments. Her mood dipped even lower.

'If you could do anything, what would you choose?' Eva asked her.

'Well, I've found a couple of cute cottages for sale … but really it's always been my dream to live on a boat. When we first moved to Richmond, right by the river, it was amazing. Thank God it was all those years ago. We couldn't afford to buy here now!'

'There's loads of boats by the bridge, they do day trips and weekend hire.'

'David gets dreadful seasickness. He once threw up on a surfboard!'

'Poor baby,' Eva said sarcastically. 'Look at it this way – it's a plus in the life without David column.'

Rachel nodded and shared a silly thought. 'I have this fantasy. It's nuts, but sometimes I think about the future and tell myself: what if? What if, perhaps, maybe, I could get him to fall in love with me again? And we could get married properly this time.' The drink had loosened her lips.

Eva frowned, not following.

'And then you'd divorce him?'

Rachel hadn't actually thought about the divorcing part; most of all she wanted David to love her, to hold her like he used to. She gave a half-hearted nod.

'That's evil,' Eva said, followed by, 'I love it!'

'It would be great, wouldn't it?' Rachel mused.

'I think it's genius. You should definitely do it.'

'Thanks, Eva. You've really cheered me up.'

Eva drew up a battle plan. It was simple:

1) Rachel would be the nicest, sexiest wife she could be and make her husband fall madly in love with her again.

2) They'd renew their vows.

3) Then she'd divorce him!

Rachel thought it was a good plan in theory but voiced some concerns about actually going through with it – *what was the point?* It wouldn't work and she was already embarrassed and felt like shit. She was tired of it, of him, of their sham marriage. She couldn't handle any further rejection from David. Unperturbed, Eva persuaded her at least to try!

Although the idea had started as a joke, it lodged in Rachel's mind. What if she could get him to fall back in love with her? They could get married properly this time. And – this was the bit she couldn't tell Eva – even live happily ever after. Without an unpleasant divorce at the end. Was that too much to hope for?

Rachel checked her phone again.

'Quick – it's time to go.' She pointed to the blue beacon on her phone. 'David's already at home!'

'But how—'

'Come on!'

Rachel tried to order an Uber but there were no cars available. Typical. Eva hailed down a black cab for

Rachel and gave her a hug. She shouted 'thanks' as she climbed in unsteadily.

'Home, Jeeves!' Rachel laughed, and the driver switched on the meter and chuckled with her.

'Remember, love, the longer it takes you to remember where you live, the more I get paid.'

She gave him her address and allowed herself to day-dream in the back of the taxi about her and David growing old together. She knew that he was her Achilles heel and hated herself for such weakness, but what if . . . ?

David was sat at the breakfast bar, bent over his laptop when Rachel sashayed in. It was an entrance intended to project a sense of sobriety she certainly did not feel.

'Someone is heavily refreshed.' Rachel slowed to investigate David's face – he was joking, there was a twinkle in his eye. She kissed him on the cheek.

'I thought you were going for drinks after your squash game?'

'Barry got a last-minute date. What about you, what time do you call this?,' he joked as he tapped his watch.'

'Eva and I needed to brainstorm.'

'Do people still do that? I thought it was all mind-mapping and such.'

David looked up from his laptop for long enough to stare at his wife as if seeing her for the first time. Rachel improved her precarious posture and gave him a twirl.

'What?' she asked.

David shook his head.

'What is it?' she asked again.

'Are you seeing someone?'

Rachel kicked off her heels and laughed hard. It blasted through the room like a foghorn. She couldn't stop laughing; the question was absurd. When she had collected herself and her breathing returned to normal, she asked, 'What – you mean, an affair?'

'It was a joke. You've been different and you look great.'

It was a genuine compliment. Beauty sleep was real and tangible. *Why didn't more people bang on about how great sleep was?* Even if for her it was chemically induced with sleeping tablets most nights, to give her brain respite for eight hours, but at least she was well rested.

'Why? Are you jealous? I once read: you know who gets most suspicious – those who are having affairs themselves. Something to do with the laws of duplicity; when one is up to no good, they automatically thinks everyone else is too. Perhaps the husband doth protest too much?'

She was immediately rewarded for the boldness of her remark. David's mouth dropped open. Rachel pretended to scroll through her calls, as his cheeks flushed. He blustered about removing something from the fridge, Rachel didn't hear what. But whatever *it* was, it had to be at room temperature right away. David's unease coloured the air as Rachel watched him try to squeeze the worms back in the can.

He helped himself to a cold lager and guzzled it down. He didn't know that Rachel had swapped the labels and he was drinking the non-alcoholic version of his favourite brand. She sat watching. The beer wasn't producing the magic release David was expecting. He opened a second bottle and wondered aloud if it was beer consumption adding to his waistline. Rachel gave his practically flat stomach a stroke and tried to pinch an inch.

Before bed, she watched as he brushed his teeth. The toothbrush head débacle still worried her. Only recently she'd thought he deserved a fate worse than death; today he might actually get it. He could die from dysentery and she would be responsible.

But she forgot all about David's potty mouth when he unexpectedly kissed her gently on the mouth. His warm tongue pressed against her lips, seeking an invitation. Her body automatically arched towards his. The warm haze of attraction was instantly dispelled when her brain kicked into overdrive, besieging her with thoughts of the other woman and her firm young body. Rachel had visions of the sex David had had with the redhead, the positions, the sounds he and his lover would have made.

She ducked into the bathroom with her mobile phone. She must message Eva and ask what to do. Rachel really did want to sleep with her cheating pretend-husband but would she regret it in the morning? This could all play into the plan to get David back ... It was almost as stressful as the decision to lose her virginity. No, she wouldn't call Eva. She didn't want to be told it was a bad idea.

Rachel returned to the bedroom and the decision was made for her: David was asleep and gently snoring. For once she didn't need sleeping tablets nor had she dosed his water with caffeine pills. They both slept dreamlessly, side-by-side.

The next morning, guilt about the toothbrush-in-toilet incident still plagued Rachel. She called Dr Lester's surgery. The lovely dental receptionist, Julie, answered the phone in her sing-song voice. She asked if Rachel would like the slot in two Saturdays' time at 14:30.

She called up the stairs to suggest this to David.

'I went recently.'

'When?' she shouted.

David didn't answer so she booked him the appointment and hoped a first-world case of dysentery wouldn't develop in the interim.

'When?' Rachel repeated up the stairs, although it would have been far easier for her to venture up them to have the conversation.

'December. When I had that toothache.'

'Where was I?'

'I don't know. On your spa thing?'

Her annual spa retreat; the thought immediately relaxed her posture. Rachel and three friends spent two days at a luxurious spa every December, unwinding in preparation for their nerves to be shredded over Christmas. It helped to ease the stress of cooking for more than twelve guests, coping with in-laws, still-frozen turkeys, Boxing Day games, too much sherry, and piles of unwanted gifts.

'That was nearly six months ago,' Rachel told him. 'I've booked you an appointment.'

Rachel wanted to Google the possible repercussions for drugging one's spouse but she hardly needed Stephen Hawking's intellect to realise it was a stupid idea and most probably illegal; plus she didn't want it left on her internet search history. She knew she should hand herself in at the nearest police station for spousal abuse. *Do not pass go. Go directly to jail.*

Rachel got to the office an hour earlier than she usually did as she had promised Eva she would try harder. She put her head down and checked in with all her clients, sending emails offering them a complimentary mid-year review. It was amazing the productivity that could be achieved when she was alone in the office.

She managed her inbox, deleted all the spam, and scrolled through the headlines. She couldn't concentrate on the details. Where was the good news?

Lydia bounced into the office and was delighted to find the clone of old-Rachel waiting for her. They spent the day working on her PA's brainchild: a new vodka launch.

Rachel didn't fancy cooking and David hadn't sent a message to say he was going to be out. She looked at the Marks & Spencer's website for inspiration and found they had a meal deal. She headed over to choose two mains, a side, dessert and bottle of wine for the magical price of £10.

Ready to woo her faux-husband, she skipped home and was informed by a note on the kitchen worktop that David had gone to the gym. Any non-verbal communication, whether it be handwritten, a text message or an email, was surely his way of avoiding the lie showing in his face. She opened her phone and searched for his location. There was no beacon of hope that he was in fact at the gym or anywhere else – his phone was switched off.

She left David's dinner in the microwave and went to bed. By ten she'd taken a sleeping tablet and arrived at the Land of Nod.

David

19

David was sitting in a meeting he wasn't sure he'd been officially invited to when he excused himself and walked out. He wasn't any use at work; they had no need for him now that the buy-out was all but finalised.

He was useless at home too. Rachel was slipping further away from him day by day. The reality of the situation hit David; he was an idiot who'd been led by the contents of his boxer shorts – the same boxer shorts that were now feeling unusually tight. There wasn't a time in the last fifteen years when he hadn't had his wife to help him through any challenge he encountered. Now he wrote a list of all the problems that needed to be addressed, one by one. His main worry was that he'd left it too late and any day now he could expect to be exposed for the lying cheating bastard he was. David decided he needed an action plan. He called Barry for advice.

Barry said he'd have to be quick, he was with a client.

'Are you around later?' David gulped. 'It's important.'

'D&D, six.'

Their code for meet at the Dog and Duck at 6 p.m.

Barry was not in the best place to be doling out relationship advice but David could trust him to be honest and, most importantly, non-judgemental.

Beers with Barry turned out to be a waste of time. David didn't confide any more in Barry beyond that he thought Rachel was acting suspiciously and wondered if she was going to leave him. Barry didn't ask for the details – he was more of a big-picture man. In fact, it turned out that he was utterly useless when it came to affairs of the heart. His advice was summarised: keep your head down and don't rock the boat. He said that if he hadn't let Gina find out about his tomfoolery, then he wouldn't have been thrown out of the marital home, and wouldn't currently be living in a studio smaller than his former two-car garage. Even more depressing was when he showed David his Tinder dating profile. He had swept right, or was it left, to indicate interest – and got nothing in return, not a sausage.

'And not even from the ugly ones,' Barry said. 'I thought it was gonna be great. Bachelor around town. Do you remember uni? We were the dog's bollocks.'

David nodded. He didn't want to be reminded of being single and in his twenties. Barry was literally a combination Ghost of David's Past and Future.

'Let's have a look at that.'

He scrolled through the hundreds, HUNDREDS, of available women. In spite of the different pictures, ages, locations, for him the profiles all merged into one.

'Why have you filtered women between the ages of eighteen and fifty?' he asked his friend.

'*You* dated an eighteen-year-old. Fuck, you married her!'

'That was fifteen years ago. And she was nineteen.'

'It's a numbers game. All the women our age have loads of kids or are desperate for kids.'

'I thought you had a date the other day?'

'That was, uhm, a different site. They're a bit less fussy over there.'

Barry didn't elaborate further and David wasn't sure he wanted to know where the less-fussy people were situated.

'Might be nice to meet a single mum.' David suggested.

'Do you know what I really want? For Gina to take me back. I miss her so much. I want to live and die in her bosom.'

'Good luck with that.'

'How about another game of squash this week?'

'I'm useless at it – last time you beat me ten–one.'

'Don't be a sore loser. It's a no-brainer. I need a partner to play with and you need a place to let out your frustration.'

'Maybe you're right.'

It was David's round. He gave Barry a £20 note and asked him to get the drinks in while he called Rachel. The stark reality of his friend's lonely plight ignited something in David. He had left a note to say he was at the gym, which was where he was planning to be before he'd called Barry. Now David wanted to be honest with Rachel and tell her his change of plan. He didn't want to lie anymore, even unintentionally.

He tried to unlock his phone. It was no use, the battery had died.

Barry sat with two pints and a packet of pork scratchings in front of him. He offered a fried pig trotter to David. The hairy smoky bacon bit in Barry's outstretched fingers turned David's stomach. He didn't feel like he could ask his friend for the change.

The next morning David called his office to remind them he had a medical appointment. The kind receptionist asked if he was okay – and commented that he'd seemed a bit peaky the day before.

At the heart assessment clinic David waited for his name to be called. He looked at the electronic display. It showed 156. He checked the paper token in his hand: 164. Why did they allocate appointment times and then run over an hour late? He hadn't brought a book or his iPad. Instead, he played solitaire on his phone. What was taking them so long?

He looked up at the wall. The digital display jumped straight to 161.

He couldn't concentrate on the card game and scrolled through his friends' WhatsApp group. Mainly it was harmless banter and memes taking the piss out of each other. Every now and then there was genuine cause for concern. Earlier in the year, Tom broke a leg hiking Snowdonia and for a while it had been touch and go. There was hushed talk of having to amputate some of the limb. Barry had been too hasty in making a legless joke. The rest of the group severely admonished him, although they privately acknowledged his quick wit, however inappropriate.

'Mr Chatsworth. Mr David Chatsworth.'

David realised his name was being called.

The woman was holding a clipboard and asked him to follow her to a testing suite.

'Can you take your shirt off?' she asked as she closed the door. She introduced herself as Lucy and explained her role as a Cardiac Physiologist.

David pretended not to notice how pretty she was. He wanted to ask for a male Physiologist but that would involve admitting he was uncomfortable with her. He took off his shirt and folded it carefully. He held in his stomach, not that she'd be interested in him but she really was pretty. He was acutely aware of their closeness in the small treatment room. He tried to remember whether he had eaten any garlic or onion recently ...

She walked him to a treadmill.

Why was his right nipple erect? It was like a bullet. It could have someone's eye out.

She blew on her hands to warm them then attached electrodes to his chest and fixed a blood-pressure cuff around his left bicep.

David wasn't particularly hairy, with only a dusting of inch-long dark hairs on his torso, but one of the pads caught a chest hair.

'Ouch!'

She apologised but said it would probably hurt more to move the electrode now it was stuck. He was primed for further pain to come at the end, very aware of his top-less state. She switched on the treadmill and he started walking. The test got steadily faster and the gradient more severe.

'You're in great shape . . .'

Was she flirting or being polite? He didn't want his heart rate to increase because of her proximity.

David wanted to say thanks but chose not to in case he showed he was out of breath. Not that he need have wor-ried; Lucy upped the speed and increased the ascent angle. He matched the new steep incline, step for step, with no slowing down.

'. . . for your age,' she continued.

No, definitely not flirting. Talk about kicking a man without his shirt on.

David had only joined the gym to punish himself for the guilt he felt. He'd had severe insomnia after his one-night stand with Amelia-Rose and the sleepless nights filled him with despair. He was glad his newly acquired fitness level could compete with the NHS monitoring equipment. Forced to talk when Lucy asked some follow-up questions, he gave short answers concerning his stimulants intake (coffee and alcohol) and exercise regime. He underestimated the former and exaggerated the latter. She asked him to describe his chest pains and any feelings of anxiety.

'Any problems at work? Or at home?'

My wife is planning to leave me and I will be destroyed.

'Personally – nothing of note.' David spoke slowly to hide his exertion, and brushed off the question by giving a broad statement that society was stressed as a whole. He was overworked but wasn't it the same for Everyman?

When she asked about medications and drugs, he shook his head.

'Do you smoke?'

'Quit twelve years ago.' After she congratulated him, David didn't think his recent dalliance with nicotine was worth mentioning.

'Anything harder? Cocaine or cannabis?'

'No.'

'Viagra?'

David wished the floor would open up and swallow him whole. He envisaged ripping off the electrodes and storming from the room like the Incredible Hulk, his favourite comic book character when he was a kid. He looked anywhere but at Lucy and tried to keep his dignity intact. 'No,' he said in a small voice.

'In your patient records, it says—'

'I got a prescription from the doctor, just in case.' David could feel sweat drip down his back and leak into the waistband of his boxer shorts.

'In case . . .?'

He caught her eye. 'Look, there's nothing wrong there!' he said before losing his balance and stumbling. He came flying off the treadmill. The wires ripped from his chest and he ended up sprawled in a corner of the room, legs akimbo.

'Oh, my God!' cried Lucy. 'Let me get some help.'

'NO!' His body was battered but the damage to his pride was far worse. He couldn't bear anyone else to witness his humiliation at careering off the running machine like that. He pretended that the chest hairs that had been ripped out didn't bother him and ignored that both his right elbow and knee were throbbing. Lucy helped him up. David gathered his shirt and quickly covered himself. If she noticed, she didn't mention that his buttons were done up incorrectly but waited patiently until he had recovered.

'It's not what you think.' He needed to clarify this with her. 'Me and my wife are trying … going to try for a baby, and one of my friends said that he was expected to, you know, perform, morning-noon-and-night at the drop of a hat. Whenever the thermometer dictated. I didn't want to …' He struggled to find the right words. '… I didn't want to let her down, is all. When I said no, I meant I haven't needed it yet. I haven't even filled the prescription'.

Lucy gave his hand a reassuring pat. David felt his arm hair prickle.

'I'll send your results to the doctor.'

David asked how long it would take for the GP to get them.

'It can take a week, maybe two. Off the record – it's my view there's nothing physically wrong with you but you've experienced some mild panic attacks.' She suggested relaxation and breathing exercises for when he felt overwhelmed. And told him to lay off the coffee.

'Stick to *single* espressos, and no more than two per day. I don't want to see you here again,' Lucy said with a smile.

'Great. Thanks,' he said before he rushed out of the room. He meant it too. He could have kissed her. David knew he could deal with panic attacks. *It was all about breathing and shit.* He had been petrified he wasn't going to live to see his forty-sixth birthday. Like his father hadn't.

As the fresh air hit David's face he already felt better. Placebo effect, maybe? Yes, he was a sweaty mess and had been thoroughly humiliated, but he hadn't died and he wasn't going to for the foreseeable future. Lucy had said he was in optimal condition for his age category, he had the body of someone five years younger easily. Although Lucy's test sample were probably not the healthiest of specimens, all being men referred to her for heart assessments.

David tried Rachel's number. He wanted to hear her cute voice. He wanted to ask if she still loved him. He needed reassurance that only she could provide. His call was sent to voicemail. *Where was she?*

He called Jim and asked if he wanted to have a celebratory-not-going-to-die-anytime-soon drink. Jim was reliable. Quiet and shy, he hid most of his face under a hipster beard. Jim would be able to give actual advice. Solid, down-to-earth advice, not the stick-your-head-in-the-sand type that was Barry's forté.

When David got to the pub, he was disappointed to see Jim sitting at a table with Aaron and Barry. Then Lee appeared with a tray of drinks. Jim, the anti-social mole of the decade, had invited all and sundry. Tom was busy and Alfie was stuck on a job in Edinburgh. But there sat four of David's oldest friends: Jim, Lee, Aaron and Barry.

Why, Jim, why?

'Dave – I was just saying, you sounded a bit blue. What better excuse for me to round up the troops!' Jim raised a glass to him.

'Thanks, Jim.'

Barry seemed more than happy to spend another night away from the solitude of his single man's studio, having quickly tired of bachelor life. Lee, vying for stepfather of the year, could fit in a swift one before he picked up the girls from the babysitter. And Aaron said he was always up for a cheeky beer on the way home, but to Barry's delight had already partnered his pint with a whisky chaser.

'Do we need to talk? Jim said you were suicidal,' Barry mouthed to David.

He looked askance at Jim, who couldn't hear their conversation but gave two thumbs up from across the table.

'Nah, he got the wrong end of the stick. I had an ECG today but it's fine – full bill of health. He must have misunderstood my *joie de vivre*.'

'That's what I thought,' Barry said unconvincingly. 'But let me know if the black dog visits.'

Aaron got the next round of drinks and everyone found himself a whisky on the side. Barry was made giddy by this determination to have fun. He didn't need a partner in crime, but he always welcomed company.

'How's the sale?' Jim asked David.

'Nearly there. This time next month, I reckon.'

'Then what?'

'Then what?' David repeated.

I don't have a frigging idea. The realisation he could be losing Rachel and his business at the same time was too much for him to take in.

'Have you checked your fantasy football?' Lee interrupted.

'Think so.' David nodded, thinking, *Couldn't give two shits about fantasy football.*

'You haven't seen it then. If you had you'd know you were in the lead by fifteen points!'

'What?' He checked his phone. That was unheard of. David usually bobbed about in the middle of the group. He had never peaked higher than third (Tom and Lee took pole position interchangeably) while Jim was always last. The rest of them floated up or down the league table.

'Something to do with Brighton FC,' Lee told him.

David realised that outside big occasions, weddings and funerals and even birthdays, he hadn't had a drink with these guys for over a year. And with the big events came wives, girlfriends, children, so they could hardly talk freely then. Time out had to be organised especially and diaries consulted, with in-laws-cum-babysitters booked months in advance. Their WhatsApp banter was a convenient alternative.

Lee's phone buzzed. It was a message from the child-minder. He showed David a picture of his stepdaughters. The two girls wore matching dresses and held up a hand-written message reading – WE MISS YOU DADDY LEE! Barry rolled his eyes and made a derisive gesture, imply-ing Lee was under the thumb. But David had never seen his friend happier, so it was obviously working for him.

Lee showed him another picture – this time at Lego-land. And then another, of Lee being buried in sand up to his neck and the two girls in fits of laughter. They were both missing their front teeth and dressed as pirates.

David wondered who would be the first of them to become a grandfather? Aaron had two girls under five years old. Barry had a ten-year-old, a twelve-year-old and a fourteen-year-old. Tom had tweens and Jim had a one-year-old, who slept through the night. Barry said that any kid with Jim for a dad would sleep through the night and most of the day, to avoid his boring musings. Bit harsh, David thought. Jim was his most loyal friend. And the most sensitive of them. David had once seen him save a ladybird from a pub bench. He was a keen member of the local Hedgehog Preservation Society and he tried to be vegan (and mainly succeeded).

David nodded along with Lee and smiled but it hit him in the gut, the thought of children. He'd told himself off for putting on weight. His underwear was too tight – that couldn't be good for his sperm count, could it? He'd read that somewhere. Or was it one of his friends here who'd told him – Aaron and his missus had had trouble conceiv-ing, although at the time Aaron had laughed it off as getting in extra baby-making practice. David pushed at his stom-ach. His jeans weren't digging in, but his boxer shorts were definitely tight. He blamed the extra beer. And missing the gym to wallow in self-pity of his own making. He fidgeted in an attempt to free the jersey cotton from his arse crack.

He looked at his phone and searched for Rachel's ovu-lation app. David had proposed it would be nice if they both tracked her cycle. He clicked on the icon. His phone buzzed in disagreement. Error: incorrect login. He tried the icon again. Incorrect login again. He deleted the saved password and manually typed *TwoBecomesThree* and the error message caused his phone to vibrate a third time.

What did it mean? Why couldn't he see when Rachel was ovulating? It made little difference. They hadn't slept together in the last month. Like a child, he used his fingers to work out how long it had been. Had four weeks really passed without sex? Lee downed his pint and pushed his shot glass towards David.

'Are you drinking that?' David nodded at the honey-coloured liquor begging to be drunk.

Lee shook his head and winked. 'Driving,' he said, and waved good night. Four became three.

David took the glass and downed the harsh nectar. The realisation hit him like a truck then. Why was he thinking about ovulation calendars and children WHEN HIS WIFE WAS GOING TO LEAVE HIM? David had been given a clean bill of health, but what did it matter IF RACHEL WAS GOING TO LEAVE HIM? She had been talking to a solicitor about a separation agreement for fuck's sake. The warning bell in his head was getting louder. He got up to leave.

'Come on mate, stay for one more. Aaron, get Dave a drink,' Barry said before David could make his escape.

His friend's command gave him breathing space. He didn't have to make a decision straight away. He had to sit and finish whatever drinks were put in front of him. Another shot arrived and was downed. Two more glasses, one little, one large, appeared. And maybe another pair. Barry had said something funny. Everyone at the table was laughing. David smiled and said 'good one', without registering the joke.

He tried to tap out a message to Rachel. He'd spilled beer on his phone and the space bar was sticky. The predictive text made it impossible for him to type out the words he wanted to use. He wanted to say he was with Jim and Barry and wouldn't be back too late. And that he missed her and he loved her very much.

David: Iminthevb wiry jamsbalry andieontbebacklqtw imisuouqne Iveuoua veyrmhxxx

Jim asked if anyone was having another pint, which caused Barry to take to his feet and celebrate this decadence with a tap dance.

'Are you alright, D?' Jim asked.

'Yeah, can't complain.' *No, I'm not alright. I'm fighting for my life, my marriage, everything!*

'And what about Barry?' Jim nodded towards the inebriated Barry. They watched as he continued his dance over to the next table. The women there looked to be having a serious discussion about literature and didn't want to entertain his Riverdance antics. It was all about the shin and calf muscles, he kept repeating to them.

'Have you been to his new place?' David asked.

'Gina's not kicked him out again?'

'You know Barry's motto: better to ask for forgiveness than permission.'

'How's that working out for him?'

'IKEA must make a mint out of temporarily excluded husbands.'

It was Barry's round, but David could see the anxiety on his face.

'Need a hand, B?'

At the bar David asked his friend if Gina had thawed towards him.

'Not a chance.'

'And the bank?'

'The same. My credit card is at its max. I'm covering all the direct debits on the house and the kids—'

'What do you need?' David offered.

'That would be great. It shouldn't be much longer.'

David checked his wallet. He had £70 and change. He handed over the notes to Barry.

'You'll pay me back.'

Barry nodded.

Back at the table, Jim asked David if he was really okay. David looked him in the eye and told him not to worry. Afterwards he wasn't sure why he spent the entire night convincing his friends he was fine and didn't need to talk when the opposite was true.

David staggered home. He tried to avoid the cracks in the pavement. It was something his kooky art teacher had told her pupils to do, to avoid being cursed. When he turned from the main road to Sycamore Rise his big clumsy foot crossed a line. *Cursed*. He moved his leg back, only to cross another line. *Cursed again*.

He paused at his front door and realised how drunk he was. The last thing he wanted was to try to enter the wrong house. The car outside the garage was his. The door was red as was his. The brown mat said WECLOME. The typo was a purposeful nod to one of Rachel's favourite comedy shows. The numbers on the door were a stylish *one one four*. Yes, this was his house. He tried multiple pockets for his keys then found them in his hand.

'Always the last place you look,' he said aloud. He slowly opened the door and headed clumsily upstairs. When his right foot connected with the creaky step, he loudly shushed the stair and told it to go back to sleep. The heat from the whisky was oozing out of his pores. He checked his breath after brushing his teeth and decided that he would need to brush again. David found it difficult to brush while simultaneously yawning. He allowed the wall to help hold him up. He needed a shower, but first he must lie down. Fully dressed, he climbed onto the bed. His head spun.

He stared at his sleeping wife. She was beautiful. The Cupid's bow of her lips was aimed towards him. Her faint outbreath was minty. He realised that this was what home smelled like for him: mint and the patchouli of her night cream. He wanted to breathe in as much of it as possible. He wanted to wake her up. He wanted to tell her everything. He wanted to tell her she was his everything. He hoped he would remember all the things he wanted to tell her. He opened the email app on his phone and started typing.

Dear rahxe
I liwvyiuso much and I neverwabtotbewithoutou.
Imaprryforwveurjjnti have otyouthrugh and I
wanttputpknowyhatiwollnevhuetypuragain.

Pleaseofforgbmw
Aavid cxx

He couldn't read what he had written and squinted hard at it. Nope, it still didn't make sense. He pressed save; he'd send it in the morning.

David took a photo of Rachel asleep so he could remember this special moment. He allowed his breathing to fall in with her rhythm and prayed to God he wasn't too late to save their relationship.

Rachel

20

Rachel had left a whisky-laden David asleep on top of the covers fully dressed when she crept out of the house. The bedroom smelled of alcohol and garlic sauce. His shirt buttons were wonky. She didn't want to hear any more of his lame excuses.

Although it was the beginning of summer, she was planning Christmas strategies for a number of independent gift shops. She loved that, for her and her team at least, Christmas wasn't restricted to December. She had a playlist prepared for inspiration. Her mood was lifted superficially by the jingle of bells. Eva wasn't a complete grouch but she had put a strict ban on playing Chris Rea's 'Driving Home For Christmas'. Rachel added hazelnut syrup to her coffee, with a sprinkling of cinnamon to bring Christmas that little bit closer.

She put on her headphones and selected her new Christmas playlist. Starting with the traditional Bing Crosby and working through the decades with nods to Slade, Elton John, Wham and Mariah Carey, before ending with Jeff Buckley's cover version of 'Hallelujah'. Rachel found herself nodding in agreement to Wizzard's 'I Wish It Could Be Christmas Everyday'.

At the beginning a young and inexperienced Rachel had been briefly reluctant to get involved with David. Jojo had often regaled her with stories about the wayward elder brother. He might as well have come with a 'bad boy' t-shirt and a 'will break hearts' warning. Not that it made any difference. Rachel developed a crush on David from the moment they met; the cliché, the best friend's older brother. He was tall, handsome, amusing, and had the most amazing eyes, deep pools of blue she could drown in. But she was too young for him. Not only was she more than ten years his junior, she acted her age and stayed quiet so as to avoid saying stupid things in his company.

David always said that he too wanted to be with her from the moment they met, but like her was worried about the age gap. But he was certain, one hundred per cent sure, that he wanted to be with her. This was a dramatic distinction for him: he wanted to be with her. Not have sex with her, not have a fling, but *be* with her, by her side. He told her that he'd made a solemn vow to himself to not even look properly at his sister's room mate, but became immediately besotted with her when he did. He thought she was perfect. She was gorgeous, and funny, and smart. And after that he tried to avoid Rachel whenever Jojo asked for his help – first it was to fix her shelves, then it was to take them both to B&Q, and then when he picked Jojo up at the end of the autumn term, she asked him to drop Rachel home as well.

Rachel said she should buy him a drink to say thank you.

Jojo finally agreed to give them her blessing when she discovered it was Rachel who'd asked David out. She'd been given a detailed rundown of why Jojo's idiot brother was a highly unsuitable suitor and *still* wanted to go on a date with him.

'Just for one drink!' Rachel had laughed.

The office was empty. Rachel savoured the quiet, waiting for Eva to return from the printer's. Lydia had the day off and Timothy wasn't due in. It wasn't long before procrastination took hold. Rachel was alone, which meant one thing: uninterrupted access to the Internet. She succumbed to the sidebar of shame clickbait and lost half an hour.

Guess what Charlie's Angels look like now? She clicked the link and was surprised it wasn't the 1970s actresses but the 2000 reiteration of the Angels: Liu, Diaz and Barrymore. Had it really been nearly twenty years?

50 facts about One Tree Hill. The video was eight minutes long. Eight minutes Rachel wasn't ever getting back.

19 ways to know if your relationship is in trouble.
Why nineteen? The odd number bothered her more than the substandard content. But still she read on.

Click.

Scroll.

Click.

Scroll.

What a waste of time. Not one site told you what to do when your partner was a cheating asswipe.

Rachel found herself starting to resent Facebook – or Faceboast as Eva called it. It was a valuable work tool and she liked to see what friends were up to. But lately she'd been feeling overwhelmed by those glimpses of other people's lives, the greener grass and all that. She saw glamorous holidays and ambitious home décor projects. And the babies – *all the bloody babies*! Rachel understood the pictures. The ubiquitous set of cards that would identify that a newborn had reached a milestone – 'I'm one month old today' – with the appropriate card precariously balanced above the child's head, or how an infant had walked its first steps, done its first shit in a potty. Not that it was comparable, but she had been known to dress up her cats as felines from history and post pictures. Oscar in particular was highly suited to this treatment – he was black and white and had a small dark patch under his nose, resembling a Charlie Chaplin/Adolf Hitler moustache. And more recently she had outfitted Neville in a scarlet cat coat and the caption 'Simply Red'. The result: 23 likes. David had renamed them 23 lame likes.

She clicked on more article headings:

Women who have kids using IVF are more likely to develop breast cancer, study warns.

Air pollution may affect number of eggs ovaries can produce.

Rachel wondered if there was a test she could take to count her remaining eggs. *How much time did she have?*

She searched 'How to tell how many ovary eggs left 34 years'. Google returned more than 3,800,000 results. The first ten confirmed that over 35, women are screwed.

Rachel was already 34 years and 7 months old. That meant she only had five months of optimum ovaries left! If she separated from David it might take her a year to find someone special. And even that could be a serious under-estimate, based on her friends' dating escapades. But say she was lucky and found someone in a year, she'd be 35 years and 7 months. They'd have to date for ... what? A year? A year before they could start the baby-making. So she'd be ... what ...? 36 years and 7 months, leaving her with nineteen months past their prime, mediocre, good-luck-with-those eggs, and that's assuming she got pregnant on the first try. It wasn't just a case of not taking the pill. And what if she wanted a second and third child?!

She was counting down the days until David left her. The plan, the ingenious plan to get her husband to love her again, was laughable. She'd never seen less of him. He'd come home with buttons done up wrong, stinking of booze, and was apparently hanging out with Barry the newly single man about town. She'd barely had an opportunity to woo David, and he had no time to spend with her. She imagined him busily planning his escape. She'd assumed he would leave her and immediately move in with the mistress, but now it crossed her mind that he was going to get a bachelor pad with Barry where they could relive their hedonistic twenties. She scribbled more calculations. Things did not look good for her ovaries whichever way they were presented.

Maybe she could go it alone and be a single parent? She'd talk to Jojo and Beth: they'd gone down the IVF route. How easy would it be to find a suitable sperm donor? Maybe she could use a surrogate – it was very en vogue for celebrities after all. All of a sudden, she saw the plight of the infertile everywhere.

Procrastination was all too tempting with easy online access.

Rachel searched for David's Facebook page. He didn't post often, and her heart swelled a little when she saw that most of his posts were of things he'd done with her, or else about her. But then again, there was no documentation of the arguments or the constant compromises between them. No tears, no shouting. None of the never-marriedness nor his bloody cheating. His profile was an e-statement of the good times, the fun moments and the funny pictures. It was nothing but a one-sided lie. No wonder people were emotionally exhausted by social media.

Rachel tortured herself some more by looking up David's ex-girlfriends. When she first met him, they'd shared everything including their respective back-stories. It was liberating for Rachel to be going out with an older man who was self-assured enough not to be jealous. Looking back, it might have been because he had nothing to worry about; she'd had few lovers in comparison with him.

Rachel opened a new page and searched for Adam McDonald. Her first kiss.

Adam: 34 years old. Lives in Basingstoke. Married with two children. Not many pictures of the wife. He had aged well; still played sports and was quite dishy.

Search: Craig Tennant. Her high-school boyfriend.

Craig: 34 years old. Lives in Chelmsford.

Also married, also with children. He looked ridiculously happy with his lot.

Search: Dan Pettigrew. Her college crush.

Dan: 35 years old. Lives in York.

He was a primary school teacher. FOUR(!) children but separated from Lindsey, his soon-to-be-ex-wife. Balding and his posts exuded toxic bitterness. He'd turned out to be a complete arsehole. But at the time she had loved him more than life itself. She clicked through the hundreds of gym selfies. His posts were on right-wing politics, busty women he'd 'like to bang', and low-carb beers. *What a douche.*

Search: Gavin Thompson. Her university boyfriend.

Gavin: 35 years old. Lives in London.

Rachel couldn't really remember why they broke up. First term: met in the queue for her first lecture, six weeks of bliss and then a fade out. He was too nice. Being too nice at that age was considered a fatal flaw but it was the opposite later in life. His photos were lacking a significant other. He didn't look like the kind of man who would cheat on his wife. He played cricket, he followed the snooker, and had a horde of gorgeous nieces and nephews. She clicked on a link to Gavin's Instagram profile and accidentally followed him. *Shit!* She quickly cancelled the follow, wondering if he would get an email notification to say she'd followed him for all of nine seconds.

A pop-up message appeared on her screen:

Gavin: *Hey stranger.*

Rachel deliberated before replying. She flicked through his photos and was reminded of his puppy dog eyes, long lashes and honest face.

Rachel: *Hi!*
Gavin: *Wot u up to?*
Rachel: *Not much, at work. You?*
Gavin: *U look exactly the same x*
Rachel: *You've aged pretty well yourself. What are you doing? Didn't you want to be an astronaut?*
Gavin: *Ha! Good memory. NASA never called, so working for my old man, plumbing supplies. With some DJing at weekends. Wot about u?*

Rachel: I have a small events company. Does your dad
           still look like Luigi from Mario Kart?

Gavin: Ha! He still has the eighties 'tache – but now
           grey. Gr8 4 u! Let me know if u ever need a DJ
           – I'll send you some of my stuff! We should
           catch up, u know 4 old times x

A photo popped up showing Gavin's dad with a wiry grey moustache. She laughed out loud.

Eva knocked on Rachel's door and walked into her office.

'Jeez, you scared the life out of me!' Rachel slammed her laptop shut, hoping she didn't look anywhere near as guilty as she felt.

'Look at these!' Eva presented the proof wedding invitations for Jojo and Beth. They were beautiful and perfect, due to the fact that Jojo had designed the artwork. There were two pencil drawings of her and Beth, encapsulated in a wiggly heart. Rachel was over the moon with the final finish.

'Are you ready?' asked Eva.

She looked at her watch and nodded. With Eva's solid back-up, Rachel felt full of new resolve. She was ready to put the make-my-husband-fall-back-in-love-with-me-again-plan into effect. Eva locked the office door behind them and together they went shopping.

David was still annoying her but Rachel bought him a new face wash to replace the one she'd tainted with chilli powder. She also bought him replacement underwear and some socks.

She wanted a new lipstick, something bold. And she needed a tube of beauty flash balm. The beauty consultant on the counter complimented Rachel's skin, saying that presumably she adhered to a strict skincare regime. Rachel agreed – a smug untruth. She had toners but rarely used them; she only exfoliated when she could remember.

'And I even take my makeup off most evenings!' Rachel added.

The consultant gasped in horror, lamenting piously that sleeping in one's makeup was akin to smoking twenty cigarettes a day. Rachel was quick to lie and insisted she'd only been joking. In her head, she calculated how many nights since *FuckingAwfulHusbandGate* she had slept in her makeup. The total was shockingly high. The girl then asked which moisturiser Rachel used. She nodded towards her beauty purchase. The girl looked confused and repeated the question.

'The flash balm,' Rachel reiterated. 'The beauty flash balm! The. Thirty. Pound. Tube. I've. Just. This. Second. Bought.' She heard her voice rise to a frequency that maybe only dogs could hear.

'A beauty flash balm has no significant moisturising qualities. It's a radiance skin booster, a complexion-perfecting measure,' the girl with the artificial complexion prescribed.

Rachel was unsure if she was going to implode or explode. Eva joined them, smelling like a brothel, having tried on a variety of perfumes with horrifying results.

'Is there a problem, Rach?'

'Yes, you could say that. It seems that the moisturiser I have been using religiously . . . the very expensive moisturiser, may I add . . . isn't a moisturiser. "Apparently" it's a mere balm. And I've been using it for . . .' Rachel did the mental arithmetic. 'Nine years! Right here on this counter, nine years ago, I first bought it. That's nine years I haven't applied adequate lubrication to my face or neck. NINE years! MORE THAN HALF MY ADULT LIFE! My neck, my poor neck . . .' Rachel checked it in the counter-top mirror and pulled at the skin under her eyes. 'At twenty-five years old, I allowed my skin to age prematurely. Thanks to . . .' Rachel didn't really know who to blame. But she had a sneaking suspicion it was herself.

'Menopause,' another customer was heard to state simply.

'It's not the menopause!' Rachel shouted into the ether. 'I'm thirty-bloody-four!'

The girl on the counter was mortified. This was not how customers usually acted in a high-end skincare concession. Shoppers and staff at neighbouring beauty stations were now avidly watching Rachel's meltdown. The red-faced beauty consultant quickly added some tester-size samples of genuine moisturisers to Rachel's purchase.

'Some moisturisers I can try nine years too late?! Well, thank you. Thank you very much.'

Eva tried to calm the situation by guiding Rachel away from the counter, saying,

'One day we'll laugh at this.'

Rachel was already embarrassed by her outburst. Eva reminded her she had ten minutes until her appointment for a cut and a colour and they should get moving. Eva had booked an appointment with her own favourite hairdresser and suggested Rachel should try having her hair styled into a more modern cut instead of her normal boring bob.

'Rach, you share a haircut with your mum. Hey! Don't look at me like that – Mrs K looks great for her age, but you've got to have a change ...'

The dour hairdresser picked up her scissors and in a Glaswegian accent introduced herself as Janice. She looked at Eva from slightly wonky eyes, which seemed to be saying: *Not much to work with here*. Eva let her own eyes reply: *Do your best*.

Rachel coloured her hair every twelve weeks; she liked the way the new thin grey strands that were appearing mingled with her highlights. She told Eva they made her feel distinguished.

'That's sweet. It's also completely insane,' her friend replied.

'But this is who I am. The age I am. I don't want to look like ...' Rachel's words trailed away.

'Like?'

Rachel didn't trust herself not to upset Eva by replying honestly, so mentally filed away the word *mutton*. And she didn't even mean Eva in particular. She was after all the exception to every rule. She always looked amazing. Her skirt was tailored and short but it didn't look slutty. Her makeup was carefully applied but looked natural. Rachel, with her knowledge of cosmetics, knew it took time and precision for makeup to look *that* natural. Eva's hair always looked like she lived in the hair salon. Or was at least bonking a hairdresser. Not Janice though. That woman had the emotional development and skin tone of Edward Scissorhands. Ironic, when Rachel thought about it.

'Should I dye my hair blonde – platinum blonde?' she asked.

'How do I say this . . .' Eva picked up a glossy magazine. 'It's a lot of upkeep, and I'm not sure you'd have enough commitment for the maintenance required. It's not for everyone.'

Rachel knew Eva was right.

'What if I promise to work at it?' she pleaded with the hairdresser, who looked petrified at the prospect of trying to turn this nondescript client into Marilyn Monroe.

'You'd need to come in every six weeks for me to do the roots.'

Rachel immediately backed down.

'What about some more dramatic highlights then?'

Eva looked over the top of the magazine at her and shook her head. Rachel stuck out her bottom lip in protest. But she knew her friend was right.

Janice positioned the mirror to show Rachel the back of her head. She gave a polite nod. It was the obligatory glance at the back of her own head – she never made a comment about it, what was she supposed to say? It looked like the back of a head and the swish-swish of the mirror was performed too rapidly for her to register any register any detail. Janice suggested moisturising the back of her neck twice-daily, noting that her short hair-style exposed her neck line to the elements, and called attention to any – er – lines. Eva saw Rachel struggle to suppress the fire behind her eyes. She wasn't sure if it was from fury or distress, but she knew her friend was still sore following the beauty counter fiasco. Eva quickly paid, shooing Rachel's purse away.

'My treat.' She hustled them both out into the street.

They finished the afternoon in a sex shop. Not on the high street; Eva directed Rachel to a back alley. They entered through an unmarked door, which added a sinister feel to their shopping experience.

'Welcome to Tassie's Tassels!'

The shop owner, Graham Tassie, a heavily tattooed Mediterranean hunk of a man, greeted Eva by name. He was wearing a kilt, adorned with a studded leather sporran. Rachel wondered: *Did men really not wear underwear beneath their Scottish skirts?*

Graham said Eva's order had come in but she shushed him; today was about Rachel. Eva explained that they needed something enticing, but innocent-seeming. No leather, no PVC, no chains, no bolts.

'Lace and silk, with holes and straps. Think: classy role-play, not dungeon dominatrix.' Eva had suggested Rachel pay more attention to common bedroom proclivities. She'd used a horrid analogy about milk and cows, and then reiterated it using burgers and steak to hammer home the point. Rachel couldn't help but stare at the wondrous items on display. Big, sexy, oppressive, potentially harmful, downright odd ... She looked at a few things and wondered where some of the toys would go.

'What's his thing? What does he like?'

'He likes shoes.'

'Foot fetish?'

'No, nothing like that.' Rachel gave a haughty chuckle. 'He's not a weirdo. Normal shoes. He likes it when we go out ... when I dress up.'

Graham replied with a knowing smirk. He whizzed around the space and picked out items from the rails and out of drawers.

Even Eva was impressed with his choices. He was the master of his domain; a sexy fairy godfather. Rachel's blushes had subsided by now and she examined the chosen items.

Lace-topped black stockings

A pearl choker

A pair of six-inch scarlet patent heels

A black silk negligee with a lace trim

A maroon push-up bra with matching suspender belt and thong.

Well, Graham said it was a thong, but who did he think he was kidding? The practicalities of having to move while she wore cheese-cutting underwear made Rachel feel apprehensive, and that was before she'd even donned the flimsy garment. She would definitely need to do some serious work on her bikini line.

'Listen, the great thing about men,' Graham confided as if disclosing the world's biggest secret, 'is that they are simple, visual beasts.'

Simple and visual ... For Rachel he had curated the median between what a man would find stimulating and she would see as elegant. Graham said that often what men bought for their wives was in no way what the women wanted to wear. He had introduced a system whereby a man could buy his wife (or girlfriend/lover/ prostitute/friend/other – no judgement!) an afternoon with Graham, inspecting and trying on the items that pleased them. It was meant to be empowering rather than degrading. In business terms it resulted in fewer refunds and a healthy stream of repeat visits. Rachel blushed at the thought of the cheap French Maid's outfit discarded at the back of the wardrobe.

She had to hand it to Graham, he knew his stuff. The touch of the silk felt soft and luxurious; she envisioned being cocooned in the expensive lace and felt her erogenous zones awaken.

She thanked Eva for her support and for the new ... well, everything!

At home, Rachel drew herself a bath and washed, shaved and buff-puffed herself to within an inch of her life. Addressing her bikini line, she tried to leave a landing strip but it was a bit skew-whiff. It looked almost like a wink. When she finally drained the water, it looked like she had shaved a yeti.

She'd never felt so naked as when she perched delicately on the sofa, in her negligee and the assorted undergarments and accessories from Graham's erotic grotto. She was transformed and didn't recognise herself in the mirror. She couldn't wait for David to see her like this. She prepared a gin and tonic, turned on the television and selected the next episode of *Game of Thrones*. It was a box set she was sharing with David on Sunday nights like clockwork. It had helped that she had read the books. However, she found she enjoyed watching the series without him rather than having to pause every five seconds to explain the storyline and many characters and their respective backstories. It was the beginning of the final season. The sex and violence washed over her as the thong string became less comfortable and more intrusive. She kept checking her phone. She wondered where her never-husband was. She resisted the urge to call him.

With every minute that passed, she felt increasingly foolish about being dressed up as the proverbial mutton. She checked her phone again in case he had messaged in the ten seconds since she'd last checked. She used the GPS app to locate his phone; he was somewhere near the station. Finally, she gave into temptation and phoned his number but the call didn't connect, sending her straight to voicemail.

You've reached David ...

She finished the gin and tonic and the episode. She would be done with her marriage quicker than finishing the entire *Game of Thrones* series. Rachel switched on the Bluetooth speaker David had surprised her with, wondering if it was perhaps a gift to ease his guilty conscience? It was voice-activated, which meant for the first few days she'd thought the house was haunted. Alexa was her only constant companion.

'Alexa, play "Ladies and Gentlemen".' She made herself a second drink and danced just as she pleased. No one was watching. George Michael's 'Jesus to a Child' brought her to tears.

'Alexa, turn down the lights.'

'Alexa, turn up the lights to half.'

'Alexa, why am I such a pathetic excuse for a wife?'

'Alexa, please let me know when my wayward husband finally gets home.'

'Alexa, is the gas off?'

'Alexa, what should I listen to, to mend a broken heart?'

'Alexa, please never let me listen to Al Green again.'

'Alexa, no! Stop playing Al Green.'

'Alexa, delete *Al Green's Greatest Hits*.'

'Alexa, have you ever been married?'

'Alexa, don't get married.'

'Alexa, have we run out of gin?'

'Alexa, can cooking sherry be used in case of emergencies?'

'Alexa, I'm so tired. Are you tired? Do you get tired?'

'Alexa, did you know?'

'Alexa, did he bring her here?'

'Alexa, have you met her?'

'Alexa, who is she?'

'Alexa, do you know ...'

Rachel fell asleep on the sofa and woke a few hours later. The earth was cooling as it patiently waited for the sun to reappear. In her semi-dressed state, she shivered. The television glared its fuzzy nothing-to-see-here shine.

The sexy lingerie was stuck to her and the thong had reached the unreachable. She was alone and remnants of her eye makeup were smudged all over a plush cushion. She assumed David had left her to sleep. Rachel clambered up the stairs to discover the bedroom was eerily empty. She checked her phone again. There were no messages to explain or account for David's absence. She removed her costume, for that's what it was. Alluring plumage. The role of tonight's try-hard sex kitten was played (unconvincingly) by Rachel, a soon-to-be-cat-lady from Richmond. It was a desperate parade of attempted sexiness worn to grab the attention of a faux-husband with a short attention span. She changed into her PJs, and folded the delicate items and put them in a hatbox in her side of the wardrobe. She felt a fool. All of it had been for nothing. She had played along with Eva's plan, with no result. She wanted to get David to fall in love with her; she wanted them to renew their vows and live happily ever after. Fat chance of that.

It was over an hour later that she felt him crawl into bed beside her. She pretended to be asleep but lay awake for hours, unable to face the false dawn of her shattered dreams.

David

21

David woke up fully dressed. He called Barry to ensure that he wasn't the only one suffering from a painful hangover.

'Great night, mate! Banging head ... nothing a few Dioralytes couldn't fix,' Barry boomed from the end of the line.

'What?'

'Dioralyte – blackcurrant flavour. Get them from the chemist. Helps with the electrolytes.'

Barry might as well have been speaking in tongues. David asked why no one had mentioned that his shirt was buttoned up wrong.

'Didn't notice. But even if I had, I probably wouldn't have said anything – you've got enough on your plate.'

'Thanks – but next time, tell me. I might be a mess but I don't want to look like one.'

'Righto! Gotta go speak to a man about a land disagreement.'

David made a coffee and paced the garden. He had found a box of cigarettes in his jacket pocket and lit one. He knew Rachel would love to have a birdbath in the garden, but it was impossible with Oscar and Neville's predatory instincts. They'd be human accomplices to the mass slaughter of local sparrows, tits and robins.

He dialled Jojo's number.

His sister was an illustrator of children's books; she worked from home in a small fusty shed at the bottom of her garden, which was her pride and joy. She loved her (wo)mancave.

Jojo had travelled the world before her degree and the gap year changed her thinking. She was once on track to read Classics at university with the intention of going into politics. After much deliberation, she'd decided the world wasn't ready for a gay woman in government. Jojo didn't want to hide who she was or the woman she loved. Times had since changed and sometimes she thought about pursuing a second life in public office.

David loved his sister but she had the ability to annoy the hell out of him. He knew he'd have to suffer self-righteous spiel and some harsh home truths once he confided in her. Then, and only then, would she give up the golden nuggets of advice David needed in order to win back his wife.

'Whassup?' The voice at the end of the phone was amplified. He was on speakerphone.

'Can you talk?' This was code for: please let me know if your other half is within earshot.

'Shoot.' Jojo gave him the go-ahead to speak openly.

First David tried to ask after Beth, and the proposal, and the baby, in an attempt at polite conversation. Jojo told him to cut straight to the chase.

'I have something to admit. I've fucked up. Really fucked up.'

'Woah, bro, where's the fire?' Jojo asked.

'Promise to hear me out before you say or do anything,' he whispered.

'Slow down, and start from the beginning.'

David gave her the bare bones of his predicament, omitting all the damning evidence and concentrating only on the necessary facts. He opened up to her and laid his ugly cards on the table. He was a bad man, who had made bad decisions, which now left him to face the bad consequences. Jojo was intrigued. He could hear she had stopped working and picked up the handset.

'Say that again?' she asked.

'The thing is … Rachel and I may not … well, I know for a fact we aren't actually married … not in the legal sense. I, well, never got round to telling her, but I think that she may have found out and … Jojo, the truth is that we're not—'

'Married, yes, I heard you the first time. I just didn't believe my ears. You're not married? Is this some sort of game to you? Why? How could you do this to Rachel? To me? You made a promise. You vowed to me on Mum's life you wouldn't hurt my best friend. I trusted you!'

'Yes, I made a mistake. Big time. But it was simply an administrative error. I didn't find out until ... Long story short, I need your help. I can't lose her over this.'

'What did Barry say?'

David said that Jojo was his first point of call.

'I'm flattered. So he was useless, I presume. And I'm the second choice? Shit husband of the DECADE award aside—'

David winced. 'Yes, but it's not as bad as it sounds.'

'As an outsider, it doesn't sound good.'

Jojo lectured him for a solid ten minutes about how he should not, SHOULD NOT, and would not be allowed to take wonderful Rachel for granted.

David explained sheepishly that the not-being-married might not be his immediate problem. Not the one he'd called Jojo about anyway. He told her Rachel was acting differently. Explained about Stefan Stratos and the separation agreement.

'What does it mean? I mean, I'm not stupid – I know that it *means* Rachel is almost definitely going to leave me – I think I'm gonna be sick.'

'Uh-huh.'

'I can feel her distancing herself and it's only a matter of time before she finds out it's not a legal marriage and then she won't have to divorce me, she can simply walk away.'

Jojo disagreed. This wasn't about Rachel. This was about how David made Rachel *feel*. It wouldn't be the albeit big fuck-off misunderstanding about the filing of a wedding certificate that finally drove her away; it would be David taking her for granted.

David wished he hadn't called his sister. He'd forgotten how self-righteous she could be. Like she was the encyclopaedia of women, which was, of course, why he had phoned her in the second place.

'Darling brother, you live in a man's world. Try opening up to your wife. Give her your undivided attention. Take an interest and put all of your energy into that one simple task. Do you have a pen?'

'Wait a minute.' David checked the conservatory for anything to write with and on. He found a marker pen and a Chinese takeaway menu. 'Got one.'

'Six words: get Rachel to renew your vows.'

'Funny.' David rolled his eyes at Jojo's pomposity. He could have done without the reprimand, but it was a great idea.

'Gently woo her, make her remember everything she fell in love with about you in the first place. And, David? Don't fuck it up.'

'Thanks, Jojo. I don't know what I'd do without her. I doubt I'd survive five minutes. I do love her. She's my everything.' But if he was looking for atonement he was not going to find it from Jojo. He was greatly relieved they were having this conversation over the phone.

David asked if she and Beth wanted to come for dinner one night that week. It was the sort of thing he did without thinking to check his diary or Rachel's plans. Jojo thanked him for the invite but said, to be honest, she wasn't too keen to waste a precious pre-baby night, especially for one spent smack bang in the middle of a non-marital battlefield.

David was left feeling despondent; this wasn't how he expected the conversation to go. He hadn't even shared the worst of his woes. Jojo's reaction told him she was unlikely to be sympathetic or understanding about his one night stand with Amelia-Rose. He needed to end the call. He walked to the front door, opened it and pressed the doorbell. He told his sister someone had arrived and he'd see her soon.

'I'm not sure you deserve her,' were Jojo's cold parting words.

David felt chest pains, again. He took a deep breath and exhaled. He let his chest relax, as prescribed by the pretty Cardiac Physiologist. It was more than likely a panic attack, he told himself as he repeated the breathing exercises. Panic caused by the thought that he was having a heart attack. Even Alanis Morissette would call that ironic. Why wasn't the breathing working? He put his head between his legs. It didn't help. He lay on the sofa with his legs up against the wall. Slowly his heart rate returned to normal and his chest relaxed. He wondered if it could be heartburn. He chomped on two peppermint Rennies; immediately the bitterness of the pills infiltrated his mouth. Confused, he reached for his reading glasses, and looked at the small print on the rectangular packet to discover he'd taken two paracetamols. At the kitchen sink, he spat out the chalky white remnants and gargled with water. He slumped back on the sofa and chewed an actual indigestion tablet and waited to be cured or die.

David called Jojo back and begged her to meet him. He tempted her with strong fruit beers brewed by Trappist monks. Jojo recognised the code red emergency, a secret communication from their adolescence that this was serious enough for her to change her plans.

Jojo was late. David paced the hall restlessly as he waited. He checked the window in response to every noise from the street. But he was going to have to come clean with her. Jojo hadn't rung the bell when David opened the door and rushed her inside, through to the conservatory. He gently closed the door behind them.

'I have one question – why?' Jojo asked, immediately on the offensive.

David was trying to remember the words he'd prepared while he was pacing. Instead, he echoed, 'Why?'

'Why are you such a shit husband? I don't get it. When did you become so lazy? What did you buy Rachel for your anniversary?'

'A fountain pen.'

'A pen?

'It was expensive – Montblanc.'

'What did you get her for Christmas, a bucket of coal?' Jojo snorted.

'No. I got her an electric toothbrush.' David's face crumpled. 'It had Bluetooth,' he added, increasing his self-defence perimeter tenfold.

He tried to justify his utilitarian gifts by saying that Rachel wasn't into flowers and things like that. He then blushed with embarrassment at the memory of the enthusiasm with which they'd once made love on a rose-strewn four-poster bed in Paris. And how her face had lit up while they were walking through lavender fields in Provence.

Jojo countered that Rachel was a grown woman, and doubtless had long given up dreaming of being swept off her feet by a Disney Prince, but suggested a little romance goes a long way.

'Seriously, Dave. Why are you—'

'Don't say it again.'

Jojo lowered her voice. 'You're my brother and I love you. But she's my best friend and, frankly, I think she can do a lot better than you right now.'

He looked so stricken then that she *almost* felt sorry for him. Jojo said she needed time to process the situation and suggested, 'Let's go and get a pint.'

David locked the back door and wrote a message for Rachel:

Gone to the Plough with Jojo.
If you get back in time, join us x

The flimsy post-it note floated to the floor and, unknowingly, he took it with him under the sole of his trainer.

The Plough stood opposite the station and was always busy. Ever since the new manager had put up a screen showing the train times, the commuter clientele had doubled. If David and Jojo wanted to be seated in the dining section, they would have to wait. They sat at the bar and the waitress promised to call them over when a table became available. She brought them two bottles of strong Belgian ale while they waited.

David had drawn up a battle plan to win back his wife. He had written down all the ways in which he was romantic and come up with a pretty crap list. First step then: he'd have to admit romance wasn't his forté.

Jojo looked at the shoddy list.

'How did you ever get her to marry you in the first place? Is this really the best you can do … you *used to* leave notes in her suitcase when she went away? You make cocktails for her?'

'I'm an idiot. I'm going to make it better. I'm going to get her to marry me.'

'Won't she notice she's already been there and done that? Maybe she doesn't want another David Chatsworth t-shirt.'

'I need your help. Please.'

'Maybe you should have thought of that before you fucked over my best friend.'

'I didn't mean to. I can feel her slipping away. I've been too caught up at work. Listen, I have a plan. I'm going to come clean and ask her to marry me – for real this time. We'll do it for the second time and live happily ever after.'

'Hold your horses there, Mr Confess All. I know I said to be honest with her, but that's when you are trying to salvage a marriage. If there isn't an actual marriage to save … Look, I'm not for keeping stuff from a spouse but that's a lot to put on Rachel. What do the invites for an

I-love-you-and-I-only-pretended-to-be-married-to-you-for-fifteen-years-so-let's-get-married ceremony look like? Rachel's *a smug married . . .*'

Here David tried to interrupt but his sister held up her hand, warning him not to.

'Let me finish! She's not in your face about it but she's had a good life, with a good husband. She's never been the subject of gossip or speculation. She's never had to explain to friends – or, God forbid, strangers – that her husband isn't really her husband. I don't know how she'll react to this. You are her world. Before you crush it, you need to tread very carefully.'

'Tell me what to do to make it better. What do women want?'

'Go get some more drinks, this is going to be a late night,' Jojo laughed.

Then she shared with him a list of the things she knew Rachel liked. Between them they devised a get-your-wife-back plan.

Rachel

22

It was the anniversary of her father's death. Rachel sent her mother a message asking if she wanted to join them for dinner. Norma responded with one word: a terse *no*.

The same invitation was extended every year. And declined every year. The thought of her mother being on her own on this day never ceased to perturb Rachel. She was also undeniably relieved. She hadn't seen Norma in person since the fateful wedding anniversary weekend and knew she could crack under close maternal scrutiny.

She wandered through Marks & Spencer's food hall. Her basket was full of food she didn't need, but she persevered. Rachel knew in her brain that all was lost. But somehow her heart kept hanging on in there. She thought of the old joke – *denial ain't just a river in Egypt*. David still hadn't explained his mysterious evenings out.

Rachel's pocket vibrated. By the time she had fished out her mobile, the phone had, of course, stopped ringing. Four missed calls. All from her mother. Guilt rushed through her. She couldn't remember when they last spoke ... wasn't it the other day? Shit, was Rachel meant to have phoned her back?

Rachel balanced her shopping basket precariously on the shelf against rustic breads ... *oooh, artisan sourdough*. She added a leaden circle loaf to her basket and called her mother.

'Hello?'

'I have something to tell you.' As usual Norma came straight to the point. 'I've got a date.' She released a heavy sigh after she'd made the announcement.

'Is that the emergency? Four missed calls! I thought you'd fallen down the stairs.'

'You kids, with your lurid imaginations! So what do you think about it?'

'Think about what? The date?' Rachel asked.

'Yes, of course the date. What do you think about Roger.'

What an awful name, Rachel thought, but hoped she hadn't said that aloud. 'I haven't met him!'

'You have. He was there at the end of the Boxing Day walk. The one with the beige gilet.'

'Him?'

'Yes – what did you think?

'I must have seen him for all of one second, across the car park. Was he the short one?'

Rachel had never known Norma fuss before; it was refreshingly human. She organised a date for Rachel and Kevin to meet Roger. Rachel tried to say it wasn't necessary – he looked quite normal from a hundred-metre distance and most probably was not a serial killer.

'Is this why you didn't want to celebrate Dad's ... you know?' Rachel still hated to think of his passing.

'Not at all,' Norma said before she ended the call.

Rachel tried to think what she might do when she finally found herself single, alone, and left on the shelf. Spinsterhood seemed a more alluring option than trying to catch an elusive man. Yes, she'd be unmarried Rachel with her two cats. She assessed the man queuing in front of her. No temptation away from her single state to be had there. In the next checkout was a tall man with broad shoulders. He had a decent shoulder-to-waist ratio. Dark hair with a smattering of grey. Rachel couldn't see if he was wearing a wedding ring ... As he turned around, he saw Rachel, nodded and smiled. She politely returned the smile before she recognised him.

'Hi there, Dr Parry-Wilson.'

'It's Luke, as well you know.'

Rachel smiled. He didn't look like a Luke. It was probably short for Lucas or Lorcan, she imagined. He was too posh for a Luke.

'I'm glad I bumped into you,' Rachel attempted to say across the conveyor belt but it was pointless and politeness got the better of them. They waited until each had finished paying for their over-packaged groceries.

They walked together towards the car park. After they'd made small talk, she nonchalantly asked him about feeding the cats with tins of tuna. Which was better? Tuna in brine or tuna in oil. *Stop waffling, Rachel!*

'Why don't you book an appointment and we'll see how their diet is doing.'

Rachel stared at his face and took in his features and how they were framed by his dark hair. His nose was on the small size. His chin was that of a Disney prince, completed by a small jaunty dimple. His eyes were a brilliant green, but were they too close together? She concluded that the whole of Luke's face was greater than the sum of its parts. Somehow the nose worked on it, and his forehead was strong. She wondered if she found this man attractive, now the blinkers were off so to speak.

Not that it mattered. But, say, in the name of scientific research, she did find him appealing? He was conventionally good-looking. Eva had described him as rugged. She couldn't help but compare him to David. Luke was taller, not as lean, with a bulkier build. His smile was wider, his lips thinner. More important than any physical attribute, though, he was kind. It had struck a note with Rachel. Eva had mentioned that among her (extensive) online dates, the majority of men were jaded by life and bitter about their past experiences with women. Many a first date ended after just one drink because a bitch of an ex-wife or a witch of a baby-mama was named and viciously insulted. It was extremely off-putting.

'Anyway, enough of this jibber-jabber,' Rachel said. 'I expect you've got patients to see. I'll be sure to book an appointment.'

'Or we could discuss it over a drink?' Luke offered.

'That would be nice,' Rachel replied, blushing as she handed him her business card. She knew that the plan to win David back was probably no more than wishful thinking. Maybe, just maybe, there were more fish in the sea.

Rachel was wrestling with a lump of pastry. She had read the recipe and asked herself how she was supposed to shape the dough without touching it too much, as instructed. She put it in the fridge to cool down. The doorbell chimed loudly and she tutted. David often thought it was easier to ring the bell than locate his keys. Easier for him, that was for sure. Rachel's hands were covered in flour and butter. She used a clean-ish little finger to twist open the Yale lock.

Rachel was surprised to see Norma bobbing about at the front door, and even more surprised that she had with her a navy suitcase.

'Hi, Mum, I thought ... You came!'

'Yes, I did.'

Norma wiped her feet on the mat and walked past Rachel. She took off her coat and headed to the kitchen with the vintage leather case in tow.

Rachel closed the front door and followed her in silence.

'Are you okay?' she asked. 'Would you like a drink? Tea? Or something stronger?'

Norma switched the kettle on and sat down on a breakfast barstool. Once the water had boiled she said she had changed her mind and asked for a sherry – a small one.

'Are you driving?'

'No, I got a lift. Where's David?'

'He's at the gym.' Rachel let the lie tumble from her mouth – that's where she assumed he'd *say* he was going. Rachel saw how Norma's shoulders dropped and she physically relaxed, knowing it was going to be just the two of them.

Rachel washed her hands. It would probably do the pastry good to be abandoned for ten more minutes. Her mother's behaviour was starting to alarm her. Rachel poured them both a small measure of fancy Christmas sherry. Rather than sit down with Norma, she continued to chop vegetables and put marinated chicken in the oven. She prepared garlic mayonnaise, all the while watching her mother nurse an inch of sherry. Rachel eventually broke the silence.

'Shall we make a toast to Dad?'

'No. I need a minute.'

More silence ensued.

Rachel mused on how much of their relationship was pure silence, awkward or otherwise. Her mother was a rare bird, a natural stoic. To her, words were to be used sparingly, as if subject to wartime rationing. Norma's mother, Nana Babs to Rachel, had been evacuated as a baby and always maintained it hadn't done her the slightest bit of harm, either physical or emotional. She was the epitome of the Keep Calm and Carry On motivational government message from WWII, the one now plastered over mugs and tea towels. Keep calm and drink tea/gin/ coffee/Porn-star Martinis. Nana Babs had passed on the same emotional restraint to her only daughter, Norma. How had Rachel ended up so normal? Although she supposed her recent behaviour might be said to prove otherwise.

'You moving in?' She nodded to the suitcase.

Norma opened it. Lined with baby pink satin, it smelled of rosewater. She removed six outfits from the suitcase and organised them for Rachel. They were a selection of near-identical three-pieces; skirt, blouse and cardigan/ jacket combos, in a rainbow of pastel hues. Rachel had never noticed before how her mother's taste in fashion was clearly inspired by Coco Chanel and Jackie Kennedy.

Rachel took the pastry from the fridge and rolled out four seven-inch circles. The time out had made the dough nicely pliable.

'You mentioned something about a date?' she asked to fill the silence. 'And now the mystery fashion show?'

'Yes, about that. I thought you could help me choose.' Her mother looked desperate.

'You should remember, I haven't been on a date myself since I don't know when. Not since the early noughties; Pope John Paul II was still alive. Tony Blair was prime minister ...'

Norma made the sign of the cross and mouthed, 'Father, Son, Holy Spirit.'

'And it was before Beyoncé unleashed "Crazy in Love" on the world,' Rachel continued.

'Which one's Beyoncé?' Norma asked.

'The one after Madonna!' Rachel laughed.

'Mary from the WI was saying I should have my skirts taken up – you know, to show a bit of leg.' Norma looked disgusted by the idea.

'Probably means Mary's an utter trollop. Case in point – she's on her third hip replacement. Need I say more? And showing some skin ... who does she think she is?' Rachel saw Norma thought she was being serious. 'Mum, it's a joke. You know what I really think? Be yourself. He asked you out without seeing your knees first so he must like you. Don't change for anyone. You're a God-fearing woman, with a God-fearing wardrobe. Just be you. And don't listen to that Mary-three-hips.'

'I can be myself?' Norma toyed with this novel suggestion.

'Is that why you changed your mind and came tonight. Because you want to start dating?'

'I don't know. I like my life the way it is. I'm not sure I want to share it again. All that compromise. Men can be so ... You're lucky, you and David.'

Rachel tried to gulp down the awkward frog in her throat.

Norma couldn't look her daughter in the eye and instead stared at the kitchen curtains. 'I feel I need to tell you something. I didn't want you to be unhappy like I ...' Then Norma clearly felt she had said too much, too directly, and came at it again in a roundabout way. 'You know, your father was idolised by so many people.'

It was true. Joseph Keatley Esq., Queen's Counsel, had been revered. He'd been the QC with a conscience, famous for helping striking coal miners in the mid-1980s. All the work had been pro-bono and he lost many a legal friend in the process, but he said he couldn't stand by and watch injustice being done without trying to help. Norma explained it had been difficult for her to match his hero's status with the reality of being married to him. Rachel didn't know how to ask the question that was on the tip of her tongue. But she did. As if the words weren't leaving her mouth. Like they were a speech bubble on a cartoon.

'You mean, he ... ,' Rachel paused.

'Many times.'

'No?! When? Why didn't you tell us?' Rachel was stunned. She wasn't sure how to feel. It didn't change her love for her father but it explained everything about Norma. Rachel swapped looks with her mother: the small, demure, devout Catholic. Sitting straight-backed on a kitchen stool, her feet didn't touch the floor. She looked like a child who had carried a lifetime of obligation on her shoulders. Norma had always been handsome. Rachel took in her mother's regal features: with her face relaxed, Norma was striking. But as quickly as her beauty had appeared it vanished under a scowl. The mask slipped firmly back into place.

'You and Kevin loved your dad and I didn't want to spoil that. And he always came back to me, didn't he?'

Norma held Rachel's gaze. *Did her mother know? Was this her way of saying: I've been there? My husband was a cheating bastard too.*

'I know I haven't been David's biggest fan ...' she continued.

Rachel smiled at the understatement of the century.

'The reason I never liked him was that he reminded me of your father. Of course, it's a notion that women marry their fathers. But David is different, I can see that now, and he obviously makes you happy and I hope—' Norma struggled to continue.

'So, who is this fella?' Rachel interrupted her, changing the subject. If her mother carried on talking up David, Rachel might lose the plot once and for all. 'Roger? You said he was there on Boxing Day?'

'Well, he's the opposite of your father.'

Not a lying cheating scoundrel then? Rachel thought.

'He's nice and, well, kind.'

'Sounds like a good start.'

'I suppose.'

'What is it, Mum?'

'I'm not sure I'm ready to share again. The fridge is full of food I like. There's no mess. I don't want to be bullied ever again. To be told what to think, how to act ...'

Rachel waited patiently, checking the oven while her mother sought to explain.

'I don't want to be disappointed again.'

Rachel had nothing to add to that. No funny anecdote, no holistic advice. 'Let's eat,' she suggested instead.

As they sat down, David crashed through the front door. He winced when he saw his mother-in-law but Rachel saw him try to give Norma a welcoming smile.

'Norma.'

'David.' She matched his tone.

He kissed Rachel on the cheek. She felt warmed by the show of affection and then hated how much she still loved him and craved his attention. He was jaunty and giddy. Rachel tried to decide if he was post-orgasmic. She thought she could smell beer on his breath. He was famished after his supposed gym session and surprised Rachel with a bunch of lilies produced from behind his back. She stood up and collected the bunch of stems into a vase, thanking him as she did so. She didn't question why he had bought her flowers, but it was nice that Norma was here to witness the gesture.

There was one negative, though – Rachel hated lilies. They reminded her of the first funeral she'd attended. She was ten years old and it was a service for a great-aunt she couldn't now remember meeting. The pungent smell of the long-stemmed flowers had lodged in her nose and she was devastated when the bright burnt-orange stamens stained the white silk sash tied around her dark funereal dress.

David served himself a portion of the Mexican-inspired dish and Rachel watched him *ooh* and *aah* and enthuse about the moistness of the chicken. Norma thought there was a word for people who use the word 'moist' at the dinner table: heathen. Until now, Rachel hadn't noticed that David was one of them.

23

Rachel allowed herself the freedom to enjoy organising Jojo and Beth's wedding since they wouldn't be the sort of clients who would be demanding or ungrateful. On Pinterest, she made separate mood boards for them both. She found wildflowers and organic material for Beth, and concentrated on tailored designs and geometrical shapes for Jojo. Somehow Rachel managed to merge the two ideals.

Jojo phoned her minutes after Rachel had sent over the link.

'You're a genius, a bloody genius – has anyone ever told you that?'

Rachel was warmed by the praise. Jojo was a tough cookie at times, but she knew she'd hit the jackpot with Beth and was willing to make whatever compromises were necessary to ensure the happiness of her wife-to-be. Rachel could tell this reaction was no concession – Jojo was truly excited.

'Tell me about your wedding.'

'Mine? It was an age ago …'

'I know, so why do I think you're living out your own wedding wish list vicariously through your clients?'

'I never thought of it like that.'

'Not tempted to renew your vows? Mum would love that.'

If she let slip to Jojo her plan for getting (re)married, Rachel wondered, could her sister-in-law edge David in the right direction?

'Are you suggesting a double celebration?'

'Ha! That would be perfect. But, no, not with Beth's gun-toting family to contend with! I'd stay clear of that one if I were you.'

Case closed, Rachel thought.

She ran through some other options and asked who would sign off on the menu (Beth), the flowers (Beth), the seating plan (Beth), the centrepieces (Beth), the photographer (Beth).

'And let me guess – the DJ?' Rachel asked.

'Beth!' they both said simultaneously.

Rachel laughed aloud. She was surprised to find herself wanting to tell Jojo everything

'Ooooh, talking about the DJ – guess who emailed me over his playlists and some videos?'

'Who?' Jojo was not one for guessing games.

'Gavin Thompson.'

'Gavin from uni? Your Gavin? Camel eyelashes and rugby thighs Gavin?'

'The very same. His stuff is really good.' Rachel could tell by the pause that followed Jojo wasn't convinced. 'I'll send you some links. He said he could even make a country music list to keep Beth's parents happy!'

'Okay, when Beth's back I'll get her to take a look. Thanks for doing this.'

'It's an absolute pleasure, Jojo.'

'We should catch up, just the two of us.'

'I'd like that. Before you're a kept woman.'

Jojo laughed as she said goodbye. Rachel was left feeling lonely when the call ended with the David-shaped elephant still in the room.

She browsed a few more wedding blogs but was distracted by the memory of her own wedding.

It was the first time she and David had been away together outside of city breaks. A real holiday. She was petrified of flying but excited to be spending two weeks in a banda *located directly on the beach. They had too many glasses of wine on the flight and arrived feeling dazed. As they exited the plane, they were welcomed by a warm breeze. It was a dream location, straight out of a travel documentary. The calls of the birds and crickets kept time. The sand was golden and as soft as wool. Sky and sea merged into the same blue. The lapping waves woke them each morning.*

On their third night, while they were dancing in the moonlight, David looked deep into her eyes for the answer to a question he hadn't asked. He fell to his knees in a comic pose and asked Rachel to marry him. She was shocked and couldn't answer immediately. Her heart urged her to say yes whilst her head struggled with the speed the relationship was going. David apologised for not planning anything in advance – there was no ring. It was a moment of pure spontaneity. Rachel nodded to show that she understood and whispered, 'Yes! Yes, yes, a hundred times, yes!'

David called over their favourite waiter, Johan, and ordered Champagne. None was to be found. There had been an important wedding over the weekend, a bigwig statesman from the mainland whose festivities had cleaned out the island. Eventually a bottle of sparkling wine was located. They sat side-by-side watching the reflection of the moon dance on the sea. Rachel wished she could take back her cheesy line that their love flowed as easily as the wine. David told her he didn't want a long engagement. He wanted her to be his as soon as that could be arranged. He knew he had to marry her. He was certain.

Rachel loved David with all her heart. The only small niggle in her mind was the fact that her mother disliked him intensely. And what would her friends say? It was a whirlwind romance. They hadn't lived together yet. Did they know each other well enough? Like, really enough? Enough to spend the rest of their lives together? She'd never see another penis. Surely that was a good thing. And what about university? She was still a student. David told her not to worry, he'd support her.

Before the bottle of fizzy wine was finished, they'd planned to marry that week, on the perfect beach where David had proposed. Johan joined the celebrations as unofficial best man, maid of honour and wedding planner. His sister was a seamstress who would make the dress. The owner of their resort also had a craft shop for tourists. It sold the usual tat, but he had a metal workshop and made two simple bands using Indonesian gold from the Grasberg mine *in Papua. More sparkling wine was located and a floral headdress was designed. On the eve of their wedding Rachel and David wrote their respective vows on linen napkins. They sat at the same table, giggling with glee, while they hid their respective declarations of love from one another.*

Here Rachel's memories were interrupted by vivid mental images of David having sex with other women. She wanted to scream. Rachel forced herself to calm down and try to approach the situation with maturity. Could she have forgiven an emotional affair over a physical one? Was it the love he was giving this other woman that hurt the most? Was it the lies and the betrayal? Or simply the fact that the redhead was young and beautiful? Whichever it was, Rachel's self-esteem had taken a serious battering.

She had never cheated on David, nor on anyone else. There might have been more of a case to answer when it came to emotional infidelity. She didn't feel non-physical acts counted as actual cheating and certainly weren't as bad as sleeping with someone other than her husband; a high and mighty opinion dictated from her pious pedestal. She thought of the emotional interactions she'd had with other men. There was one in particular that haunted her. It was seven years into their marriage and David was always working or at home talking about work. He was distant and distracted. For a time she'd had strong feelings for another man. She unashamedly lusted after one of her suppliers but finally dismissed the notion as the seven-year itch. She found herself doodling his name in her notepad one hundred times and finding excuses to

226

call him to place extra orders. It had reached the point where she had to take her business elsewhere and allow her heart to heal. But she had never acted on her feelings – was that better or worse? Maybe it was worse.

Amongst her numerous online searches, Rachel found a TED talk that explained the driver of romantic love came from the craving part of the mind and was a similar process to cocaine addiction. Was that it? Was David addicted to love? She tried to take a metaphorical step in his shoes. They weren't as uncomfortable as she would have expected. She understood why he might want change, but why couldn't he have simply told her: *it's been grand, let's end the marriage on a high?*

David

24

By the time Rachel emerged from her slumbers the next morning, David had made himself a solemn promise to be a better husband. The best husband ever. He wanted to be the husband Rachel deserved. He made a list of things he thought would make her happy. He started by making her a coffee, which was promptly abandoned on the kitchen top. Rachel kissed him on the cheek and rushed out, citing a breakfast meeting.

This was suspicious. Rachel hated breakfast meetings more than anything. She was a creature of habit and enjoyed waking up to a cup of coffee and a perfectly poached egg on one slice of wholemeal toast, apart from on her 5:2 fast days. On those mornings she didn't even like to open the fridge. David could see washing had been left in the machine. Rachel ran a tight ship; the house ticked over like clockwork. She handled the cooking, laundry and vacuuming. David looked after the bathrooms, dishwasher-emptying, bins and the garden.

He drank Rachel's tepid coffee and opened the email app on his iPad. He changed the account from his own to that of his wife and found that he was locked out. She had changed her password. He would rarely snoop. They had each other's email log-ins for printing confirmations: e-tickets, boarding passes and what not. David could only think of nefarious reasons why Rachel would have changed hers. She was hiding something from him. He pushed down the jealousy he felt, which was hypocritical he knew. What if Rachel had sent erotic images to another man? They met long before the advent of 'sexting', although he had a few faded Polaroid photographs of Rachel. His sexual prowess was what Amelia-Rose termed *vanilla*; she thought he was sweet. He'd taken offence at that. She had taught him a lot in the space of one evening – mainly, that he liked being vanilla when he wanted to make love to his wife. He missed their intimacy, their *normal* sex. The freedom to make proper love. Rachel knew how his body worked and how to get the best from it, and vice versa. He regretted everything. How he wished he could turn back the clock.

Rachel had laughed in his face when he'd suggested she was seeing someone. Nevertheless, fear spread through David. He was determined to find out what she was hiding from him. The thought of Rachel kissing, never mind sleeping with, someone made him physically retch.

He felt he had to see her.

David flashed his best smile as he walked into the offices of Keatley Marketing & Events. He nodded to Eva and Lydia and put a finger up to his mouth to urge them not to give him away. He knocked on Rachel's glass door.

'Surprise!'

He interrupted her daydreaming and she looked like a rabbit caught in the headlights when he appeared unexpectedly. Since when did a husband have to ambush his wife for a lunch invitation?

'Fancy some tapas? You know, like the old days?'

The old days had been great, especially when they'd worked from a small garden flat, just the two of them. They'd bring the landline on its forty-metre extension lead into the garden and picnic on deli cheese, meat and olives.

'Or we could order a takeaway and sit by the river?'

Rachel closed her laptop. She nodded and asked David to give her a second, saying she'd catch him up. She asked him to order her favourite dishes – *Croquetas de Espinacas, Pimientos del Padron* and *Patatas Bravas*. David did as he was told and he found himself humming cheerfully to himself as he left the office.

Rachel joined him at the restaurant as their order was being packed. They stopped in a quiet spot and ate slowly, staring out at the passing river traffic. Rachel spotted a black swan. It was the first time either of them had seen one on the Thames. After eating, she rested her head in David's lap and he stroked her hair, wondering where it had all gone wrong. *Was she going to leave him? What could he do to make it better? Why was he such an idiot? Why had he listened to his cock? What was she up to?* He alternated between regret for his own misdeeds and wild unsubstantiated suspicions of infidelity on her part.

Rachel jumped up when she noticed it was nearly three o'clock. They had been eating watching the world go by lazily for more than two hours. She gave him a kiss and thanked him for a lunch pass to the old days.

David waited impatiently for Rachel to return home. He called Jojo to tell her his perfectly laid plan. He'd wooed her with lunch and made one of her favourite dinners for this evening. And in a fortnight's time he was going to whisk his wife away to Paris – he had two first-class Eurostar tickets in his pocket already.

'Are you smoking?' his sister asked.

'No,' David lied as he threw the lit cigarette into a rosebush. He returned to the kitchen to check the pans and stir the gravy for the fiftieth time. Rachel hated lumpy gravy.

'Don't you think you should ask her first? She doesn't like surprises.'

'But you forget, we got married spontaneously.'

'Yes, exactly! And look how well that turned out.'

David was disappointed by this reaction.

'I didn't mean for you to unleash all the romance in one fell swoop on the same day!'

He heard a key turn in the lock. 'She's back, I've got to go.'

At the door, he took Rachel's coat and bags from her. He gave her arms a firm rub and kissed her on the lips. He presented her with another bunch of lilies and passed her a champagne flute. He had made them each a Lemon Fizz.

LEMON FIZZ RECIPE
25 ml Champagne*
25 ml Limoncello
25 ml ginger liqueur (Giffard Ginger of the Indies is superb)
15 ml freshly squeezed lemon juice
1 tsp finely grated fresh ginger

* can be replaced with fizzy wine

The oven timer interrupted their toast. David checked the dinner; the roast chicken was golden and surrounded by potatoes and vegetables cooked in the meat juices. He tested the temperature of the chicken and set the oven timer for a further ten minutes.

He gave Rachel's shoulders a short massage and asked after her day. He didn't really listen to the details of Jojo and Beth's wedding preparations. Instead, he found himself staring at his wife's face trying to ascertain why she'd changed her email password.

'How's work?' she asked.

David had one last task to complete for the new Board of Directors. It was called a final delivery meeting but he knew it was to justify why he should stay on as an expensive advisor.

'Fine!' he said, too cheerily. 'You know, Rome wasn't built in a day, and neither was DC Computing sold to a big multinational.' He asked if Rachel would like to see his presentation.

'Go for it.'

David was suddenly nervous. Rachel took a seat at the breakfast bar. He should tell a joke. Rachel loved his jokes, didn't she? She had heard them all a million times before but she always laughed. *That had to count for something?*

'How many software consultants does it take to screw in a light bulb?'

Rachel stared at him blankly.

'The answer depends on the fee structure, are we being paid by the hour or by the job? And what are the call-out charges?'

Rachel gave a small laugh. It wasn't funny, it was the way he told it. He went through the rest of his presentation with aplomb. He directed his pitch straight to her; and thought he saw her blush when he didn't break eye contact.

When he'd finished she gave him a standing ovation. She had a few small notes: he had forgotten to state their biggest challenge and their best solution. She advised David to leave a pause between each of the benefits, to allow each one to hit home. Also to explain what the sixty-day invoice plan meant for cash flow, not to mention the rolling monthly contract. You know your customers are loyal when they voluntarily renew the product – not because they are under the cosh with a five-year agreement they can't wait to expire.

David's phone buzzed notifying a text message.

Jojo: *So? Paris???*
David: *You're right. I should check with her first. Bottled it.*
Jojo: *Chicken!*
David: *Yes, roast chicken.*
Jojo: *Ha!*
David: *You told me not to surprise her!*
Jojo: *You've been listening. Bon voyage!*

Rachel

25

Rachel was laden with bags of shopping. She collected tote bags now to use instead of plastic. She found David in the hall. He was practising speaking into the mirror. He started with Robert De Niro impressions, he couldn't help himself. *'You talkin' to me?'* She could see he was attempting to keep his eyebrows still. A colleague had once mocked his habit of arching them dramatically and he'd been paranoid about it ever since.

David followed her into the kitchen and massaged her shoulders. She asked after his day and was pleasantly surprised when he suggested running through his presentation with her.

'Was this why you made dinner? Trying to butter me up?'

David pretended to be offended by her presumption.

'It was a joke!' Rachel laughed at his dramatic response, and gave him the go-ahead to try to sell her his wares. David was a natural salesman with a twinkle in his eye; she bought every word and her heart fluttered when she observed his snake hips. *He still had it, ladies and gentlemen.* She was persuaded by the sales pitch. David's eyes had their own weather system. They could be cold and piercing or a warm, seductive shade of Cerulean blue. From across the room, she could see his bright eyes dancing and was excited by him in a way she hadn't experienced in a long while, though doubt swiftly crowded back in. He stared at her and smiled.

'Why are you selling the company again?' she asked.

'You knew I thought it was time.' He stared directly at her.

'What is it?' she asked.

'You. You're great.'

'It's not that.'

'It is that.' David fiddled with something in his pockets. He did his nervous twitch and cracked his knuckles.

'What was that show you wanted to see with the bloke off the telly? Book tickets for it. We can go the week after next.'

Rachel nodded in agreement. Everyone had been raving about the play and the performances. The tickets had sold out months ago. But his suggestion had thawed her.

Before dinner, they caught up on each other's respective news. She empathised with his stories of nightmare clients. She was having such a lovely evening that she'd forgotten all about the plan to get him to love her again.

*

The next afternoon Rachel heard a beep from outside. She looked out of the window and saw Kevin's car.

'Last chance – do you want to come to Mum's with us?' she asked David.

He responded with a rude gesture implying he'd rather not.

Rachel kissed him on the cheek and wished him luck with his presentation. He then took her aback by saying he might have to stay overnight in Swindon if it was looking like a late one. She was left speechless. Unable to respond, she merely nodded. At that moment, she made a decision. She said goodbye and left the house.

Her brother drove an Audi with a matt black finish. Kevin was proud of it but Rachel thought it looked naff, and she had told him the only person to pull it off was Christian Bale – and only when he was pretending to be Batman!

Rachel slipped into the passenger seat. She unlocked her mobile phone and drafted a reply to a message she'd received earlier.

Rachel: Yes, it is short notice, but tonight would work. Let me know where and when.

She thought about adding a kiss but decided against it and pressed send.

'Please tell me the seat warmers aren't on?' The last time Rachel had grabbed a lift with Kevin she endured a very uncomfortable five minutes. She thought she'd lost control of her bodily functions; it transpired the seat warmer had been turned on full blast. Kevin nodded towards the house. She shook her head to indicate David wouldn't be joining them.

'Long story.' Rachel couldn't go through the rigmarole of explaining why her never-husband had strayed then stayed. There was a danger of her brother wanting to confront David on her behalf. Kevin's nicknames at school were Hothead and Fisticuffs.

'We have an hour.'

'Where's Louise?'

'Long story.'

'We have an hour,' she said, mimicking her brother's tone.

Kevin and Louise were still finding their feet as a new couple. Rachel and Louise were polite and chatty with each other but had nothing in common; Louise was a doctor and always on-call. She was tea-total and seemed a little bit absent most of the time. Rachel didn't take it personally. If she were a heart surgeon, she'd have better things to gossip about than neighbours she'd never met. Kevin was separated from his third wife and Louise was his first foray into mid-life dating.

Understandably, Kevin wasn't keen to introduce another new girlfriend to their mother. Norma was a hard nut to crack. Lesser women had been broken by her imperious stare. Not to mention the high bar and the backhanded compliments Norma was renowned for. Kevin liked to ensure the relationship was solid and the girlfriend in question could handle the scrutiny before a home visit was scheduled.

*

Their childhood home had endured regular refurbishment over the decades. The latest was in the usual vein (floral) and most of the furniture was the same (dark, mahogany) and now probably considered antique. There was a painting of Pope Paul VI over the fireplace. Norma didn't like the faces of the more recent popes; Pope Paul VI was her firm favourite. Rachel thought the portrait looked sinister. His eyes seemed to follow you around the room, reminding her of a Hammer horror vampire.

The sideboard had a concealed drinks cabinet. Kevin had already drawn the short straw by driving them there. He and Rachel now played rock-paper-scissors to determine if he would drive home too. She cast paper, and Kevin tried to turn his rock into scissors, an underhanded move he had got away with for most of Rachel's childhood. She caught him cheating and cackled victoriously. She poured herself a gin Martini (extra dirty) and offered Kevin a Virgin Mary. He declined; there was no fun in tomato juice without the vodka. Their mother was nursing a small tot of sherry while giving the beef stroganoff a final once over – five more minutes. When the doorbell rang, she ordered Rachel and Kevin to stand up straight.

'Kevin, why are you wearing jeans?' she fussed.

Norma tucked Kevin's shirt into his jeans, and tidied a wayward strand of hair behind Rachel's ear.

Roger Halliwell blast straight into the house, giving the impression he was already very familiar with Norma's lounge. Roger had a high forehead and thick dark hair (more pepper than salt). He was tall (not short at all,

Rachel noted), with broad swimmer's shoulders and narrow hips. He was wearing a salmon-coloured jacket with beige chinos and a pair of large dark-rimmed glasses (à la Dennis Taylor circa 1985). He had huge sausage-like fingers and wore a garish pinky ring.

Rachel wanted to hate him. She wondered if this was the default position of any potential stepchild. *Was thirty-four too old to be a stepchild anyway?* Roger presented Norma with a bottle of wine (white, chilled) and a bunch of flowers (roses, yellow). It was clear that he wanted Rachel and Kevin to like him as much as they wanted to dislike him. Hard as they tried, it was impossible. He was absolutely charming, with a great smile (veneers) and endless stories about his former lives.

Kevin tried to trip him up with questions about his suitability to be Norma's 'boyfriend'; Norma and he both preferred the term 'gentleman friend', it seemed. Roger passed the Kevin and Rachel test with flying colours. He was looking to settle down and not afraid to disclose to the world it was Norma with whom he wanted to share his winter years.

They discovered he was born in the late 1950s; his birthday coincided with the release of the film *The Bridge on the River Kwai*, and he relayed a funny story about his mum going into labour before the opening credits and how ever since she refused to watch the David Lean classic. He'd had a short stint as a history teacher at the end of the seventies before joining the British Navy and being on the frontline during the Falklands. When a broken ankle saw him honourably discharged from military service, he worked as a photo-journalist for the remainder of the eighties and opened an art dealership in the nineties. He knew nothing about paintings – but he loved to be surrounded by talent and beauty, he said as he winked at Norma. He had a wealth of self-effacing stories about incredible situations he'd found himself in. She had never seen her mother as animated and alive, certainly not with Rachel's father.

Rachel and Kevin left feeling warmed by Roger's friendliness.

'What do you think of him?' Rachel wondered aloud. 'Do you think he's a spy?'

'I don't mean to be funny but what does he see in Mum? They're a bit chalk and cheese,' her brother said.

The journey home was filled with old memories and stories from their childhood. They still argued about who broke the light fitting in the attic. But they were in total agreement that they couldn't fault Roger. He was larger than life. He was fun and, more to the point, he made their mother smile.

Rachel thanked Kevin for the lift. She found the house empty. She headed straight to the shower.

Rachel wore a green cocktail dress and a pair of vintage pearl earrings. The sunset added atmospheric light to the riverside. The glass-fronted restaurant twinkled with tea-lights and lamps. Luke stood up when he saw her directed to his table.

'You remind me of Audrey Hepburn in *Breakfast at Tiffany's*,' he whispered into her ear as he held out her chair. The song 'Moon River' filled her head. *Wait, was Holly Golightly a prostitute?* She couldn't remember. Luke ordered a bottle of the recommended house wine. The Argentinian Torrontés was flashed in her direction; she gave the waiter a polite nod although she hadn't studied the label.

Luke recommended a selection of plates and then suggested they share them. He was happy to make conversation. Rachel tried to keep track of his life story. They chuckled when it turned out they both had an older brother called Kevin.

Luke wanted to know everything about Rachel. He asked question after question, which appeared like actual interest in her rather than an inquisition. He didn't pry when she said there had been problems in her marriage. He assumed she was separated from David and she didn't correct him.

Rachel wondered how her husband lived with his guilt. Here she was having an *innocent* dinner and it felt as if David was primed to jump out of the bushes at any moment and shout GOTCHA! Not that it mattered, she reminded herself, because she and David were NEVER MARRIED!

When Luke placed his fingers over hers momentarily, she felt protected by the strength and warmth of his hand. The shackles of depression seemed to have dissolved. She felt herself wanting him to touch her hand again.

They shared plates and laughed together. Rachel couldn't remember the last time she had laughed so hard.

'Do you want dessert?' the waiter asked.

He tried to tempt them with a sumptuous chocolate mousse but Rachel politely declined, she could hardly explain that she had already had a huge beef stroganoff lunch with her family.

Luke walked her to a taxi. She was a little tipsy and wondered if they would kiss. He pulled out a money clip and gave the driver two notes. He gently kissed Rachel goodnight on the lips and said he would call her in the morning.

The journey home was filled with anticipation and confusion and disappointment. She touched her lips where she sensed the ghost of Luke's kiss. She saw a message on her phone from David confirming he was staying in Swindon overnight. *God, how much time could he spend bonking his mistress?*

At home she wiggled out of her dress and threw it straight in the washing machine. Desire radiated from her loins. She still had butterflies from that kiss and knew that having dinner with such a man could not be dismissed as an innocent outing. She felt conflicted for craving Luke's touch, his kiss. She pushed any thoughts of her own culpability aside as she dreamed of Dr Luke Parry-Wilson, his soft lips and caring hands.

The next morning Eva immediately noticed a difference in Rachel.

'What's happened?'

'What do you mean?' She tried to appear indifferent.

'One – you have matching shoes on, two – your make up is subtle, your complexion is great, and three – is that a wiggle in your walk? If I'm not mistaken, Rachel, I would say you got laid!'

'Hardly!' she said, and blushed. She and Eva agreed to meet for drinks after work when Rachel decided she would tell all.

Rachel was more than tipsy when she returned home. Her recent behaviour was not in keeping with their weekly meal plan. On her 5:2 diet, Monday was normally a fast day but it hadn't worked. Her husband had still found someone thinner, taller, younger. She could work at being thinner, and she had heels for being taller. But she could never be younger.

David had gone out again. At least he'd left a note:

Fed cats
Supergreens salad in the fridge,
Gone for a jog.

Rachel ignored the salad; she had devoured minisliders and thick potato wedges after the over-consumption of wine with Eva. She drew a hot bath with more of Eva's oils. The bathroom floor was wet from when David must have showered. As she dipped into the steamy bath, her phone buzzed. She couldn't be bothered to check – assuming it was David, with another lame excuse for being late. *Where was he jogging? To the Moon?* What if it was an emergency? She lifted herself out of the hot water.

Dr Luke: Next time – let's leave room for dessert.

Finally! She noted that he didn't sign off with a kiss – what did that mean? She was desperate to reply but unsure of the etiquette. Rachel had heard different rules about waiting one day, three days, and even five! She'd forgotten to ask Eva. Luke said he'd call in the morning and now it was gone 8 p.m. *What did it mean?* She returned to the bath and put her crime novel aside, her mind too full of thoughts of Luke, his hands and his soft lips against her cheek. She'd forgotten the sensual pleasure that could be gained from even the smallest of touches. She closed her eyes and recalled conversations, meetings, messages and touches from Luke. When he held her hand, and her gaze too long. And the way he looked at her legs, set off by expensive heels ... She imagined him turned on and how the fire behind his eyes would burn brighter. Her breathing heightened, the hot water surrounding her enhancing her lust. She wanted Luke. Wanted him to hold her, to kiss her. To touch her. More than that – she wanted him to desire her. The thought took a strong hold over her body, and then she felt something else, a shadow of shame. She hadn't fully come around to the idea of thinking of another man in that way.

Rachel picked up her book again. She found her place and familiarised herself with the plot once more. She was enjoying the novel; the protagonist had framed her husband for a double homicide. Pure bliss. She fantasised about David being set up for a murder. Then pictured him in Tudor stocks and herself throwing rotten fish and mouldy tomatoes at his face while his hands were shackled.

David pounded upstairs and disturbed her glorious reverie. He shouted through the bathroom door. He sounded agitated, something about a client and Swindon. Rachel dried herself in the bathroom instead of the bedroom. She applied body lotion all over her body, something she always meant to do but somehow forgot. She dressed in full-length silk pyjamas. She was still basking in the warmth of Luke's text message.

David was still going on about the client when she slipped into bed. Mr Franklin wanted an extra report that wasn't part of his monthly contract agreement. Rachel didn't see the problem: give the customer what he wants. And the new owner was hardly likely to want to have a customer leave in the first month without you! Her advice was brief and to the point. David told her he was so wrapped up in the drama that he hadn't thought of that simple solution. He said he missed working with his wife, kissed her lightly on the nose and headed for the en-suite.

David was in the shower, again! With each wash she grew more suspicious. She had to assume he was washing away the scent of his mistress. He emerged from the bathroom with a towel wrapped around his waist, and there it was: the first sign on him of middle-aged spread.

Tonight, she hated him a little less.

David

26

David's week passed without much interaction between him and Rachel. David was busy wrapping up the company sale, but was aware his wife seemed to be avoiding him. He complained to Rachel that the grey in his hair had almost doubled recently. She pretended not to hear him, which was ridiculous since she was chopping vegetables less than three metres away. Finally, she replied that grey hair can result from stress, and suggested a massage to relieve any tension.

'You do look after me well.' David gave her a kiss on the forehead, and said he would find some oil.

'I meant a sports massage at the gym.'

'Oh, of course.' David didn't know how else to respond, and nodded weakly.

Rachel started to cook spaghetti bolognese as David prepared cocktails in the conservatory. He had a new recipe.

ROSE MARTINI RECIPE
35 ml Gin
20 ml lychee juice
15 ml rose infused water
10 ml freshly squeezed lemon juice
5 ml rose syrup
1 rose petal to garnish

'Have you seen the new neighbours?' David had been updating Rachel about the removal van comings and goings for over a week and there was still no sign of the new arrivals, the Jessops. The SOLD sign had been removed but so far Rachel hadn't seen the couple for herself.

David was determined to get back on track with his wife. Lately it seemed the harder he tried, the more she pulled away. It was making him second-guess his every action. He'd tried being amorous with her before dinner; gave his signature moves. First, he stroked her neck and gently nuzzled behind her ears with his mouth. When Rachel spilled red sauce on her white blouse she completely overreacted. He went upstairs to find her a new top. Rachel's work shirts were lined up in a row on her side of the wardrobe. He rummaged through some drawers but could only find her exercise garb. He somehow ended up knocking a jacket off the rail, which took four more with it as it fell to the wardrobe floor. David cursed as he bent down, leaning deep inside the wardrobe to retrieve the tangled hangers. It was then that he noticed the box. In it, he found something that shocked him to the core.

Rachel called up the stairs, 'Have you found something for me to wear?'

David quickly chose a grey t-shirt that she wore for yoga and tossed it down to her. He told her he'd be down in a minute and phoned Jojo.

'Can you talk?'

'We're about to Skype with Beth's parents.'

'What's worse than a code red?'

'I dunno, we've never needed higher than that before, officer.' Jojo put on her *Star Trek* voice. 'Captain's Log: unknown territory.' She laughed. At least she was amused.

'I've just found—'

'How's it going with Rachel?'

'She's got someone else.'

'I don't believe—'

'There's a box full of underwear and things I've never seen before. Sexy things.'

'Maybe she bought them for you.'

'Na-huh. I've never seen them before and I think they've been *worn!*'

'Don't tell me about it – talk to *her*.'

Rachel

27

Rachel loved cooking. She had prepared fresh tagliatelle and a bolognese sauce using a pound of minced steak and an entire packet of pancetta. She used lard instead of oil and grated a huge serving of Parmesan cheese. It was comfort food fit for the Gods.

She showered before dinner and applied tinted moisturiser, red lip stain and a swipe of mascara.

David had a new cocktail recipe. She stopped herself from asking the inspiration behind the drink, assuming it was the *other woman*. When he presented her with a Rose Martini, she silently ground her teeth. He was so transparent. When David wasn't looking, she added another shot of vodka to her pink drink. She wanted to anaesthetise the pain that was rising within her. Two cocktails would stabilise her mood. A third would be the ideal numb-to-happy ratio. A fourth would tip her over the edge. And a fifth would set off waterworks. She finished the Rose Martini in two gulps. *That felt good.* She promised herself she'd stop after the third drink.

'Have you put on weight?' David asked.

WHAT THE ACTUAL F—?

'It suits you,' he added. 'Reminds me of when we met. All boobs and bum.'

Rachel downed the rest of her cocktail, unable to think of the correct retort.

For God's sake, she thought to herself when she spotted red dots of rich Italian sauce across her white linen blouse. The liquid had spread already. The top was ruined.

'Calm down, it's only a shirt.' David passed her a napkin.

Rachel took off her top; the sauce had stained her bra too. She asked David to find her something else to wear. He threw down an old t-shirt that she wore for yoga and finally returned in a mood. He wolfed down his dinner before telling her he needed to work. Rachel sat in her French Connection skirt and crappy old t-shirt and wondered what she was still doing with him?

Rachel poured her morning coffee into a flask. 'Can we talk later? I've got to go, I've got Jojo's dress fitting.'

In contrast to his sulk the night before, this morning David had given her a long speech about being happy and ended with a suggestion: he wanted them to go to Paris. Rachel said she'd think about it. She couldn't decipher his mood swings. Was he leaving her? Did he want to let her down gently? Had he been dumped by Little Miss Redhead? And then he gave her some spa vouchers.

Rachel wanted to believe in David's sincerity. They were a team, a good team, or they had been once. She wanted to trust him. She wanted to believe in him, and in his faith in them as a couple.

She asked David if he wanted to join her and Kevin for Sunday lunch with their mother. David mumbled something about preferring to stick hot needles in his eyes. She kissed him goodbye and told him again she'd think about Paris.

Rachel flicked through the rail of assorted wedding dresses. Pippa's Bridal Emporium was the only go-to for wedding attire. Rachel owed her for fitting in a quick turnaround for the two dresses.

'I will be demanding your everlasting soul in return,' Pippa cackled before she left Rachel with Jojo's wedding dress and a glass of Champagne.

Jojo rushed in red in the face – not exactly the look suited to a wedding boutique. She didn't apologise for her lateness. It was a given; Jojo was always late.

'How can you stand *this*?' Jojo nodded at the selection of exclusively white, cream and ivory gowns. 'And you have to do it all again next week with Beth.'

Pippa appeared silently with a glass of Champagne for Jojo and like an apparition was gone again.

'You know what? I actually love it. Weddings are so joyful, and even the Bridezillas – not that you or Beth would ever be considered that – when you see the looks on their faces as they walk down the aisle, and cut the cake, and the first dance, and throwing the bouquet … it makes it all worthwhile.'

'That's … that's beautiful,' Jojo said, surprised by her own heartfelt reaction.

'I didn't have you down for a secret romantic, Jojo. So, are you going to try it on? It's the final fitting – no eating whatsoever until the big day,' Rachel joked.

Jojo went behind the curtain into the changing room.

'How is everything?' Jojo asked.

'Fine.'

Rachel was glad she was hidden on the other side of the curtain. She had mental flashes back to her date with Luke and winced with embarrassment.

Jojo looked beautiful in the magnificent dress and pretended she didn't have a tear in her eye when she gazed at herself in the mirror. Rachel agreed. The dress was gorgeous as was her best friend.

Jojo nodded to the other dresses on display and asked, 'Which one has Beth gone for?'

'You know a magician never reveals her secrets,' Rachel said giving Jojo a wink. The bride and bride had picked almost identical dresses without any inkling of it, albeit Beth's dress was roomier around the waist thanks to some guess-work alterations. No one knew quite what size her bump would be by the wedding day.

'And for the finale …' Rachel made a trumpet noise '… put your hands on your hips.'

Jojo found a small opening. 'No way!'

'It's Pippa's pièce de résistance, a secret pocket.'

Rachel ordered Jojo a coffee. She sat in silence and waited for the inevitable.

Her friend played nervously with a napkin and folded it into an origami boat.

'I've been speaking to David quite a bit lately. Anyway, I know you hate surprises, which is the only reason I am telling you this. He is going to surprise you with a trip to Paris. I didn't want you to have other plans. He's spent the last couple of weeks organising it. Don't worry about our wedding and everything is in hand. Nothing is going to go wrong if you take the weekend off.'

'But—'

'But nothing. It'll do you good – time to reconnect.'

'Yeah, he's already mentioned it to me earlier as I was on my way out.'

Rachel thought back to the recent times David had slammed his laptop shut when she entered the room, the sneaky phone calls . . . and wondered if he had been speaking to his sister?

'Great – did you say you'd go?'

'I said I would think about it.' Rachel took a deep breath. 'So you know then?'

Jojo nodded.

'Sorry, I was going to tell you – but I didn't want to say anything before the wedding. You shouldn't have to deal with our mess. Let's get your wedding out of the way first.'

'Look, if you need to talk, you know where I am, and that goes for Beth too. Especially if you need some time away.'

Rachel nodded, afraid she might cry.

'I'm really proud of you.' Jojo squeezed Rachel's hand.

Rachel slept like the proverbial log, unaided by sleeping tablets, through until morning. She had amorous dreams and saucy entanglements with a faceless lover and woke with a crimson blush. She had overslept. Her phone had multiple messages and missed calls from Kevin. And one message from David.

> *Kevin (three hours ago): I'll be there at 11:00 to pick you up.*
> *Kevin (two hours ago): I'll be there at 11:00 to pick you up.*
> *Kevin (ninety minutes ago): Did you get my previous messages?*
> *Kevin (one hour ago): You better be ready.*
> *Kevin (twenty minutes ago): I'm leaving. See you in twenty minutes.*
> *David (now): Heading back from the gym. X*

Roger sat in the living room wearing house slippers when they arrived. Rachel raised an eyebrow in her mother's direction. Norma flapped away any suggestion of impropriety.

Roger looked surprisingly dapper. His outfit was similar to something David had in his wardrobe. The salmon jacket had been replaced by a navy version, the financier's blue shirt with white collars and cuffs exchanged for a white linen shirt with a granddad collar. His glasses were now a manageable size and no longer tinted, and his signet ring was absent. And he was wearing a cravat.

Rachel joined Norma in the kitchen and watched her prepare lunch: roast beef – served pink.

'Your brother didn't bring Louise, she's a heart surgeon, you know?'

Rachel tried to nod and shake her head simultaneously. Kevin had broken up with Louise. He said it was because of her doctor's on-call hours, but it was an excuse for their not being enough for each other. Kevin had told her, 'Life's too short to be riding the wrong horse.' Rachel was tempted to give her mother the gossip but decided it would be best coming from the horse's mouth.

'Was it Kevin's fault?'

Rachel ignored the question. 'This thing with Roger is all moving very fast,' she said with a hint of naughtiness.

'We've known each other for decades. We used to go on holiday together, you know.'

'No, I didn't know.'

Rachel had visions of her mother conducting a forty-year-long affair with Roger the teacher cum sailor cum photographer cum art connoisseur cum prospective stepfather. Had Rachel and Kevin not looked so much like their father and his side of the family, Rachel would already have been ordering online DNA tests.

'Pass the mustard.'

Rachel found the jar and passed it to her mother.

'We went with Roger and his wife, me and your dad. To the coast.'

'What happened to the first Mrs Halliwell?'

'Cancer.' The C word wiped the Cheshire cat smile from Rachel's face.

Rachel went to check on the boys. She could see through the crack in the door to the lounge that her brother was being kept enthralled by Roger's stories until he whispered that he had been meaning to talk to Kevin on his own. It was all very cloak and dagger. Rachel watched Kevin move forward conspiratorially. Roger removed a ring box from the inside breast pocket of his jacket and divulged his sincere intentions towards Norma. He made it clear he understood very well that she wasn't the sort of woman to enjoy an unwedded dalliance. Roger wanted to make an honest woman of her. Rachel covered her mouth to silence a gasp.

'Keep it under your hat, old boy.'

The drive home was filled with family gossip. Rachel told her brother Norma hated living in sin; she was atoning for it every other day.

'They're already living together?!' Kevin exclaimed.

'Where have you been all afternoon? It's all very proper and above board – he's in the spare room. Now, what did the ring look like?'

'It looked like a ring.'

'Kevin! What size and shape?'

'I don't know, it was an engagement ring. Old-fashioned, antique, the stone was square.'

'Don't you think Roger looked different – like his edges had been smoothed?' Rachel asked. Kevin admitted he hadn't noticed the house slippers or the second toothbrush in the bathroom. Or the mug with Roger's name, or Roger's post in the basket by the front door. Kevin hadn't imagined her being interested in love and romance and all that again at her age. He couldn't imagine her wanting to return to housewife mode. He also didn't want to think of his mother with a man other than his father, as ridiculously old-fashioned as that sounded.

Rachel told him that their mother couldn't wait for Roger to make it official. Not that Norma had a clue he had already chosen and purchased a ring.

David

28

David was manic. He thought he was making headway with Rachel, but it was one step forward and ten steps back. He replayed the conversations with Jojo in his head. Rachel did deserve better but what if he was too late? *He couldn't be alone. He didn't want to turn forty-six on his own. He was too old to start again. What if his charm couldn't win her round? What if one chicken dinner wasn't enough? What if he'd ruined it with Rachel forever?*

'I was thinking,' David said as he pushed open their office door with his feet. He was holding two coffees. Rachel looked up from her tablet and accepted the proffered mug.

'Again?' he asked, nodding towards the wall.

The new, still unseen neighbours were going at it. The Jessops made love like it was an extreme sport. The carnal grunts and sighs of gratification gave Rachel the giggles. David suggested they communicate with Morse code.

'Do you need help?' he said to the wall. 'Tap once for yes or two for leave us alone.' He starting gently tapping. Rachel stopped him and they both collapsed into laughter.

'Sorry, what were you saying?'

'I was thinking—'

'Me too.'

'You first.'

'No, you first,' Rachel said.

David conceded. 'I get the impression that you're not happy. I want to be a better husband. Also I need to let go of DC computing, they're all so young there and have these mad ideas. I don't work without you. I've already stepped away from the company. It was a temporary thing. They didn't need a former CEO moping around the office. It wasn't great for morale. I have less than a month before the handover is official, but everything is signed already. I'm looking ahead to the next challenge and I want you to be part of it. I miss us.'

Rachel nodded and said they should talk about it when things calmed down.

Rachel

29

Rachel called Eva to ask if she fancied joining her for a spa weekend. Rachel had been so busy executing her master plan lately that she hadn't taken the time to spend the vouchers. It was an oddly thoughtful gift from David whose presents were normally mundane, perfunctory and kitchen-based. *Had he been trying to get rid of her so he could have another of his precious shagfests? Or was it one of Jojo's suggestions?*

'Come on, it's our last weekend before open season on weddings,' Rachel almost pleaded. Eva did not need asking again.

The spa was heavenly. It was clean and light. Even the atmosphere was pristine. Women floated by silently in white robes and cotton slippers.

Rachel had booked the weekend package; one night, two delicious days. They checked into their room. Two beds, an oversized bath and luxurious skincare miniatures. Eva claimed the bed nearest the window and they changed into swimming costumes and robes. There was a plate of chocolate-covered apricots and strawberries alongside a welcome note. There was nothing the spa staff hadn't thought of.

When Rachel unpacked her toothbrush and eye mask she found an envelope in her Breton holdall. It was a greetings card of a pug having its claws painted a shocking pink. And inside were the words: *Relax. Love David xxx*. She let out a big sigh and remembered the words of her acupuncturist: *a sigh is negative energy stored in the chest*. She tried to breathe out all the negative energy and only stopped when she had nothing left to give. Rachel checked her phone one last time. No important emails, no messages from David. She packed the phone away in her bag.

Now she would *finally* get the time to enjoy the books she had been meaning to read; she felt she needed to escape with the help of Jack Reacher's brawn and wayward streak. She dreamed of being alongside him, no baggage, just the two of them on the open road. *Utter bliss*. A gentle knock on the door interrupted her Reacher fantasy. Susie, head spa co-ordinator, welcomed Rachel and Eva with a glass of Prosecco and presented them with the relaxing programme they had pre-planned plus some complementary group sessions they could enjoy.

She gave them vouchers for the restaurant to be used for afternoon tea (with more Prosecco) and highlighted their treatment times for Rachel's hot stone massage and a calming facial, and Eva's mud wrap and rejuvenating facial. They investigated the labyrinth of steam and sauna rooms. Rachel started with the foot baths. The jets of water tickled her toes. Next she sat in the hot dry salt sauna and allowed the tears to fall unobserved. She swam in the pool. Washed away the hurt in the rain walk. Read on a waterbed. Recuperated in the mineral steam room.

The spa's serenity was momentarily disrupted by a gaggle of women on a hen party, all tittering with excitement and whispering loudly. She left the hens to it in the sage-infused sauna, dousing herself in cold water, which was warm by the time it reached her hot taut skin. The spa was working its magic; already she could feel the stored feelings of insecurity, sense of betrayal and bitterness seeping from her pores. Rachel and Eva had arranged to meet for a complementary mini-spa experience. They gave each other the look that said: 'Please can we live here?' Rachel felt the weeks of angst wash away.

The session was taken by Spa Head Girl, Susie. It was in essence a sales pitch as Susie got the spa goers to try different products on various parts of their bodies, in the hope they'd order an overly-expensive facial exfoliant and body oil (to be used on face, body and hair) that afterwards would be stored in the bathroom and forgotten. The instructions for use were beyond Rachel. Masks that should be left for twenty minutes at night but only ten minutes if applied in the morning. She tried a facial exfoliant that needed to be left to dry before she gently rubbed away the dead skin cells. Her robe was left covered in face dandruff. *No, thank you!*

She was taken by the mineral serum, though, and the lavender toning mist induced her into a state of total calm. The £40 price tag soon brought her back to a state of clear-headedness. Eva was impressed by a particularly fragrant aromatherapy body oil, and Rachel made a mental note to buy her the set as a thank you present. Soon they were joined by the increasingly raucous hen party. Eva rolled her eyes as she nodded towards the group's matching robes and slippers, which were personalised with #BettyBride stitching.

Susie described how a certain invigorating wash shouldn't be used on any sensitive areas and she gave the bikini area as an example; she blushed when the hen party started giggling delightedly. Rachel couldn't help but notice how young they were, without a single trace of wear on their faces or bodies. One of the women untied her hair and red curls danced around her shoulders. She looked vaguely familiar – a celebrity perhaps? Rachel did a double take. Could it be *her?*

The bride, Betty, confirmed with the others in her group the running order for the rest of the day. 'Amelia-Rose and I have massages now.' She hooped her arm round the redhead's.

Astounded to be face-to-face with her husband's lover, Rachel might have whispered, 'It's you,' but she still wasn't quite sure. She seemed to be existing a little outside herself, feeling light-headed and giddy from the potent aromatherapy oils and the hot sauna. Amelia-Rose was such a beautiful name ... It suited her. A beautiful name for a beautiful girl – and she was just a girl really. Rachel actually laughed. She couldn't help it. It was that or cry. She was transfixed; Amelia-Rose was even more stunning up close. Tempted to reach out and touch her face, Rachel attempted a smile towards her mortal Nemesis.

'It's her!' she screeched at Eva when the hen party had dispersed. Rachel still sat glued to her seat.

'Who?'

Rachel was mesmerised as her gaze followed Amelia-Rose's confidently receding figure.

'Who?' Eva repeated.

Rachel was having a hard time concentrating on both the conversation in hand and the calculations in her head. She was distracted by thoughts of Amelia-Rose's rosebud mouth and cute-as-a-button nose.

'Her! Her, her, her ... She ... It's *her*!'

'This is getting difficult to follow, do you need some water?'

Rachel pointed in the direction of the bride-to-be and her wing-woman. 'She's David's girlfriend.'

'The redhead over there?'

Rachel nodded. 'Did you see her perfect breasts?' she said aloud.

'What is wrong with you?'

'What? But look at her. How can I compete with ... that? With those?' Rachel shielded her own breasts as if to protect them. 'And did you see her neck?'

'Do you know what I think?'

'That I'm a self-obsessed crazy lady who should adopt twelve cats and be done with it?'

'No, that's not what I was thinking. But now that you mention it, you have two cats and a philandering husband. You already have the cat-lady starter kit.'

Rachel shot her a faux-hurt look.

Eva continued, 'I was thinking that your husband is a dick. Look at it a different way and it makes sense. Not to me. But it makes sense *because he is a man*: he's forty-five, right? In my experience, men go a bit cray-cray after any birthday with a zero or a five in it. My ex-husband, number three ...' she clarified. Rachel wasn't sure she wanted to hear an anecdote that involved ex-husbands enjoying life after divorce '... he went mental when he hit the big four-O and was never the same since. And as for your one – dick-for-brains – he's had a life-changing few years. Now he's selling his business, so asset-rich but meaningful-life poor. This was never about your marriage; it's all about him.'

'It's not my fault?'

'It's not your fault. It's *not* your fault,' Eva repeated.

'Are you trying the *Good Will Hunting* technique on me?' Rachel asked in a small voice.

'No. But glad to know you wouldn't fall for it if I tried.'

The remembrance of the pain and hurt she'd been through pushed Rachel to the brink of losing it.

'Do you want to leave?' Eva asked.

Rachel took a deep breath.

'No,' she said, 'not yet. Call me nuts, but I want to get another look at her.'

Eva nodded, but she didn't look convinced.

After thirty minutes of breathing exercises Rachel was calm enough to leave the tranquillity of the spa, and Eva walked her to the restaurant protectively. Still in their robes and slippers, they ordered their Prosecco afternoon tea. The majority of tables and chairs were filled with people, women mainly, also dressed in soft white towelling robes, expressing their inner-calmness in hushed tones.

The next table had a Reserved sign and within minutes team #BettyBride arrived and sat mere metres from Rachel and Eva. Amelia-Rose and Betty both showed the after-effects of their massage.

Betty's treatment had left her euphoric; she told the other girls she had reached a higher plane, as if she was looking at her own life from the outside.

'Deep,' one responded.

Eva urged Rachel to leave.

Betty went on to complain that she was having second thoughts. *Wait, shit just got interesting.*

Amelia-Rose chimed in with light-hearted complaints about her own boyfriend. He was a pretentious music snob, obsessed with chicken dinners, and she hated his hair – it was so old-fashioned. Betty's fiancé wasn't *that* bad, she added. And then, something terrifying happened. Betty the bride invited Eva and Rachel to join in the conversation. Rachel shouldn't have been surprised. She would have done the same in her position, in such relaxing all-female quarters. What was perhaps more horrifying, though, was the bride's opening gambit. She began by asking their opinion on marriage. Rachel froze, but Eva joined the discussion. She lifted her left hand to display an empty ring finger. 'Married three times, divorced three times. Broke up with my boyfriend this week.'

Rachel turned to her. 'I didn't know that. What happened to Terry the Fireman?'

'You've been a bit busy, shall we say?'

'What about you?' Betty asked Rachel. 'You're married?'

Rachel nodded.

'How did you know he was *The One*?'

'She didn't. And you won't. You have to trust your heart,' Eva cut in, 'and be prepared to have it broken!'.

The hens cooed at the advice, despite the fact that it came from someone who had moments before self-declared as a terrible source when it came to matrimonial guidance. They muttered support for Betty and her frankly foolish-sounding fiancé.

Rachel couldn't stand it any longer. 'And hopefully, after fifteen happy years, you won't catch your husband kissing another woman!'

The hens gasped and giggled, and Rachel caught one of them whispering 'She's mental' from behind her flute of Prosecco.

That flipped Rachel's switch.

'My advice? What I wish someone had told me before I was stupid enough to get married to some waste-of-space cheating lowlife?' Rachel got to her feet.

'Men are the worst – don't waste your time on them. In fact, ditch the wedding. Save yourself a lot of heartache. Take your stunning maid of honour, and I mean stunning

– *Red* over there – on the honeymoon instead. Thelma and Louise the shit out of your lives. Be happy. Otherwise you'll end up like me. I can see how you're looking at me with your woe-is-you eyes. I used to be like you and now I'm so self-centred and obsessed with the end of my marriage that my best friend – here – didn't even tell me she'd broken up with her gorgeous fireman boyfriend.'

'You need to chill out, lady,' said the girl who had whispered about her. 'Not everyone is as bitter as you.'

'Yeah,' added Amelia-Rose, 'you're spoiling my friend's special day.'

Rachel turned to face this woman who'd ruined her life and realised from the expression on her face that Amelia-Rose had no idea who she was.

'Don't say I didn't warn you,' said Rachel, shaking with emotion. She and Eva scurried out of the restaurant and went straight to the outside pool where Rachel allowed the water jets to massage her taut muscles.

'You broke up with Terry, what happened?'

Eva ignored her question. 'That was incredible. I reckon you should give motivational speeches to women. It was truly empowering.'

Rachel covered her cheeks with her hands. 'What is wrong with me? I might have ruined that poor girl's life.'

'Fuck it. She was already having doubts. She'll think twice, that's for sure. And give yourself a break. You've had a shock.'

'Did you see her? Amelia-Rose?'

Eva nodded in agreement.

'She's beautiful.'

Eva nodded.

'And so young.'

Eva nodded again. There was nothing she could say that could or would placate Rachel.

'Tell me about Terry.'

There was a minute of silence.

'I'm sorry. I liked Terry,' Rachel added.

'I liked Terry, but it wasn't going anywhere. And you were right – I need to find someone more age appropriate.'

'Why didn't you tell me?'

'You had a lot on your plate and, honestly, there's no drama. Nothing to talk about, no revenge to take. I'm a bit sad, but I'll be okay.'

Eva's supreme grasp on reality helped Rachel come to terms with meeting the young, pretty girl who had stolen her husband's heart. She felt defeated though. How could she compete? She obviously knew nothing about her husband if that was who he wanted to be with.

Eva reminded Rachel it was time for their next treatment. The hot stone massage promised to rub all the stress from Rachel's body. *Good luck with that!* Surprisingly though, it did help, albeit temporarily.

A feeling of calm stayed with her for the journey home but evaporated the moment she opened the front door. David wasn't in. The fridge was empty; there wasn't even enough milk for a cup of tea. The house was silent and she was alone. Rachel sat in her armchair, stared out of the window at the quiet cul-de-sac and sobbed. This was a taste of the David-less future she had to look forward to.

'Alexa, play songs for the broken-hearted.'

The first song on the playlist was Fleetwood Mac's 'Go Your Own Way'.

Rachel hadn't seen the point of streaming music. Why pay for things she already owned in other formats? But here she sat, listening to the magic that was Fleetwood Mac without having to turn CDs to MP3s, and transfer them from laptop to phone. She had a deep feeling of FOMO as her nephews would say. Her *fear of missing out* wasn't about being away from David but the fear of missing out on another life entirely. A better life; one without a cheating husband in it. Then she could spread her wings and fly. 'Alexa, play Wind Beneath My Wings.'

The breeze outside caused the trees to dance – they too seemed to be admiring the timeless song. The branches of the hundred-year-old oak moved in time with the music. What was the point in having this garden, this house, without having David to share it with? Say he had died, she couldn't have stayed in the house without him. She'd loved their first place together. As newlyweds, they moved to a small flat in Tufnell Park. The eight-foot patch of grass that justified its description as a garden flat was just big enough for a table and two chairs plus a mini-barbecue. It was David who later on wanted a garden the size of a small park. He wanted to recreate his childhood. Heavily influenced by his grandmother's green fingers, he wanted somewhere to grow roses for Rachel.

She watched a ring-necked parakeet hopping in the garden outside – these exotic wild birds were common in the area though not originally a native species. Rumour had it that they originally escaped from Heathrow airport, or Ealing Studios, or that an aviary had collapsed during the big storm of 1987 and allowed its exotic inhabitants to fly free. Nonetheless, she enjoyed their visits. With their pleasing bright green plumage and often a ring of red around the neck, they looked rather distinguished – as if they were wearing ties. They were sexually dimorphic, she remembered reading, and the necktie was how you could tell them apart – the males wore the ties, or maybe it was the other way around?

Neville and Oscar were primed for attack, like little lions on the plains of their own private savannah. They worked as a tag team – Neville was the distraction, herding the unwitting bird towards the cherry tree in which Oscar sat waiting. Rachel raised her hand as if to warn the bird but it was too late. At the last second, she looked away, unable to watch the cats play with their prey.

Her thoughts returned to David, and Rachel was suffocated anew by the feelings of betrayal.

'Cheat on me once, shame on you. Cheat on me again and again, shame on me,' she told herself. She would have to get the slogan printed on a t-shirt to warn other wives of wayward husbands.

Still, she missed her never-husband. She missed the friendship, the partnership, their intimacy and their stupid in-jokes. She missed the feeling of being in love. Then the thought hit her, like a lightning bolt or a fast train: she couldn't trust a word David said. She had overheard Amelia-Rose tell her friends she was planning to move in with her boyfriend. Rachel couldn't believe she was *still* giving him the benefit of the doubt. She wanted to tell him all of this. She wanted to scream and shout at him.

She missed everything they used to have but it was time to accept it was never coming back.

30

Eva opened the door to Rachel's office. As she did she called out to their PA, 'Lydia, could you join us for a second?'

Lydia was printing out tasting sheets and asked for a couple of minutes to finish. Eva said to take her time and closed the office door again.

'What about Kegels?'

'Who …?' *Was he a footballer?* Rachel thought.

'Kegels … pelvic floor muscles. Are you exercising them? They're the first thing to go.'

Go where? 'Oh! Ke-gels! All the time.' Rachel fibbed.

'Does wee ever escape when you sneeze?

'Uhm, no. I don't think—'

'Can you trust yourself on a trampoline?'

'I think so …' Rachel couldn't recall when she was last on one and doubted it would have been to test her pelvic floor.

'That's great. But you *must* add them to your daily routine. I'm doing mine now.'

Lydia came bumbling into the office, struggling with a heavy cardboard box marked DELICATE on each side. Rachel thanked God when Lydia interrupted them and the conversation ended, hopefully never to be revisited again. Rachel tried to tighten her pelvic floor and was worried that Eva would read the activity on her face, so stopped.

'What have we got here?' Rachel asked. She hadn't wanted to bid for the VD Vodka launch. Apparently it was the best British vodka since sliced bread, yet the packaging was tacky, there were endless spelling mistakes in the social media, none of the images on Instagram made sense – it was a mess of an account. Rachel had initially dismissed it as being too much work for very little reward. Not to mention that the brand name was an abbreviation for VENEREAL DISEASE! It was Lydia who'd pushed for the pitch and made the initial assessment of the brand. She seemed sure they could turn it around as the name was apparently so *hipster*.

Rachel rolled her eyes. She increasingly felt she had lost touch with the younger generation. She had been married to David before she graduated. All her uni friends, apart from Jojo, soon stopped inviting her to do normal young people stuff as, to them, being married at nineteen was frankly a little dull.

Lydia wanted vodka to be the new gin. The recent ginaissance had done wonders for the drinks industry. She was sure that if crafted and marketed in the correct way, vodka could easily overtake gin in sales and popularity. Lydia spent the whole weekend before the pitch getting it perfect. She had identified forty-two key dates of the year for a social media calendar and designed ten working partnerships in and around the capital to boost the new brand. When they finally won the account it was thanks to her great work – Rachel was super proud of her progress. Lydia was definitely ready to manage her own accounts.

The box contained six large bottles of high-end vodka. VD Original came in three strengths (39%, 45% and 52% – or *God help us* as Rachel privately referred to it) and there were three VD Flavours (pineapple, vanilla, cherry). Rachel touched the packaging. It really was bad. When competing against no-frills suppliers such as supermarket own-brands, which already undercut craft alcohol on price and quantity, she was going to have to face the owner head on with a difficult conversation about branding. Eva had three mugs ready for the tasting but Lydia would have none of it. She produced small shot glasses, seemingly from nowhere.

'Ready?' She gave them her widest smile.

First up, VD Original 39%. At half-past four in the afternoon, it really was too early for them to be drinking. But what the heck? They needed to know their product. They each took small sips and marked the liquid on the nose, taste, after-taste, taking into consideration depth and complexity of the spirit.

Rachel commended Lydia for a thorough marking sheet, and asked where the mixers were?

Lydia laughed nervously. 'All vodka tastes the same with Coke and bitter lemon. We have to taste the true flavour.'

Rachel nodded, as if she had only been joking about the mixers. She wasn't great with neat spirits, and was very much, *1 tequila, 2 tequila, 3 tequila, floor*!

'Lydia, I was wondering if you could help me with something . . .' Eva asked.

'Of course.' The girl was always so eager to please.

'How do you track someone down on social media?'

'It depends . . . it's harder if they have a name like Laura Smith because there are a gazillion of them. Who do you need to find?'

'A girl.' Eva was being elaborately casual about it. 'Her name is Amelia-Rose, she might live near here, she's about twenty-five?'

'Ooooooh!' Rachel was intrigued by this idea.

Lydia said she'd have a go but a few further details would be useful. 'Write down everything you know about her.'

She prepared the second tasting: VD Original 45%. They all took larger sips this time and scribbled down their scores.

Rachel could tell the difference. This stronger one was much nicer. 'What's the price point on this, Lyds?'

'It's twenty-seven pounds a litre.'

As Lydia tapped away furiously into her phone, researching anyone with the name Amelia-Rose, she said casually, 'You say she was at the spa last week, on a hen weekend. And the hen weekend was called . . .?'

'Hashtag-Betty-Bride,' Rachel and Eva sang in unison.

Lydia spent a few minutes more on her phone, her thumbs a blur of scrolling, flicking and typing. She squinted at the screen, finally selected a profile and showed the picture to Rachel.

'It's her!' she squealed. 'How did you find her?' Rachel took Lydia's phone to examine further.

'Easy-peasy. If she's local, there's a good chance she'd complain about South West Trains on Twitter, add that with the first name and hen party hashtag – and *voilà*!'

Eva looked at Lydia with newfound respect.

'Her full name is Amelia-Rose Springer,' Rachel read aloud. 'According to her social media, she is twenty-two years old. TWENTY-TWO!' Amelia-Rose's Facebook account was public (average two posts a day), and so Rachel was able to scroll through hundreds of posts. She next searched for her Twitter account (average eight tweets per day), and then found her Instagram (average four photos per day).

'She's a Francophile. Of course she is! And she owns a beret. Who does she think she is? Fleabag?! Only Phoebe Waller-Bridge can pull off a beret.' Eva gestured for Rachel to apply some volume control and willed her to stop shouting. Lydia didn't comprehend the gravity of the situation and was happy to have impressed Eva.

'Twenty-two!' Rachel repeated in a quieter tone. 'She'll be twenty-three in December. She's a Capricorn.' She made a yawn gesture, dismissing all Capricorns as second-rate citizens. 'According to her Instagram, in her spare time she's a yoga instructor. She teaches a hot yoga class a few times a week. IN HER SPARE TIME!' Rachel continued without a pause. She noticed that photos of Amelia-Rose's boyfriend were mysteriously absent with only the odd appendage in shot, a male arm or leg. There was one photo of a man, but Rachel couldn't tell if it was David. He was in fancy dress, hidden behind a huge moustache and a wide-brimmed sombrero. Pain seared through her chest. What if her husband had been to a party with Amelia-Rose and her friends? What if he'd been socialising with twenty-two-year-olds? To make matters even worse, David normally hated fancy dress!

Rachel whispered 'twenty-two' again, then added, 'I'm going to bury him.'

This got Lydia's attention. 'Bury who?'

'It's a long story,' Eva deflected her. 'What's next?'

Lydia held the new bottle up to her eyeline: 'VD Vanilla.'

'Bring it on.' Rachel held up her tasting glass, all the while flicking through Amelia-Rose's various online profiles at manic speed.

'How old are you?' Lydia asked Eva, fuelled by Dutch courage.

Eva softened her habitually harsh retort to any such query. 'None of your beeswax, my lovely little Liverpudlian lamb.'

'Eva, you old lush, I think that's the nicest thing you've ever said to Lydia! Lyds, I think Eva is a bit sloshed! Is there any cake?' asked Rachel.

Rachel craved cake. On her twice-weekly 5:2 fasting days, she fantasised about a life full of cake: living in cake town, working as chief cake taster in a cake factory. Right now, she needed cake. Any cake would do.

Eva tried the biscuit tin and Lydia tried the bread bin, both coming back empty-handed. They were all out of carbs.

Rachel found the company credit card and ordered a pizza. It was the only sensible solution: extra pepperoni, extra chilli and extra mozzarella. A worthy contender to cake.

Eva and Lydia cheered at her decisive leadership.

'What's next?' Rachel asked.

Lydia tried her most sensible tone of voice. 'Back to the beginning – VD Original thirty-nine percent.'

'A second opinion?' Eva asked.

'Always a good idea to be thorough,' Rachel confirmed.

The hangover was a killer. Nobody beyond their teens should have to endure a Wednesday morning hangover. Rachel was tempted to phone in sick. She cajoled herself into the shower and had two coffees before she could even contemplate getting dressed. She found sunglasses, and said aloud, 'Ahhh, that's better.'

She left her car in the driveway, worried she might still be over the alcohol limit, and walked to work in the beautiful spring weather. Eva and Lydia were both disgustingly chipper. Rachel pretended to work until lunchtime. She tried inhaling biscuits – chocolate, plain and garibaldi – but none of them had any effect on her mood, her blood sugar, or her ability to keep her head up straight. She gave up and pretended she would work from home. It took her a good thirty minutes to walk slowly to the local hospital. She regretted not stopping for a remedial cheeseburger and fries en route. Sometimes an unhealthy ratio of fat to carbs to sugar is the best medicine.

Rachel knew she had put off the inevitable long enough: being tested for sexually transmitted diseases. The shame. Although there was no itch to scratch, Chlamydia and other sexually transmitted diseases were supposedly symptomless; it was impossible for her to tell whether she had been infected or not. She used to be proud of the fact that she had reached the age she had without once getting a bout of anything nasty down there. She couldn't go to her own GP – it would be far too embarrassing.

Rachel and David didn't use condoms and hadn't in fifteen years, but the knowledge of his extramarital activities weighed heavily on her. She had stopped taking the pill one month earlier, when they'd had the big talk about starting a family, and now bitterly wished she had not.

The local hospital was a maze. She had called NHS Direct and was given details for a GUM clinic within Kingston Hospital. She then had to Google what GUM stood for: genitourinary medicine. *Sexy.* Rachel looked around cautiously as she neared the unit. She didn't expect to encounter anyone she knew at the hospital, but what if this was the one where Kevin's ex-girlfriend worked? How would Rachel explain her presence if they bumped into each other?

She walked behind two teenagers, hand in hand, wondering if they could be heading in the same direction. First loves, looking for birth control? She tried to follow the blue arrows, through departments, up in a lift and past some blood-testing stations. Her hunch had been correct; she found the same young couple there in front of her in the sexual health services reception area. Apart from Romeo and Juliet, starry-eyed and holding hands, the waiting room was filled with men. *Was that normal?* Everyone was avoiding eye contact and silently judging one another.

When it was her turn at the reception window, Rachel was greeted by a whispering receptionist holding a clipboard. The first question was to confirm her GP's details – she was only there because she wanted to avoid her doctor and close-knit staff knowing. She was given a form to fill in and put down the name Eva Jenkins and then crossed it out and wrote her own fake-married name – Mrs Rachel Chatsworth. She conscientiously ticked boxes (no symptoms, no discharge, no pain, no assault), and handed back the clipboard. She hadn't experienced symptoms other than an annoying itch every time she thought about the possibility of catching something. The roomful of patients reduced gradually one by one and eventually a nurse called Rachel into a consulting room. Gemma (as her name badge announced she was called) was professionally polite. She looked through the form and then asked some intrusive questions. Had Rachel:

Engaged in sexual activity with any foreign national? No.
Engaged in anal sex? No.
Engaged in selling sex or engaged in intravenous drug use? Yes!

Rachel instantly regretted making the joke about it; she'd only been trying to lighten the mood. Gemma didn't even smile.

'I mean, seriously, no. I haven't been injecting drugs. Or selling sex. Look at me.'

The nurse looked up. Rachel was a recognisable type, a mid-thirties professional woman … but Gemma must see all sorts in this treatment room.

'Sorry, but it was such an absurd question,' Rachel continued. 'The reason I'm here is … m-m-y husband has been b-b-b-bonking a young … Someone else. It's okay—'

'No! It's not okay,' interjected Gemma, 'my advice? You need to tell that jackass where to get off.'

Rachel let out a stifled laugh. She had found an unlikely ally in Gemma. She interrupted the serious nurse. 'I needed to … wanted to check … I'm here because I read some things online about diseases … infections with no symptoms and what not …' Rachel whispered. 'And that Chlamydia can affect fertility?' She suddenly felt very self-conscious.

Gemma explained that because of the lack of symptoms, Rachel could administer a self-swab kit. She showed her the enlarged cotton bud and gave instructions on how to take a sample and place it in the envelope, which already had Rachel's details printed on it.

'Anything else I can help you with today?'

Rachel shook her head. She knew that Gemma couldn't give her what she really needed, which was:

- to get some proper rest without pharmaceutical aid;
- to close her eyes without the never-ending cycle of worry repeating itself;
- not to have to compare herself to a beautiful, younger woman.

Left alone in the room, Rachel struggled to *swab* her uterus, accidentally stabbing herself a number of times as she poked the cotton bud along her vaginal wall. She assumed the pain meant she had hit the correct depth.

She added the sample to the tube provided, put it in the envelope and posted it through the letterbox by reception. She was grateful to escape into the fresh air outside.

Rachel walked along the riverside path through the deer park, enjoying the views and the proximity of the deer. There were dozens of the handsome animals though the stags were largely absent as the females tended to their new-born fawns. Rachel picked wildflowers and basked in the last of the afternoon sun.

On the way back, she noticed the church on the corner. The rays of the sinking sun had created an apt and striking halo around the belfry. She hadn't intended to go inside. Rachel had long ago abandoned organised religion. She had found enlightenment through yoga and liked to think of herself as spiritually aligned with Buddhism, although some of her recent behaviour was at odds with its teaching, and she knew she needed to take a long hard look at herself and her actions. She realised now she sometimes missed the rituals of religion. Norma didn't hold back from showing her disappointment that

Rachel stopped attending Mass and worried aloud that her only daughter would end up in Hell. Rachel was suddenly flooded with deep-rooted guilt.

For her, lapsed Catholicism was a void that had never been filled. Her close friend at university, Emma, fell pregnant and chose to have an abortion. She confided the details in a man of the cloth whom she'd trusted to keep her secret, but before long found herself the subject of damaging rumours and gossip. Emma was subsequently ostracised by the Church. Appalled by what she saw, Rachel gave up the Church too. She didn't want to be part of a religion whose God refused her friend support and understanding.

Rachel pressed down on the solid metal latch and pushed open the church's heavy wooden door. Her footsteps echoed through the empty building. She allowed herself a few minutes of reflection, sitting in a pew next to the aisle, and felt the stress of her afternoon gradually leave her. The resentment she had once felt towards the Catholic Church melted away. She sat there for half an hour, taking in the special atmosphere of the tranquil space. She dropped a pound coin in the collection tin and lit a candle. She closed her eyes and whispered her father's name. She hoped he was at peace.

Rachel noticed a shadowy figure emerge from the vestry. A priest. Could he sense her estrangement from her religion? Was he daring her to approach him? Without thinking, she stepped into the penitent's side of the confessional box. It had been nearly two decades since her last Confession. She was in desperate need of spiritual redemption. Rachel confessed all. She didn't hold back. She admitted not only her questionable actions, but the ugliness of the thoughts she was nursing towards the man she had loved and the young woman who had tempted him away.

After taking a moment to reflect on Rachel's Confession, the Irish priest advised twelve Hail Marys and urged her to seek out the kindness within her heart. She thanked him and said she wouldn't leave it so long next time. It wasn't a lie; she'd been genuinely comforted by her visit. It was a reaffirming experience. She left the box thinking about how to change her life for the better.

When Rachel opened the front door, she was annoyed to find that David had gone out and left every light on. Then she saw him lying asleep on the sofa and her irritation dissolved. He looked so happy as he slept, a man at peace; she found a chenille throw and placed it gently over him. Then she tiptoed out of the lounge and went to the bedroom to catch up on her own forty winks. *Working from home, ha!* After a two-hour nap she thought it odd to find David still asleep. She called out his name. When he didn't respond, she shouted his name. He didn't wake. She prodded him with her stocking-clad foot. He didn't move. She found a pocket mirror and placed it under his nose; it didn't register any sign of breathing. She stepped back to look at his chest. She couldn't detect any visible movement.

'Oh my God, have I killed him?' she whispered as she punched him hard in the arm. Surely messing with his caffeine and sleep patterns couldn't have finished him off? 'Please don't be dead, please don't be dead. I love you. I'm sorry, I'm sorry I was mean to you. I should have let you go. I should have given you to the ginger goddess. She can have you.' Even in the midst of her rising panic, she gleaned some pleasure from punching him a second time.

Rachel straddled his stiff torso and attempted to administer CPR. It had been more than a few years since she'd last undertaken a first-aid course. She found the position of his sternum and laced her fingers together. Backed up by her body weight, she pushed down hard onto his chest. She had to get into a rhythm of one hundred compressions a minute – or was it ten? She struggled to remember. The aim was not to kill someone while trying to save their life. *Think. This is important. One hundred compressions or ten? Come on. Rachel, keep it together. Think. Think. Think.*

David flinched. Rachel screamed and jumped up, elbowing him square in the scrotum. He pushed her, hard, and she was thrown from the sofa onto the floor. She let go of the breath she hadn't realised she was holding.

'You're alive! You're alive!,' she exclaimed as she hugged him and planted small kisses all over his face. She wasn't going to prison after all. She wasn't going to be a widow. She was mightily relieved, but less impressed by his grumpiness.

'Of course I'm alive.' She pushed him for answers. He said he'd been exhausted but couldn't sleep, so he took one of Rachel's strong tranquillisers that she'd been prescribed for her fear of flying. It had left him disorientated. She lambasted him for making her think he was dead and questioned the number of pills he'd swallowed. In a huff David went upstairs to finish his sleep in the comfort of their bed.

'They're not bloody sweets!' she shouted after him.

David

31

David woke up suddenly to find Rachel pressing down on his chest. She counted with each compression: 'One, two, three …' Squashed under her weight and with his arms pinned under her thighs, he couldn't breathe. Panic set in. He tried to access the oxygen needed to breathe and let out a loud strained cough, which scared Rachel. She punched him in the balls and he doubled over in pain, accidentally shoving her off him. *Was this a horrible dream? No, his balls were truly pounding with pain.*

David was groggy and downright confused as Rachel demanded answers from him. As he stumbled upstairs, she called after him, 'They're not sweets, you know.' He wasn't listening properly as she continued shouting, something about going to Norma's for dinner.

David couldn't get back to sleep. But he couldn't get out of the hazy fog that immobilised him either. He tried a cold shower. Under the freezing water, he had an idea; he would ask Norma's permission to (re)marry Rachel before proposing, especially as no such courtesy was paid the first time. That would get him into both Norma and Rachel's good books. When he heard her shout goodbye through the bathroom door, David regretted remarking he'd rather stick pins in his eyes than ever go to his mother-in-law's.

'Wait! I'm coming!'

Rachel told him not to bother.

'I said I'm coming! Give me a few minutes.' David quickly dried and dressed.

They left the house together and had already double-locked the front door when David said he had to go back inside.

Rachel looked at her watch. 'We're going to be late.'

He ignored her, unlocked the front door and ran to the kitchen. Then he packed a chilled bottle of Champagne into a cool bag. He ran upstairs to the office and grabbed the hidden turquoise ring box and slipped it into his pocket.

Norma was surprised to see David on the doorstep with Rachel. Her first thought was she hadn't enough food for tea. She pointedly told her son-in-law she had only been expecting Rachel and Kevin. She had defrosted four pork chops and would struggle to make them stretch to five. She told him it wasn't fair, and now it meant *she* was unprepared, it was very selfish of him to show up unannounced. David reminded her that, with God's help, everything was possible.

'Look at Jesus – he knew how to feed a crowd.'

Rachel slapped his arm and told him to behave, then placated her flustered mother. David asked Norma if he could put a bottle in the fridge. She flapped her hand towards the kitchen without so much as a glance at the bottle.

The proposal was already not going to plan. David's strategy relied on getting Norma firmly onside. He hovered in the kitchen and offered to help her, but she didn't want his assistance and kept brushing him out of her way. He tried to make polite conversation about Bridge Club (an unpopular topic as Norma ranted that Annie had lost her game since meeting her new man, Sandra 'forgets' to pay her way, and Jeremy is hopeless). When Norma complained again about the rationing of pork chops (which of course was his fault), David offered to ease the problem by making an omelette for himself, an idea she dismissed outright. As a last resort, he mentioned the recent nice spell of hot weather (the sun had dried out her herb garden while she was in Bath for the weekend). When he asked about her weekend away, Norma told him to mind his own business.

He had a speech prepared about how much he loved Rachel and his plans for the rest of their lives. How he was going to look after his wife. He wanted Norma to see he wasn't the bad egg she'd always viewed him as. The thought of Amelia-Rose suddenly plagued him. He *was* a bad egg. He tried to dismiss memories of all the times he had upset Rachel over the years. He couldn't erase her lip quiver from his mind. It was the few seconds' notice that she was about to cry. Her bottom lip would droop of its own accord before she gave way to her misery.

Roger appeared from upstairs. He shook Kevin's hand with his Lancashire sausage fingers and held Rachel's shoulders as they hugged. Finally he shook David's hand.

'Good to meet you.' David thought the handshake was on the soft side but Norma and Roger made a presentable couple.

When the doorbell rang Roger rushed to the front door. It was a florist with a huge bouquet of two dozen red roses. Norma assumed the delivery girl had the wrong address.

Roger presented Norma with the unwieldy array of flowers. She opened the small envelope attached to them. The note had been written in cursive script. Norma couldn't help but smile, making David wonder if he'd ever seen Norma actually happy before.

Rachel gently took the card and read aloud: *'Beautiful flowers for a beautiful woman. Always, Roger x.'*

Norma blushed as she thanked him.

Roger brushed back his hair and winked at Kevin as he slowly sank down on one knee. The pressure on an old ankle injury threatened to destabilise him for a moment but Kevin steadied him obligingly. David could not believe his eyes. He'd planned his proposal in advance, although not as well as Roger had, it seemed. He was being upstaged by his own father-in-law-to-be. This was not how today was supposed to pan out. Roger had only been seeing Norma for ... what? A matter of weeks!

'Norma, will you make me the happiest man in the—'

'Are you kidding me?' David whispered to Rachel.

'Get up before you do yourself an injury,' Norma said.

'Mum! That's not an answer,' Rachel admonished her.

'Yes.' Norma's mouth stayed tight-lipped for a moment but she allowed herself a smile eventually. It might even have reached her eyes.

'When did you two meet?' David asked.

Norma ignored the question.

'Let's celebrate!' Roger said.

Kevin was one step ahead. He opened the fridge and popped open the chilled Champagne. David's Champagne. The Champagne David had brought with him to celebrate his own proposal, to his own wife. He looked on in horror as Roger and company splashed back his expensive fizz.

'Did you know about this?' David whispered into Rachel's ear.

'Isn't it exciting!' She clapped her hands together.

'Why didn't you tell me?' he said through gritted teeth.

Rachel stared at him nonplussed.

'You're not interested in anything Mum does.'

'I certainly would have liked to know about *this*.'

Roger suggested going down the road to celebrate at the newly refurbished gastropub, which served beer-battered fish and chips for an exorbitant price. The fish and chips were certainly good, but David wasn't convinced they were £25 good.

'Weddings are like buses – none for years and now, what with Jojo and Beth's and this, two come along at once!' Kevin quipped.

'And after we've eaten, David can help Roger set up the new PC.' It was a statement rather than a request from Norma.

David thought that really took the biscuit. He smiled, but had no intention of helping Roger do anything. As they waited for Norma to get ready to leave the house – this needed a change of lipstick, shoes and clothes, including for some reason a different pair of tights that looked identical to the originals – David texted his sister:

David: *Guess who got engaged?!*

Jojo: *Amaze-balls – so happy for you both xxx*

David: *Guess again.*

Jojo: *Oh, no – WTF? What have you done? I get Rachel in your faux-divorce. This is me officially calling dibs on her.*

David: *Can you imagine, the righteous Dowager Keatley is engaged?*

Jojo: *The ice queen?*

David: *The very same.*

Jojo: *You got pwned by Roger!*

David: *Yes, please laugh at the further destruction of my sanity.*

Jojo: *Send the ice queen my congrats!*

Rachel

32

Rachel finished applying her make up and covered herself head-to-toe in body lotion. It was for a special occasion rather than a new routine for her impending journey into even older age. She could never actually adopt a body moisturising routine – there were too many other distractions in life. How did anyone have the time? In the morning she couldn't wait for the cream to be absorbed before getting dressed and at night she didn't want to mess up the sheets.

Why did she need to try to look ten years younger? The anti-ageing industry's job was to reinforce the idea that ageing was bad, and sure, surgery and lotions and potions might help in the short-term. But nothing was going to change the inevitability of getting older or time passing.

Rachel accepted she was the age she was and tried hard to leave behind all the bullshit pressure. That said, she was agonising internally over her neck folds when the doorbell rang. She wrapped herself in a dressing gown. Surely it was too early for guests?

Eva couldn't stop; she was dropping off the replacement cake toppers (the company had sent two grooms instead of two brides by accident) and still had a blow-dry appointment and a manicure to fit in. She was now firmly Rachel's friend first and colleague second. Rachel didn't know how she would have coped without Eva's strength to fall back on.

As Rachel walked her to the front door she watched in slow motion as Eva opened it, Kevin stood on the step outside with his finger poised to ring the bell, and Eva let out a high-pitched shriek. Kevin smiled, unperturbed.

'Hi, I'm—' he said, holding out his hand to shake hers. Eva didn't return his gesture but left his hand hanging. 'Whatever you're selling, we're not buying.'

'Actually, I'm here for Rachel, is she in?'

'Rachel?'

'Rachel – my sister.'

She popped out from behind Eva.

'Eva, this is Kevin, my numbskull brother.'

Rachel noted with glee Eva's icy expression as she took the measure of the man standing in front of her. Eva was in four-inch stilettos and her eyes were level with Kevin's. Rachel was sure they had met before but obviously not properly. Now they were eyeing each other up like cowboys duelling at high noon. Eva told Rachel she would be back in time for the celebrations. She shooed Kevin out of her way, leaving his arm still outstretched.

'Who was that?' he asked as he watched her sashay away in her pink heels.

'Keep away from my office manager.'

'Wait, is she the nymphomaniac?'

'Who told you that?'

'You did!'

'Actually, she's not a nympho – she's just very in tune with her . . . look, it's a long story – and don't try to change the subject. You've got work to do.'

Rachel changed into a tuxedo onesie. She had her wedding outfit packed for later. She gave Kevin a list of errands. He was happy to be helpful but continued to ask questions about Rachel's aloof office manager.

'She'd eat you alive. And she's had more husbands than you've had hot dinners.'

'That's a LOT of husbands.'

'It was a figure of speech.'

'Your phone is flashing like a seventies disco.'

'Pass it here.'

Beth was incoherent. She was blubbing and wheezing to the point where Rachel had difficulty hearing what was wrong. Beth said she couldn't phone Jojo because it was bad luck. Rachel could hear her mother-in-law, Lillian, trying to calm Beth in the background. Rachel ran through a mental checklist. Everything was checked, double-checked and triple- checked. All except one thing.

'Is it the baby? What's wrong?'

Beth tried to talk but the hysteria was too strong.

'Beth, please breathe. Do I need to phone an ambulance?'

She was finally able to squeeze out the words: her parents had missed their plane from Texas.

'It's fine. We can delay, what time will they land?' Rachel was relieved, missed flights she could deal with.

'Tomorrow! They won't get in until tomorrow.'

Rachel thought they could delay by a few hours but not by an entire day.

Shit! Think, Rachel, think.

'Beth, we have two options: one – we postpone. We have wedding insurance, we can find another venue, and there are always last-minute cancellations.'

'We can't cancel! I can't do that to Jo.' Beth still sounded distraught but at least she had reined in her sobs.

'Okay – second option, we go ahead and then have another celebration, say a big dinner party with your parents, once they arrive. What do you think?'

'But who will give me away?'

Rachel wanted to say David, but he already had Best Man duties. She looked at her brother and found the solution.

'Kevin! He's here, he loves you. He'd be honoured … and he looks great in his morning suit.'

Kevin looked panicked by the unknown prospect that Rachel was pimping him for. His eyes begged for reassurance, but Rachel flapped away his alarm and Beth quickly agreed to her suggestion. Rachel asked Beth to put Lillian on the phone. She instructed her mother-in-law to:

1) Keep Beth calm,
2) Ensure the bridesmaids left on time, and
3) Wait with Beth until Rachel and Kevin arrive.

Rachel tried to get Eva on the phone while urging David to hurry up.

'We're going to be—' Rachel shouted up the stairs. 'Oh, Eva, thank God – we have a change of plan. Beth's parents are stuck in Texas ... hold on a minute, David's saying something.'

'Why don't you go on ahead?' he bellowed from the bedroom.

'We can't be late.' *What was taking him so long?* 'She's your sister! And you're the Best Man!' She returned to her call. 'Eva, you know what to do ... yep ... Kevin is going to step in. See you here at two.'

Rachel glanced at an ashen-faced Kevin. 'We can do this,' she said unconvincingly.

David came down the stairs and Rachel gave him a list of things he had to do. She alluded to the drama with Beth's parents but warned him not to tell Jojo until the very last minute. 'The very last, do you understand?'

'Jojo will want to check Beth is okay,' Rachel instructed. 'Do *not* tell Jojo until you absolutely have to.'

David gave her a look that said, 'I'm not stupid'.

He studied his list and began packing various boxes into the car.

David came back in to say goodbye and kissed Rachel on the left eye. 'What did you do that for?' She checked her face in the hall mirror – he'd smudged her mascara. She resembled a lopsided panda. She huffed her way up the stairs, mumbling about not having enough time to redo her entire face.

Rachel and Kevin arrived at Beth and Jojo's exactly on time. Rachel gasped as she saw Beth who looked amazing in her wedding dress, albeit a little red around the eyes. She was wearing an ivory strapless mermaid gown with a long train that had been altered to accommodate the delicate baby bump. Beth was positively glowing, although she found it difficult to walk longer than a few minutes without needing to sit down. The pregnancy was taking its toll, and she had severe hyperemesis gravidarum. Lillian was more than happy to explain to Kevin that Beth suffered from the same morning sickness as the Duchess of Cambridge.

Kevin told Beth he was proud to be walking her down the aisle, and she relaxed in his comforting presence.

Rachel tried not to look at her watch. She had promised Eva they wouldn't be late and could feel her phone vibrating in the small clutch bag. Beth's bump wasn't even that big, yet she waddled like a swan – more gracefully than a duck, but only just. They managed to get her out of the house, but then her bladder decided to throw its own curveball. And back inside they went.

Kevin looked the other way as Rachel and Lillian tried to squeeze into the bathroom with Beth along with the train of her dress. They tried not to laugh at Beth's minutes-long racehorse wee. Despite the number of events she'd managed, Rachel had never before had to adjust a bride's knickers into place. She pulled up the maternity underwear (something blue) over Beth's bump, straightened the ivory garter (something old), and smoothed the dress (something new) into place. Lillian finished the look with a family heirloom, a pearl bracelet, which she fastened to Beth's small right wrist (something borrowed).

They tried not to rush Beth, who was wobbling towards the car like a giraffe with broken legs.

'Are we late? What time is it?' Beth gasped.

'We're fine,' Rachel lied. 'And they'll wait.'

They reached the entrance of the eighteenth-century manor house where the civil ceremony was taking place. Rachel smoothed Beth's hair and kissed her on both cheeks. 'You're gorgeous. Enjoy your day. Now I'm going to hand you over to Kevin.'

Beth asked for a moment before she vomited violently into a bush of lilac rhododendrons. Rachel stroked her back as she tried to keep the veil away from Beth's face.

Beth apologised profusely between retches. Rachel messaged Eva with a live-to-the-minute update, while Kevin appeared with a bottle of water for the sick bride, who swilled some water but didn't want to risk drinking any. *What goes down must come up!*

'I'm ready,' she advised.

Kevin held Beth's elbow. 'Let's do this.'

Rachel was flittering at the back of the room as Kevin and Beth took slow and delicate steps. Between them Eva and Rachel were keeping track of the catering, the registrar, the DJ, the Champagne toast, the free bar, parking, the presents, the environmentally friendly alternatives to confetti. She was organising the wedding instead of participating in it – this was the best present she could bestow on her best friend.

She slid into the end of a row of seats to her right. David gave Rachel a wink and her heart ached as she thought about her own never-marriage.

There was a moment of amusement when both brides realised they had chosen near-identical dresses. The registrar had to give a small cough to ease the tittering among the guests.

David

33

David was given strict orders not to tell Jojo about Beth's parents' absence until the very last minute. He was undecided how to say goodbye. Should he kiss Rachel on the mouth, or the cheek, or simply pat her affectionately on the bum? He'd decided to kiss her on the cheek when she turned suddenly and his lips landed square on her eye.

'What are you doing?' she shouted at him.

He put up his hands. 'I didn't mean—'

Rachel pushed past him to check her make-up, complaining that she didn't have time to start again. It was clear that he'd been dismissed. David tried to laugh it off as Kevin stood awkwardly watching the interaction.

David sat in the car and slapped his own cheeks. He didn't want troubling thoughts of his relationship with

Rachel to ruin his sister's wedding. But it was going to be difficult to keep it together.

'*You can do this, you've got this,*' he said to himself. The question he was trying to avoid was flooding his brain. *What was he going to do?*

His phone beeped.

Jojo: Where the hell are you?!?!

David walked his sister down the middle of the ornate drawing room of the wedding venue and they stood before the registrar waiting for Beth.

'I'm not nervous,' she declared.

'It's okay to be.'

Jojo whispered that she had butterflies, but in a good way; they were butterflies of happiness. 'I was never expecting to get married. What with it being illegal and all that,' she continued. 'Seriously, until the law actually changed, I thought ... maybe it wouldn't happen. Maybe I'd never marry a woman. And I'd got used to it – the idea of *living in sin*. Or hiding a secret union.

'It may not be a church but this room is beautiful. Now I want the ceremony to be over because I can't wait for the rest of my life to begin! I can't wait to be Mrs Elizabeth Taylor and for Beth to be Mrs Joanne Chatsworth or for us both to be Mrs Chatsworth-Taylor. Sorry – I'm babbling. David – can I ask you a small favour?'

'Go for it.'

'I know you are barely suppressing the urge to declare yourself to Rachel all over again, but please don't propose to her during Beth's and my wedding. '

'As if I would – it's your day!' Jojo raised an eyebrow at him, unconvinced. 'I promise.' Deep in his jacket pocket, David's fingers were crossed. He hadn't planned to upstage the brides, but if he found the right time and place today, somewhere quiet and private, he would definitely ask his wife to marry him. He patted his breast pocket; the ring box reassured him with its presence.

'Are they late?' Jojo asked in a small voice. 'My watch didn't suit the dress. What time is it?'

David smiled at the thought of Jojo's metal Casio watch from yesteryear and squeezed her hand. Rachel had promised him to secrecy, and she'd also promised him that Beth would be on time, so there was no need to worry Jojo with the details.

'You know what women are like.' He rolled his eyes.

Jojo gave him a huge smile. 'Cute, did anyone ever tell you that?' She thumbed the small dimple in his chin, before adding nervously, 'She is coming, isn't she?'

David had never seen his sister scared before. Loud recorded organ music began bouncing off the walls and ceiling. Jojo looked at David who had turned to face the door.

He nodded. It was time.

David pressed his handkerchief into his sister's palm; he knew she would need it.

'Can I look? What's the etiquette? Or is it bad luck?'

'Relax, take a deep breath.'

'Sorry, I'm still babbling.' Jojo stayed facing forward. The wedding guests could be heard whispering with excitement.

'One last thing,' said David. 'Beth's parents didn't make their flight. But it's okay! Kevin will be escorting her in.'

Jojo turned to face him. 'What the actual f—?'

'Eyes forward! Beth didn't want you to worry. But also, she didn't want you to freak out. So breathe in and suck it up.'

'I hate you so much right now,' his sister whispered.

'I love you too. Come on, you're up!' he whispered back.

Kevin lifted Beth's veil and David winced as his brother-in-law tried to secure the delicate lace clumsily with a hair clip. When he'd finished he sat down quietly and David saw that Jojo's little finger was intertwined with Beth's. Jojo and Beth looked at each other in their matching dresses and similar bouquets, and they giggled and laughed, until the registrar gave a small cough. Jojo gave David a knowing glance as she used his hankie to dab away her tears of happiness.

David caught a glimpse of Rachel in the front row. He knew he was at fault. He had deprived her of a loving ceremony like this one in front of their friends and family. What a selfish bastard he had been. Well, not anymore.

The festivities were raucous for everyone bar the wedding couple. Poor Beth was exhausted and stayed seated for the evening celebrations, Jojo sitting protectively by her side. People danced around the blushing brides. David watched with amusement as Kevin followed Eva around the party like a puppy. Rachel was in full work-mode and dished out orders to everyone – she threw her phone at David and charged him with recording a message for Beth's absent parents. As he fumbled with the video settings, he started saying: 'Hey, Mr and Mrs ...' and then paused filming when Beth's surname slipped from his mind.

'Taylor!' Jojo reminded him.

'Of course it's Taylor.' He held the phone steady to start recording again, when a notification popped up on the screen.

NHS-NoReply: THANKS FOR USING THE WOLVERTON CENTRE HEALTH SERVICES – YOUR TEST RESULTS ARE NEGATIVE.

What tests?!

He searched Rachel's text messages and couldn't find anything more from the hospital. Flustered, he deleted the offending message accidentally as Rachel was walking towards him. On autopilot, he quickly recorded a video clip for Beth's parents, again stumbling over their surname. It would have to do. He handed back Rachel's phone.

David hid in a recess by the bar and Googled 'Wolverton Centre'. His worst fears were realised: it was a sexual health clinic. He asked the bartender for a double Jack Daniel's and downed it. Questions filled David's head. *Did Rachel know about his infidelity? Was she seeing someone else – he'd asked her and she hadn't actually denied it, but laughed it off. Was Rachel having an affair?* He felt doubt punch him in the stomach. David looked over and saw his wife hugging the wedding DJ. The man was short but extremely good-looking, even David had to acknowledge it. He was built like a tank, all muscle, like Tom Hardy on steroids. Did he imagine it or had the DJ's hands lingered too long on Rachel's waist?

David ordered another double Jack Daniel's and headed towards the DJ booth.

Rachel

34

Rachel was cornered by Gavin, who thanked her for getting him the gig. She told him it was no problem, and said she'd use him again. And she meant it. He was a great DJ. More importantly, he didn't let his ego get in the way. If the client wanted 1980s cheesy tunes, that's what they got, even when Gavin obviously preferred 1970s rock.

'Babe, seriously! I'm having such a great time. This is all I want – being paid to play tunes.' He went in for a hug.

Rachel was awkward in Gavin's arms. The embrace felt alien. They didn't fit together in the natural way that she and David did. She didn't feel comfortable. She didn't feel at home.

'Let's get a picture.' Gavin whipped out his phone and took ten consecutive selfies of himself with Rachel. 'These are great.'

She left Gavin to his tunes. Rachel was overwhelmed by the wedding fever all around. Today's joining of Jojo and Beth. Her widowed mother engaged again. She was truly envious. For the first time she admitted to herself that she resented not having had her own traditional wedding ceremony. No big celebration with friends and family. Instead she had fallen in with David's wishes. She had agreed that everything was okay, that her needs were being addressed. She had even fallen out with her mother about it.

Eva clicked her fingers in her friend's face. 'Earth to Rachel, Earth to Rachel!'

'I was just thinking … It's great isn't it? Everyone is happy, right?

'Rach, you have done an amazing job. I was thinking we should write to a couple of the bridal mags and blogs and show what you've achieved at such short notice. Only a couple of months. You could be the queen of last-minute weddings!'

'What *we* have achieved. Talking about thinking, let's discuss the business when we're finished here and have caught up on some sleep. Let's concentrate exclusively on events from now on.'

'Whatever you say, boss.'

'And less of that. I want you to be my business partner. I meant what I said: I could only have pulled this off with your help, Eva. And if I'm honest, I wouldn't even have a business if you hadn't been there these past weeks. You don't have to say anything now.'

'Sounds like a—' Eva interrupted herself. 'Rachel,' she said, pointing, 'what's David doing? He looks like he wants to lamp the DJ.'

'What?' Rachel followed Eva's gaze.

David was heading, eyes narrowed, towards the booth.

'Maybe he doesn't like Simple Minds?'

'False alarm!' Eva laughed, as she and Rachel watched David swerve the DJ booth and circle back to the bar. 'Anyway, you owe me some gossip. You didn't tell me about the rest of your date with hunky Dr Doolittle—'

'It wasn't a *date*, and he's hardly my type—' Rachel was interrupted by one of the blushing brides.

'Are you talking about the DJ – who knew nerdy Gavin would turn into such a beefcake?' Jojo joined in the conversation.

'What? No.' Eva explained they were talking about the hot new vet in town before Rachel waved away any mention of Luke.

'It's nothing,' she said.

Jojo was still David's sister after all. Realising her faux-pas, Eva found a reason to excuse herself and went to rescue Beth from an over-zealous religious uncle.

'What's this about a vet?' Jojo asked.

'Long story involving an accidental dinner.'

'Rachel, you sly fox!'

'Nothing like that.' *A little bit like that.* She liked Luke, but it was David who gave her butterflies in her stomach.

'We need to catch up properly when you're back from your honeymoon.'

Jojo raised her eyebrows. 'I know you and David are having a hard time, but …' She held her hand up then as if to say she didn't want to interfere. She gave Rachel a hug. 'Thank you so much for all you've done. You're a wedding goddess. But would you mind awfully if Beth and I slip off now?'

'It's your wedding!' Rachel looked over and saw Beth attempting to keep her head up and pretending not to yawn. It was gone midnight.

'All she wants is a foot rub!'

'Welcome to married life. I'll find you a driver. All the presents have been packed away, I'll drop them off when you're back. I've saved the top tier of cake for—'

'Baby's christening? You're amazing.'

Jojo and Rachel helped Beth to her feet and somehow got her to the car without anyone noticing.

Rachel and Eva finally sat with a glass of Champagne each and enjoyed the last of the party. Kevin and David seemed to be having a dance-off competition, with David self-proclaiming himself the winner. Afterwards Kevin came over and asked Eva to dance. She looked at Rachel, who checked her watch.

'You're officially off the clock, go dance!'

Rachel was envious of Eva's dance-like-nobody's-watching attitude, as her and Kevin threw middle-aged shapes on the dance floor.

In the taxi home she held David's hand and marvelled at the way their palms still fitted together perfectly.

*

Rachel woke after a long sleep. Although they were exhausting, weddings tended to bring out the best in people. She called Eva, who was also still in bed, and they discussed the clean-up that needed to be done. Rachel asked if Eva managed to get much sleep after their late night.

'Hmmmm, about that ...' Eva said.

'Hello, sis,' came her brother's voice from Eva's end of the call. Rachel was lost for words as she put two and two together and got Kevin and Eva in bed.

'Well, I never! Please can you put Eva back on?'

'Don't judge,' Eva insisted.

'I wouldn't dare, so long as ...' Rachel was going to say, so long as Eva was happy. If all they wanted was some fun together then so be it, and if they found they wanted more then great, but she didn't want to see either of them hurt. She didn't want to ruin their post-coital morning, though, and kept her thoughts to herself. 'No rush, I'll see you when I see you. Lydia's holding the fort at the office.'

Rachel smiled, thinking of Eva and Kevin, and hoped it was indeed the start of something. In spite of her protestations about being an independent woman, Eva wanted someone to look after her and Kevin wanted someone to be better for. She could warn her friend about his past but actually, on reflection, they had trodden similar paths and might well be perfect for one another. How had Rachel not seen it before?

Rachel picked up her to-do list. It was two pages long. She really should get out of bed. She ticked off 1. CALL EVA.

Now for 2. CALL CLINIC.

She Googled the number for the Wolverton Centre. After a glut of automated options, she was connected to a real person. She gave her name and date of birth and waited for the computer to catch up. The receptionist said she should have already received a text with the results, but confirmed Rachel had been given the all clear. Thirty-four years old and still no sexually transmitted diseases (bouts of cystitis and thrush aside)! She celebrated with a small whoop.

She looked back at her list: 3. CALL GAZEBO GARY. Rachel decided that could wait until after a cup of coffee. Items 4, 5, and 6 could too.

Rachel floated down the stairs on a calm cloud until she heard David wheezing, groaning and gasping for air. Renewed guilt washed over her. He still showed the bruises from when she'd attempted to administer CPR to his apparently lifeless body. Scared of what she might find, she ran into the kitchen.

'What are you doing?' Rachel watched him trying to wrestle Neville into a submissive position. There was an empty box of chocolates on the floor. And David was trying to smell the cat's breath.

'Did you leave the chocolates out?' Rachel accused him.

'I didn't mean t—'

'You know chocolate can be fatal for cats.'

'Yes, Rachel, I know it can kill them,' David said flatly. 'Like I said, I didn't mean—'

'You're going to have to take Neville and Oscar to the vet's straight away! I've got to clear up after the wedding ...' Rachel looked at her watch, pretending to be pressed for time. Any excuse. She didn't feel ready to see Dr Luke just yet.

'I'm on my way out too,' David said unhelpfully.

Rachel didn't ask where.

'What's wrong?' he asked.

'The vet is a dog man.'

'And?'

'And nothing. It's your fault an entire box of Belgian chocolates might or might not have been devoured by one or both of our cats.' Rachel hoped David didn't notice her blush at the memory of the dinner date she shared with Dr Luke, and how she felt when he kissed her on the lips as he put her in a taxi.

David left the kitchen, mumbling he was going to be late.

'The least you could do is help me get them into the cages!' she called after him. It was too late, David was already out the front door.

Rachel was left in the empty house, accepting it was over between them and it was never coming back. She'd thought she could win her husband all over again, but it hadn't worked.

They should sell the house and divide their possessions. David could have the coffee machine if he wanted. She was done. He would always be a part of her life but sadly not of her future. She hoped with time their friendship would survive. She braced herself at the prospect of encountering Amelia-Rose at family gatherings. Or maybe Rachel would be slowly phased out and would have to see Jojo and Beth in secret.

She knew she needed to have it out with David once and for all. It was time to call time. If it wasn't his birthday weekend coming up, she might already have had the courage to say all the things she was thinking.

Rachel called the vet's office and asked for an emergency appointment. Her fear of seeing Dr Luke had subsided. She wondered if she had time to apply lipstick and mascara?

Neville and Oscar had been living the high life. Rachel had offered them treats every time she felt low – she had been comfort-feeding them. She felt immense remorse at being labelled a feeder, one of those people she had seen in a documentary. Admittedly, it had concentrated on human relationships, but she was obviously a person who gleaned pleasure from feeding others with complete disregard for their obesity or compromised health. She loved to feed her (not-so) little cats. They danced around her legs when she shook the treats tin. They loved her so, but Dr Luke had practically accused her of killing them with kindness.

Rachel collected the cat boxes from the garage and braced herself for drama. She sympathised with their plight, she wouldn't want to be shut up in a cage either. She went to close the kitchen door to thwart any dashes for freedom, just in time to hear David come blustering back in through the front door.

'I'm here, I'll take them.' He swiftly placed both cats in their respective boxes without further altercation. To her surprise, David kissed Rachel on both cheeks and proclaimed that he loved her, he loved the cats and he loved their life together. She watched as he carried both cats, one box in each hand, to the car and drove off.

David

35

David couldn't sleep after the wedding and stayed up after Rachel went to bed. He poured himself a final nightcap and opened a box of Belgian chocolates, an early birthday present from his mum. 'They were on offer,' she'd told him.

He was distracted by thoughts of Rachel. What about the DJ? She'd said they had recently rekindled their friendship. How recently? How rekindled? How friendly? Rachel wouldn't invite an ex-boyfriend to DJ for Jojo's wedding if something was going on. Would she? Or had she hired him *because* something was going on? David wished he hadn't deleted the message from that clinic. He needed to study it for clues.

Grudgingly, he'd accepted Gavin 'The Gecko of Grunge' Thompson's business card and now he was glad he had. He didn't have to investigate, the card provided direct links to all of Gavin's social media. There were already photos from Jojo's wedding posted including a selfie of Gavin and Rachel together with the comment 'ThanX to the hostess with the mostess. Gr8 gal!' followed by a row of red hearts.

David's last whisky was relegated to a penultimate drink as he added a second tot to his glass. He thought he knew Rachel's type, and Gavin wasn't it. Except he was wrong because once, apparently, at university for six weeks Gavin had been. David had lost all hope. And thought maybe the answer might lie at the bottom of the bottle. He added a third tot of the smoky Laphroaig to his glass.

David hardly slept. He woke hourly to find his heart pounding. He lamented his over-indulgence in food and alcohol, and acknowledged his sheer mental exhaustion, and prayed he wasn't having a panic attack. He tried breathing exercises and finally crashed to the tune of the dawn chorus. He woke suddenly after two hours of much-needed REM, dragged himself out of bed and switched on the coffee machine. It was clearly a triple espresso morning, but with the Cardiac Physiologist's advice ringing in his ears, he reduced it to one large espresso. He asked the cats to quieten their meowing, as he explained to them how much alcohol he had foolishly consumed. He was adding a layer of cat biscuits to each of their bowls when he spied the overturned box of chocolates. He tried to recall how many of them he'd eaten. It was more than a few. But the whole box? He shut the kitchen door as he circled Neville, who was chomping happily on his biscuits and caught unawares as David scooped him up. Neville struggled to escape, and David was shouting at him to stay still until Rachel interrupted their clinch.

She was near-hysterical, reasoning Neville and Oscar were both poisoned and on the brink of death. She demanded David take them to the vet at once. He momentarily shut down. It was all too much: the hangover, the lack of caffeine, plus the hopelessness of the situation – he had to get out of there.

David left the house having decided to walk the two miles to the station. He was a mess. He checked his pockets for cigarettes knowing he didn't have any. It wasn't fair to call Jojo, she was leaving for her honeymoon. They were spending two nights in the village of Portmeirion, home of the television series *The Prisoner*. And to make matters worse (for Jojo), Beth's parents had decided to join them there, to make up for missing Beth's big day. They had proclaimed that a honeymoon didn't need to be a private affair when one bride was already with child.

As if by magic, David's phone started to ring. He was delighted to see Jojo's name on the display.

'Hey, I was just thinking about—'

'I can't talk for long,' she whispered, 'we're about to leave, and I've promised no phones. Listen, I was wrong. I know I told you to slow down with Rachel, but I was wrong. You know what got her attention the first time around – BIG FUCK-OFF DISPLAYS of affection, spontaneity and a whirlwind proposal. That's what worked. I was wrong. You have to woo the shit out of her! And tell her everything, and I mean everything. Fuck what I said before, she needs the honest you. Give her your heart, your soul, your entire being.'

'What's changed your mind? What has she said?'

'Just make it better! I'm counting on you not to fuck this up. And, David, whatever you do – do *not* let her near the vet. I've got to go.'

'What about the vet?'

But Jojo had ended the call. David looked at his watch. He was already going to be late for the office, what difference did it make if he was late or really late? He jogged back to the house, out of breath by the time he reached the front door and struggled for his keys.

'I'm back,' he shouted. Without any fuss, David put the cats in their cages and left for the vet's. He told Rachel he loved her as a parting shot. He presumed it was too little, too late, but Jojo had given him an injection of hope.

As it was an emergency Dr Parry-Wilson agreed to see Neville and Oscar during his lunch hour. David interrupted the vet finishing an avocado wrap.

'I'm vegetarian but I'm thinking of going vegan.'

David nodded. *Of course he was going vegan*, he thought to himself sarcastically. He was going to reply with some controversial facts about veganism and the environment and climate change, but the moment passed.

'Hello, Neville and Oscar, what have we got here?' Luke talked directly to the sulking felines and then turned his attention to David. 'So you know what to expect when you see the invoice, we take poisoning, potential or otherwise, very seriously. I'm going to do a physical exam and take blood and urine samples. It's going to be around a hundred and fifty pounds. Each.'

David hoped his face didn't react negatively to the £300 bill coming his way.

'How about I throw in an ECG for free?'

David didn't know if the vet was joking.

'Sorry, in all the rush, let me introduce myself. I'm the new vet in charge, Dr Parry-Wilson. Please call me Luke. And you must be Kevin.'

'No. No, I'm David.'

'Oh, Rachel's ex-husband, yeah? Nice to know the pet-sharing—'

'What? No. You're mistaken. Not *ex*. Very much married. Her husband. I'm Rachel's husband. And she's my wife!' He shouldn't have to explain his circumstances to Dr Parry-Wilson but it felt very necessary. David heard the words tumbling from his mouth while his hands gesticulated wildly to hammer home the emotion he was trying to convey. 'I'll have you know that Rachel and I are very happily married. We're going to renew our vows and go to Paris!' David felt like a Bond villain, giving away his master plan without any agreement from Rachel. 'Not all at the same time,' he added. 'And you know what? I'm taking Neville and Oscar somewhere else. I don't want you anywhere near my cats again. Come on, boys, we're going.'

Neville and Oscar were shrunken versions of their garden psychopath personas but showed no inclination to help David as he tried to cajole the cats back into their cages. Neville was suffering post-traumatic shock and dug his claws into David's jeans where they took root in his right thigh. Luke moved forward to help.

'Don't touch him! Don't *you* ever touch him again' David warned.

Luke stood uncomfortably as he watched David's attempts to coerce the cats back into their transport cages.

David's face reddened as Luke tried to look anywhere but at the violence playing out on his treatment table. It took nearly ten minutes for the cats to be rehoused securely in their cages, but finally David was finished. He uttered a breezy goodbye and made an unwieldy exit with a cat box in each hand.

Neville and Oscar stayed silent as David sat in the car and asked them what he should do next.

David missed Rachel. He missed it all. And the worst of it was, he didn't know how to get it back. Jojo had advised him to follow his heart, but it was now fractured.

David was fussing in the kitchen when Rachel opened the front door and instead was greeted by Neville and Oscar.

'My boys! You're home!' he heard her exclaim, happy to see them alive.

They curled their tails around her legs, which David interpreted as protest against the drama he had caused at the vet's. He was relieved they couldn't tell on him.

David waited as Rachel she dropped her handbag and kicked off her heels in the direction of the shoe cupboard under the stairs, but they didn't quite make it to their destination. She went through to the conservatory to take in the sunset.

He stood behind her and put his arms over her shoulders. She squeezed his hand. Was it in solidarity? In love? Or was it a pity squeeze, and she was planning to tell him she was leaving him for the 'Guru of Grunge'?

David retreated to the kitchen and reappeared with two Blood Orange Martinis.

BLOOD ORANGE MARTINI
50 ml blood orange juice
50 ml Vodka
30 ml Cointreau
50 ml fresh lime juice

He had prepared pan-fried duck in cherry sauce, one of his three signature dishes. Before she could ask what the special occasion was, he clinked his glass against hers.

'You'll never guess what?' Rachel asked.

Questions ran through David's head. *You're leaving me? You're bonking the vet? You want a divorce? You want to see other people? You fucked the wedding DJ?*

He took a gulp of his drink to steady himself.

'Give up?'

David nodded.

'Guess who got lucky at the wedding?'

God, you did sleep with the DJ! At my own sister's wedding. That is inappropriate on so many levels. Since when was Rachel cruel? And when could she have found the time?

'Give up? Eva and Kevin!'

'Thank God for that!' David was relieved to find he was not the answer to the *guess who lost their marriage overnight* game.

Rachel looked at him oddly.

'I mean, that's great, isn't it? You always say Kevin needs someone more brain-appropriate,' David continued.

'It is great, isn't it!' She clapped her hands and asked, 'What's the special occasion?'

'Does there have to be one? I wanted to thank you for being you. And for what an amazing job you did for Jojo and Beth. Thank you. It really was a day to remember!'

'Sounds like you'd forgotten how brilliant I am?' Rachel winked at him.

'You're not going to ask about the vet's?' he enquired.

Rachel swooped down to gather Neville in her arms and swung him like a baby. 'I didn't need to ask – look at them, they're alive! Was it expensive? Do you want me to do dessert?'

David had so many questions to ask but was afraid of the answers. He nodded half-heartedly and Rachel collected the ingredients for a dark chocolate sauce.

David served the duck. It was a perfect pink in the centre. 'Rare Duck Pink' could be its own dedicated Pantone.

'You know, call me an old romantic, but what with the wedding, and … everything … maybe we should think about … only if you want to … We could renew our vows if you wanted. Before friends and family this time. What do you think?' he asked.

David, stop waffling!

Rachel

36

When Rachel arrived at the office, Eva skirted around the subject of Kevin.

Rachel raised a hand. 'I don't need to know about what went on with my brother unless it's serious and not a one-off bit of fun. I don't want the sordid details. I don't want to hear a whisper of sweet nothings. And knowing you both as I do ... No, I've said enough.'

Eva mimed putting a lock on her mouth and throwing away the key. 'You okay?' she asked.

'Eva, I'm glad you're here. I feel like I need to confess everything to David. It's all such a mess. I'm so embarrassed. You know the vet—'

'The dashing Dr Doolittle? Go on.'

'Well, this morning it seemed that one or both of the cats might have eaten chocolate.'

'Is it potentially fatal, like it is for dogs?' Eva interrupted.

'Exactly. I couldn't bear to face Dr Luke, so I sent David. Well, I asked him to go but he left to catch a train, then ten minutes later came running back in superhero mode and took the cats. He was acting all magnanimous, like he's up for Husband of the Year or something.'

Eva cackled. She went into the office kitchen and brought out Jaffa Cakes.

'What happened then?'

'Nothing.'

'Nothing? What did David say about the dishy vet?'

'*Nada*. He cooked me a special dinner, made me a cocktail. And it was a lovely night ...'

'Oh, it was, was it?' Eva smiled.

'David, in a roundabout way, suggested we renew our vows.'

Eva gasped and clapped her hands. 'It's worked! The plan's worked!'

Rachel urged her cheeks to stop reddening and asked to change the subject, saying she didn't know what she wanted anymore.

'Can I say something? You might not want to hear it, but I think you avoided the vet because you no longer want revenge. You want to get married to David and stay married!'

'No!'

'Yes! Admit it!'

'I don't know! I mean, maybe!' Rachel pretended the thought had just crossed her mind.

'It's okay, Rach, you don't have to be a mean, bitter old shrew just because I am!'

'As if! And not according to my brother! But we're not going to talk about him.' Rachel winked. 'Do you think I'm weak, a walkover?'

'No, but only you can walk in your shoes. You have to do what's right for you and no one else. How did it happen? Do you think he suspects you're on to him?'

'No! I don't think so. Or I didn't – not until you just said it …' They were interrupted by Rachel's mobile ringing. Eva gestured for Rachel to take the call, and returned to her desk.

'We're back!' Jojo sang down the phone to Rachel. She continued, 'what's that … you need to meet me today? I'll see what I can do.'

Rachel was puzzled and asked Jojo what she was talking about.

Jojo whispered that she needed to escape. She loved Beth's parents, but only in thirty-minute segments on Skype when they were all the way across the Atlantic Ocean. The last seventy-two hours had depleted her reserves of politeness. And please, please, please, could Rachel save her?

Rachel was delighted to step in. Jojo suggested they meet for a coffee at The Brew.

Jojo gave Rachel the biggest hug.

'I've missed you,' she said, stroking Rachel's hair. 'This is cute – it suits you.'

'Yours too!'

They ordered coffee. A cappuccino for Rachel and an Americano for Jojo.

'How was the honeymoon?'

'I'm not sure I'm ready to go there. Let's just say it wasn't the romantic break I was hoping for. A new wife, horrid morning sickness, the Texan in-laws from hell, and ten hours on a train without a working toilet! Do you know what Beth's dad said when we got back?'

Rachel shook her head.

Jojo attempted a Texan drawl. 'Excuse the poor accent, "*Now can I take a dump in peace? We've been on a train since, I don't know when, yesterday some time.*" I'm sorry, I shouldn't complain. Ed's actually lovely, except when he's overtired or in Wales it seems. But more importantly, and please don't interrupt, I need to apologise . . .'

'What do you need to—' Rachel tried to ask.

'For everything.' Jojo released her inner neuroses. She started at the beginning – when she and Beth first decided to have a baby, they were so scared it wouldn't work, or at least wouldn't work first time, they'd made a vow not to tell anyone. 'And then when the egg fertilised and grew, it was even more special with just the two of us knowing about it. But we completely abandoned you, didn't we? You're my best friend and you're amazing . . . The wedding was perfect. Thank you! A million times thank you. But I realise I've been so wrapped up in my own life, I didn't stop for a minute to check how you were doing. I wasn't even aware you and David were having problems. Not until—'

They fell silent while the waiter delivered their coffee order.

'I'm a selfish friend. Will you forgive me?' Jojo said when he had gone.

Rachel weighed up this speech and joked, 'Well, I suppose you have been horribly self-centred . . .'

'Ha! How about I give you my shortbread biscuit?'

'Deal!' They hugged again.

'Now tell me, what has my stupid brother been up to? Do you think you can get through this? I've already told him that if anything happens, we get to keep you and he has to find another family.'

Rachel was warmed by her friend's loyalty to her.

'Well . . . and I guess this is down to you . . . I've been besieged with flowers and special dinners lately, and last night he floated the idea of us renewing our vows.'

Jojo tried not to take credit for that but Rachel could see she was inwardly jumping for joy. 'Dare I buy a hat?'

Rachel tried to conjure a smile, to give her friend her biggest, widest beam. But it wouldn't come. Instead Jojo brought Rachel to her chest and gave her a bear hug.

'What is it? Is it about the vet Eva was—'

'No! That was just Eva being, well, Eva. It was smack bang in the middle of the Hoo-hah with David. Luke-handsome-vet-extraordinaire suggested a drink and I said yes.'

'And?'

'And nothing.'

'Got a picture?'

Rachel Googled the veterinary surgery's website and showed Jojo the picture of Luke on the *About Us* page. He had a stethoscope around his neck and was holding the world's longest sausage dog up to his face.

Jojo laughed. 'Wow, he really is good-looking. What a big sausage!' she joked. 'And you're really saying nothing happened?'

'Really, truly, seriously. Dinner, that's all. With not even a hint of tongue.' Rachel tried to make light of this conversation but she was only kidding herself. Luke *had* kissed her. She had fantasised about her tongue touching Dr Luke's, and she'd be lying if she said she didn't find him very attractive. 'Jojo, be honest. Do you think David's cheated before this? You'd tell me, wouldn't you? My whole adult life hasn't been a lie, has it?'

'What?'

'Do you think David's—'

'What did you say?'

'Do you think he'll do it again?'

'He's cheated on you? David has?'

'Yes, why, what did you think he'd ...'

'I *think* I'm going mad? My brother, David Ross Chatsworth, has cheated on you, Rachel?

'Please, for the love of God, keep it down.'

The waiter was hovering again. Rachel waved him away. Jojo was visibly fuming.

'Wait, if you didn't know about *that*, what did you think was going on?'

'David told me that your wedding might not have been strictly legal.'

'So he knew about that all along?'

'I don't think so. Something about an admin error. I got the impression he only found out later.'

'I've been so stupid.' Rachel filled Jojo in on the whole messy story. She started with the kiss she'd seen in the high street, and her trying to follow David; the sneaked calls and his nights away. 'It gets worse. I bought all this stupid lingerie and he didn't even come home that night.' Rachel breathed in deeply, hoping not to cry. She flapped her hands to cool her face, which then garnered further unwanted attention from the waiter. Jojo shooed him away curtly.

'When was this?' Jojo asked.

'I dunno. Before the bank holiday?'

'He might have been with me.'

'What?'

'He's been worried he was going to lose you – like *really* worried. Now I know the real reason, no wonder!'

'Really? Do you promise? You're not covering for him?'

Jojo stated formidably, 'I swear on my beautiful wife, I will never lie to you and I will certainly not lie *for* him.'

'And then … oh my God, this is awful! Maybe I shouldn't say.'

Jojo tried to call over the waiter but he wasn't falling for that trick again. 'I'll be back in a sec'.' She went to the bar and came back with an ice bucket, a bottle of rosé and two glasses.

'I bumped into his girlfriend. She was at a hen weekend at the same spa and I went batshit – and I mean absolutely batshit. I feel sick thinking about it.' Rachel covered her face with her hands. 'Jojo, I'm so confused, I don't know what I want. Sometimes I want everything to return to normal and at other times, I wonder if the relationship is even worth fighting for? I kept expecting him to leave. But he stayed, and then when he suggested Paris, and renewing our vows, from the bottom of my heart I wanted to say yes, but I couldn't help thinking about him with this other woman. I've got to listen to that, right?'

'You sure do, kiddo. So what are you going to do? What did you say to him?'

'I said we'd talk after his birthday.'

Rachel couldn't find the courage to say what she was thinking, but she wanted to thank Jojo for trying to make David a better husband. Thank her for the candles, and the flowers, and the dinners. But she didn't want a husband who had to be taught how to be romantic.

She also wanted to say she'd miss her sisters-in-law because both Jojo and Beth meant the world to her. And she would miss spoiling the soon-to-be-baby-on-board, the niece or nephew who wouldn't be hers to spoil. And she wanted to say: *let's stay friends*. But she didn't say any of those things. She didn't want to make promises she might not be able to keep.

Rachel blotted her blotchy cheeks with a napkin and took a deep breath.

'Are you going to be okay?' Jojo asked.

'You know what? I am. I don't need a David, or even a Dr Luke, or anyone else. I'm ready to be on my own.'

'Good for you! You're so strong, Rachel. You remind me of Norma when you're like this.'

Rachel rolled her eyes.

'I'm going to kill him! I'm going to fucking kill him,' Jojo said to herself.

When Rachel got home she saw David had left a note saying he was going to his sister's. That might be the last anyone saw of him. Rachel would not want to be in the path of Jojo's wrath. She'd never seen her sister-in-law so angry.

David

37

David stood at the bar waiting for Jojo. She'd texted to say traffic was bad and to order her a G&T with a fancy T. David didn't know which tonics were deemed 'fancy'. He selected the one with the nicest bottle, when Jojo appeared and ordered a different one.

David was about to say hello. He was going to ask after Beth and the in-laws. He was going to ask about the honeymoon. He was going to ask what time she was coming over at the weekend for his birthday. He was going to make conversation. Instead Jojo pushed him down into a chair.

'Sit down. I've got some questions for you. First, why did you cheat on your beautiful wife? Second, how could you do that to Rachel? And for the hat trick, what the fuck were you thinking?'

'What? How do you …? But—'

David was transported back in time to when he was up in front of the headmaster for letting off firecrackers by the staff car park. He squirmed in his seat, praying that his mum wasn't going to be called.

'When you came crying to me because you thought your marriage might be up the spout, you didn't think to mention your mistress? This whole time I've been thinking that it was all some innocent misunderstanding. But it's not, is it? God, I can't even look at you right now.' Jojo downed her drink and left the table to go and stand by the door. David could see her tapping her feet, working out if she would stay or go. There was nothing he could say that could change Jojo's opinion of him right now. She nodded for him to follow her.

They walked along by the river in silence.

'What happened?' Jojo eventually asked.

And David told her how he was wooed by Amelia-Rose, and how young and sexy she had made him feel, until Jojo stopped him and told him off for sounding smug and unrepentant. He apologised and tried to redeem himself. He explained how lying to Rachel had made him feel awful. How he'd punished himself in the gym. How he still loved Rachel, and now that he'd tasted the forbidden fruit he was certain he'd never be tempted again.

'Do you still fancy her?'

'I … It's comfortable. But, you know, it's not fireworks going off every night. It's been a long time—'

'That's a no then. Do you still say, *I love you*?'

'Look, it's weird having to say this to your sister. Yes, I love her. Yes, I fancy the arse off her. I might not be good at remembering to tell her. But I don't need to be told what a bastard I am. I know what a tosser looks like – I have a mirror. I fucked up.'

'My advice? Let her go. I'd prefer to be dumped at thirty-four than forty-four, especially if I found out my partner had porked some young strumpet.'

'How do you know she's young?'

' – I took a punt. You've always been obsessed with new and shiny gadgets. I'm betting she's no different. She's as beautiful as a doll, with a carnal sexuality straight out of a Victorian bodice ripper. Am I right?'

'It's not like that.' David had run out of steam. He didn't have the bravado to answer her honestly. Jojo would see through him straight away and would call him out on it. And now he could add *arsehole who disappointed his younger sister* to his ever-growing list of flaws.

'Is this helping?' Jojo asked. She tried not to sound judgemental. 'Or is it too close to the bone?'

David wasn't sure.

'Okay – all you need to do is be honest.'

'Why?'

'Rachel's an intelligent woman: share your woes about getting older. I see you're more salt than pepper these days. She's still hot and if you can't see that—'

'It was a moment of madness. Like an out of control hourglass and I was unable to curb the free flow of sand.'

Jojo laughed at his absurd pomposity.

'I promise I've learned my lesson.'

'Have you cheated before?'

David shook his head. They headed for a small riverside pub. It wasn't the type of establishment that served decent wine or stocked fancy tonics. David ordered them two pints of Doom Bar.

Jojo told him, 'I thought you two were happier than ever. You said you were thinking of trying for a baby.'

'We are! I mean we were planning to … I made a horrible mistake. I hadn't touched new flesh in years and it was frankly exhilarating. But it wasn't real. It was a sexual out-of-body experience. I don't know what I was thinking. I can't explain it. Haven't you ever been tempted?'

'All the time, but then I remember the blonde bombshell waiting for me at home. You could have told me about the affair, you know?' Jojo was deadly serious.

'It wasn't an affair!'

'And you're not still seeing this other woman?'

'It was a one-off! A one-night-stand! I haven't seen her since. Well, once in the street. It was nothing. It meant nothing.'

David downed the remainder of the warm English ale and stared miserably into the empty pint glass. He explained everything, right from the beginning. 'I'm sorry. I'm sorry my dick got caught in an extramarital black hole.'

'That's not what Rachel thinks. She believes you've got a mistress. That's right, she thinks that you had an affair, and you're STILL having an affair. She thinks you want your cake and to eat it. She thinks you're a sick fuck for continuing to lead on two women. She's met the girl-friend. Yeah – the redhead. They've shared words. It's OVER! It's too late. I told you not to fuck it up, but you just couldn't help yourself, could you? Do the decent thing and stop playing with Rachel's feelings and hurting her. You need to let her go.'

David couldn't make eye contact with his sister. It was too much to take in. He didn't answer her, he had everything and nothing to say. David took a large gulp of Jojo's pint. He was a failure. Here he was – one week shy of his forty-sixth birthday and everything he wanted was destroyed. The one thing he was scared of most was happening. He couldn't undo his actions. He was a shit, and the fear and the shame of everyone knowing the truth, well, that cat was well and truly out of the bag. The only person he wanted to protect from harm, Rachel, had found out, and now she wouldn't forgive him.

At the bar he ordered two more drinks and saw an advert in the local paper that piqued his interest.

'We need to see a man about a boat.' David showed Jojo the newspaper.

She ignored him. 'Not so long ago you asked me what it is women want? I've given it a lot of thought. How about: not to be thought of as a puzzle to be solved. Not to be used or taken for granted. Not to be fooled. Women don't want to be part of an equation; it's not Men + flowers + compliments + love = sex. They want communica-tion, collaboration and companionship. They want their partners to be present. And, above all, not to fuck other women.'

'Noted. But, to be fair, it was you who advised me to buy her flowers.'

'Shut up, David.'

Rachel

38

Eva smoothed the tablecloth and Rachel gently pushed her away from the table.

'Please! It's not your job, you're here as a guest!'

The doorbell rang. Most of the guests had now arrived. They were only waiting for Jojo and Beth, Beth's parents and Kevin.

'Do you want me to get that?' Eva asked.

'Funny! Please enjoy yourself.' Rachel could see her friend was trying to act nonchalant when at any moment Kevin was going to arrive and blow Eva's *cool girl* cover.

Jojo and Beth both beamed when Rachel opened the door to them. She couldn't wait to have a proper conversation with them, but that would have to wait.

'Wow, look at you two – married life obviously suits you!'

Jojo gave Rachel a hug that was too long and whispered into her ear, 'Let's not tell Mum or Norma yet.'

Rachel laughed, and agreed that David's birthday was designated a drama-free day!

Jojo ground her teeth as behind them a giant of a man complained about the cool English weather and asked if there would be sweaters at this party.

Jojo rolled her eyes. 'Rachel, have you met Ed, my *hilarious* father-in-law?' Ed it seemed did not get British sarcasm. 'He would die for a Long Island Iced Tea.'

'Ed, welcome—'

'Rachel, I heard a lot about you. Rachel this, Rachel that.'

'Please come in.' She closed the front door.

She whispered to Jojo, 'A Long Island Iced Tea is just the contents of the drinks cabinet with a splash of orange and a splash of Coke, right?'

'That'll do it.'

Rachel accompanied Jojo's new in-laws through to the conservatory and asked David to prepare the drinks. Jojo disappeared into the kitchen to help him.

'Hi, I'm Rachel.' She held out her hand to Beth's mum.

'Don't be offering me no hand! Come here an' give me a hug. I'm Patrice, but all my friends call me Patty.' Rachel wondered if she and Patty were now friends? Could she call her Patty too? Then call-me-Patty grabbed her in a squeeze so tight Rachel felt her ribs compress. 'I heard you did a great job on the wedding, and it was your idea to get people to record video messages for us? That was so thoughtful. And look at my lovely daughter – you sure are a guardian angel looking over her, and I'm glad she has found love in your family!'

Rachel turned to look at Beth, who was trying and failing to balance on a barstool. 'Pregnancy suits her,' Rachel agreed.

The doorbell rang again. Finally, it was Kevin. Eva blushed like a teenager with a crush.

'Go get him.' Rachel could see her friend was itching to.

Jojo snuck up behind Rachel. 'Since when are Kevin and Eva a couple?'

'Ha! Since the magic that was your wedding.'

'I see what you're doing.'

'What?' Rachel asked innocently.

'You've already lined up a new sister-in-law!'

'Don't worry, no one can replace you. You and Beth, you're two for the price of one!'

Kevin kissed Rachel and Jojo on the cheek and grabbed hold of Eva's hand. To the shock of everyone watching, he took the opportunity to introduce her to his mother.

PEACH BELLINI RECIPE
Ripe peaches, stoned and diced
25 ml fresh peach purée
100 ml Champagne/Prosecco/sparkling wine
1 tablespoon freshly squeezed lemon juice

About an hour in, Rachel refilled her glass and gazed at the guests celebrating David's forty-sixth birthday. It made her teary-eyed to think that this was the last time she would be with her friends and family in this house. It was the last time she would celebrate David's birthday by his side. It would be the last time these people would think of David and Rachel as a couple. She had resigned herself to the fact that she might lose some of these friends. Rachel looked at the couples. She thought about their marriages, the pitfalls some of them had survived, and wondered why hers couldn't work. Marriages survived worse things than infidelity. Some of these people had been able to rebuild trust. Then she looked especially at the second wives and husbands. They had managed to make new lives and new memories for themselves. Would it be so difficult for her?

David crept up behind her and put his chin on her shoulder. She could sense the sadness emanating from him without seeing his expression. She turned and clinked his glass with hers.

'Happy birthday!'

'Cheers.' He looked drained. 'Thanks for everything.'

'You're welcome – happy birthday.'

'No, I don't mean the party. I mean everything.'

'Barry brought Gina. Are they making another go of it?' Rachel asked.

David nodded. 'You look beautiful.'

'I'm going to see if Eva and Lydia ...' Rachel escaped from his melancholy mood.

She had rallied the troops from work and now thanked them for coming to celebrate David's birthday. They too were family and now she would need them more than ever. She'd promised to do right by them. Her clients had remained largely unaware of Rachel's personal difficulties, with only one jumping ship. Heck, you can't win them all.

'Eva, have you given any thought to what I said about us being business partners?'

She nodded. 'I'm in.'

'We'd have to rebrand. What sounds better, Keatley Jenkins? Jenkins Keatley? Or KJ?'

'What about Sunshine Events?'

'Sunshine Events,' Rachel repeated. 'I like it.'

David smiled at Rachel. He tapped a spoon against his glass and demanded everyone's attention. The next few minutes passed in a blur. When David asked Rachel to marry him her friends and family looked happy and hopeful, even her mother was smiling. She was unprepared for his proposal, but could hardly turn him down publicly. Instead she opted for a courteous nod that was received with rapturous applause by everyone around.

Afterwards Rachel went to the bathroom to splash cold water on her face. She added a dusting of bronzer and a swish of red lip stain. 'You can do this,' she told herself as she eased her face into a smile.

David

39

David was pleasantly surprised to see Barry had arrived with Gina, and it looked like they had more than made amends. Proud as punch, Barry told David he was back in the marital bed, and Gina elbowed him in the ribs.

Gina gave David a kiss on the cheek and wished him a happy birthday, afterwards whispering in his ear, 'Thanks for looking after B.'

'Thanks for coming,' David said.

'We couldn't miss your birthday, mate.' Barry said, as he slapped David on the back.

'What did you get me?'

'Our presence is your present, isn't it Gina!'

'Does Rachel know about the boat yet?' Gina asked.

'Sshhhhhh! Not a word.' David checked Rachel was out of earshot.

Barry told him not to worry. 'Now, let's get this party started!'

David could hear a commotion at the front door. He'd been expecting Beth's parents and here they were, literally larger than life. It didn't help that her father was dressed in khaki green; he looked like the Jolly Green Giant on a hunting trip.

David held out his hand, which was shaken so violently it felt like it had been through a tumble dryer.

Jojo followed him into the kitchen and gave him a forgiving smile and a big hug. He was relieved to have his confidante back. He explained he didn't want Jojo to have to keep any secrets from her best friend. And he also didn't want to jeopardise his relationship with his sister. She shooed away his apologies.

'Last night we took Ed and Patty to Pizza Express. You know, the one in Covent Garden. Ed likes jazz and everyone likes pizza, what could go wrong? The first thing he does is grumble the music coming from the cellar bar is too loud. And when the food arrives, he calls over the manager to complain. He points to the unsliced pizza and asks, "What are we, barbarians?" Ed looks to us to back him up. We all smile politely and the manager has a waiter slice Ed's pizza for him.'

David laughed as he finished preparing two Long Island Iced Teas for his new in-laws. Jojo tasted one. It needed more whisky.

'What are we, barbarians?' David mimicked. 'But I already put—'

'Trust me. It'll quieten him down.'

David did as he was told and received no complaints from either recipient. Patrice thanked him and insisted he call her Patty. Jojo tried to introduce David to her new in-laws, but Ed brushed him away as if he was a hovering waiter. Ed was busy reiterating the story of their delayed flight and how it was the fault of some idiot at airport security.

'They were meant to change at Atlanta and the whole of ATL had to be closed down because some jock joked about having a bomb in his carry-on. IT WAS A FRICKIN' JOKE! But could anyone see that? I feel for that college kid – now he's all over that face-tweet. So we were diverted to LAX, just missed the flight to London, couldn't get on the one to Paris and missed our only daughter's wedding.'

Patrice was an older version of Beth. She was also tall and blonde, with a lovely calm disposition. She must have heard Ed's stories countless times, but kept her hand loyally on his arm and smiled along with his raucous gags.

David clinked his glass to get everyone's attention. 'When Rachel asked me what I wanted for my birthday, I couldn't think of anything. Because I'm lucky, I already have everything I want. But then I thought about it. And actually, I do have one question I want to ask.' David glanced at Norma and once again regretted not consulting her in advance.

He looked to Jojo, who shook her head.

Beth's face crumpled.

Rachel stared on aghast.

David dropped to his knees. In the palm of his out-stretched hand, he held a turquoise ring box. He looked up with excited eyes and a wide smile.

'Mrs Chatsworth, will you marry me?'

Barry added 'again' for humour.

'Again,' David repeated.

'Ha! Who cheated?' Roger heckled cheerfully. An awkward pause followed. He quickly clarified that he was only joking, and went on to over-explain that the only couple he knew to renew their vows did it after someone – who was he kidding, it's always the fella – had experimented with some extramarital how's-your-father!, he said with a big wink.

David nervously laughed off any suggestion of infidelity.

Rachel stood frozen to the spot as he pulled at the white silk ribbon and opened the small box for her. Inside was a Tiffany ring, encrusted with diamonds and pearls. He kissed her hard on the lips before he felt her squirm out of his arms.

'Another wedding!' Lillian cheered.

'One we're invited to this time?' Norma said sardonically. Beneath the sarcasm David could see she was delighted.

Rachel nodded. 'I'll be back in a minute.'

David was filling glasses with fizz when it occurred to him that Rachel hadn't actually said yes.

When all the guests had left, the house was full of empty bottles and mountains of washing up. Rachel and David retired to the sofa. Without thinking, they let their legs intertwine. David untangled himself and paced the living room. He downed a glass of flat fizz.

'I need to explain something. I know you know. And . . . And I should have told you. It should have come from me. I didn't know we weren't married. Not at first anyway. No one said we had to get the marriage certified.'

Rachel snorted into her glass.

'I found out about ten years ago,' David continued. 'When I was organising the pension. Everything was in both our names – we'd never needed to prove we were legally man and wife until then. Your dad had just been rushed to hospital. When he died, I didn't want to rock the boat.'

'So why didn't you tell me later?'

'As time passed – what did it matter? We were happy. We already shared our lives. It's just a piece of paper. I didn't want anything to change.'

Rachel pulled her cardigan closer around her, shielding herself from the emotional ambush.

'What should I have said? *"Guess what? We're not actually married."* Maybe you'd have seen it as a reprieve – you know, time served. End of a chapter, move on, get a new husband. A better one than me, that's for sure. Maybe even one who knows your favourite colour.'

'Who cares what my favourite colour is?' Rachel asked.

'If I was subjected to one of those immigration interviews, it's safe to say it wouldn't go well. I know nothing about you. I don't know what colour your hairbrush is and I see it twice a day. I don't know your favourite food or drink. I don't know your favourite flower. I get to the florist and I ask the girl to recommend a bunch, or as a safe bet, buy lilies. Don't you see? I still don't know, after all these years. And yet you still love me and look after me. You make my favourite dinners. You buy my preferred beer and make sure it's chilled in the fridge. You know everything about me.'

Rachel scoffed. 'What you don't seem to get – is that none of that mattered to me. I was happy. I thought *we* were happy.'

'And I didn't want you ever to question that because what if you didn't want *us* anymore? I wouldn't want anything without you. Take the money, take the house. But, please, take me with you. I love you, Rachel. I will always love you. I want what we had. I want it to be like before, but better. And I'll make it better, I promise.'

David paused for a long time before he continued, 'and the other thing, I'm really embarrassed that you know ... that Jojo knows. That I'm a dickhead. I can't even say the words aloud.'

'You're going to have to,' Rachel replied quietly.

The drink loosened David's tongue. 'It wasn't you – you're beautiful, caring, everything. It was me and my stupid reaction to finding myself in my mid-forties. The overwhelming certainty of my own mortality scared me. It literally weighed me down.'

Rachel arched an eyebrow.

'I'm ashamed but I want to try and explain.' David closed his eyes. 'Dad didn't make it past forty-five. I felt fated, doomed. Then someone I went to school with died.'

'You didn't tell me.'

'Simon. We played football together as teenagers, he joined the army and I did A-levels. Besides, what could I say? "This might be the year my number is called?" He had a stroke. Forty-four years old. On holiday with his wife and kids. Just like that. Gone.'

'I'm sorry.'

'No, I'm sorry.' David tried to look Rachel in the eye but she evaded his glance. 'I'm sorry I hurt you.'

'It's okay,' she whispered.

'It's not. Look at me . . .'

'Look at our boring life?'

'It was never boring.'

'You said you felt like you were dying.'

'But not because of you. We talked about kids. What if I wasn't there to see them grow up?' David continued.

'I don't make you feel alive? You can't be alive with me?'

'That's not what I meant. It was madness, like I was a different person. And only now I'm the other side of it can I see it wasn't me. It was a desperate attempt to . . . I dunno.'

'But . . . what if it happens again, with . . . someone else? I'm not dense, but I still don't actually know what happened to us,' Rachel said as apprehension tightened her throat.

'Why didn't you kick me out?'

'Because I didn't want it to be true.' Rachel's bottom lip quivered and tears began to stream down her face. David used his sleeve to mop them up. 'What should I have said? "Hey, guess what? There's a meal deal in Marks & Spencer – and by the way, are you fucking someone else?"'

50 points to Rachel.

David felt each of her words pierce him like a knife.

'And what about your girlfriend?' Rachel pulled up Amelia-Rose's Facebook page on her phone.

'It. Was. A. One. Off.'

'When?'

'The conference at Christmas.'

Rachel scoffed. 'I'm not an idiot. I saw you snogging in the street on our fucking anniversary!'

50 points to Rachel.

'What?' David had been caught out. 'But that was nothing, I promise.'

'Like the sex was nothing?'

50 points to Rachel.

'It was a one-night thing. I'm not proud of myself. It wasn't good, it wasn't a porno or anything. The opposite, in fact. This woman hit on me. Told me I was "vanilla". And then fobbed me off.'

'And if she hadn't fobbed you off—'

'I didn't mean that! The moment I was in her room, I regretted it.'

'But you fucked her anyway. How gallant of you.'

'It wasn't like that.'

'So tell me, David. Why was shagging this *girl* worth ruining our marriage?'

Challenged like that, what could he say?

100 points to Rachel.

'I am never going to be able to explain or defend those three hours—'

'It lasted three hours? What a bonkathon! Was she better than me? I mean, if you had to score out of ten?'

150 points to Rachel. Rachel felt vindicated, even though she froze inside at the thought of David with Amelia-Rose.

'No! Listen. From the time we left dinner and I called a taxi to take me home, it was three hours.'

'Did you mention your wife to her at all? I guess we know now why you feel uncomfortable wearing a wedding ring. It must get in the way of all the extramarital fucking.'

200 points to Rachel.

'That's enough, Rachel. I've said I'm sorry. I have been trying to make it up to you every second of every hour of every day since it happened. I didn't tell you because I didn't want to hurt you and because it was my mess. I love *you*. I want *you*. If that's not enough for you to give me a second chance ... If it's not enough to say fifteen years were more important than a regrettable evening with someone for whom I have no feelings whatsoever, then I don't know how I can change your mind. But, Rachel, please don't give up on us. Not now.'

David cupped her face in his hands. She wriggled free.

'I need a minute.'

Rachel

40

David continued to talk as Rachel opened the patio doors. 'I don't have a crystal ball. I know I need to earn your trust again, I can only promise you with everything I have that I will never hurt you again. Sorry, I'm rambling. Please, if we just can stay together, and I can prove, something ... I don't know what to say to make it better, but I promise in time, you will see. Do you think you can find it in your heart to forgive me?'

'You're still rambling.' Her head was reeling. It was a one-night stand? That changed everything, didn't it?

She was transported back to the stuffy hospital room that smelled of disinfectant and out-of-date vanilla yoghurt. Rachel was still haunted by the memory of her dad jaundiced from chemotherapy. The crepey skin on his big hands and bony wrists. Saying goodbye to him was the hardest thing she had ever had to do. David was right. She wouldn't have coped with the news that she was not married to her husband.

Is this what she wanted, a life with David?

Rachel couldn't afford to drown once again in David's deep blue eyes, however tempting it was. She tried to understand how he felt. She'd wanted the truth. Could she trust him with her heart again?

When she went back inside David was lying on the sofa, Rachel moved his legs to sit beside him. She smiled at the discarded birthday balloons. The number four bobbed up and down on the ceiling, and the six rested on the floor as if tired from all the excitement.

David held her long and hard. The type of hug that promoted a sense of security but also incited lust and desire deep within her. Rachel slowly undid the top button of his shirt and into the depths of his neck whispered, 'I don't know ...'

David put his arms around her and squeezed hard, telling her he was never going to let her go.

'What if it's too late?' she whispered. 'What if the trust is gone?'

David took a deep breath. 'I'm not the only guilty party here.'

Rachel removed herself from his embrace. 'What on earth is that supposed to mean?'

'I saw the text message – from the sexual health clinic. And what about the lingerie, the secret phone calls!'

50 points to David.

'You've been going through my phone?'

'It flashed up.'

'And then you deleted it?! The STD test was because my husband was sleeping with someone else. The lingerie was for you, you idiot. I was trying to make our sex life exciting because you were off having *interesting* sex elsewhere.' Rachel became more incensed. 'The phone calls were to friends supporting me through the drama of NEVER BEING MARRIED, and … Wait, I don't need to justify anything, it was YOU who had an affair! A fucking affair. *And* you shaved off your pubic hair.'

'I did that for you!'

'You had an affair for me? Thank you very much!'

'No, the manscaping. Barry said it's what women w—'

'And look at Barry! He's hardly—'

'Can I finish?' David relayed that Barry had told him things had changed since he was last single. He was David's only conduit to the modern world of dating. He said that nowadays men *trim it like Beckham*! It was all about keeping a clear and tidy man-bush.

10 points to David.

'And stop calling it an affair. It wasn't an affair. It wasn't love. It happened once and I regret it from the bottom of my heart. What about you and the vet? The self-righteous going-to-turn-vegan prick of a vet?'

50 points to David.

'What about him? I didn't have *sex* with him!'

'He thought we were divorced. He assumed I was bloody Kevin!'

Rachel covered her mouth and let out a short laugh at the thought of what must have been an awkward encounter. David took the opportunity to kiss her. Rachel was instantly at home in his arms. His tongue tickled hers as he pushed open her mouth with his lips. Her mouth submitted and allowed his tongue access.

'I thought we were going to start trying for a baby,' David whispered.

15 points to David.

'I thought we were *already* trying for a baby!'

100 points to Rachel.

'I'm sorry. Rach, I'm so fucking sorry. For everything. This is all my fault.' David stared at the ceiling and let out a huge sigh. 'I miss us. I miss how we used to be.'

Rachel untangled herself from David. She was exhausted. She tried to think, but her head and her heart were competing for attention. 'But I think . . . it's too late,' she whispered.

'Please don't say that.'

'I don't know! I don't know what to think, or what to say. Everything between us feels poisoned. BECAUSE YOU HAD SEX WITH SOMEONE ELSE! You had your penis inside . . . I can't even say it. You did that. And now I'm supposed to trust it will never happen again? What about all the secret phone calls?'

'They were to Barry. He was helping me with something . . . Come with me, I've got something to show you.'

'Where are we going? It's the middle of the night.' Rachel was confused.

David grabbed their coats in preparation for the cold night air. He held out his hand and after a moment's hesitation Rachel accepted it. David rushed them down towards the river. She had to run to keep up with his long strides. When he stopped at the deserted moorings, it was like a ghost town. Rachel was chilled by the silence. Even the River Thames was sleeping.

She watched as David got down on one knee. She held up her hand as if to stop him from speaking. If a proposal was everything she wanted, why was her stomach tying itself in knots?

David clasped one of her hands in his and at the same time presented her with an envelope. 'Rachel, please do me the honour of accompanying me to Paris. It's all I want for my birthday.'

25 points to David.

'Another one of Jojo's ideas?'

50 points to Rachel.

'No, this one is mine. All mine.'

100 points to David.

Rachel rubbed her hands together to keep warm. 'What are we doing here?'

'You'll see,' David said with a smile. He showed her to a boatshed and began struggling with two oversized padlocks. Finally, he pulled open the door. Inside the shed was dark and dank and smelled of paint stripper. David fumbled for a light switch.

'And as useless as Barry can be, he's a dab hand with a toolbox.'

David stepped aside and let Rachel peer into the blackness where she saw the silhouette of a boat. There was a 24-foot Motor Cruiser supported on scaffolding and blocks, tall and proud. Rachel was speechless.

'She's a Walton! Do you want to know her name?' David pointed to the starboard side where the freshly painted letters shone: *RAQUEL*. 'I was going to call her *Rachel*, but her documentation said she was built in Spain, so … But she's yours, she's all yours. Whether we stay together or not. And give it a couple of weeks, she might even be sea-worthy!'

500 points to David.

'But why?'

'I thought your dream was to own a boat?'

'It was. A gazillion years ago. But that was before we married and … What about your seasickness? '

'Apparently there are pills you can take – who knew? Or I could adopt the Captain Jack Sparrow method with a bottle of rum for when we cruise up and down the Thames.' David gave an awful impression of a pirate.

Rachel could feel her eyes well up.

'How did you remember?'

'Please don't cry. Don't you like her? I'm sure I can give her back. I'm sorry. I was trying to do something, anything … to … to show y—'

Rachel brought David close to her. She felt tears roll down her cheeks as she kissed him. For minutes their faces were pressed close together, separating only briefly to come up for air before they went back to the kiss. They sighed with delight and yearning. Their tongues met, each of them emitting a small moan when they found the other.

'Is this some kind of bribe?' Rachel pointed to *Raquel*. 'You can't buy me a boat every time you cheat on me.'

'I couldn't afford to!'

'Ha!'

'Seriously, Rach, I love you and I will never leave your side ever again. Not for a moment.'

'That sounds annoying!' she joked.

'I know you don't like surprises but ... Paris? It's all booked. The tickets are for tomorrow. Please say yes?'

'Tomorrow?' Rachel checked her watch. 'Don't you mean today?'

It was David's turn to check the time. 'We'd need to leave in six hours! Come on, let's live spontaneously!'

'What about work?'

'I've cleared it with Eva and—'

'You what?'

David explained he'd asked Eva to hold the fort and she gave her blessing – her exact words.

Rachel accepted the challenge though a dozen worries were already running through her mind. She'd need to find passports and currency ... They ran home to pack.

Rachel liked romantic breaks and she liked city breaks; but in her mind, they were two very different holidays. In Paris, Rachel and David could spend all day in bed, leaving the hotel only for sustenance and sometimes not even then thanks to the magic of room service. There they were free to make love all day and to eat and drink extravagantly. Of course, they could do that at home without having to tell tall tales to friends about the cultural activities they had indulged in on the continent. Having been to Paris more than a dozen times over the years, not once had they visited the Arc de Triomphe or the Louvre. They hadn't managed a boat ride along the Seine, nor seen inside the Moulin Rouge.

They always stayed in the same boutique hotel: a small family-run place above a bakery. It was worth every cent for the balcony's picturesque view of Paris. As the sun rose behind the Eiffel Tower, they'd devour warm croissants for breakfast before falling back into bed. It was bliss.

Paris was *their* city: 'Rachel and David's romantic hideaway'.

The Eurostar terminal was packed and the imminent journey conjured a mix of memories. Rachel found herself feeling jittery and out of sorts. It was Monday morning and they treated themselves to breakfast in the long Champagne bar as they waited for the 09:25 train. The clink of the toast followed by the first sip of bubbles eased Rachel's anxiety. They watched commuters and passengers disembark from the trains and made up stories about their respective journeys. It was people watching at its purest.

David had splashed out and booked first-class tickets. The journey was fast and they looked like they could be loved-up honeymooners. Rachel relaxed, finally enjoying herself. This was what fun used to feel like.

They arrived in Paris in no time, joined the long queue for taxis outside the Gare du Nord terminus. The manager, Marie, welcomed them with open arms when they

arrived. It was a home from home. Their room was perfect. Rose petals covered the four-poster bed.

Rachel felt nervous. In normal circumstances, Paris was
the green light for debauchery. By now, they would have
ripped each other's clothes off. Rachel waited for David to
initiate things, but the air felt stilted between them and
she could sense he was holding back. He suggested a walk.
Paris was picturesque as ever. They strolled along the
tree-lined streets, kicking the fallen leaves. They picked a
brasserie with an ambitious menu and sat outside. Rachel
ordered two glasses of wine in her best French accent. The
waiter was appreciative that she had attempted his native
language. The *carte du jour* was a salad, served with different hams and cheeses, topped with fried potato and served
with fresh baguette and lashings of creamy, salty butter.
Who knew salad could be so delicious? It was divine. After
eating they were serenaded by a street violist playing
Tchaikovsky, as they were served small strong coffees.

They walked along beside the river and ambled in the
direction of the Musée d'Orsay. For the first time they found
themselves venturing inside the former Beaux-Arts railway
station, where they passed the afternoon bewitched by the
artworks inside. Having only seen the famous paintings in
books, Rachel was amazed at how big and beautiful they
were in real life. In the gift shop, she sought out postcards
of Van Gogh's *Starry Night Over the Rhône*.

When Rachel's phone buzzed, David raised his right
eyebrow. She was momentarily distracted by the message
and apologised to David with her eyes.

Kevin: I've officially asked Eva to be my girlfriend. She still hasn't responded!

Rachel: Give her time. X

She had already added two and two and made ten, knowing Eva would make a great girlfriend for Kevin, not to mention a wonderful future sister-in-law. Rachel mimed turning her phone off and returned it to her handbag. They crossed the Seine to the Île de la Cité, home to the Notre-Dame Cathedral, where they playfully disagreed if it was pronounced *dame* or *dahm*; the damage from the recent fire was still heartbreakingly evident.

They walked, and walked. They found themselves at the bottom of the hill of Montmartre and raced up the steps, trying to beat the funicular to the top. They were both out of breath when they spied a wedding party posing in front of the Sacré Coeur.

'Let's get married here,' David said. 'We could elope again.'

Rachel stared at him. His wide smile faded slowly as he wondered whether he'd broken the spell of their magical day.

'Don't we owe a proper ceremony to our families? As I recall they weren't happy being left out the first time around!' Rachel rebuked him, but lightly. He sighed in relief.

They stopped at a ticket booth – that evening's show at the Moulin Rouge was sold out, instead the ticket girl recommended a concert in a small jazz bar tucked away in a nearby alley. She said it was off the beaten track for tourists. A taste of real Parisian life. And Henri would look after them. She told them to tell him Camille sent them.

A rickety staircase led down to a long room with small tables set either side of the aisle. A jazz quartet was already playing: piano, vibraphone, double bass and drums. David's French was much better than hers; he glanced at the wine list and ordered fluently. Some time later a bottle of Sancerre, two glasses and a bowl of olives appeared. Rachel tried to imagine this place before the smoking ban. The music was entrancing. She thought of her jazz-loving granddad and they raised a glass to his memory. Rachel reflected that for someone who'd loved the sounds and colours of the world, he'd hated to travel far outside his own front door.

David mentioned Camille's name and the bartender, Henri, winked and made them two sublime cocktails. Later David would try to recreate the simple recipe Henri generously wrote down for them.

FRENCH MARTINI RECIPE
35 ml Vodka
20 ml Chambord black raspberry liqueur
50 ml pineapple juice

They walked hand in hand back to the hotel. The room door hadn't closed before David was kissing Rachel. He was grabbing at her coat buttons. The urgency between them mounted. When they stood in front of one another in their underwear, there was a moment of mutual hunger. David wiggled his hips and his boxer shorts fell to the floor. Rachel was distracted by the Marks & Spencer's label protruding from the dark cotton, together with the acute angle of David's erection, and she started laughing. David couldn't see the funny side, and he attempted to reclaim his underwear.

Rachel had the giggles, she couldn't stop herself. She thought of Marie Kondo's advice about minimalism: *touch something and ask yourself, does it give you joy?*

She tried to explain through the self-induced hilarity.

'Sorry, David ... It's just ... Marie Kondo ... does it bring me joy?' Rachel had to stop talking, she felt a stitch coming on. 'Yes, it brings me joy. Your penis brings me joy ...'

She took a huge breath and addressed David's penis in her most serious and formal voice. 'I want you to know: you bring me joy.' Then she gave the tip a small kiss.

The following morning Rachel awoke with David's hardness pushed into her back. She turned to face him. They kissed. It was a small peck. And then another. Rachel wasn't sure who was first to slip in a tongue. This would usually have been the point where one or both of them would have scrambled out of bed to brush their teeth, but neither of them wanted to break the spell. Tongues and hands moved freely; there were gasps for air as they moved closer to each other. Rachel cupped David's balls in one hand while the other stroked the base of his shaft. He pushed down her knickers. She pulled at his boxer shorts and undid the button, releasing his cock through the fly of the cotton. She circled the tip with her thumb. He groaned 'Oh, God' into her ear. He used his knee to gently nudge hers apart. They kissed as he removed his boxer shorts and finally her knickers escaped from her legs and onto the floor.

He asked if she was sure she wanted this. She nodded, she wanted him, and urged him to continue. Soon Rachel could feel the orgasm build inside of her. David's face was alight with pleasure.

'I'm not done with you yet,' he said as he thrust, fast, then slow, then fast, then slow.

There was unspoken satisfaction in the musky post-coital air; a surreal call-back to their former sex life. Their legs remained intertwined as they silently exhaled deep post-orgasmic breaths of release. The physical reconnection had shaken her to the core. Rachel thought she might cry.

The return journey to London was slow and full of signal delays. Rachel allowed the rhythm of the train to lull her to sleep with her head resting against David. He woke her to say goodbye to France.

David fumbled and dropped something and Rachel saw him pick up the familiar turquoise ring box. On his knees in the aisle, he opened the box and asked if Rachel, the love of his life, would consider marrying him. He told her that he felt compelled to propose to her again now everything was out in the open. And it wasn't because he was scared of losing her. And not because he didn't want to start again at forty-six.

'I know this isn't perfect. I'm sorry I'm not outwardly romantic. I wish I could be your Prince Charming. But what I do know is that I love you and I want to spend the rest of my life with you. So here goes: Rachel Norma Keatley, from this day forward, for better, for worse, for richer, for poorer, in sickness and in health, until death do us part … Will you marry me? For the first time, and the second?'

She allowed a comedy pause before exclaiming, 'Yes! I mean, *oui*!'

Their neighbouring passengers couldn't believe their eyes. They cheered and applauded. Someone offered to take a photo.

David told her he was the definition of a middle-aged idiot. He told the entire carriage that he thanked his lucky stars he hadn't lost this wonderful woman and urged them to keep their own loved ones close.

They were falling in love (again) and, Rachel decided, it would be okay. They would file the last year as the bad one amongst fifteen good years. That was enough for her. She stared at her reflection in the glass and wondered if she should have added some colour to her lips. It didn't matter. She was happy. From the bottom of her heart she could say: this was all she wanted.

Epilogue

Eight Months Later

Norma was fussing with flowers.

Hilda, the genial wedding planner, announced: 'Ten minutes.' However, her softly spoken words made it clear they could wait all day if they had to – it was Rachel's day.

'That's enough, Mum. You're going to destroy the bouquet.'

'I'm guessing bossy pants,' Norma nodded towards the door, 'has a spare.' Norma didn't know what to do with empty hands. There was a silence that couldn't be filled.

'Leave Hilda alone – she's lovely. Have you thought about where you and Roger will get married?' Rachel deflected her.

'I thought maybe a little register office. We've both had the proper weddings and, you know, long marriages. And …' Norma paused. 'And we've both lost spouses. But now, here, seeing all these flowers, I think maybe a church wedding in front of God would be nice after all. A small church, mind. He's God-fearing, you know, Roger is. What do you think? Would you mind?'

Who was this woman in front of Rachel? Would she mind?

'Do you mean, you want my blessing?'

Norma gave a movement so small Rachel doubted it could it be categorised as a nod.

'I just want you to be happy, Mum.'

Her mother was wearing less makeup these days. She still looked perfect (as Norma would add – 'for a septua-genarian') but Roger had thawed the ice queen, brought out a new, warm and caring woman. One Rachel wasn't quite ready for.

'He'll never replace your dad, I know.'

'Of course not, but then maybe you don't need a replacement either. Roger sounds like an upgrade. As husbands go, that is.'

Rachel's wedding dress from all those years ago had not been appropriate after all; it was too short, too white and too translucent.

Lydia helped her choose a new dress, after Rachel had bookmarked what seemed a million different options on Pinterest, and they quickly narrowed the style down to a Hollywood design in champagne. It was a gown that would have been perfectly modelled by Greta Garbo or Lauren Bacall. It was timeless, but could also be worn to a black tie event. If it was dyed, of course. *Who actually ends up dyeing their wedding dress?*

Norma kissed Rachel on the cheek and told her she was going to find Roger. Hilda popped her head around the door again. She wasn't interrupting, she said, in a voice as gentle as a summer breeze. 'Hilda, tell me . . .' Rachel hesitated. 'Have you ever had a fail? Has there been . . . anyone not, you know, finished? Not made it down the aisle? I mean, has anyone not gone through with the ceremony?'

'We've had last-minute cancellations and such.' Hilda paused as she took in the possible significance of the question. She looked momentarily like a stricken mouse in amongst a herd of elephants. 'But you're already married!'

Hilda had not planned for this conversation. How could she have? To the outside world, her clients were already married. The renewal of vows was often seen as a saccharine and self-centred gesture, certainly an unnecessary one. Hilda's brain was working overtime for strategies to solve this unforeseen hitch in proceedings.

'Do you want to . . .' she started. Rachel could finish the sentence in any number of ways; leave, go home, eat, drink, sleep?

On the outside Rachel beamed with radiance – thanks to the hair and makeup. She ignored her own inner turmoil and told Hilda she was ready. The short portly wedding planner let out an audible sigh of relief.

'But first, I need your help.'

'Anything,' Hilda said sincerely.

'Mr Ahrens is a registrar, isn't he?'

Hilda nodded.

'An official one? Legally?'

Unlike a wedding ceremony, the renewal of vows didn't require a certificate or witnesses. But Rachel asked if the registrar could prepare a marriage certificate, a real one.

Hilda's mouth dropped open; she had seen it all now. She did a strange walk-run as if she wasn't in a hurry and collided with Kevin as she rushed from the room.

Kevin sat with his sister and twisted some of Rachel's hair between his fingers.

'You look smashing. Wait, no, don't you dare cry, you'll ruin your face.'

'Do you think I'm an idiot?' she asked.

'It's been a tough year for you both, but you've survived. Better than ever. I reckon David'll think twice before doing anything that stupid again. And if he doesn't, he'll have me and the twins . . .' Kevin nodded to his balled fists '. . . to answer to.'

Rachel laughed at her brother's protective streak.

'I've got something to show you.' He removed a ring box from his jacket pocket and showed Rachel a solitaire diamond ring.

'For Eva? Does she know?'

He shook his head. 'What do you think?'

'She might not say yes. You know what she's like.'

'I've planned for that. I'm expecting a rejection first time round but I'm just going to keep asking until she says yes. Fourth time lucky for us both, I reckon.'

Rachel tried to hug her brother but her arms were confined by her lace dress.

'Go get her! She's worth it.'

*

For the ceremony Rachel had found a beautiful chapel dating back to the 1300s. The medieval building was near the River Thames. It was small and intimate, with beautiful stained-glass windows and a vaulted ceiling. When there was a cancellation less than a month ahead, David said to book it. Norma demanded assurances that the tone of the long-awaited, overdue matrimonial service was not going to be disturbed by the puerility of his friends, namely Barry. None of them was to make a speech, which was just as well as his friends had been planning a slideshow of embarrassing photos and video.

Hilda returned, out of breath, and interrupted the siblings' embrace.

'I've spoken to the registrar and it seems that David, Mr Chatsworth, has asked the same thing. It's all been taken care of.'

Rachel didn't think she was waiting for a sign. But if she had been, this would have been it.

Kevin offered to walk Rachel down the aisle.

'I'm serious,' Kevin said. 'I know you didn't want a big song and dance entrance, as you're meant to be renewing your vows and everything, and I'm not Dad but I'd really like to and you deserve to be walked in. And I'm sure Beth will give me a glowing reference!'

She nodded and told him he was going to make her cry if he carried on with the sentimental mush.

He held out his arm. 'Ready?'

Rachel nodded.

She gave her biggest smile to friends and family. In the congregation her eyes sought out Eva. She was reassured when her friend gave a discreet thumbs up. Next to Eva, Beth bobbed Baby Phoebe on her lap, and Jojo held up Phoebe's chubby little arm to wave at Rachel. Norma smiled as Roger clasped her hand and kissed her palm. Lillian was crying with happiness and searching her handbag for a tissue. Stefan Stratos looked fit to burst with glee; some divorce lawyer he turned out to be.

David turned and blew Rachel a kiss. He first complimented her face, her dress, and then her in the dress. He told her she took his breath away. The registrar steered clear from religious whatnot, and before long the audience were being asked if they knew of any reason why Rachel and David should not be wed, again. The silence was affirmative. Vows were exchanged and they sealed their union with a kiss. A chaste peck on the lips. Rachel and David were directed to sign the marriage certificate. Kevin and Eva witnessed the signatures. The volume of chatter around them escalated.

'I've got something to confess,' David addressed the room as he raised his glass.

Rachel nearly choked on the Champagne in her mouth. She looked at Eva with eyes that said, *What the f—?*

'I've been selfish,' David continued. 'Many moons ago, there I was on a beach in Bali, and the most beautiful woman in the world had agreed to marry me. I didn't want to give her a moment to think twice. I was worried she would discover my flaws and change her mind, or worse still, get a better offer.'

A small cheer came from Barry, followed by a heckle from Kevin: 'Yeah, she would have done.'

David cleared the frog from his throat.

'Call me a soppy romantic – but I love this woman and she's put up with more than her fair share from me. I promise to be a better husband to her from now on.' There it was again, a crack in his voice and the threat of tears in his eyes.

'When Rachel suggested then that we write our own vows, I was stumped. I had mistakenly given her the impression I was some sort of high-brow Lothario.'

'You wish!' came another jeer from Barry. Norma glared at him.

'I was caught unawares and the only poem I knew off by heart was "If" by Kipling. Somehow I made it work. I think you'll all agree Rachel is the main reason I can keep a level head. And there's a line in it that goes: *"And so hold on when there is nothing in you/ Except the Will which says to them, 'Hold on!'"* Now – I'd like to raise a glass to Rachel.'

A brief silence followed by a schmaltzy smattering of applause was cut short by the clinking of David's glass against Rachel's.

'Rachel, thank you for holding on.'

The room once again filled with applause. And Rachel's heart swelled a little as she took a sip of her Champagne to allow a moment to compose herself.

'Thank you David. And to you all – to friends, to family, to those who are both.'

Her brother stood to take a dramatic bow, which gleaned the attention-seeking laughter he was after.

'Kevin – you can sit down!' Rachel ordered, setting her glass aside. 'To everyone … Love isn't perfect, but then again, neither is life. Who knows if they're going to make it?' She looked to David. Her wide eyes looked petrified. 'But we did and we're here, and …'

Rachel wasn't sure she could continue. David passed her a linen napkin. Rachel smiled at his thoughtfulness.

'What I mean to say is: thank you for sharing our special day, sixteen years on, almost to the day.' She looked down at the material in her hand and froze as she gazed at the thick cotton. It had discoloured with age. She felt a lump form in her throat. She hadn't seen this piece of material since the night of their Indonesian faux-ceremony all those years ago. David had kept her vows all these years.

She could make out most of the words she had bastardised from Elizabeth Browning's Sonnet 43. How did she love him? All those years ago, she had counted twelve. The words swirled in her head. Now there were a few more to add. Love shone through those hastily written vows, pure unadulterated emotion. David squeezed her hand, giving her the power to continue. He whispered in her ear the three words that she longed to be true. 'I love you.' She searched his face in return, for signs she could trust him, for the truth. In his eyes she found all the security she was looking for.

'When I met David, he quickly became everything to me – my sun, my moon. But he was more than that too. He was the way ahead. He didn't smother me. In fact, quite the opposite. He gave me the freedom to find my own path; comforted me when I made mistakes; above all, he offered me his unconditional support. I am who I am today thanks to his love. And, David, for that I thank you.'

Their friends and family revelled in the romance of the moment and clinked their glasses in appreciation.

'To David!' they shouted with glee.

He leaned in to Rachel and almost inaudibly said, 'Thank you, Rachel. Thank you for giving me a second chance. I'll never hurt—'

'Don't say it! Not today. It's behind us now.'

David presented her with an envelope wrapped in ribbon. She pulled at the ribbon and found he had booked them a second honeymoon. Two weeks in the blue and white Greek island of Santorini.

'Something blue,' Rachel whispered.

'Something blue,' David repeated.

Rachel joked they should sail *Raquel* all the way to Greece. David nodded obediently until he saw the smile on her face and laughed with relief.

'It's not Bali,' David joked.

'Too soon!' Rachel laughed.

She allowed herself to drown in his blue eyes. She drank in his familiar smell. The musky scent tickled her nostrils and left her with goose pimples. She nuzzled into his neck and whispered into his ear: 'Don't let us down. This is the last time I'm going to marry you, Mr Chatsworth.' Rachel and David started the next chapter of their lives with a kiss.

'For the record, your favourite colour is fuchsia.'

'Nice try, it's teal.'

'Teal?'

'And for the record, I bloody hate lilies!'

Acknowledgements

It's a dream come true to have my debut novel published. First, I have to thank my mother, for instilling a passion for books and reading with our weekly trips to the local library. Fullwell Cross Library was also home to my first job as proud Saturday assistant.

I would like to thank my publishers, the wonderful team at Arrow – Selina Walker, Emily Griffin, Isabelle Ralphs, Alice Spencer, Natalia Cacciatore. Thanks also to my incredible copyeditor – any mistakes that made their way into the book are definitely my own. And three cheers to my unwavering editor extraordinaire Sonny Marr!

Being shortlisted for the *Daily Mail* Penguin Random House First Novel Competition 2018 changed my life! Thank you to my agent, Luigi Bonomi, and his wonderful enthusiasm, and to the very supportive team at LBA Books. Luigi's first call in September 2018 will always be in my heart.

I am indebted to the Romantic Novelists' Association – and an early draft of *How To Marry Your Husband* was reviewed through their amazing RNA New Writers Scheme. I couldn't have done without the RNA Facebook group and I can't wait to be upgraded to fully-fledged member!

My journey as a writer started at primary school where I thought that my reinterpretation of Chitty Chitty Bang Bang would get me a gold star (it didn't). The first of many rejections! In 2017, I took a sabbatical to establish a non-profit to conserve wild chimpanzees in Uganda, the Bulindi Chimpanzee & Community Project, with my then-boyfriend, now fiancé. After three months, my job was no longer available and we ended up moving to Africa. It was in Uganda that I was able to write up the ideas that had been dawdling in notebooks for years. This story had been in a state of scribbles until I was inspired by NaNoWriMo (National Novel Writing Month) to write 50,000 words in one month, and I was able to complete the first draft of *How To Marry Your Husband*.

Thank you all my friends and family who had to endure early drafts! Thank you for staying friends! And to Anne Gilchrist, who told me … Well she knows what she said.

This book would not exist without those who spurred me on and provided time, advice, unconditional love and support. Special mentions (sorry – the list is long!) go to Adrian & Helen Jeckells, Alison May, Andrea Wylde & Adrian O'Brien, Alan Thorne, April Rohen, Catherine & Ben Gosling-Fuller, Cece Beyer, David Quammen, Emily Griffin, the lovely Gareth Smith (and his mum Janice),

Gazz & Kuli, Helen Lederer, James Duncan, Jo Dickinson, Joyce McLennan, Kathy Wylde, Kelly Pearce, Kim Mendez, Luigi Bonomi, Ma Rohen, Monica Burgess, my lovely spa ladies (Andrea, Julie & Lesley), Nancy Merrick & Gary Lairmore, Paul Savident, Pippa Batt, Rahel Noser, Ralph Bogard, Richard Lumsden, Rosie Walsh, Sally Howe, Selena Walker, Sinead Wall, Sonny Marr, Sue Msallem, and Susan Raasay.

A million thanks go to Matt McLennan for putting up with EVERY draft and my constant tea and coffee demands!

And last but not least, thank YOU (the reader) for joining me on this journey!